THE BITTERWEED PATH

The Bitterweed Path

With a New Introduction by John Howard

THOMAS HAL PHILLIPS

The University of North Carolina Press   Chapel Hill and London

First published by The University of
North Carolina Press in 1996

© 1949, 1950 by Thomas Hal Phillips
New Introduction © 1996 by The University of
North Carolina Press

Originally published by Rinehart & Company, Inc.

Manufactured in the United States of America

Library of Congress Cataloging-in-Publication Data
Phillips, Thomas Hal, 1922–
The bitterweed path / by Thomas Hal Phillips;
with a new introduction by John Howard.
p.   cm.   Includes bibliographical references.
ISBN 0-8078-4595-7 (pbk.: alk. paper)
1. Social classes—Mississippi—Fiction.   2. Country
life—Mississippi—Fiction.   3. Gay youth—
Mississippi—Fiction.   I. Title.
PS3566.H524B5   1996   95-42508
813'.54—dc20   CIP

The paper in this book meets the guidelines for
permanence and durability of the Committee on
Production Guidelines for Book Longevity of the
Council on Library Resources.

This novel was started on a fellowship granted by
the Julius Rosenwald Fellowship and completed on
one granted by the Eugene F. Saxton Memorial
Trust.

Excerpts from this novel were combined into a short
story which appeared in the *Southwest Review* under
the title of "A Touch of Earth."

00   99   98   97   96   5   4   3   2   1

This book is

for my mother

and my father

introduction

In the middle of the twentieth century, American life was marked by contradiction. On the one hand, prosperity reigned and Americans appeared united in their belief in God, country, and family. On the other hand, economic disparities along lines of race and gender became more apparent; doubters and nonconformists expressed their views, often suffering harsh repercussions. After a long, painful depression and a horrific war overseas, happy days were here again, but nagging social ills persisted, new fears surfaced, and a sense of danger and mistrust filled the air.[1]

The year 1950 marked the beginning of a decade that later would become valorized, if also satirized and scrutinized, in American popular culture. Television, the defining entertainment medium of the fifties, today reflects the era back at us through sitcom reruns that tell a part of the story. Yes, the Cleavers represented a genuine demographic trend: divorce rates were going down, birthrates were going up, and suburbia was expanding. Legions of housewives, epitomized by Donna Reed, confirmed a widespread domestic ideology and a postwar government campaign that coaxed working women back to the kitchen and demanded they be happy there.[2] After all, father knew best, especially in the "real world" outside the home. Men educated on the GI bill, the heads of single-income households, would assure the United States' prominence as the wealthiest nation on earth. Strong, masculine, assertive men would attest to its position as the mightiest military power on the planet.

But those who want to understand the great variety of experience in post–World War II America, especially those who were born after the 1950s, must look beyond the television. We must diligently examine the past in order to understand the complexity of social and economic arrangements and to recognize the victims of political philosophies and practices purportedly born of consensus. The positive aspects and images of the fifties often concealed within them equally negative realities.

The abundant dollars fueling the postwar boom passed less frequently through black hands than white. Economic disempowerment pointed up systemic inequalities pervasive in all institutions of daily living. In the American South particularly, most communities contained two distinct but interwoven domains— one white, the other black; one privileged, the other impoverished. African Americans and other racial minority members courageous enough to question the prevailing order often met with the severest consequences. Emmett Till, the black Detroit youth murdered in Money, Mississippi, for talking to a white woman, was just one of countless persons lynched for defying local custom, or for no other reason than racial hatred.[3]

A revolution in leisure and luxury was launched in the 1950s. The new car symbolized the consumer impulse among people of means. The interstate highway system, the auto lobby's great victory, affirmed a seeming collective commitment to individualism and the nuclear family. Gleaming new roads enabled the suburbanite's commute to the urban center and connected far-flung cities together. But like the railroads before them, they also helped tie previously self-sufficient agrarian communities to larger national and international markets, steering farmers increasingly toward cash cropping—often in the form of sharecropping and tenancy for poor whites and blacks. This post–Civil War phenomenon endured through the post–World War II era.

The 1950 U.S. Census asserted that the South on average was finally, like the rest of the country, made up mostly of town and city dwellers.[4] But low-income, Deep South states like Alabama and Mississippi remained predominantly rural. Male elites in these states devoted their Saturday leisure time to college football, anticipating the annual showdowns between rival, all-white institutions of higher learning—Auburn and Alabama, Mississippi State and Ole Miss (so named after a slave term for the plantation mistress). Meanwhile, country folk and other working-class Southerners ordinarily labored six days a week in the fields and mills.

Across class lines, Sundays were spent in church. The South was already deeply religious—"Christ-haunted" in the words of Flannery O'Connor—but the nation as a whole witnessed dramatic increases in church membership beginning around midcentury.[5] Again, consensus seemed prevalent. But conflicts appeared when Judeo-Christian precepts were interpreted to advance narrow, usually conservative, political agendas.[6]

Stirred into the complicated mix of race and gender, region and religion, class and ideology, sexuality proved peculiarly vexing to the American "consensus."[7] The Kinsey reports demonstrated the great frequency and variety of American sexual expression, shocking polite segments of society unaccustomed to discussing such matters. Sexual deviancy—a term applied to any number of commonplace feelings and behaviors—became a prominent public concern. Sex scandals rocked numerous American localities, and newspaper and magazine exposés kept readers well informed.

With unusual candor, politicians and civic leaders voiced precise views on how to have sex. Senator James O. Eastland of Mississippi declared that white persons should have intercourse only with white persons, and black with black. Miscegenation ostensibly led to the "mongrelization" of the races and the decline of the "white race." White supremacists' efforts to thwart a budding civil rights movement employed sexually charged rhetoric, deflecting attention from serious issues of social and economic justice. Black and white intermarriage remained illegal in every Southern state.[8]

Sex should happen only within the bonds of marriage, most popular media suggested. Reporters warned that petting was rampant among young people and that shadowy "teenage sex clubs" encouraged them to lose their virginity. Husbands and wives routinely found intimacy outside the home. Beyond legitimate concerns over the sexual abuse of children, which was allegedly on the rise during the period, observers implied that any intergenerational sexual intercourse was suspect.[9]

Perhaps foremost among prescriptive sexual advice, however, women were to have sex with men, and men with women. Homosexuality was out—outlawed by sodomy statutes in most states, outside moral tenets according to many clergy, and out of the question in terms of socially acceptable practice. Still, word was out that homosexuals were everywhere. And they were a threat.

So potent was the threat that homosexuality became linked in American public discourse to the overriding preoccupations of the day—communism and atomic warfare. Homosexuals not only threatened to molest vulnerable children (a despicable late-1930s fabrication, revived in the war's aftermath). They not only endangered traditional family structures (by demonstrating the arbitrariness of prescribed gender roles and the range of sexual desire). They not only jeopardized their neighbors' psychological well-being (or, more to the point, complacency). *They imperiled the nation.*[10]

Homosexuals, the reasoning went, led double lives. Of necessity they had to hide their "perverse tendencies" while otherwise engaged in "normal," sometimes respectable, pursuits. They were ripe for exploitation by enemies of the state. Communist spies could use them, make them do their bidding, under threat of exposure.[11] Indeed, Senator Joseph McCarthy insisted that this was happening. A study done by Senators Kenneth Wherry of Nebraska and Lister Hill of Alabama found that the prevalence of homosexuals employed in federal government agencies warranted a special investigation. A wave of purges resulted—inquisitions, firings, public rites of humiliation. It spread from Washington to state and local governments and to large and small businesses and communities throughout the land.[12]

The chain reaction initially flared with an off-the-cuff remark made by John E. Peurifoy, a federal employee in the State Department. As reported in the *New York Times* on 1 March 1950, Peurifoy told a Senate committee that left-wing subversives recently booted out of the State Department because they were security risks were mostly homosexuals.[13] The statement was uttered; the connection was made. Homosexuality represented the worst evil.

During the onset of this torrent of hysteria, at the same time, almost to the day, that Peurifoy testified that the State Department was firing gay staff members, Rinehart and Company of New York published a novel about love between men in the American South, a story of intimacy—sexual intimacy—called *The Bitterweed Path*, by Mississippian Thomas Hal Phillips.

In the far northeastern corner of Mississippi, on a farm situated between the communities of Theo and Kossuth, Thomas Hal Phillips was born on 11 October 1922. He was the third of six children, one of five sons, born to W. T. Phillips and Olive Fare Phillips. It was a lively household, always stirring with activity. It was a place that Hal Phillips would always refer to as home.[14]

In addition to farming, Thomas Hal Phillips's father built roads using mules, as his father had before him. W. T. Phillips was the descendant of English settlers, a stern, imposing figure. Hal's mother, however, doted on her children. She was, as Hal remembers, "a remarkable person . . . always pleasant." She worked as a schoolteacher and demanded respect for education as she demonstrated its joys. Hal began schooling at the age of three, and he grew to eagerly anticipate new reading material. His mother frequently surprised him with "an armful of books," and she also arranged for him to borrow books from a friend's library. Lessons in right and wrong were taught at the "little church right within sight of our house"—Tishomingo Baptist.

Hal likewise learned about physical labor early on. The Depression had come to the rural South long before Black Thursday, and Hal joined his sister and brothers in helping tend the family garden, feed the livestock, and cultivate the ever-depreciating cotton. His parents maintained their jobs through those lean years. So although Hal sensed that the family was "poor," the children were "not deprived."

Hal felt a competitiveness with his brothers, who were more "physically gifted." Thus, while he excelled in his studies and joined both the debate team and the writing club at Alcorn Agricultural High School in Kossuth, he found time for sports as well. He played right guard on the football team and "liked it." Still, he flourished under Henry Dalton, his English instructor. He remembers soaking up the "basics of creative writing," and by graduation he "was already ready to write a novel."

Nonetheless, Hal Phillips majored in social science at Mississippi State. He supplemented his scholarship by tutoring in mathematics and working at the YMCA, a campus hub. When he obtained his bachelor's degree in 1943, he joined the Navy. He served as a lieutenant in north Africa and southern Europe and was a part of the invasion forces at both Anzio and Elba.

At the close of World War II, an early draft of a novel secured Phillips's admission into the well-regarded creative writing program at the University of Alabama in Tuscaloosa. There he studied under the influential Hudson Strode, whom he revered, and under Edward Kimbrough, with whom he developed a close working relationship. He submitted his master's thesis entitled *The Bitterweed Path* in 1948. With the help of grants from the Julius Rosenwald Fund and the Eugene F. Saxton Trust, Phillips later revised the work, which became his first published novel.

He meanwhile taught creative writing at Southern Methodist University in Dallas from 1948 to 1950. After the release of *The Bitterweed Path* in early 1950 and with the affirmation of a Fulbright scholarship to Paris and later a Guggenheim fellowship, Hal Phillips devoted himself full time to writing. He put out nearly a novel a year through the mid-1950s: *The Golden Lie* in 1951, *Search for a Hero* in 1952, *Kangaroo Hollow* in 1954, and *The Loved and the Unloved* in 1955—all generally, though not overwhelmingly, well received. While *Kangaroo Hollow* was published only in Great Britain, the *New York Times* praised the four American releases for "their mature understanding of life and character, their humor and compassion, and their sound craftsmanship."[15] A handful of Phillips's short stories were anthologized.

Then Phillips's literary production stopped. He began to disperse his efforts across a variety of areas, seemingly in response to chance opportunities. When moviemakers expressed interest in screen adaptations of his novels, Phillips explored the possibilities of film work, developing Hollywood contacts that would continue to benefit him for decades to come. In the late fifties, he wrote the story and screenplay for *Tarzan's Fight for Life*, a fortieth anniversary commemoration of the Tarzan series.

In 1958 Phillips was lured into politics when Mississippi governor J. P. Coleman appointed him to fill his brother Rubel's unfinished term on the state Public Service Commission. He won election to a full, four-year term in 1959 and was eventually named chairman. Phillips managed Rubel's 1963 Republican gubernatorial campaign—a barnstormer the two spent circling the state, seeking "smooth pastures" for landing their small, twin-engine airplane. Rubel surprised pollsters by garnering 40 percent of the ballots, the largest state vote cast for the party of Abraham Lincoln since Reconstruction.

Phillips's personal and professional concerns continued to multiply. Reporters noted that he remained a bachelor, while he kept up homes in both Jackson and Kossuth. Near his birthplace, he rented out most of his fields and spent time deer hunting with his beagle pack. He confessed to repeated trips to St. Louis to watch Cardinals baseball. And he confided to a friend that among his "accomplishments for 1962," he had "won a silver cup in golf at the Jackson Country Club" and augmented his "Black Angus herd to an even fifty."[16] Increasingly successful in business, he became president of a life insurance company. He also was named the first head of the Mississippi Film Commission.

Phillips worked on a number of movies in a variety of capacities—as consultant, actor, writer, or often unacknowledged "script doctor"—during the 1960s, 1970s, and 1980s. Among the most well known were *The Autobiography of Miss Jane Pittman*, *Ode to Billy Joe*, *Walking Tall II*, and several Robert Altman pictures. Phillips developed and played what is arguably the most famous nonappearing character in the history of American cinema, the populist presidential candidate Hal Phillip Walker in

Nashville. It is Phillips's voice that eerily radiates from speakers atop the campaign van during the Altman classic.

In 1971 Phillips told his respected mentor, Hudson Strode, that he was cutting back on his business commitments to allow more time for creative work: "I *am* on a daily writing schedule— a novel I've had planned for some time." As late as 1978 he was reportedly at work on an as-yet-unfinished manuscript, tentatively entitled *A Road through a Cemetery*. But Phillips never completed the novel. Contented in later life to retire from his disparate vocations, he considered his most significant output to have been his five novels from the fifties. And he judged his most daring and provocative novel, *The Bitterweed Path*, to have been his best.

Now in his seventies, Thomas Hal Phillips still lives in the county where he was born, still attends the church where he was baptized. He remembers with astonishment the boldness he had as a young writer, the audacity with which he broached a seemingly unspeakable topic in his first novel: "I just wonder now how I had the nerve to complete it."

Thematically, the inspiration for *The Bitterweed Path* did not flow from other works of fiction. As of the late forties, Phillips had not read the few American novels addressed specifically to love and intimacy between men. Nor had he read the ambiguous early works of Southerners Truman Capote or Tennessee Williams. He was pleased nonetheless when many critics compared him favorably to such writers. His treatment of the subject, they said, wasn't as lurid or dark; though realistic, it wasn't as morbidly tragic. *The Bitterweed Path* eschewed the formulas of the Southern Gothic. When Phillips began the novel, he felt as if he were operating in a vacuum. He felt that he had "found" or "discovered" a plot line that was "new."

At the same time, Phillips consciously drew from an age-old

tale, the Old Testament story of David and Jonathan, which he had read as a youngster in Sunday school. As told in the book of 1 Samuel, Jonathan, a warrior and son of King Saul of the Israelites, had a great love for David, who was described as ruddy and handsome. David achieved fame in battle against the Philistines, notably slaying the giant Goliath. Saul favored David, offered his daughter to be David's bride, but ultimately grew jealous of David's popularity. When Saul plotted to kill the future king, the spurned son Jonathan kept his "covenant" with David, helping protect him from Saul. With its curious phrasing, portentous silences, and suggestive interpersonal relationships, this narrative, Phillips found, was open to multiple interpretation: "Now, you can make of David and Jonathan anything you want to." While no less subtle, Phillips's story of the postbellum South extended the narrative possibilities by suggesting sexual relations between golden boy Darrell Barclay, the son of a sharecropper, and Roger Pitt, the prosperous landowner's son—as well as between Barclay and the landowner, Malcolm Pitt, often jokingly referred to as the "king."

Yet it is the very subtlety of Phillips's novel that accounts for publishers' initial interest, the critics' warm reception, and the book's eventual fall into obscurity. In manuscript form *The Bitterweed Path* attracted attention from major New York publishing houses. Both Hudson Strode's publisher, Harcourt Brace, and Edward Kimbrough's publisher, Rinehart, vied for the project. Phillips chose the latter and the opportunity to work with respected editor John Selby. The book appeared in early 1950 priced at three dollars.

While not spectacular, early sales justified a paperback edition, and Avon brought out a thirty-five cent version of *The Bitterweed Path* as part of its Red and Gold Library. Though sensationalistic by late-twentieth-century standards, the cover design and copy hardly outshone the bombastic competitors on the drugstore shelf. In meager typescript, the teaser on the back read: "This is the story of the deep affection an older man and his son held for a youth on one of their farms—and of the girl that the youth wanted to love, but could not, because of the strange emotional tie that bound him to the two men." While this hinted at and distorted the principal themes of the novel, the prominent cover illustration was downright deceptive. The artist, signed "Fullington," apparently depicted a minor scene from part three, chapter three, set in the cotton gin. Darrell Barclay and Malcolm Pitt's daughter, Miriam, lie on the ground, surrounded by a discarded shovel, work gloves, and sacks of cottonseed. In the foreground, lower right, is Miriam's poke bonnet, which they have just angrily thrown at each other. In the text, the two kiss and make up. Miriam rubs her hand over Darrell's bare stomach, forcing an erection, which he covers with his shirt. Miriam leaves. At odds with the author's characterization, the rendering suggests a highly seductive Miriam, alluring and vampish. Though Darrell is clearly leaning back, defensively, the image insinuates that Miriam will eventually seduce him. A casual shopper might have assumed this to be any other spicy, heterosexual romance novel.

Critics tended to agree with publishers' assessments that Thomas Hal Phillips was a skilled wordsmith who convincingly portrayed Southern life and landscape. Writing for the *New York Times*, Thomas Sugrue asserted that Phillips "knows the country he describes, its colors and moods and seasons, its odors and winds and dirts, its flowers and trees and grasses."[17] The subject of homosexuality and its proper handling in this literary genre concerned a number of reviewers. *The Saturday Review of Literature* found it nearly impossible "to fashion a novel out of one emotion"[18]—presumably same-sex love—whereas the *New Yorker* faulted *The Bitterweed Path* for "too much emotionalism."[19] Even the most flattering reviewers couldn't resist a gibe at the taboo topic, given the era's intense hostility toward it. Coleman Rosenberger of the *New York Herald Tribune Book Review* wished Phillips had "chosen a more rewarding theme for the display of his obvious talents."[20] It was "a pity," said a critic from the *Montgomery Advertiser*, who otherwise lauded the local author.[21]

As these carefully phrased comments demonstrate, however, reviewers were as successful at dancing around the issue of homosexuality as Phillips was at addressing it. The comments of John W. Wilson of Dallas's *Daily Times Herald* were typical. He described Phillips's writing as "sincere" and "honest," the book, "excellent."[22] Yet the lengthy article obscured the novel's central themes. Wilson, like so many others, parroted John Selby's dust jacket descriptor and commended Phillips's "pleasant lack of attempted sensationalism." Phillips's removal of the action of the novel to an earlier period — a good fifty years prior — re-emphasized the story's fictive nature and made it less threatening to contemporary sensibilities (while it also implied historical antecedents to the fifties' much-maligned "pervert"). But this critical consensus around the "delicacy" of the subject matter and the "dignity" of Phillips's treatment (not "a suggestion of vulgarity") was perhaps the novel's undoing.

All told, *The Bitterweed Path* generated a respectable critical and popular response. Indeed, fan mail showed that Southerners, other American readers, and even reviewers had much to tell the author about their inner, visceral reactions. A North Carolina critic heaped praise on Phillips in a personal letter, since "time and space [and propriety?] do not always allow a reviewer to say as much as he would like to in a review."[23] But contrary to the *Advertiser*'s prophesy that the book was "bound to cause controversy," it was a lack of controversy that scuttled it. The novel's subtlety assured its quiet acceptability as well as its unheralded demise.

Phillips never again explicitly addressed homosexuality in

his novels. Had it marked his career? He isn't sure. But he thinks Strode, and maybe others, would have extended far more invitations for reading and speaking engagements had one of his subsequent novels—challenging in their own right—been his first. Phillips's four other works demonstrated his enlightened positions on class and race, especially as measured against other white Southern writers and thinkers of the time (although his representations of women remained problematic).[24] Sexuality proved the more encumbering issue, however. Even so, *The Bitterweed Path* would be remembered by the author as a risk that he felt impelled to take.

Thomas Hal Phillips and I speak different languages. Sure, our mother tongue is the same; we both write in standard American English and talk with Southern accents. We are born of the same place: Mississippi. But we came of age in different times. Our vocabularies are different.

When I told Mr. Phillips that I wanted to help bring *The Bitterweed Path* back into print, I felt obliged to explain my purposes, my motives. First, I had to introduce myself, tell him who I am, identify myself. I am a writer of lesbian and gay history, a teacher of literature, an activist. I'm gay. So I would like to offer my community another look at an important precursor to contemporary gay fiction. I want other social and cultural historians to have an additional window on earlier ways of living, earlier means of expression. With what I hope will be an even wider audience for this extraordinary novel, I want to forward a political agenda based on human dignity and equal treatment.

Thomas Hal Phillips never uses words like "lesbian," "gay," or "homosexuality." He has never answered reporters' annoying questions about his personal life. Certainly, his spiritual commitments have bearing. For an author who once confessed to backsliding, to attending services "not more than a dozen times in the past year,"[25] religious values hold sway: "I was brought up during the period of hellfire and damnation, and I think that had a considerable influence on me—and still does. I don't know what I believe about things like that. I just don't know what I believe."

Here is a researcher (in the late twentieth century of identity politics) committed to self-disclosure as an openly gay man speaking with an author for whom such clear distinctions, such categories, were not as often or as easily articulated in his own time (midcentury) or, even less so it seems, during the time about which he was writing (the turn-of-the-century). Implicit in this postmodern exchange between two individuals and their two worlds is not just two, but a multitude of ways of viewing, interpreting, and labeling human experience. This despite some social constructionists' insistence that a remarkably fixed, readily definable, decidedly urban "modern homosexual" appeared around the end of the nineteenth century—and lives to this day.[26] Within those hundred some odd years, discrepancies and complexities of time and place must be accounted for. Differing constructions of masculinity and homosexuality according to race, class, and region must be considered.

The Bitterweed Path helps us in this regard. The novel helps us imagine. With it, we can speculate about loves, liaisons, meetings, unions, and emotional ties of various sorts between men—rural men, farmers, and white Southerners—who have yet to fully emerge from the historical record of the postbellum era. The story renews our efforts to revisit our diverse individual and collective pasts and thereby allows us to re-envision our personal and public futures.

John Howard
Atlanta, Georgia
1995

Notes

I have been privileged to work with Thomas Hal Phillips, whose kindness and wit made this project a pleasure. I owe much thanks to community activist, local historian, and antiquarian Patrick Cather, of Birmingham, Alabama, for first suggesting I read *The Bitterweed Path* and for offering invaluable assistance along the way. I am grateful to Margaret Rose Gladney and Paul Skenazy for their assistance. And for perpetual support, both financial and emotional, I am permanently indebted to John D. Howard, Sr.

1. Of the numerous survey texts and monographs on post–World War II America, my discussion here is most informed by William H. Chafe, *The Unfinished Journey: America since World War II*, 2nd ed. (New York: Oxford University Press, 1991); John Patrick Diggins, *The Proud Decades: America in War and Peace, 1941–1960* (New York: W. W. Norton and Company, 1988); and Elaine Tyler May, *Homeward Bound: American Families in the Cold War Era* (New York: Basic Books, 1988).

2. Although, in fact, "the number of women workers first declined sharply after the war . . . [it] picked up in the late forties, and continued to increase throughout the fifties" (Diggins, *The Proud Decade*, 212).

3. On the plight of black Mississippians during the first half of the twentieth century, see Neil R. McMillen, *Dark Journey: Black Mississippians in the Age of Jim Crow* (Urbana: University of Illinois Press, 1989). On African American political action in the state from the close of World War II through the period more traditionally associated with the Civil Rights movement, see John Dittmer, *Local People: The Struggle for Civil Rights in Mississippi* (Urbana: University of Illinois Press, 1994). On Till, see Stephen J. Whitfield, *A Death in the Delta: The Story of Emmett Till* (New York: Free Press, 1988).

4. A useful overview of the South in the twentieth century is Earl Black and Merle Black, *Politics and Society in the South* (Cambridge, Mass.: Harvard University Press, 1987). On the urban South, see Blaine A. Brownell and David R. Goldfield, eds., *The City in Southern History: The Growth of Urban Civilization in the South* (Port Washington, N.Y.: Kennikat Press, 1977).

5. Flannery O'Connor, "Some Aspects of the Grotesque in Southern Fiction" (paper delivered at Wesleyan College for Women, Macon, Ga., Fall 1960).

6. On the efforts of Baptist and Methodist clergy and laity to regulate sexuality in 1950s Atlanta, for example, see my article, "The Library, the Park, and the Pervert: Public Space and Homosexual Encounter in Post–World War II Atlanta," *Radical History Review* 62 (Spring 1995): 166–87.

7. The most comprehensive historical study of "sexual meanings, sexual regulation, and sexual politics" in the United States remains John D'Emilio and Estelle B. Freedman, *Intimate Matters: A History of Sexuality in America* (New York: Harper and Row, 1988). For more detailed representations of homosexuality during the 1950s, see John D'Emilio, "The Homosexual Menace: The Politics of Sexuality in Cold War America," in his *Making Trouble: Essays on Gay History, Politics, and the University* (New York: Routledge, 1992), 57–73, and Estelle Freedman, "'Uncontrolled Desires': The Response to the Sexual Psychopath, 1920–1960," in *Passion and Power: Sexuality in History*, ed. Kathy Peiss and Christina Simmons (Philadelphia: Temple University Press, 1989), 199–225. The following discussion is drawn largely from these sources.

8. Robert Sickles, *Race, Marriage, and the Law* (Albuquerque: University of New Mexico Press, 1972), 64.

9. "Must We Change Our Sex Standards?" *Reader's Digest*, June 1948, 1–6; "Teen-age Love Clubs," *Ebony*, April 1952, 83–88.

10. "Queer People," *Newsweek*, 10 October 1949, 52–54; "Object Lesson," *Time*, 25 December 1950, 10; "Investigations: Files on Parade," *Time*, 16 February 1953, 26.

11. In 1957—in one of the few documented cases of espionage and homosexual blackmail—the Soviets were unsuccessful in their apparent attempt to enlist a prominent American newspaper columnist. See Edwin M. Yoder Jr., *Joe Alsop's Cold War: A Study of Journalistic Influence and Intrigue* (Chapel Hill: University of North Carolina Press, 1995), 153–58.

12. Hearings and reports are cited and partially reprinted in Jonathan Katz, *Gay American History: Lesbians and Gay Men in the U.S.A.* (New York: Thomas Y. Crowell, 1976), 91–101. In addition to the cities mentioned by D'Emilio, Katz documents the 1955 Boise, Idaho, witch-hunt, 109–19. See also John Gerassi, *The Boys of Boise: Furor, Vice, and Folly in an American City* (New York: Macmillan, 1966).

13. Katz, *Gay American History*, 91.

14. This short biography is taken primarily from oral history interviews I conducted with Thomas Hal Phillips in Corinth, Mississippi, on 25 November 1994 and 18 July 1995. I also consulted the entry by James M. Davis Jr. in *Lives of Mississippi Authors, 1817–1967*, ed. James B. Lloyd (Jackson: University Press of Mississippi, 1981), 370–72; also, Lewis Nichols, "Talk with Mr. Phillips," *New York Times Book Review*, 28 August 1955, and "Mississippi Writer to Make Hollywood Trip," *Memphis Commercial Appeal*, 13 January 1965; and E. J. Mays, "Hal

Phillips H'wood Bound to Discuss Filming Novel," *Jackson Daily News*, 14 January 1965.

15. Orville Prescott, "Books of The Times," *New York Times*, 19 August 1955. Rinehart was also the publisher of Phillips's second and third books. *Kangaroo Hollow* was published in London by Allen. His final novel, *The Loved and the Unloved*, was published in the United States by Harper.

16. Thomas Hal Phillips to Hudson Strode, [1963], W. S. Hoole Special Collections, University of Alabama Libraries, Tuscaloosa, Alabama. There are five additional letters from Phillips in the Strode papers, dated 26 September 1949, 7 November 1961, 11 June 1963, 21 June 1968, and 28 January 1971.

17. *New York Times*, 10 September 1950.

18. *Saturday Review of Literature*, 5 August 1950.

19. *The New Yorker*, 10 June 1950.

20. *New York Herald Tribune Book Report*, 2 July 1950.

21. *Montgomery Advertiser*, [1950].

22. Dallas *Daily Times Herald*, 28 May 1950.

23. Walter Spearman to Thomas Hal Phillips, 29 May 1950, in possession of Thomas Hal Phillips. Words in brackets are my own.

24. A notable exception was Phillips's contemporary, Georgia writer Lillian Smith. Smith posited radical notions of racial equality in her essays—notably the collection *Killers of the Dream* (New York: Norton, 1961)—and in her controversial best-selling novel on interracial love, *Strange Fruit* (New York: Reynal & Hitchcock, 1944). For an insightful and engaging presentation of Smith's life and work, her loves and her views on sexuality, see Margaret Rose Gladney, ed., *How am I to Be Heard? Letters of Lillian Smith* (Chapel Hill: University of North Carolina Press, 1993).

25. Thomas Hal Phillips to Willie Orval Talley, 12 June 1945, Archives and Special Collections, John Davis Williams Library, University of Mississippi, University, Mississippi.

26. A useful critique of this model and a survey of its proponents can be found in Eve Kosofsky Sedgwick, *Epistemology of the Closet* (Berkeley: University of California Press, 1990), 44–48. Though an early article by George Chauncey is cited therein, perhaps no other historical work has done more to instantiate the great variety of homosexual categories, meanings, and identities in twentieth-century America (in one particular locale) than Chauncey's impressive *Gay New York: Gender, Urban Culture, and the Making of the Gay Male World, 1890–1940* (New York: Basic Books, 1994).

THE BITTERWEED PATH

· ONE

one

He was nearing the edge of Vicksburg where the buildings lay scattered along the knolls like stalks from wild seed. Below him, at the water's edge, a white circle of smoke lifted above a boat, and after a moment he heard the damp chill whistle. He hurried on, for already he was late. He had told his father they would be late, but he knew that his father did not care. Now, alone, he rushed toward the edge of the canal that branched away from the river like a small swollen teat and he could see the crowd lined along the bank where the track stretched away—a long table of smooth dry silt. At the far end of the track, hanging between two poles, was a wide, waving canvas bearing the label: VICKSBURG SPRING RACES.

His heart quickened with each step but a sense of easiness was coming over him, for he thought, It's all over—I won't have to run. When he reached the uneven fringe of the crowd, he heard the deep-reaching voice of the starter: "First call for eighth-grade contestants, the final and last race. . . ." He pushed through the crowd, holding his bundle in his hand, and came to the starter. He stopped quickly and his lips stalled, for

3

the man held in one hand a list of names and in the other hand he held a long bronze dueling pistol. The starter looked down, his round face seeming to jut forward. "You in this race?"

"Yessir."

"What's your name?"

"Darrell Barclay."

"You better hurry, Mister. Got your suit?"

"Yessir." He held up his bundle.

"You dress in the boathouse. Race starts in five minutes."

"Yessir." Darrell ran to the boathouse and entered a long narrow room where a row of clothes hung from pegs in the wall. Quickly he stripped naked, placed his jersey coat and shirt and knickerbockers on a peg, and put his shoes directly beneath his clothes. He stood up and his fingers fumbled to untie the bundle which held his track suit and a sandwich that his grandmother had prepared for him. He had meant to eat the sandwich while he rode in the surrey to Vicksburg, but he had not been hungry. Suddenly he caught his breath and the bundle slipped a little in his hands. Hardly three yards away from him a boy stood smiling; he was very still and naked and the light seemed to bounce away from the pale fullness of his loins. Along the lean body the neat muscles moved faintly. Darrell's gaze measured the body slowly, cautiously; it was almost the size of his own, not quite so heavy or so brown. The eyes before him were a little lower than his own and the head of short dark hair was clean and tangled and soft. They stared at each other and slowly their faces began to redden.

"Hello," the boy said.

"Hello."

The boy lifted his right foot and put it on the bench near Darrell. "I sprained my ankle in the broad jump." He looked down at his foot. His eyes were very dark.

"Is it swelling?" Darrell said.

4

"No. It's not bad."

"I'm sorry," Darrell said. He leaned over a little, and then stopped abruptly. He had meant to touch the ankle. Quickly he turned away and untied the bundle, took out his suit, and placed the bundle between his shoes. He jerked the suit—a pair of trunks—on quickly. "I have to go. I'm in the next race." He ran out of the boathouse and toward the dozen barefooted, short-clad contestants talking easily with one another at the end of the track. He did not enter the group. A few yards away he stopped and looked at their suits and wondered whether anyone would know that for his own suit his grandmother had cut the thick durable cloth of a feed sack. She had dyed the suit blue and trimmed the edges and sides with pokeberry red. He looked away from the bright-colored shorts and back toward the boat-house, remembering the body he had seen hardly a minute ago. The late March sunshine struck his shoulders in a warm flood but the silt was cool to his feet. He watched the door of the boat-house, thinking he would see the face again; and suddenly he heard the starter's voice and he wheeled toward the sound.

"Allen Edgeworth, Waycrest Grammar School."

"Here, sir."

"Take the first lane."

"Kenneth Randall, Moccasin Branch Grammar School."

"Here, sir."

"Take the second lane."

"Roger Pitt, Leighton Grammar School . . ." The starter looked up for an answer. "Roger Pitt . . ."

Through the crowd came a figure tall and strong and broad-shouldered in a bright leather jacket. Darrell's look fastened on the solid brown chin, the deep hard-twinkling eyes mocking above the flushed cheeks.

"Roger can't enter," the man said. "His ankle's sprained."

"You Malcolm Pitt?" the starter said.

5

The man nodded. His eyes were steady and firm, and a small cleft dented his chin.

"Since your boy's not running, how about helping us a little? You tag the number one man at the finish line."

"All right, sir," Malcolm Pitt said. "I'll be glad to."

Darrell watched the broad shoulders turn; they were wider by a fraction than his father's but he was not afraid of them.

"Darrell Barclay, Otho Grammar School . . ."

He was trying to match the face in the boathouse with the face he had just seen, and the feeling of some new and fleeting tenderness came over him. The broad shoulders were moving down the track away from him toward the finish line.

"Darrell Barclay . . ."

"Yessir . . ." He spoke quickly.

"Can't you answer up, Mister?"

"Here, sir."

"Move over one and take lane three."

"Yessir."

"Arlin Meeks, Lone Pine Grammar School . . ."

The names went on and Darrell knelt in lane three and dug little starting toe holds. He was trying to remember what his teacher had said to him after he had won the race at school yesterday: left foot slightly forward, right knee touching, hands closed . . . and then, elbows close to body, fists straight out. . . . Far down the track he saw a figure limp across the layer of smoothness toward Malcolm Pitt and he knew it was the one he had seen in the boathouse. A little shiver ran along the inside edge of his suit and seemed to touch him like a drawn finger. He began to breathe deeply and he could hear the starter's words not very clearly. He waited, looking down; his knuckles were like white cotton-locks.

The starter was talking again. Darrell trembled.

6

"On your mark . . . set . . ." The dueling pistol thundered and Darrell was faintly aware that already he was running, and the pounding thighs seemed to engulf him. But ahead of him, no more than a streak of light, was a narrow, narrow passage. He could not hear his own breath; he could hear the breath of others, ahead of him, a stride ahead of him. Suddenly he saw the broad shoulders at the finish line, and the face—the chin and the lips and the eyes—as clearly as he had seen it when it burst through the crowd. And he knew he would win. Through the sunlight and the space his body seemed to arrow forward, and he could no longer hear the breathing about him. He knew they were all behind him—all of them. And as if to leave them forever he gave one last splurge; then the cord broke across his chest.

When he turned, Malcolm Pitt was coming toward him, the steady eyes laughing now. Darrell looked down to the track, as if he had won unfairly, but for the moment he could not remember why he was ashamed. Malcolm Pitt put his arm around Darrell; the big sleeve of the leather jacket was cool but the fingers were warm against Darrell's naked shoulders.

"You walked off with the blue ribbons, boy. You get a prize for yourself and a prize for your father. What's your name?"

"Darrell Barclay."

"Thad Barclay your daddy?"

"Yessir."

"Well, I'll swear. You better find him and go to the judge's stand, over there. The judge is Bertran Wilcox. He'll give you your two prizes."

"But my father's not here. He brought me to Vicksburg, but he had to see Mr. Biggs about renting a place . . . he didn't have time to watch the races. He . . ."

"Come on. I'll go with you."

They went toward the stand built of raw two-by-fours. The second and third place winners were receiving their ribbons and the crowd was cheering.

Bertran leaned over the rail of the judge's stand and looked down at Darrell. The bald top of his head was like a bare knee. "First place?" he said.

"Right here," Malcolm said.

"This another one of your boys?" Bertran said.

"Yes," Malcolm said.

"I didn't know you had two boys."

"I've got the finest two boys in the country. Isn't this a good-looking one?"

"He's too good-looking to be your boy. Son, don't you start trusting Malcolm Pitt. You hear?"

Malcolm caught Darrell's arm. "He's a banker and a politician, Darrell. He's the one not to be trusted."

"Come on up here and get your prizes," Bertran said.

Darrell crossed the platform. He could feel the ribbons in his hand and could hear the crowd and could see them moving in toward the platform. Then suddenly Malcolm Pitt lifted him down and they moved out of the crowd.

"Roger?" Malcolm called.

Darrell looked around and he saw Roger coming toward them, limping slightly. His dark hair was well-parted now. Slowly his eyes met Darrell's.

"This is my boy . . . Roger," Malcolm said.

They stared at each other. Roger was now in a brown coat and knickerbockers. Darrell's heart quickened again. He wondered whether Roger would say that they had already met. A careful smile came to Roger's face. "Hello," he said. It was all like some secret between them.

"Hello."

"You can sure run."

8

"He sure to hell can," Malcolm said.

Darrell looked at the son and then at the father and he was suddenly ashamed again. And he was afraid. Quickly he said, "I have to go. I have to get dressed and be at the wagon yard by three o'clock."

"Is your daddy going to be there?" Malcolm said.

"I don't know, sir. But Mr. Metlock will. I'm going to ride home with him."

"It's a long time till three o'clock," Roger said. "You could go to the Showboat with us."

"Sure," Malcolm said. "It's for all you boys this afternoon. You go with me and Roger. It's a treat. We'll celebrate your victory." Malcolm took from his pocket a rich brown cigar and bit the end of it and lighted it. "Come on and let's get some clothes on you. We have to hurry."

He went into the boathouse a step ahead of Roger and Malcolm and when he came to his bundle he stopped and looked back at them. They stood a few feet away, waiting, and watching him. His face began to grow red and damp and suddenly he turned his back to them and pulled off his shorts and dropped them on his bundle. Quickly he dressed and rewrapped his bundle and wondered if they could know that he had brought along a sandwich. Then he went out of the boathouse, walking between them.

A few yards away from the Showboat a man came toward them, his face tight and shadowy and his broad ascot tie flowing back against his chin. He caught Malcolm's arm and all of them stopped. "There's going to be trouble at Waycrest, Malcolm . . ."

Malcolm Pitt looked up and down the man. "There's not a damn thing going to happen at Waycrest unless somebody makes it happen."

"A dozen niggers are armed already."

9

"You're stirring up trouble again, Clifford. You and Bert and Th . . ." He stopped quickly. "Go on. I'm taking these boys to the Showboat."

"You wouldn't be afraid to fight?"

"I'm just as ready to fight as the next fellow when there's something to fight about."

Clifford grinned and put his hand on Malcolm's shoulder and his eyes were like the horseshoe stickpin in his ascot tie. Malcolm caught the arm and flung it away from him, shoving Clifford a step backward. "The trouble is, Clifford, that you don't want to realize the War's been over thirty years. We'll soon be fifty years old and that's about time for a man to quit fighting."

"I hope they fix you sometime. They will. They'll fix you good."

"Come on," Malcolm said. He looked down at Darrell and Roger.

They went on. Darrell walked a step behind the two. It was as if some circle was being defined for him so that the area outside that circle would always be alien ground to him. He wondered what his father would think if he knew about this. And with the uneasiness was also the certainty that something was safe about these two—something about them could never be touched by any angry hand.

When they went into the musty-odored saloon of the boat, for Darrell it was like going into a dark cave where only the brave entered. The thought of it made little shivers go up and down him again, like the pressure of tiny fingers. They found seats, he sitting between Roger and Malcolm. The master of ceremonies, the only white-faced man upon the stage, was thrusting his arms and clenched fists downward commanding his performers: "Gentlemen, be seated." As his arms snapped still the roll of drums began; and when the roll had ended he

10

stretched taller in his plain frock-tailed coat, looked out over the crowd. "Ladies and gentlemen, I now call forth for you that golden-voiced tenor of the South, who will charm us with a new rendition of *Alabama*." The black-faced man, his frock-tailed coat striped with red, danced down the center steps of the stage. His red lips parted slowly, "Al . . . a . . . bam . . . a, stretched in the sunshine . . ."

Darrell could feel Malcolm Pitt shaking beside him in the low ladder-back chair, as if all the healthy laughter inside him could not come out easily.

You heah bout de boll weevil dat flew outa de double-tree and perched on de dash board and says: "Mista, lemme drive yo buggy?"

De white man says: "You can't drive no buggy. Goan home."

"I done lef home."

"How come?"

"My pa done whop me cause I couldn't take two rows at a time . . ."

More than once Darrell felt the big hand on his knee in a slight grip, and Malcolm Pitt was leaning over to him to whisper, "You like this show, son?"

When they came out into the sunlight again Malcolm stopped to light a cigar. Then he pulled out a gold watch and held it in his hand. Darrell looked at the watch and the open palm and the face, and some spring seemed to unspin itself within him.

Roger caught his father's arm and said, "Let's show Darrell where you swam the river."

Malcolm looked down at him and laughed. "Boy, what are you doing, boy?" He looked at Darrell. "All right," he said.

They turned and walked along the slope toward the water. The whistles sounded on the river, and when they came nearer

11

to the water's edge they could smell the dark mud. They stopped. Darrell thought he should be gazing across the wide space of water toward the tupelo trees on the bank beyond, but he was watching, instead, the arms and shoulders of Malcolm Pitt.

"It's a mile, isn't it, Father?"

"About."

Roger turned to Darrell. "Nobody ever swam it but Father. And with his clothes on too. Tell him, Father. Tell him why you did it."

"Why . . . to prove the man I am." He began to laugh. "No. It was to win a little bet." He held his coat open for Roger and Darrell to see the label: *Kingley & Kingley.* "They bet me the finest suit in Vicksburg. So I took off my shoes and coat and set out." He turned away from the water's edge.

Darrell was the last to turn, and when he did, his eyes fastened again on Malcolm Pitt's arms and shoulders, and then on Roger's face.

Malcolm looked down at Darrell. "Roger will go with you to the wagon lot. I've got some errands to do."

"I know what it is," Roger said. "You're going to the Yellow House."

Malcolm reached down and tousled Roger's hair. The little chills moved along Darrell's body again—he wished the hand would touch him too.

"We'll see you again sometime, Darrell. . . ."

"Yessir." There was nothing else to say. Then Malcolm Pitt walked away with that determined graceful movement that belongs only to very strong men.

"What's he going to the Yellow House for?" Darrell whispered.

"To get a bottle of wine . . . and whiskey."

"You ever tasted any?"

12

"No."

"I haven't either."

They began to walk slowly toward the wagon lot and when they had gone a little way, Darrell could see that the surrey was there, waiting. A stone's throw from the surrey Darrell stopped and faced Roger. "Mr. Metlock's waiting . . . he's ready to go." He was not certain that his words were loud enough for Roger to hear. They kept looking at each other.

There was a tiny ripple about Roger's lips. "We could see . . . don't your father ever bring you to Vicksburg?"

"No."

"Not ever?"

"Almost never . . ."

Roger's eyes seemed to blur. "Goodbye," he said and quickly turned away. Then he stopped and faced Darrell who had not moved. "Could I . . . could I see your ribbons again?"

"Yes." He took them carefully from his coat pocket. "Papa won't look at them. I'll give you one . . . if you'll take it."

"No. They're yours." Roger took the ribbons, his fingers passing gently over the cloth; then he gave them back to Darrell. His hands trembled a little. They did not say anything. Roger turned and walked away, limping slightly in the afternoon sunlight.

The surrey seemed to crawl along the road. Darrell sat beside Mr. Metlock and tried to listen to him, but his mind kept leaping back to the hour before, and to those faces; and he thought, I wish he'd hush . . . I just wish he'd hush. The voice went on, "Yessir, they tell me they buried a live woman in that Shiloh graveyard and somebody heard the scratching or something one night, and it was the next morning before they done anything about it and by that time she'd died again." Mr. Metlock leaned over and pulled off his shoes—he did not wear any

13

socks—and propped his feet on the dashboard. He rubbed a few streaks of dirt from between his toes and wiped his fingers on the knee of his overalls. "I was down at the gin last fall and saw this feller firing the boiler standing there barefooted in the middle of November and somebody said to him, 'You're standing on a live coal.' And he turns his face a little and says, 'Which foot?'" Mr. Metlock's laughter rang out and seemed to ricochet from the sharp red clay banks probing the late afternoon sunlight.

Darrell was glad when he was away from the voice and was walking up the path toward the rusty-tin-topped house, for then he could remember the hours which had been more real yet more uncertain to him than anything his mind had ever built. He could bring each minute to life with flesh and blood, remembering: *I've got the finest two boys in the country . . . the big hand on his knee and the face leaning to whisper: You like this show, son? The faint limping in the afternoon sunlight . . . the blur in the very dark eyes . . . the light bouncing away from the pale fullness of loins . . .*

He did not want to walk into the room where he knew his grandmother would be waiting, because he was afraid that once inside he would have to forget everything which had happened to him that day. When his foot first touched the porch his grandmother called, "Darrell, is that you?"

"Yes, ma'am."

He went into the living room. His grandmother was standing beside the mantel, tall in her plain gray crepe dress which was too good for daily wear, too old for Sunday; and along the front of the dress down to the bodice was a line of small buttons like new green peas shining in firelight.

"Where's your father?"

"I don't know. He didn't come back with us. He said he'd catch another ride."

14

"Did he see Mr. Biggs?"

"I don't know. He said he was going to . . ."

"Mark my words it'll be April here and no place rented. It should have been done three months ago. Wild fool notions in his head. He's not thinking about a place. Get your good clothes off now; you've got lots to do. Carry up the water . . ."

"I won the race, Grandmother. I won first place. Don't you want to see the ribbons?"

"Yes. Put them on the dresser. I'll look at them after a while."

He laid the ribbons on the dresser and went into the kitchen where his bed was, and where the black walnut wardrobe was, and changed clothes. He brought in the wood first and then brought the water from the spring, and on the last trip when he had reached the yard he saw his grandmother coming through the kitchen doorway to meet him.

"Set the water down there," she said. "He's back and he's calling you to find his riding quirt. I'll help you in a minute."

He put the water down quickly and when he passed the corner of the house he saw his father at the lot gate, his shadow very long and dark across the earth.

"Darrell!"

"Yessir . . ."

"Where's my riding quirt?"

"I don't know, sir."

"You've done something with it. Skin out here and find it."

He began to run, for his father's horse was already saddled, waiting. When he came closer to the gate he saw that the lines about his father's eyes now were like heavy pencil marks. The bulge was in the wide jumper pocket and he knew it was his father's pistol.

"It might be in the crib," he said.

His father followed him toward the corn crib. Darrell un-

15

chained the door and pulled it open, and a little to the right of the doorway he saw the wrist-loop of the quirt. He reached out his hand and then leaped back against his father. Inside the quirt a long black body moved.

"What's the matter with you?"

"A snake . . ."

"Where?"

Darrell's lips twitched. Like a streak of water moving along an uneven floor the long black body slid down through a rat hole.

"There . . ." Darrell said. "There . . . through that hole." His father was towering over him now.

"The plank's loose. Lift it up. I'll shoot it."

He saw the gun in his father's hand; his own hand twinged, for he could feel the sleek body, the fangs needling into his fingers. "Let me get a hoe. I can raise the plank with a hoe . . . I'm afraid to put my hand . . ."

"You want it to get away?"

He looked at the quirt. "It might . . ."

"Lift it!"

His hand moved slowly and he could almost feel something dripping from the end of his fingertips; slowly his fingers went down through the crack, curled, and jerked the plank upward in one terrible breath. A few inches from where his hand had caught, the snake moved along the sill. The pistol fired. The long black body coiled and wriggled and finally lay still. Darrell turned from the doorway quickly and lowered his head as if he would vomit onto the windswept clay. He could hear his father breathing deeply and then his voice, "It's only a chicken snake . . ."

Darrell raised his eyes and saw his grandmother standing quietly behind his father, fingering the shawl that covered her shoulders. "You're awfully brave, Thad Barclay. It does my old heart good to see what a fine brave boy I've raised . . ."

"Stop it!"

"Now get on your horse. Go on and meet the Klan . . . and beat some niggers and show them how brave you are. You can't stop fighting. You and Clifford Meeks and Bert Terrell . . . I've raised you and I can say tonight with my face lifted to God it's a pity you didn't die at Vicksburg in the place of your father. But ride on. We haven't had enough trouble already. Look at the hovel we're in now. Sometime they're going to get you—and if not the blacks, then somebody . . ."

"You're a woman. You don't know anything about it." He picked up the quirt and turned to Darrell. "Take that off with a hoe and bury it." He went to his horse and mounted quickly and looked down at the grandmother.

She lifted her hand in a little wave. "Ride on. March is all but gone and you with no place rented."

"Hush," he said. "Just hush. I've rented a place. From Malcolm Pitt."

Darrell caught his breath. He watched his father's face, and then his grandmother's. She took the shawl from her shoulders. "I thought Malcolm Pitt told you last week he didn't have a place to rent."

"I guess he changed his mind. I'm telling you what he told me today. Only two hours ago." He reined the horse quickly and galloped out of the lot and down the bare red knoll.

They watched the horse and when it was out of sight the grandmother said, "Of all the places he might have chosen, he would settle with Malcolm Pitt."

Darrell slowly knelt onto the ground and looked up at his grandmother. "Is there anything wrong with him—Mr. Pitt?"

"No. Nothing's the matter with him, and he's got good

17

land. He's just not a man of God. I doubt if he ever goes to church. He drinks, and plenty. I know about him."

"I saw him today at the races. I liked him."

"Yes. Most everybody likes him. But I hope you'll be spared the ways of the Pitts. I know what drink can do, that and a little goods to go with it. I've seen it in your own grandfather." She moved to put her hand on his head but he drew away.

"I don't care what he does. I like him. When I won the race today he was there and he went with me to get my ribbons and he took me to the Showboat. Papa wasn't there. He didn't even ask if I won. He didn't care. I wish Malcolm Pitt was my father and I wish Roger was my brother . . ."

"Darrell! That's an awful thing to say. You'll take what God's given you and be pleased. At least your own father doesn't drink. You don't wish any such thing."

"I do."

"Get off that ground and get your work done and stop such talk."

But he kept kneeling and looking up at her, for something beyond her face held all his mind with a wild tenderness.

two

A sadness was about him as he ran and he knew it was not caused by his father's voice. It was something that lay ahead of him, like a shadow but not clearly defined. For a moment, it seemed that he might look ahead more clearly than he could look back. But he saw only the shadow. It was like remembering when his mother had died, remembering the casket and the handles and the smell of fern, but not remembering her face.

18

Then the moment passed and he ran on until he reached the creek.

The sun was down and the wind was rising, but it was not yet dark when Darrell waded across the creek on his way to Malcolm Pitt's house. There was no bridge and no foot-log, and though the water was cold to his feet his body was free from the March wind until he climbed up the clay bank and started through the pasture. The thick dead tops of the bitterweeds caught between his toes and he hurried because his father had said, "You go to Malcolm Pitt's and you tell him we got moved all right today. Tell him we want some groceries, some lard and sugar and coffee. You take the path across the pasture and hurry back so your grandmother can get supper. I mean hurry. You hear me?"

"Yessir," Darrell had said.

"Four pounds of lard, quarter's worth of coffee, quarter's worth of sugar . . ."

"Yessir," he had said again and turned away from the ferocious sound of his father's ax biting into the hickory poles hauled up for firewood only an hour before.

He could hear the solid strokes until he had reached the creek, but now that he had crossed the water, he could no longer hear them—as if the sound had stopped precisely on the opposite bank.

He was walking now beside a rail fence where cedars grew. They tapered upward through the dusk like church towers. At any other time he would have walked slowly and counted them. But now he must hurry. He noted, however, that there was a sadness about the cedars and wondered if the stars would be bright above them when he returned. Then he felt lighter as he ran, for he remembered the faces he would see.

Once he stopped and stooped over to remove a bitterweed top that had caught between his toes. His fingers touched his damp foot and he thought first of heavy dew before he remembered that only a moment ago he had waded the creek. When he started on again the wind was stronger against him. It seemed to sweep him toward a time and place where he would lose the uneasy sense of strangeness forever about him.

He started to run again, for he could hear the words shaking in his mind, "And I mean hurry, boy . . ." He was afraid not only of the words but of the physical strength behind them: the strength which bit so fiercely into the hickory poles.

He did not think of being tired now, though the moving had been long and slow. He remembered his seat high on the cotton mattress in the second wagon which Malcolm Pitt had sent, along with Yancey, to help with the moving. Except for three places (when Yancey had said, "Now, Mista Darrell, you bettah let me take the lines heah") Darrell had driven all the eleven miles from Otho without lunch or water. He and Yancey did have three baked sweet potatoes, cold and waxy, one for each and one divided.

The barn loomed ahead of him in the dusk and Darrell began to walk. At the lot gate he waited, seeing no one. Then suddenly he saw Roger beyond the rail fence, standing motionless, his back against a post, watching something which he himself could not see. Darrell crawled through the gate and went toward him, more mindful now than ever of the cold spring wind around his bare ankles.

He stood in the lot a little behind Roger and saw that Roger was watching Malcolm Pitt curry and brush a rakish bay saddle horse. After a moment, Roger, sensing that someone else was present, turned and looked full into the face of Darrell.

"Darrell . . ." Roger moved a step toward him and stopped. Then they began to smile, both their faces full of a brief tremor.

20

Darrell whispered, "Did you know we moved on your place today?"

"Yes . . ."

They moved, as if to touch each other, when a sudden, childish laugh broke the stillness. A girl leaped from the barn loft onto a pile of hay in the alley.

"That's my little sister," Roger said. "Miriam. She's always down here when I don't have any corn to shuck."

She looked at them and then she ran out of the lot, laughing, and the streamers of her dress trailed her in the dusk.

Quickly Darrell said, "I came to see your father."

"Father!"

Malcolm Pitt stopped currying and turned from the horse. He drew his forearm across his mouth as if the lips might have tasted dust. He said, "Yes, what you want?" Then he saw Darrell and all his face seemed to give a quick salute. "Well! Hello there. I thought we'd see each other again. Didn't you?"

"Nossir."

"You didn't?"

"I don't think I did."

Malcolm came toward them and the arms in the bright leather jacket seemed stronger than Darrell remembered. The eyes were still mocking above the flushed cheeks.

"You get moved all right today?"

"Yessir."

"Good. You want something out of the store?"

"Yessir, sugar and lard and . . ."

Malcolm changed the curry-comb to his left hand which held the brush, and with the right hand brought out a ring of keys. "Roger will take you to the store and get whatever you want." He handed the keys to Roger. "Put it on the books, on the green book by the scales. It's already fixed."

"Yessir," Roger said.

They walked past the edge of the pond toward the big house almost hidden behind the grove of oaks and pecans, and Darrell kept one step behind so that Roger would not look down at his feet.

"That's a big pond," Darrell said.

"Sure," Roger said. "We'll go swimming when April comes. You can go with us."

"You have to have clothes on?"

"No. We go naked. Father said all the trouble in the world started, anyhow, when folks put on the first fig leaves."

Roger opened the front gate and waited for Darrell to go first. He did not close it. They went around the house and crossed the backyard toward the garden. Roger stood on the steps of the storehouse and turned the key easily in the padlock. He pulled the chain, pushed the door back, and entered ahead of Darrell. In the semi-darkness was the smell of dust, of empty nail kegs and coal oil. The shelves to the right were stacked with food—four-pound buckets of lard, small twenty-five cent bags of sugar, cans, glasses, sacks of meal and flour piled high toward the back of the room. On the left the shelves were filled with gear and lines and tools.

"Sure is a lot of stuff," Darrell said.

"Sometimes it's packed full." Roger picked up the green ledger by the scales and walked to the door. "I'll put it down now so I can see," he said.

"Four pounds of lard, quarter's worth of sugar, quarter's worth of coffee," Darrell said.

Roger wrote slowly, touching the pencil once to his lips. Darrell stood beside him and watched. He saw the name *Thad Barclay* was already written at the top of the ledger sheet. He watched the pencil slide easily, the top moving in wider sweeps than the point. He wanted to say, "I wish I could write like that.

It's nearly as good as a copybook." But instead, he moved away, ashamed, afraid that Roger might think he was checking the entry prices in the lined columns.

Roger pointed to the silver coffee-grinder fastened to the counter. "You want the coffee ground?"

Darrell shook his head. "My grandmother doesn't like it ground. It gets old."

Roger closed the ledger and placed it back beside the scales. He opened a brown paper bag and put the bucket of lard in first, then the small bag of sugar. He stood in a cane-bottomed chair and reached toward the top shelf for the coffee. He brought down a quart jar, looked at it closely, set it by the scales and reached to the top shelf again. He put the second jar in the brown bag and then he laughed. "I almost gave you peanut butter for coffee."

Darrell laughed too. For the first time the feel of things about him did not seem strange. It might have been Roger's look which had caused the change. "I wish you had. I like it nearly better than anything."

"Then buy some peanut butter too."

"No." His answer was quick and final. "I can't buy anything but this . . ." He reached out for the brown bag.

"It's only a quarter. I'll put it on the books."

"He told me . . ." Darrell said. "He told me just to get lard and sugar and coffee." He looked down at the brown bag squeezed under his armpit.

"Here," Roger said. He held out the jar. "We got plenty of peanut butter. You take it and I won't put it on the books or nothing. It's a present."

"I can't take it. I don't want you to give me anything." He backed away toward the door.

"You got to take it. It's just a present." Roger pushed the jar into his hand and Darrell stood by the door looking down

23

at the dark round glass. He turned it in his hand, feeling the smooth surface against his fingertips until he heard a quick drawing of the chain through the lock-hole. Darrell jerked his head up to see Miriam come slowly through the door, walk beside the counter and drag her finger across the glass case.

"I want some candy," she said.

"You can't have any. You know what Father said about taking things out of the store."

"I heard you," Miriam said. "I heard you give away something. You give me some candy or I'll tell. I'll tell Father just as soon as he comes from the barn."

"Tell," Roger said. "Tell."

A short breath rushed through Darrell's throat. *Tell* . . . *Tell* . . . was like the biting of his father's ax and he said, "I been gone a long time. I got to go." He ran out of the door, past the house, and through the gate, not knowing why he ran. There was the urge to stop, to retrace his steps and give the jar back to Roger; and there was the thought of peanut butter clinging solidly against the roof of his mouth, filling his stomach with solid weight. So he ran with the brown bag closer under his left armpit and the jar tighter in his right hand.

At the lot gate he put out his hand to set the peanut butter down while he climbed through the fence, but quickly he jerked his arm back, holding the jar against his ribs, and set the brown bag down instead until he had crawled between the planking.

He stopped at the creek and fingered the jar again. There was the sure feel of the gift's being placed into his hands, the round solid weight. And no part of it, now that it had been given to him, belonged to anyone else.

He could sit on the sand and eat; if he hurried he could eat all of it; and if he needed water he could drink from the creek. He dropped the paper bag (the lard and the sugar and the coffee) on the sand and held only the jar, his right hand ready to turn the lid. His hands closed tighter, straining against each other, and the lid turned. But at the very moment of loosening, when all he must do to eat was lift the lid, he knew that the gift did not belong to him alone, but to his father and grandmother, too. With the same quick turning of his wrists he sealed the jar again and lifted the brown paper bag to his arms.

Before he reached the yard he could smell hot cornbread baking in the stove, and he could not think of anything but the taste of peanut butter on cornbread crust. He could sense it exactly and completely; for only three months ago, at Christmas time, they had had two jars.

He saw a light only in the kitchen, the small coal-oil lamp with a smoked chimney, and his father standing in the kitchen doorway. He hurried past the wash-pot, the pile of new split wood, to the kitchen steps and lifted the brown bag to the heavy red hand waiting above him. He felt the weight of the bag go from him to the stout arm.

"You get everything?"

"Yessir."

"What's that you got?"

"Peanut butter. Roger gave it . . ." But he did not finish. In a flash he saw the quick sweep of the muscled hand and felt the knuckles hard and solid against his cheek. "He gave it to me, he gave it to me," Darrell cried, and he felt the knuckles against his cheek again.

Then the words came, sharper than the knuckles, "Can't you never learn, can't you never learn to get what I send after and nothing else? Now don't stop till you take that back."

Darrell shrank away from the pointing finger, the wrist that might lash out again.

"I'll make a believer out of you, or die trying. You hear me?"

"Yessir." He thought he had not answered loud enough and

he said again, "Yessir." He saw the wide shoulders turn in the kitchen doorway and the bulky body limp toward the coal-oil lamp.

He did not remember this time that the water was cold when he waded the creek, nor was he aware of the bitterweeds catching between his toes. He did not see the stars above the cedar trees. He was hearing, *Your father was not that way before the War, but we have to understand what all our brave men went through at Vicksburg even if we cannot feel what it must be like to lose the use of a limb in battle* . . . How many times his grandmother had said this did not matter. For, though he was only four that night, Darrell knew it happened a long time after the battle of Vicksburg. It happened below Two-mile Creek with the Klan. He remembered two men bringing his father in the house that night, the blood dripping in the doorway, beside the bed, and the man saying, *Good God, fellow, you're liable to lose this leg.*

When he had crawled through the lot fence at the barn the second time, Darrell could see the bright swath of light from the window of the big house. It stretched across the yard to the oak trees. He knew he must walk into that light. And he felt that once it touched him it would break through his skin.

He opened the front gate, waited, started cautiously toward the front door; and then he stopped. It would be easier to go around the house and leave the jar on the steps of the store. But he tensed his muscles and advanced through the light. Then he stopped again, and through the window he could see Miriam and Roger standing beside Malcolm Pitt. Roger stood with one hand on the center table, his eyes dropped toward the rug. Miriam was saying, "Father, Roger took a jar of peanut butter out of the store and gave it away."

"Huh?"

26

"He took it and gave it away. He gave it to that little boy, but he wouldn't give me one stick of candy."

"What are you two fussing about?" Darrell saw Malcolm lay his paper aside and look up at Roger. "Did you get the groceries for him?"

"Yessir."

"Did you put it on the books?"

"All but the peanut butter. I . . ."

"Why did you leave that off?"

"I just did."

"That's not an answer." Malcolm got up and walked to the mantel. His lips opened, waited; but he did not speak. He turned and put his elbows on the mantel so that Darrell could not see his face. Miriam stood on her knees in a chair and watched Roger, who had not moved.

Darrell saw Malcolm start, not quickly but almost hesitantly, toward Roger; and he waited for the father-hand to tense, to swing in a short arc against Roger's cheek. But the hand was not raised. Malcolm Pitt only looked down at Roger, at the short black hair, and said: "Don't you know I don't give a damn for a little jar of peanut butter. But I gave you the keys —all by yourself. Then you took something which didn't belong to you. You know what that's called?"

"Yessir."

"Give me the keys."

Roger's hand went slowly into his pocket. He lifted the keys without looking up. His hand remained raised for a moment, empty; then it fell.

"What you crying about?" Miriam said.

"Can I go now?" Roger said.

"Yes," Malcolm said.

Darrell saw Roger go past Miriam. He heard the door close

27

and the quick steps across the porch. Then he saw Roger pass the oak trees, his right arm moving once across his eyes and dropping quickly. Darrell followed him and stopped by an oak, the tree's length away from where Roger sat down by the lot gate with an elbow on each knee and a cheek in each palm. He knew then, while his hands grew moist and cold on the jar, that he must slip away from Roger, around the pond and go home. He guessed that sometime he would have to say, "I ate it all by myself."

When he turned away from the tree, Roger lifted his face quickly and said, "Miriam?"

He wanted to run, but already Roger was coming toward him. He stopped and said, "It's me. I had to bring it back. If I hadn't taken it you wouldn't have got into trouble."

"How come? How come you had to bring it back?"

"Papa told me to. He made me bring it back. Maybe he thinks you didn't give it to me . . ."

Darrell held out the jar and Roger took it. "Are you going to put it back in the store now?"

Roger looked down at the jar, and even in the darkness Darrell could see the straight part running through the short black hair.

"I haven't got the keys any more." When he lifted his eyes again he said, "Come on."

"Where we going?"

"Just come on," Roger said.

They stood on the bank of the pond and the water was dark below them. Roger held the jar tightly; then he put it out toward Darrell. "You throw it."

"No," Darrell said. He could feel the jar cold and slippery in his hands; he could feel his fingers gripping and squeezing until the glass cracked and bit into his palms. "No. You do it."

He could taste the peanut butter on hot cornbread crust.

He did not want to swallow, because he was afraid that Roger would hear, but he knew that he must, for the dryness in his throat was choking. He did not see exactly where it fell, but he heard the splash and knew the water was settling in the darkness.

"I guess it won't ever bother anybody else," Darrell said. "Nobody but us."

Darrell could feel Roger still watching him, but he did not turn his eyes from where the jar had fallen. He was hearing Roger's voice, "But you could have eaten it."

"I'm not hungry."

Then Roger moved one step closer. The water stretched level and dark before them.

"You're not mad at me?"

"No," Darrell said.

"If you'll come to our house tomorrow afternoon, I'll show you something. Something Father is going to bring from Vicksburg. Will you come?"

Darrell could not answer. It was as if he lay at the bottom of the pond, thinking, *I won't go back, not for groceries, not for anything or anybody ever.*

And while this crowded in upon his mind, some old and ancient warning seemed to rise up in him, to seal his lips, so that he could only nod that he would come.

three

"Tell me what he's going to bring," Darrell said. But Roger only shook his head, as if he thought that once the secret had been told he could not keep Darrell beside him. They sat on the lot gate in the late afternoon sunlight and looked at each other. Darrell thought the terrible uneasiness which had surged in him last night would not come again to him in the sunlight, but it had shadowed him and brought him back and now it moved over him again like fingers—the fingers were larger now, perhaps as large as Roger's.

Suddenly Miriam ran from beside the crib and shook the gate. Roger swayed; Darrell reached out and caught his shoulder.

"Miriam!" Roger straddled the fence to face her. "You little sprig. You're worse than Nolie."

Darrell looked down at her eyes, heavy with a small circle of darkness—and her pouting lips. He tried to believe that her eyes were more like her father's than Roger's were, but he could not because of their fleetingness—there was something fleeting about her whole body. Yet everything about Roger seemed as if it would go on forever.

She looked up at Darrell. "You climb down and tie my sash and *I'll* tell you what Father's going to bring us."

"You climb up here," Darrell said.

"Will you tie it?"

"Yes."

"Roger won't. He likes you better than he likes me." She caught the gate and shook it again.

Roger held and looked down at her. "Go ahead Nolie Potter. Go ahead and be mean and silly and indiscreet."

She stopped shaking the gate. "Roger likes to use big words. He thinks he's grown but he's only twelve and going on thirteen . . ."

"Who's Nolie?" Darrell said.

"O," Roger said. "She's the preacher's little girl. You'll find out about Nolie . . ."

Suddenly Miriam stood straight and brushed the corn silks

30

from the front of her dress and started running out of the lot with the small sashes streaming behind her.

"It's Father!" Roger said.

They leaped off the gate, running together. Before they had reached the road Darrell stopped; it was not his father—there was no reason for him to run. He waited. Across the road, in the driveway, Malcolm Pitt climbed awkwardly from the surrey. In each arm he carried an Irish setter puppy, the dark red hair shining.

"Now," Malcolm said. "Now, what did I promise you?"

Darrell watched without moving. He did not expect a face that big and strong to smile.

Roger grabbed at the puppy in his father's right arm. Miriam stood with her hands caught behind her. Then slowly she held out her arms.

"Take it, Honey-bunny. Are you afraid of it?"

She took the puppy cautiously, held it wriggling against her. Malcolm looked across the road to where Darrell stood. "Show them to . . . to Darrell," he said. Then he motioned with his arm. "Come here."

For a moment Darrell did not move. There was a peculiar thrill in hearing Malcolm Pitt call his name.

"Come on," Roger said. "Come on." He was stroking his puppy with short hand movements.

Darrell crossed the road. A few feet away from Roger and Miriam he stopped and stood with his hands locked behind him. Until then he had not thought of his overalls, nor of his bare feet. He wanted to run away.

"I'm going to give mine to Darrell," Miriam said.

Darrell backed suddenly away. His hands unlocked and fell against his sides.

"Have you got a dog?" Malcolm said.

31

Darrell's face jerked up. Malcolm Pitt seemed to him bigger than anybody he had ever seen. "No, sir."

Malcolm bent over Miriam. "Do you really want to give it away?"

"I want to give it to Darrell."

"I couldn't take it."

"Yes, you could," Malcolm said. "A dog belongs to a boy anyway. Honey-bunny doesn't want a dog."

Miriam walked toward Darrell. He backed away again. "But I can't . . ."

She put the puppy into his arms. He heard Malcolm Pitt say, "He's a pretty thing, isn't he?" Darrell could not answer. He was afraid he would drop the dog.

"You be good to him, son. And he'll be good to you." Malcolm got into the surrey and drove toward the surrey shed.

"He's just like mine," Roger said. "We got two just alike. Tinker and Winker."

"You've got Winker," Miriam said. "He's got a white speck on his forehead and I'll bet you can't find it."

"You better take him back," Darrell whispered.

Miriam turned her back quickly to Darrell. "You can put him down now and tie my sash. He won't run off."

The sun seemed no higher above the earth than his own shoulders when Darrell left for home. He crawled carefully through the fences holding his puppy close against his side. When he got into the pasture he ran. At the creek he stopped for a moment and put the dog's face near the water. The dog lapped a few times. Then Darrell held him close in his arms again and looked for the white speck on his forehead. It was easy to see, once he had found it. "Are you going to like your name little Tinker . . . Dinker . . . Winker? Are you? You don't? Oh, you do? I'm going to be good to you. And you've got to be good to me. I haven't got anybody but you. Did you know that? You want to walk? I can't let you walk. I've got to hurry . . ." He began running again because his night work was to be done —wood to get in and cow to milk and feeding to do before his father came home.

He ran into the house, through the living room into the kitchen and thrust Winker out for his grandmother to see. "Look what they gave me, Grandmother. Look!"

In her black clothes she seemed like a tall and slender streak of darkness. "Now look at that," she said. "Who gave it to you?"

"Miriam mostly. And her father. And Roger too, I guess."

"It ought not to be in my kitchen." She came closer and put out her hand. "But it is a pretty thing. It reminds me of your grandfather. He loved an Irish setter better than anything else living."

"Papa will like it. Won't he, Grandmother? He'll like it?"

"He won't like your being gone all this late. Why didn't you come home before now?"

"I didn't mean to be late."

"You never mean to be late. Get your milk bucket, and hurry."

"Will you feed him? Can I put him down here?"

"Yes. Now wash your hands and be gone. It'll be dark here and nothing done."

Slowly Darrell bent over and put the dog on the floor. Then he went to the washstand beside the stove and washed hurriedly, turning twice to see the dog in the center of the room, sitting quietly. He took the milk bucket, with enough water to wash the cow's udder, and with one last look at his new possession, ran out the kitchen door. Suddenly he turned back to his grandmother who had stooped over the puppy.

"Grandmother. His name's Winker. And you'll feed him a lot, won't you? A lot of milk."

33

"I'll feed him in the yard," she said. "But he is a pretty thing," she whispered. She was shaking her head.

At the barn Darrell worked with a new kind of haste. It was not fear that made his hands rip the shucks quickly from the corn. It was the thought that for the first time in his life he possessed something all his own. It was something he already loved, and would keep on loving. Nobody would ever know how much he would love Winker, not even Roger or Miriam or Malcolm Pitt. Deep within, almost so secret that he could hardly let himself know, was the knowledge that Winker would be on the covers of his bed every night, where his fingers could reach out and touch the soft, dark red hair.

He hardly remembered shucking the corn for his father's horse, throwing down hay, and milking the cow. He stabled the cow; and when the horse came into the alley of the small barn, he knew that his father had come home. He latched the horse's door, took the milk and started toward the house. He could hear the sound of his father's ax at the woodpile. The sound made him hurry. Then, like the final ricocheting of a gun, the chopping ended. Darrell caught his breath. He did not know why he clung to the chain that held the small lot gate in place, but he knew that something was going to happen. He heard his father's voice, "Where did this come from?"

Then his grandmother's voice, "They gave it to Darrell."

"Who?"

"The Pitts. Malcolm Pitt, I guess."

"Why did he take it?"

"I don't know."

The chain fell from Darrell's hand. He began to run toward the house, and above the sound of his running was his father's voice again, "Suppose it went mad? Had you thought of that? Do you think I'd have the money like Malcolm Pitt to put one of us in a Vicksburg hospital?"

34

Darrell turned the corner of the house. He saw the big jumpered shoulders of his father wheel in a short arc. He heard the grating thump, the whimper, then nothing. The bucket of milk dropped from his hand. He could feel his bare feet wet, and the slight stickiness of the wet earth. The dog lay stretched a yard away from his father's shoes, as if it had died in the midst of a sudden leap. Slowly his gaze traveled up his father's leg, past the handle of the poleax which his father still held, then to his father's throat and finally to his face. He knew that in that moment he hated the face, that he must hate it. He could not cry. More than anything else he was hurt because he must hate.

"Get me a sack," his father said.

Darrell did not move, nor answer. He thought of Roger and Miriam and Malcolm Pitt. He thought of his own lips trying to say, "He's dead!"

"Did you hear me? Get me a sack. There's one on the lot gate."

Darrell looked down at his bare feet. He set the milk bucket upright, then stepped out of the milk.

"Come here," his father said.

He walked toward his father. He thought his father's hand would reach out for him, strike him; but it did not matter now. He stopped. His father's hands did not move. "What's got into you? Do you want to get bit by a mad dog? You want to foam at the mouth? You think I could send you to a hospital?" He waited for an answer. "Do you?"

"No, sir."

"Are you trying to be like the Pitts? Is that it?"

"No, sir."

"You listen to me. You'll take nothing from them. You won't borrow their books. Nothing! You hear me . . . Can't you learn you're not a Pitt? Can't you?"

"Yessir."

"Get me that sack. You'll take this off in the woods."

Darrell seemed to make himself turn. He would not look at his father's face, nor at the face of his grandmother who stood in the kitchen doorway. He saw only the dark folds of her dress, and the dark tips of her shoes. Once past the corner of the house Darrell knew that his father could not see him, yet the eyes seemed sharp against his back. He jerked the sack from the gate post and started back toward his father, like one walking through snow, numb with coldness. He would not cry now, because he thought it was what his father expected, perhaps even wanted. His teeth were set tight, yet he could feel his lips and chin move. Ahead of him his father was like a huge stump rising in the duskiness.

Darrell held out the sack, his eyes turned so that he could not see the lifeless body stretched across the hickory chips.

"Hold it open," his father said.

He opened the mouth of the sack. His father stooped. Darrell turned his head again. He felt the weight drop into the sack. Then his father was tying the mouth of the sack tightly.

"Take it deep into the woods," he said. "Beyond the creek. You hear?" Suddenly his father's voice changed. He talked low, almost whispering. "A mad dog. A mad dog could get all of us. Take it deep into the woods." He looped the string again and handed the sack to Darrell.

For the first hundred yards Darrell walked swiftly. At the edge of the woods he slowed. It was darker there. He let the sack slip a little in his hand. He was afraid. Something he loved was gone; and he was walking in the woods with death, a death that came with swiftness and sureness and ease. He crossed a gully and waded through old pine limbs that crackled. He changed the sack into his left hand.

The creek was not wide. He leaped it and went beyond the pines to the gum tree thicket. At the edge of briars and a canebrake he put the sack down gently. Slowly his fingers began to pull at the string around the mouth of the sack. He could hardly see the knots, but his fingers held on, pulling, solving a little, pulling again.

With a dry crackle something leaped within the canebrake. Darrell wheeled and ran, empty-handed, stifling a scream. Before he reached the creek he stopped. He had to go back and see Winker for one last time, to touch the dark red hair. He wondered if there would be any blood about Winker's mouth, if the white speck would be spoiled on his forehead.

The darkness seemed to thicken while he stood there; and the grinding of insects began, a sound he had not noticed before. Slowly he walked toward the canebrake. It was like going toward death, toward the fingers of a crushing hand. Still shaking, he picked up the sack, fumbled with the knots again, not seeing them but feeling them give way to the pull of his fingers.

When the mouth of the sack suddenly loosened, Darrell caught his breath. He knew then that he could not touch or look upon the dark red hair again. What he had loved, and what had been beautiful, was now a heap of death, of nothing. He began then to cry, and with the cry he began to run, not remembering the creek or the pine brush. At the edge of the woods he saw the light in the kitchen, and he slowed though he did not stop running. A few feet from the kitchen window he stopped and listened to his breathing. Now that he could see the lamplight, his grandmother and his father at the table, he began not to be afraid any more. His breathing slowed until he could not hear it or count it. He did not hear his father and grandmother speak. His father rose from the table and left the kitchen. After a moment his grandmother stood and took her plate away. Darrell could hear the rattle of dishes. He wanted to hear it; it was not at all like death. Cautiously, he went to the kitchen door and entered.

37

His grandmother turned, caught her breath a little as if shocked to see him standing in the doorway. She held a cup towel in her long slender hands. A neat white apron covered the front of her black dress, the collar of which seemed to choke her. Darrell looked directly into her face, his eyes not moving, as if she must now give him an answer to all that he needed to know. Her face seemed narrow. He had never thought of its being narrow before, except, maybe, a long time ago when she read to him. Maybe he had thought of it then. Her face was small, too, lean, not at all like his father's. It was not tender or pretty. But he liked it. It was all that he had.

"Well," she said. "It's over and done with."

"I could have carried it back to them."

"What's gone is gone. The Lord knows best."

"I was good to it. He would have loved me."

His grandmother took another plate to dry. "Your supper is ready."

He reached down to rub his foot. He would not cry before her, or before anybody. "I'm not hungry."

"You might as well eat. I reckon you've learned your lesson." She turned to stack the dish away. "And all that good milk you spilled. You'll have to milk before breakfast in the morning, even if it is Sunday. When you dropped it you bent the pail. At least it's bent. I reckon that's what caused it . . ."

That night, in his bed in the kitchen, Darrell dreamed or half-imagined that there had never been any dog at all. Everything was a little joke that his sleeping mind was playing upon his waking mind. Then he began to dream that everything was all mixed and confused, that there were only a few realities; his father was actually Malcolm Pitt, and if one dog got killed there were a hundred others to be had by the mere reaching out of a big hand.

38

He woke without a start, but with a cold soberness which tried not to give way to wakefulness. He did not want to think of anything, but he knew that tomorrow morning, before the first church bell rang, he would have to find Malcolm Pitt. He did not know what he would say, but maybe that did not matter so long as he did not cry. He turned in the bed and the sound of old springs screaking made him afraid again: like walking toward the sack or the sound of the leaping within the canebrake. He slept, fitfully, and by daylight he was awake again, lying on his side staring at the claw-shaped feet of the stove. In the faint lightness it was easy to think of the claws as real. He got out of bed and washed his face in cold water. He opened the kitchen door and sat in the doorway looking beyond the woodpile to the mist that rose above the slope.

He did not hear his grandmother come into the room. When he turned she was standing beside the kitchen table, tall and straight, her sleeves pushed high upon her wrists.

"What's the matter with you this morning?"

"Nothing. I just got up."

"To go out doors?"

"No, ma'am. I just got up. That's all."

"Does anything hurt you?"

"No, ma'am."

"Make a fire for me then."

"Yes, ma'am."

He did not mind making the fire. He wanted to. It would give his hands something to do. Then he went to the barn and milked, and fed his father's horse. When he came to the house again his grandmother had a pan of warm water for him. He washed slowly, until his father came into the room. Then he hurried, though he did not look around to his father.

They sat down to breakfast, his father at the head of the table. Before him were eggs, biscuits, gravy, and coffee.

39

His grandmother said, "There's no milk for you, Darrell. Spilled, you know. Nothing but this morning's milk and it's too warm."

"I don't want any," Darrell said. He knew that his father was staring at him.

"Are you talking short to your grandmother?"

"No, sir."

"I don't know what kind of streak has moved into you."

Darrell kept looking down at his plate. He wanted to leave the table, but he knew that his father would not let that happen. His father held out a plate of biscuits.

"Did you eat your supper last night?"

"No, sir."

"Stubbornness. Don't try to mule up with me. Now eat your breakfast."

He ate. And his throat seemed to be crying instead of his eyes. He wondered if Roger had ever been made to eat; he wondered, too, how he could tell Malcolm Pitt that his dog was killed.

After breakfast, when he had brought in stove-wood, and had gone to the barn to turn the stock into the pasture, he took a tub of water into the back yard beside the chimney and began to bathe. The water was cold though he had drawn part of it from the reservoir of the stove. The sun was not high so that there was more warmth from the chimney than from the sunlight.

When he had dried carefully he put on his underwear, then his pants, turning the cuffs up one roll until he had put on his shoes. He took the clothes he had worn and started around the corner of the house. A few yards from the doorway he stopped, breathless. The clothes dropped from his hands and covered his shoes. He screamed, at first no words at all, and then, "Grandmother!"

She came to the door; he could hear her. But he was looking beneath the kitchen steps.

"What is it now?" she said.

"It's back!"

"What?"

"My dog. It's him! I know it is." With his quick breathing he began a strange and uncontrolled little laugh. "I won't have to tell them he's dead. Will I? It's him all right." He made a step away from the clothes that covered his feet.

Suddenly his father seemed to fill the doorway, then leap into the yard, wheeling and searching beneath the doorsteps, where two eyes, glassy and quiet, stared out. His father's fist tightened. "I tied that sack. I knotted that sack. Bring my gun!"

Then his grandmother's voice was like pebbles rolled in the palm of the hand. "Now you listen to me, Thad Barclay. You've taken this thing far enough. He can carry it back if you want him to."

"Goddam that thing! You bring my gun."

"I'll not."

"Darrell!" His voice was sharper and harder than the sound of his ax had ever been. "Darrell! Bring me my gun."

Darrell did not move. His father was staring beneath the steps. Slowly his head turned. "I'll beat the living . . ." His voice became lower, "Bring my gun."

Darrell started toward the kitchen door. The dog moved, with a faint whimper.

"Not this door," his father said. "Go around the house. You want to run him off."

Darrell backed away. He could already feel the pistol in his hands, the cold dark metal. He went around the house and up the front steps, then into the living room, where his father slept, as if he might be stealing something. He knew the pistol lay in the machine drawer, at the foot of his father's bed. The drawer

41

opened easily; his hand caught the dark barrel. He lifted the pistol, as though it was very heavy. Through the window he saw his father. He knew how easy it would be: his hand trembled. He started toward the door, not breathing at all. On the front steps his knees shook; he stopped and waited.

"Darrell!" It was his father's voice at the kitchen door.

He clutched the pistol with both hands to keep it from falling, but he did not answer.

He turned the corner of the house; there seemed nothing before him except his father. He stopped, waited, like one standing before a creek, knowing that he must cross though the water is too wide for leaping. He held the handle tight, looked at his father, then the dog, then his grandmother who was standing now in the yard beside the woodpile. He looked back at the dog, as if he might find the white speck on its forehead. The dog had moved to the edge of the steps.

Slowly he put his other hand on the barrel. For the space of one held breath, long and terrible, he knew again, clearly, how easily the pistol fired. His gaze caught against his father's stare. His heart was beginning to race so that the pounding no longer seemed broken into beats, but one continuous throb. He was coming closer and closer. His father loomed. Suddenly he thrust the pistol forward. "Here!" he said.

His father's hands shook; he took the pistol and kept staring down to Darrell. His face was pale.

"I wish you'd die," Darrell said.

His father's face turned slowly toward the steps. The pistol was leveled quickly on the dog. Darrell did not move or flinch or change his gaze when he heard the four shots. He thought of the white speck, whether it would still be there.

His father put the pistol in his jumper pocket. Then he went to the steps, picked up the dog, and walked around the house. There was a little trace of blood along the ground.

42

Darrell had lowered his head, so that he could hardly see. Suddenly he knew that his grandmother was holding him, that she was crying and shaking him. "You're all right," she said, breathing and choking. "You're all right. I was so afraid."

He pulled away from her. "I'm going to tell *him* now. I'm going to tell him what happened."

He walked with a strength he had never had before, his face set, and not hurrying, and not afraid. He crossed the creek and pasture and came to Malcolm Pitt's barn. His heart gave way a little and some of the strength seemed to flow away from him when he did not see Malcolm Pitt or anyone in the lot. He did not want to go to the house, nor to see Roger or Miriam. For a moment he waited at the gate. Maybe tomorrow, when he started to school, he could tell Malcolm Pitt. But he did not think he could wait.

Then he climbed through the gate and went into the alley of the barn. He seemed to lurk from stable door to stable door. Quickly his heart leaped, for when he had reached the end of the long alley, he saw Malcolm Pitt standing beside the shed crib. Darrell stood and watched him. For the first time he knew that Malcolm Pitt was not fat: he was big and strong. He was not dressed as he had been the day before. Now his sleeves were rolled up and his shirt collar was open. His face was muscled and firm, and a faint redness seemed to make it smooth. He began to smile when he saw Darrell, and slowly his teeth shone in the morning light.

"Well, hello. You're mighty early for Sunday morning."

Darrell went toward the crib, as if it was the first time he had not stood barefooted before Malcolm Pitt. He was proud he had on his Sunday clothes. At the corner of the crib he stopped. His eyes caught Malcolm Pitt's eyes; and he wondered why they did not stare.

"I came to tell you something."

43

"All right." Malcolm Pitt reached for an ear of corn.

"It's about what you gave me."

"What is it?"

"He killed my dog . . . Papa did."

The redness was heavier in Malcolm's face then, and it made his face seem bigger and stronger. "That's the shooting I heard?"

"I'm sorry you gave it to me. But I would've been good to it."

Slowly Malcolm Pitt twisted the ear of corn in his hands, tighter and tighter, until suddenly every grain seemed to break from the cob and fall at his feet.

"Goddammit," he said. "Goddammit to hell." The cob dropped from his fingers. He put out his hand and gripped Darrell's shoulder. Darrell felt that the hand had covered him, but he did not move. Then he heard, "It's all right, son. Do you understand? It's all right."

Darrell turned and walked away from the crib. He thought that Malcolm Pitt was watching each step, and it made him feel warm, like sunlight across his shoulders.

four

Darrell marked his days by tracks across the new furrowed earth, sometimes with Roger, sometimes with Malcolm Pitt, but more often in his father's own fields carrying water, following the harrow, or sprouting with the poleax, which was too heavy for him, the five acres of new-ground along Winter Creek. When the April smell of burning sedge came to him, even though he held the poleax in his hand and the sweat streaked white along his dusty body, his heart lifted with the smoke be-

44

cause he was no longer on the red clay knoll of Otho where no white house with columns stood, where no Pitt lived; but he had come like people pictured in his Sunday School book out of the wilderness into a land rich with more than goods. Always there was for him a new skipping of the heart when he walked toward the big white house and a faint hurting when he turned away, for there was a certain exact pattern of living within the shadows of the tall columns which he stood in awe of. Yet he would not let himself be ashamed of his own small house or of the strict prophetic quotes of his grandmother over each meal. He was still moved by fear of his father's arm though for a time the cloud had lifted; the hand seldom touched his face; hardly a drop of blood slipped from his nose.

Darrell had sprawled often on the dark green carpet in the Pitt house playing jack-rocks with Roger and Miriam, or playing checkers with Roger while Miriam learned to crochet. But when Roger said, "Let's play cribbage," Darrell shook his head quickly, "I don't know how, and besides, my grandmother said I couldn't play cards."

In the fields or at the barn when Darrell and Roger sweated over the breaking of a yoke of bull yearlings, Malcolm Pitt never did more than yell, "Watch 'em boys, watch 'em. They'll take you right through a fence." But in the house, even as they sat unmoving at a game of checkers, Roger's mother always stopped sewing on her patchwork quilts (pieced from the small geometric patterns as if no scrap should be left loose in the tidy house) to say often, "Don't muss up the house, Roger," until Malcolm dropped his paper to say, "Now, Leta, who in the hell ever heard of messing up the house with a game of checkers?"

It was mid-June when Darrell first stayed at the big house over night. After he had bathed in the cold water brought in by Yancey and while he stood in Roger's room clothed only in the one piece broadcloth underwear, new-made by his grandmother,

45

Leta Pitt came through the door without knocking, a coal-oil lamp in hand, and stood looking down at him.

"I wanted to find out . . ." she said, and leaned over close to him so that he could see her black hair parted precisely in the middle of her head and could have touched, with little reaching, the buns of hair above each ear. She added in secret whisper, "Do you wet the bed?"

He stepped away from her, his face quivering almost as if his father had yelled to him, and only after his lips stopped twitching could he say, "No, ma'am, never in my life."

"Just wanted to prepare if you did," she said. "Roger does sometime. Good night." She turned and went out, her long shadow from the lamplight crawling behind her. He looked down to his stomach for a minute feeling that he no longer even wore his underwear and that he had spoken of an action seldom enough, if ever, spoken of as man to man and never mentioned to a woman, so that he could not, when Roger returned to the room, even speak of the question the mother had asked.

While he lay beside Roger, Darrell thought he might tell things now that he had never told anyone, that he might tell Roger of everything that had happened before he knew the Pitts. He would talk of the red clay knoll at Otho, the cold biscuits on a green plate, the way he could not remember his mother's face any more, or of how his father rode with the Klan. Maybe he would tell Roger how he had thrown into the bluebird's nest—not because he wanted to throw, but because he must. And the bird fell to his shadow on the moss; the gray eggs dripped on the mulberry trees. Roger would understand. But after a while he knew that Roger was asleep; he was hurt that he could not talk.

When he awoke in the morning Roger was still sleeping, close beside him, with his arm around Darrell. He moved a little and pushed Roger's arm away. Roger opened his eyes and put

46

his arm around Darrell again. Darrell lay still. Now and then he could hear sounds in the house, and around the edges of the window shades he could see the brightness of sunlight. "We better get up, Roger."

"I don't want to get up."

Darrell closed his eyes, trying to sleep again, but his eyelids quivered. Then he heard steps in the hall and he whispered to Roger, "You better move."

But Roger neither moved nor answered. The door opened and Malcolm Pitt came suddenly into the room, his face clean-shaven and two pin-points of blood shining upon his chin. His voice was loud, "All right, you two. If you're going with me you've got to roll. Drag him out, Darrell." Malcolm turned back into the hall and closed the door.

Darrell sat up in bed quickly, feeling his whole body warm. "Why didn't you move?"

"I didn't want to."

"Why didn't you move your arm then?"

"Don't be so jumpy. I'm not afraid of Father . . ."

That summer was almost gone, the watermelons were turning white in the sun, when Roger came suddenly up the path to Darrell's house, one Saturday evening, to say for the first time, "Father said I could spend the night with you." Darrell did not know at first whether he was glad that Roger had come or not, for sooner or later Roger would say, "Where is your papa?" and he thought he must tell the truth. He watched the smile that seemed to have its beginning deep within Roger and he knew that he was glad that Roger had come. The barrier was not completely gone, but at least for now he was not alone.

With the thrill still quick within him, Darrell said, "Let's go get a watermelon. We got some good ones left."

"I'll pull off my shoes," Roger said.

47

They went barefooted through the tall corn toward the creek and the watermelon patch; and there, after expert thumping, selected the right melon and took it across the dying vines to the gum tree at the end of the rows. They stripped naked, dropping their clothes on the gum tree roots, and buried the melon knee-deep in the cold blue creek. While Roger sat on the slippery rind, with the water whipping around his armpits, he said, "If this thing would be still under me, I'd show you how to make a real big frog on your arm. It gets bigger when your arm is wet." Because Darrell was not looking at him and so did not answer, Roger added, "We didn't have any good melons this year. Tinker loves watermelon."

Darrell looked up at Roger. "A dog doesn't love watermelon."

"Tinker does."

"Why didn't you bring him?"

Both their faces lit with sudden redness. Their eyes held each other, understanding. As if forced to talk, Darrell said, "Papa can raise good melons. We planted these before sunup on May the first. We always do, even when it comes on Sunday. That's when grandmother fusses, but Papa plants them then and the blooms don't ever fall off." The redness was going away from his face; for a moment he was forgetting Winker, and the white speck on his forehead, and the sound of the poleax.

"Where is your papa?" Roger said.

Darrell, kneeling in the sand, made an uneven arc about his knees. "I think he went to Otho." He did not know how he could have lied to Roger, except that a son, no matter what he thought or believed or even knew, must protect the father. Yet he remembered, without looking up to Roger, dark-of-the-moon nights when his father rode off from the house with the grandmother calling after him, "You can't stop. You can't stop fight-

48

ing. It's in your blood eating away, and pounding in your ears until you can't stop even to listen to your own mother. If you'd leave them alone they'd leave us alone. It was people like you that caused the War. No time for listening, because you're stinging inside with something you can't even bear to look at . . ."

Roger was spinning the melon in the cold water. Darrell was almost afraid of Roger's sober eyes which seemed to look, even while laughing, into the secret places that should not be. Yet he knew that Roger could not know where his father was, and could not know that only a week before his father had ridden off while his grandmother stood in the darkness on the edge of the porch predicting again: "The Klan can't rest two weeks now, can't rest for you and Bert Terrell and Clifford Meeks. Next thing you'll be riding in the wide open daylight. If there was anything to ride about Malcolm Pitt would be riding. But there isn't. You want trouble because that's the only way now to warm your thin blood; it's the only time you can live. But you'll answer sometime with more than a limb. You'll answer, Thad Barclay, because God won't let anybody trample like he owns the earth. He is quick and certain . . ."

His father had said, "Hush. What does a woman know about niggers gathering at night, the Yankees turning the black fools wild, and giving them guns as good as mine? You want them breaking through your window at night? Is that what you want?"

"If they did you ought to be here protecting . . ." but her voice had died with the sound of hoofbeats down the hill.

Roger lifted the melon, held it against his stomach, and while his eyes laughed again, he said, "Maybe your papa's with a girl."

Darrell knelt in the creek so that the water whirled about his waist, and Roger could see only his shoulders and head.

49

He said, stammering a little, "What kind of girl?"

"Just a girl, any kind of girl. Maybe somebody at Vicksburg."

The water chilled the inside of his legs and Darrell rubbed his thighs, knowing that his face was warm and red and that Roger was looking toward him again with his sober eyes while his arms strutted with the weight of the melon and the pan-muscles of his chest were tight. Darrell had reached inside himself for anger to hurl against the words of Roger, and the face of Roger, and his naked body; but he could not be angry with Roger who stood as if to say, "See how our muscles have tanned since the night we threw the jar into the pond. One of these days they'll be big, really big, and heavy like my father and when they are I'm going to have me a real sweetheart."

Darrell said quickly, "You don't know about girls like that."

"Heck, I do know." He was spinning the melon in the water again. "Is it still deep enough to dive?"

"In the lightning struck hole, it is." Darrell pointed a few yards up the creek.

Roger came out of the water and put the melon on the sand. He climbed up to the clay bank, and stood with his hands over his head.

"You ought not to be on the bank naked, Roger. It's about time for the train."

"We can get in the water when we hear the train." He stretched his arms over his head again and said, "Here I go. I'm *Friday.*"

Darrell said, "What do you mean, *Friday?* This is Saturday."

"*Friday* the man. Don't you know? I've been reading *Robinson Crusoe* this morning. What did you do?"

"Picked butter-beans."

"Oh . . ." Roger stretched his arms again and said:

50

"Dive like a rock, swim like a feather,
Go to the bottom and stay forever."

He shut his eyes and leaped. His hair formed a black mushroom upon the surface of the creek. He shook the water from his face, then turned with his stomach breaking level on the surface. "You know what my father's going to do?"

"What?"

"He's going to build a gin right below our pond. Maybe this fall. I don't know. Sometime."

"You'll be at school then," Darrell said. "At Jackson."

"I think they're going to send me, but I don't much want to go."

"Why?"

"I just don't."

"If you don't say *why*, I won't believe you."

"I don't know *why*."

Darrell looked away from Roger. He sat down in the water. After a while he looked up at the bank of cloud in the west, the heavy blackness and light yellow. "Reckon it's going to be a storm?"

"I hope it's a storm," Roger said. "I hope it's going to be a hurricane with rain and hail and racer-snake lightning. But it won't be."

"You know what makes a storm?"

"Yes. It's things doing things they shouldn't be doing."

"No. I can tell you. God stores up thunder in nail kegs. He keeps packing it in and packing it in, and boom! All of a sudden the head comes off . . ." Darrell stopped short. "Roger, I saw something moving in the willows over there."

"Where?"

"In the willow bushes there."

With short rapid strokes Roger was skimming the water

51

with the heel of his hand. "Maybe it's a snake," he said. From the clay bank of the creek and the willow-patch came high laughter, like the quick unwinding of a toy. "That's Nolie," Roger said.

They waited, waist-deep in the water. Then they saw her stand up, rising out of the willows, and still laughing. Roger said, "You better go on back, Nolie."

"Why?" she said.

"Cause we're in swimming and we're naked and . . ."

She walked along the bank and her laughter was louder. "I'm going to get your clothes."

"If you go toward my clothes, I'm gonna come out."

"I don't want your clothes. I'm going to get Darrell's clothes. He's prettier than you are." She went on slowly toward the gum tree, her head down and turned so that she watched them out of the corners of her eyes, all the time curling a strand of hair around her left forefinger. Darrell did not move.

"We're coming out," Roger said. "We're coming out." He ran through the water, first knee-deep, then ankle-deep, and when he reached the bank, Nolie turned quickly and went screaming past the willow bushes and the blackberry patch.

Darrell moved then toward the bank, his heart beating to the sound of Nolie's running. Even her name was always to him like secret whispering, like something that could not be touched and was never clear, always out of reach because he did not understand. He was looking down to the sand beneath his feet, but he could hear Roger beside him laughing. The fierce surging in him would not die. He said, "We got to go, Roger. It's already supper time."

"Nolie . . . Nolie's crazy about you," Roger said.

"How do you know?"

"She told me. She tells me everything."

"We got to go," Darrell said again.

52

"I bet she loves you and you're afraid of her . . ." Suddenly, while he looked at Darrell, his laughter stilled. Quietly he said, "Who's going to tote the melon?" Before Darrell could answer, Roger added, "You throw me on the sand, I tote it. If I throw you, then you tote it."

Darrell studied Roger, his long full muscles from neck to wrist, golden now in the dusk. "All right," he said.

Their hands touched, gripped, parted; arms and palms slipped with quick uncertain seizing. Then locked suddenly, stomach against side, thighs tangled, they rolled in the sand, and lay bound together. "Dog fall," Roger said. But neither of them moved. Their cheeks were tight together, their stomachs pressed each other, and their thighs were inter-locked. Roger began to laugh and said, "Look at the way you are."

"You are too," Darrell said. Their arms unlocked but their bodies did not move away from each other.

"What you thinking about?" Roger said.

"Nolie. We better get up. She might come back."

"Richard told me he did something once."

"With her?"

"Yes."

"Maybe he didn't tell the truth."

"He told the truth. I know the way Nolie always was at school. One time after school I was going to do something, but I didn't."

"Why?"

"It was lightning and I was afraid. Then last summer and the summer before last she stayed in Vicksburg with her old crazy aunt that's a painter. When she came back she told Richard all about a lot of things she did."

"Why didn't she tell you?"

"She told me. But she told Richard first."

"You like her?"

"In a way."

"Move."

"You move."

Darrell got up and turned his back to Roger and waded into the creek and began to wash the sand from his body. Roger lay on the sand and watched him. Suddenly in the stillness they heard the stretched voice of the grandmother screaming through the August corn: "Darrell! Darrell! Hurry here. It's your father . . ."

With clothes half-buttoned they ran toward the cry, through the lashing blades of tall corn; and when they came into the open where the cotton was no more than knee-high, Darrell could see his grandmother standing on the hill, her slender form a little darker than the dusk. When he reached the clean-swept back yard she clung to his arm, her eyes choked more with fright than with tears, while her incoherent words ranged from cry to whisper: "They brought him in; they brought him—Bert and Clifford. Bert has gone for the doctor but I know it's no use . . ." Then, as if to steady herself, she added, "You see what God does, you see. Go in to him."

Darrell moved through the kitchen without breath, sensing the moment as a dream. He could hear his grandmother coming slowly behind him, but he did not know whether Roger followed or waited. At the living room door he stopped, held to the facing. He could see in the lamplight by the center table Clifford Meeks bending toward something. Then with a deep drawing in of heavy air he looked to the left where his father lay uncovered on the bed. For a moment, while his eyes welled, he could not see clearly but stood breathing quickly through his mouth, hearing his father whimper first like a child and then struggle with the breath in his throat until the air came out in one dull hiss. He moved slowly, face quivering with each step, to the foot of the bed, heard again the dull stac-

54

cato hiss, and after that, "Not my leg this time . . . Clifford."

Darrell's lips closed, stuck tight, quivered open when he finally said, "Papa . . ."

The strained, puffed lips on the bed opened with the eyes to say, "Come here."

"I'm here . . ." Darrell said. He was afraid, even then, to move closer to the wide, blood-stained hand which lifted tall and straight for one brief breath and fell, not struggling or moving at all, but fell like the final heavy plunging of an oak earthward. And the arm was still, like the full face upon the pillow. Darrell turned. His grandmother was there, her arms outstretched to pull him to her bosom, whispering while she wept, "Gone. You see what God does. The Klan. I'm sick of the Klan. Fighting Negroes at Waycrest . . ."

Darrell pulled away from her, not crying then but knowing the blood was upon his hands now because he had lain in his bed in the kitchen and prayed: *I wish God would make him die.*

He ran from the house and toward the pines that loomed before him. When he stopped he could see behind him the weak light seeping from the house, and could hear the faint voices. He crumpled, face downward, upon the copper pine needles damp with dew. After a little while he turned on his back and looked up into the blur of limbs and heavy darkness. Time was measured by the endless drumming of frog and insect sound. The pounding in his ears became like spurting blood. He remembered again the terrible thing he prayed for: *I wish God would make him die.*

He wanted to cry, yet he could not. And even while he tried to make the tears come to his eyes he remembered Vicksburg, and a wide muscled hand that never lashed out; he remembered: *Malcolm Pitt laughing in the low ladder-back chair, the big hand on his knee and the face tilted to whisper: You like this show,*

55

son? I've got the finest two boys in the country . . . He tried not to remember the white speck on Winker's forehead.

He stood then, and leaned against the thick-barked pine. The resin was cold against his wrist. He was sure that God would eternally doom anyone who did not cry at his father's death. And he was feeling, too: He who lies dead now in the crowded room is only my father in the flesh and my real father is forever Malcolm Pitt who, alone, is tall enough to stand against God.

He heard the soft slow walking behind him like steps in a new-made furrow; and when he lifted his head, Roger stood beside him. Roger's eyes were calm, and again they seemed to look through the darkness of the night and of the mind to a thing no longer secret.

"Darrell?"

"Yes."

"Why don't you go ahead and cry out loud if you want to?"

He watched Roger's still face, saw him stand firm in the darkness as if his body was equal to a richness which he, himself, would never possess. Then Darrell, crying, though feeling that he was no longer a child of twelve, said, "I wish you'd go home, Roger. I wish I'd never seen you or your father or Miriam or anybody."

Something was dying in Darrell, too; and the first rush of man-blood surging in him wanted to reach out into nothing and crush the world between two hands. But space did not move back its walls nor did time stop; and Gabriel did not plunge feet-first, for him, through the clouds with trumpet in hand. Only the surging stilled with the cooling night.

Roger found his voice in the darkness to say, "You don't really want me to go home, do you?"

"No," Darrell said.

56

part

· TWO

one

Darrell ran along the creek bank toward Roger's house that late afternoon but he was not hurried by any voice. That voice was now falling apart beneath the ground, and the two weeks since it had died away were like two long crop years to Darrell. Sometime it frightened him to think that no voice or hand might ever bother him again. He ran now because he thought that his grandmother was going to take him away from Leighton and Malcolm Pitt and Roger.

He did not see anyone at the barn or in the lot so he stopped running and walked on toward the house. When he reached the gate the sweat was heavy on his face and he took his shirt-tail and dried his eyes and cheeks and stood waiting until his arms were dry. While he waited he could hear the stiff lumbering chords from the piano and he knew the sound was made by Roger. He went into the house and stood in the living room doorway and watched Roger's hands. They were long and smooth and the color of a new egg. There seemed to be no touch of moisture on Roger's whole body though his arms moved vigorously as he bent slightly forward. Roger was always clean and spotless. Suddenly he got up and went to the window and leaned his head against the screen. "Mother! Mother! I tell you I've got another barrel of corn to shuck."

"Don't call me again, Roger."

"I guess you want Father to come home and find it not done and beat the pee-turkey out of me."

"Roger!"

"Well, I can't practice any more. I rubbed a blister on my hand shucking corn this morning. It'll burst and fester and turn green and purple and kill me. And I hope I lie in bed four years and three months before I die and you have to come in to see me every day and remember a little old blister on my finger caused it all . . ."

"If I have to come in there to you, Roger, you'll have a blister somewhere else."

"If you'll just let me go, I'll memorize fourteen hundred lines of Shakespeare—when I get grown."

"Just one more word, young man . . ."

Roger went quickly to the piano and for a moment his hands moved madly along the keys. He saw Darrell and stood up suddenly. "Darrell," he said. "Just a minute. I'll have to play a serenade or something right quick or she'll be in here with half a hedgerow." He played slowly, his face half-turned to Darrell, mocking the sound. After a little while he stopped.

"Go on," Darrell said.

Roger turned on the bench. "Aw, I was just satisfying her."

"I thought you never played any more."

"Well, Father quit making Mother not make me practice."

"Oh. You mean he lets her make you practice."

"Yes."

"If I could do that I wouldn't fuss about it."

"Yes you would. Come over here and I'll show you something."

Darrell went to the piano and Roger took his hand and moved it along the keys. Roger's hands were soft and Darrell could feel his own face warm. Darrell withdrew his hand. He was standing over Roger.

"See if Mother is still in the flower garden."

Darrell stood beside the window. Leta Pitt was bending over a small bed of fresh turned earth and leaf mold, her long gloved fingers raking and kneading and smoothing. She was not large, but she seemed strong to Darrell and he was afraid of her. He was most afraid of her when he saw her dressed to go somewhere, usually to church.

Roger began to play hard loud chords. "Does she look like she's coming, Darr?"

Darrell shook his head slowly from left to right, and Roger stopped playing.

"Who's Darr?"

"You," Roger said.

"Why did you call me that?"

"I thought of it last night. That's a special name—for you. Nobody else." He looked down at the piano and dragged his hand along the keys. "Father wouldn't make me do a thing like this. It's Mother . . . Mother . . . Mother."

"I came to tell you something," Darrell said.

"What?"

"My grandmother is going to take me to Uncle Turner's."

"Where's Uncle Turner's?"

"That's grandmother's brother. In South Carolina."

"For how long?"

"For always."

Roger reached out and caught Darrell's belt. "You? She can't make you go. You can run away from her."

"What would I do?"

"Live with us."

"That wouldn't be right. I would live by myself."

"You'd be afraid."

"I wouldn't be."

"Yes you would. And I'd have to come over and stay with you. Would you let me?"

"Yes. If you wanted to."

"Would you want me to?"

"Yes."

Roger lifted his hand and pushed back his hair and suddenly three cornsilks lay like a web across his hair. Only the faint smooth edge of his teeth showed and along his throat flesh moved up and down. "Are you going . . . going to move away?"

"I don't know. I guess I might as well. You're going off to school."

"But not far."

They heard the surrey outside, then Malcolm Pitt calling, and then the sound of the chain on the lot gate. Darrell moved and picked the three cornsilks out of Roger's hair and held them in the palm of his hand.

Roger looked up at Darrell. "That was Father."

"Yes."

"You won't go away. I know you won't."

"How do you know?"

"Because I know. Will you?"

"If I have to go, I'll come back." He looked at Roger for a minute and then he went quickly out of the room.

He went down the driveway toward the lot and looked back once to see whether Roger was following him. He did not once hear the sound of the piano. Beside the surrey shed he stood and watched Malcolm Pitt unharness the mares and rub them down and turn them into the pasture. When Malcolm had finished the brushing he turned and drew his wrist across his lips, the way he always did, and tossed the brush into a box. His eyes caught Darrell and he said, "What's on your chin, boy?"

Darrell drew his hand across one cheek and down the side of his chin. Malcolm came over to him and pulled a cornsilk away from his lips; his hands smelled like strong horses. "Did Roger talk you into helping him shuck corn today?"

"No, sir."

He shook Darrell's shoulders playfully, and Darrell did not move away from the hand, for he did not mind the smell of strength.

"How's your grandmother?"

"She's all right. I think she's going to South Carolina. Uncle Turner wrote to her today. He asked her to come and bring me."

"You ever been to South Carolina?"

"No, sir. And I don't want to go."

"You don't?"

"No, sir. If she went and I didn't go, what would you do with me?" He held his breath until a smile gathered on Malcolm's face.

"What would you want me to do?"

"I could work. I could work awfully hard. And somebody's got to work for you."

"You want to stay that much?"

"Yessir."

"Come spring what if I put you in some of the stables spading up manure and throwing it out? Gets hot and nasty and stinking in there."

"I can spade it out. Feel my arms."

Malcolm began to laugh and for a minute he pulled Darrell against him. Then he released him. "But Roger won't be here. He's going to school."

"I want to stay."

61

"All right. You tell your grandmother I've hired you. Tell her you're one of my hands now. I think maybe we can get her to stay too."

"Yessir. Thank you, sir." He turned away quickly.

"Darrell!"

"Yessir."

"I wasn't going to let you leave anyway."

He backed away a few steps, watching Malcolm Pitt's face before he wheeled and began to run.

His grandmother was standing on the edge of the porch as if waiting for him. From a long way off she was like dark smoke, but when he came nearer he could see the neat checkered apron tight about her so that its bosom bulged and in the bulge was a needle with a long black thread swinging back and forth. When he came up the front steps she took the thread and circled it about her forefinger. "Now where have you been?" she said.

"To Roger's."

"You slipped off."

"I had to see him."

"And you saw him only yesterday and stayed so late I had to help with the night work. Well, I'm not going to help tonight. Come here. Did you run all the way back?"

"No ma'am."

"You look it. What did you go for?"

"I just went."

"Darrell. Would you stand before God and keep a little thing like that secret from your grandmother? Would you stand there and tell me you went for nothing?"

"I told Roger about Uncle Turner's letter—and told his father too."

"What a pretty thing you are. Going there with your troubles. We've got a family. What did you tell him?"

"That I don't want to go to Uncle Turner's."

"Why not?"

"I want to stay here."

"Charity?"

"I can work. I'll work hard. Mr. Pitt told me I could work for him. He said tell you I was one of his hands now."

"You listen to me before you go any further. We're going to your Uncle Turner's. The Pitts will ruin you. They've already done enough. You think more of them now than any of your blood kin. But the time will come when you'll need what they can't give. You understand? The time will come . . ." She stopped, for the tears were in his eyes and his lips twitched and his body trembled.

"If you make me go I'll come back. I'll run away. I'll come back here and live by myself and work for him."

The thread corded her finger and slowly the needle slipped from the cloth. Then she looked away from him and quietly she said, "Go on and do your night work. Go on . . ."

two

His grandmother did not go to South Carolina and Darrell very carefully did not mention the name to her. By the time the month was gone he knew that she would not go at all, for already she talked about winter and hurried with the late summer canning and at night, when Darrell came from Malcolm Pitt's hay fields, he helped his grandmother take the warm square jars to the storm pit and stack them in colored rows along the clay shelves, where the earth was warm in the dead of winter and nothing would ever freeze. Every day he saw Malcolm Pitt and Roger and there was nothing to mar his happiness except the knowledge that Roger was going away.

On the day before Roger went away to school Leta Pitt called Darrell to her room. He left Roger at the front gate, where they had been pitching horseshoes, and entered the house very cautiously. He stopped in the doorway of the room and looked at Leta Pitt who sat erect in her crisp gray dress and brushed at her hair. Almost every time he had stood before her he had felt himself a miniature, and when he looked at her she seemed far away. He was as afraid of her as if she had been his father, for he felt that she had never quite done or quite said the thing she had intended.

"Come in, Darrell." She still held a hairpin between her lips.

For a while she did not look at him but sat sidewise before the mirror and continued to brush her long black hair that fell all the way to the floor. Her hands were full and white and he remembered that he had never seen her outside the house without gloves. Along the white line of her head, where her hair was then parted, he saw a small pink mole. She let her brush play across the mole as if she had meant him to see it. Then she removed the hairpin from her lips, took her comb and parted her hair in another place. Her face was brown and smooth but a little too lean for the fullness of her body. Darrell imagined that she was very beautiful when Malcolm Pitt had first seen her. She was not now large or fat, but there was something heavy about her. He believed that she thought she ruled Malcolm Pitt, but secretly—a thing he might someday say to Roger—Darrell was certain that she did not rule him at all.

Finally she stopped her comb and took the fallen hairs from it and rolled them into a little ringlet. "Here," she said. She handed the ringlet to Darrell. "Put that in the wastebasket. There beside the dresser."

He obeyed her and stood again looking at her.

"I called you in here to talk about your not going to school.

64

Malcolm said you wouldn't go even if he tried to send you. And I said that was the way it ought to be. After all, you do have to stay with your grandmother. I just wanted to tell you not to think about not going. You just work hard and don't think about it and everything will turn out all right. Malcolm thinks you're a good worker. Here." She handed him another ringlet of hairs.

That afternoon Darrell told Roger that he was not going to the depot with him the next evening. Roger did not understand and he said, "If you don't go I won't write to you, and I won't forgive you and I'll make myself forget all about you—I'll make like I've forgot your name and I won't ever call you Darr again."

"You don't have to joke," Darrell said.

Roger's face was a sudden mold of stillness. "You are going, aren't you?"

Darrell knew then he would have to go. All the way to Waycrest the next evening he sat in the back seat with Miriam and Roger and could not find anything to say, not only because Roger was going away but also because Leta Pitt was in the front seat beside Malcolm. He was afraid that she might say something to him about his having to stay at home. But he was certain that Malcolm Pitt would understand and would not say anything.

At the depot they waited in the darkness for the train, and Darrell could think only of the long, long distance to Jackson and the long, long time until Christmas, when Roger would return. Yet the going would not have mattered so terribly if he could have been certain in his heart that Roger would ever come back to him.

The train did not come swiftly through the night, but slowly it crawled from toward the hills and the river, sounding the whistle that Darrell would hear again and again long after Roger was gone.

Eagerly and quickly Roger embraced his father and then his mother and then Miriam. For a moment he stalled before Darrell and the sureness in his face was gone.

"Hug him too," Miriam said, and the smoke from the train blew down over them and the cinders, like small shot, touched their faces.

"Maybe Darrell doesn't want him to," Leta Pitt said.

"Do you?" Miriam said.

"Will you hand my bag up to me?" Roger said.

Darrell nodded. Roger went ahead of him and climbed up to the vestibule. When he reached down for the suitcase his face seemed full of the train smoke and his hand caught Darrell's hand and held it. Finally he took the suitcase and said: "Goodbye, Darr."

"Goodbye."

The train pulled away and they could see Roger through the window but he did not once look around to them, and in the stillness Leta Pitt said, "Do you think he wanted to go?"

Nobody answered her. And all the way home she talked to Malcolm, but he did not reply often to her. They were halfway home before Miriam began to talk to Darrell. He could feel her beside him and finally she began to whisper, "Roger will come home Christmas. That won't be so long."

He did not say anything and she said, "Hold my hand."

He held her hand. It was warm and small.

"Will you think more of me now that Roger is gone?"

"Yes," he said. He looked at her and he was glad that she was beside him, but he was not sure he had spoken the truth.

"I don't think Father cares much that Roger has gone away, because you're here."

"Why do you say that?"

"The first day you ever came to our house and I told on you and Roger—do you remember?"

66

"Yes." His thumb began to feel her hand.

"Father told Mother that night that you were the finest-looking boy he had ever seen. And Mother said she hoped he never said that before Roger. I think Father got angry at her because he thought Roger wouldn't care if he said it. He came and picked me up and asked me what I thought."

"What did you say?"

"I said you were beautiful."

He held her hand tight. She seemed very sad to him and he was sorry for her because she did not have Roger now and she could not work in the fields or at the barn with Malcolm Pitt; and he was afraid that he would never really be good to her. Her hand struggled a little in his palm and his grip loosened.

When he got home that night he went into his grandmother's room where she sat beside the sewing machine with her back to the long oval-shaped mirror and with the lamplight falling over her shoulders. He walked across the room and stood near her before she finally lifted her eyes and closed the book on her fingers. He gazed into the mirror and let his forefinger rake across his chin. "Grandmother, do you think I'm beautiful?"

"Beautiful?" She got up and took the shawl from her shoulders and spread it out on the foot of her bed. And while she bent over with her back to him she said, "Now what a pretty thing to ask." Then suddenly she faced him. "But I'll tell you the truth. Yes. You're too much so. You're too beautiful Darrell Barclay, and any time the Lord gives a body too much of anything he has to pay and pay and pay . . ."

Darrell began to laugh, quietly at first and then very loudly. He threw himself across his grandmother's bed and said, "Beautiful . . . haaaaaaaa . . . beautiful . . . haaaaaa . . . beautiful . . ." He kept laughing until he got up and went across the hall to the room that had belonged to his father.

He worked harder in the fields that fall than he had ever worked for anyone, and the autumn sun kept his skin a golden brown. He did not want winter to come, except that he would see Roger at Christmas time.

A few days before Christmas Darrell and Yancey were unloading corn into the crib when Miriam climbed over the high sideboards of the wagon. Yancey grabbed her and said, "Honey, you gonna fall and bust something yet. You better be gone on back to the house."

"Where's Father?" she said.

"On the next load."

"I don't want him anyway. I came after Darrell."

Darrell was gathering up the last few ears scattered in the bed of the wagon. "What for?" he said.

"Mother wants you."

"What for?" he said again.

"I don't know."

He went with her to the house, but before he would go upstairs to Leta Pitt's room he went to the kitchen where Louella gave him a pan of warm water. He washed carefully because he was always afraid around Leta Pitt.

She was sitting up against the head of her bed with a row of pillows to her back and her heavy black hair fell about the pillows and covered her shoulders. The dark hair made her face pale but she did not look sick at all. She was brushing her hair when he entered the room. She missed a stroke or two while she took a hairpin from her mouth and said, "Come here, darling, I've got something I want you to do for me."

He could not move for a moment. She had never called him anything but Darrell and she had never been very kind to him. He had meant to close the door, but he pushed it farther open.

68

"Come here," she said again, though not very clearly, for the hairpin was once more in her mouth.

He went to the bed and stood a yard away from her. She put the brush down in the little trough that the covers made between her thighs.

"Will you do something for me?"

"Yes, ma'am," he said. He did not know anything else to say.

"Roger has had the measles. He's quarantined. Do you know what quarantined means?"

"No, ma'am."

"Well, that's all right. He can't come home for Christmas. My little baby quarantined up there all by himself. I'm on the verge of illness and I can't go, and Miriam's never had the measles and Malcolm needs to be here at Christmas time with the darkies doing the way they do at Christmas time. Will you go? And you'll take him some presents and a fruit cake—him away from home at Christmas time. You will go? Won't you?"

"Yes, ma'am."

Then she picked up her brush and looked at Darrell, and as if for the first time she said, "He's quarantined."

Darrell turned to go.

She put the brush down in the little trough again and called to him. "Oh, Darrell, I forgot. Have you had it? The measles."

"Yes, ma'am," he said.

Darrell was loaded down with presents the day before Christmas Eve when Malcolm drove him to Waycrest to meet the train. Malcolm kept the mares in a fast trot, and he said, "When I leave you, I'm going over to the Yellow House in Vicksburg and get something strong and warm for Christmas— to drink." And he began to laugh. After a while he said, "One damn fine day I'll make that train stop at my place. We'll have a little gray house beside the tracks with Leighton painted across it."

At the train Malcolm said, "You have a good time. When you get to Jackson just get a cab to Fillmore Hall. That'll be easy. And when you get back I'll be waiting for you."

Finding Roger was easy, everything except carrying the Christmas bundles up the stairs to the second floor of the dormitory. He did not knock on the door, because he wanted to surprise Roger. He opened it quickly and found Roger standing in his pajamas looking out the window.

Roger wheeled to face the door and his hand drew back a little and gripped the window sill. His face was bright and red and his hair was longer than Darrell remembered and the flaps of his pajamas blew in and out. They did not say anything. Roger came across the room and Darrell's hand slid away from the doorknob and they held each other until Roger moved back and sat on the bed and looked up at Darrell.

"I thought you were sick," Darrell said.

"I'm well now," Roger said. He began to smile and finger his face. "They were all over me but they're gone now. Today I had a bath—the first one in two weeks." He began to talk rapidly and clearly and his voice laughed with words. "It's all gone now. That smell. And my clothes are clean and my bed is clean and, oh, the whole room is clean. And here you are! Mother Bee cleaned the room today herself. We thought Father was coming. Why didn't you tell me?"

"We wanted to surprise you."

Roger moved back on the bed and drew his knees up and covered his feet with an afghan. "Sit down. Sit on the bed. And tell me everything. I'm so homesick. I was, I mean, and thought I'd have to stay here Christmas all by myself."

Darrell opened the door and brought in all the presents he

had left in the hall. But Roger did not ask about them. He only looked at them and then to Darrell again and said, "Come and tell me now. Everything about home and what you've done." Darrell sat on the bed and curled himself against the footboard and looked at Roger and did not speak. Roger pushed his fingers into his hair and said, "I need a haircut. Don't I?"

"No," Darrell said.

They stopped smiling at each other and Darrell reached out and caught Roger's hand and held it and said, "Do you practice now?"

"Yes," Roger said. "Sometimes. But only very sad music, and only when my heart hurts."

"Is it often?" They were smiling at each other again.

"Yes. Much and often. But not again until you go away."

"Maybe I've come to live with you. There's another bed."

"No. You'll leave me. You'll go away day after tomorrow. I know."

"But I have to go."

"I know that too."

Darrell nodded toward the other bed. "Who is your roommate?"

"Walter. He's had the measles. So he could go home."

"What's he like?"

"Good-natured and very dull, and chubby. There's no sadness in his eyes, like yours."

"Is that good?"

"I don't know." Roger got off the bed and went to the mirror and stood looking at himself.

"What are you doing?" Darrell said.

"Measuring myself."

"For what?"

"For nothing."

Roger turned away from the mirror and came to the foot

of the bed. One hand held a post very tightly and in the other hand he held a report card. In the center of his eyes were little flecks of white, like sparks from tombstones in an old cemetery. "You don't like me as much as I like you."

"That's a funny thing to say. I came to see you didn't I?"

"Here!" Roger thrust the report card into Darrell's hands. "I made all A's—the highest grades in school. But I don't like to study. I did it so you would be proud. That's why I did it. I just want you to be proud of me—that's all."

Darrell did not move his lips. He sat in silence against the footboard and gazed at Roger and shivered the whole curled length of his body, for Roger was the most beautiful thing he could imagine in a very real and beautiful world. And he thought, even then, it would be the kind of Christmas he would never again know.

three

After that Christmas it was not easy for Darrell to go back to work in Leighton. But he went back and worked on the fences and the ditch-banks, at terracing the fields and pruning the orchard, and at the barn. Sometimes Malcolm Pitt made him stay at the barn because of the rain or the wind or the one light snow that winter. But he did not like to stay there, alone, for then he would often sit and think of Roger's room and the other bed and of Walter and what Walter was like and what he might be saying to Roger at that very moment. Sometimes it frightened him and he would get up and shuck the corn standing because he never seemed to think quite that way when he was standing. When he was with Malcolm Pitt he never thought that way at all, so that finally he thought to himself that he would put Malcolm Pitt between him and Roger forever. That way he could keep from being afraid.

He began not to write Roger often. Sometimes when he thought about it he felt very strong, and was even glad that Roger was going away to a camp in the mountains that summer and would not be at home.

It was not long until winter was over and the trees were tipped with buds and the noise of the plows and the harness and the mules came. The Negroes began to sing again.

When the March wind was almost gone they began one morning to clean the barn, two to a stable—Fleet and Mark, Stafford and Dill, Yancey and Darrell. Their picks cut easily into the winter-packed layer of solid manure. In the alley of the barn three piles shaped up quickly and above the cone-top of each pile a thin layer of steam drifted toward the loft of the barn. Yancey and Darrell had cleaned out one corner of their stable as a starting point and Darrell was slicing off big smoking slabs with his pick when Malcolm found him. Malcolm did not come into the alley of the barn. He called, "Darrell, where the hell are you, boy?"

"Here. Helping Yancey."

"Come out here."

He went to the end of the alley and stood holding the pick, his face streaked, his hands sweaty, and his shoes caked with manure. Malcolm frowned for a minute and then he began to laugh and said, "Well, I'm a son-of-a-bitch. You don't have to do that."

"I promised to do it."

"You forget about that and go home and get you on some more clothes. We're going to Waycrest to the mule auction. I've got to have two more good mules before I can finish this crop."

They arrived at the auction early and joined a group of men beside one of the stacks of lumber. Darrell knew three of

73

them, the ones from Leighton—Eastland Street, G. Roper, and Aaron Gammel, and he liked them and disliked them in the same way he thought of their sons: Duard Street and Forrest Roper and Richard Gammel. The only one of the men he really liked was Aaron Gammel, though that might have been because Malcolm Pitt always talked a lot with Aaron Gammel and bet with him. They could curse and bet and it never seemed wrong; but that was not true of Eastland Street and G. Roper.

Malcolm pulled out five dollars. He was betting that his watch was more correct than Aaron Gammel's. Aaron's big fingers played with his leather watchband and finally he pulled his watch out of the bib of his overalls and ran his thumb over the crystal and began to laugh. "Hell, I ain't going to bet. My watch has not been set in three year."

All the men laughed and Malcolm said, "What a crawfish you are. Just an old crawfish."

G. Roper caught the sleeve of Malcolm's big leather jacket. He was tall and stooped and his hands were thin as if he had worn them lean with too much picking of cotton and shelling of corn. "When you gonna build that gin you keep talking about?"

"When I get enough cash."

"Hellfire," Aaron said. "When you get enough cash. I bet you got a roll on you now that'd choke a horse."

"A gin costs big money," Malcolm said.

"It'll make you big money too. And here we are hauling our cotton all the way to Waycrest. It's a pain in . . ." Aaron reached down and put his hand on Darrell's shoulder, then took his hand away and let his thumb catch in the side of his overalls, the side which was always unbuttoned. "You could just set down the rest of your life and let this young man manage it."

Malcolm looked down at Darrell. "When I get enough money I'll do it."

74

G. Roper laughed and pulled Malcolm's sleeve again. "You know why you're not rich—if you're not already. Because your niggers get it all. They make more out of a crop than you do."

Malcolm said, "By God, I can leave my crib unlocked and they don't steal from me. I'm honest with my Negroes. That's a whole hell of a lot more than some folks can say with a straight face."

"Don't get me wrong."

"I won't get you wrong, G.," Malcolm said.

Eastland Street had not said anything. He winked at Darrell. Aaron took a bottle from his pocket and said, "What you two need is a touch of this." He held out the bottle.

Malcolm took it and handed it first to G. Roper. He drank and then Malcolm took the bottle again. Darrell watched him taste it with his lips and tighten his face. It made little chills in him and he knew then that Malcolm Pitt was stronger than all the other men put together.

More men came and the mules were turned into the stock pen and Darrell moved away from Malcolm and leaned against the rail fence and watched. After a few minutes two men came and stood beside him. They nodded and talked low, almost whispering. The fat man who held his cigar only with his teeth and whose eyebrows were white said, "Them iron-grays is the best pair I've seen in two year. Over there by the lumber."

The tall man said, "Mare mules?"

"Yeah," the fat man said.

The tall man crouched down, as if to see better, and said, "I want 'em both mare-mules or both horse-mules. They team better that way."

"Well, I'm telling you," the fat man said. "You won't get a pair like that this side of Memphis." The two moved away toward the lumber pile, and the first pair was led into the ring. The auctioneer was a hunk of dark overcoat on the platform and his turned-up collar almost hid his ears though the spring wind was not cold at all. Darrell felt Malcolm's arm on his shoulder. "Pick out a pair, Darrell. You're going to work this team, so pick out the best. I'll see what kind of judge you are."

Darrell pushed against the rail fence, feeling his heart quicken. The auctioneer rattled on and the mules trotting across the lot stirred the dry odor of manure into the wind.

"The pair in the ring?" Malcolm said.

"Nossir. The next ones. The iron-gray pair there by the lumber."

"Well, by God. Here. Hold my cigar. I'd better count my money again."

Darrell turned quickly. "I don't want them. I just said they're the best pair."

Malcolm took a roll of money from his pocket and held it between him and Darrell.

"I don't want them . . ." Darrell said again.

"Hold still," Malcolm said. "You're going to get them if we have to unroll this down to the core." He put the money into his pocket again.

The iron-gray pair, frisking like fillies, was led into the ring and the auctioneer called, "All right, men, all right. These four-year-olds, perfect matches, well broken, no flaw, no blemish, right down the river from Saint L., come around and look at their teeth if you haven't already, but one glance ought to tell you. What'd I hear?"

"Three hundred."

"Give me a decent bid somebody."

"Three and a quarter."

"Three fifty," the fat man said. He was standing beside the lumber pile and the tall man was behind him.

"Three seventy-five."

Malcolm bit into his cigar. Then he gave it to Darrell again. "Here. Hold this. We better pitch our hat in the ring. Four hundred."

"Four and a quarter," the fat man said.

"Four fifty," Malcolm said.

The fat man looked at Malcolm. "Brother, I aim to take this pair back to Vicksburg. What you dickering about?"

"Your bid, Brother." He took the cigar from Darrell.

"Four seventy-five."

"Five hundred."

The fat man said to the tall man, "He ain't aiming to buy. He's got about as much finesse as a avalanche. Just running me up."

"His tail's dragging now," Malcolm whispered to Darrell. "He'll see."

"Five fifty."

"Five seventy-five," Malcolm said.

"Six hundred."

"Six and a quarter."

The fat man whirled away from the lumber pile and brushed into the tall man. He looked back at Malcolm. "You can have the goddamned things."

Malcolm was looking down at Darrell, laughing, and holding his arm. He pulled out his money and began to unfold the bills. "If you let the rough side drag long enough it'll get smooth." Then he leaned over and whispered, "We better not tell Miriam and her mother about these. They're just about a good suit of clothes too high."

They drove home with the iron-gray pair trotting behind the surrey, Malcolm laughing now and then. But Darrell did not really want to laugh or even to talk, because something had been purchased for him at a terrible price.

A mile and a half from home Malcolm stopped the surrey on a knoll and his arm stretched out and he said, "You see that block of land and that timber. Biggs wants to sell this place. That's a fine house and the tract of timber alone will be worth a baby fortune when the sawmills come in here one of these days. And do you know who the sawmills will belong to, will have to belong to?"

"Nossir."

"To whoever owns the gin. And we're going to own it. I furnish it and you run it and we split half and half." They rode on with Malcolm shifting his cigar and saying, "This fall when the crop's all gathered and winter sets in we're going to Memphis and buy the best gin Wentworth's got. I promise you we'll do that. And if we don't, I'll take you to Vicksburg the day before Christmas and get out in the middle of Washington Street at twelve o'clock noon and bend over and pull my britches down and let you kiss my behind—or kick it." He threw his cigar away. "Which would you do?"

"Neither one."

"You wouldn't kick it?"

"Nossir."

"That's a good boy." He put his arm around Darrell and hugged him.

Two weeks before Christmas, when all the crops were in, Malcolm and Darrell went to Memphis. The first day they were there the snow fell along the wide streets and covered the banks along the river, and covered the tools and tanks and boilers and flywheels and pipes stacked in Wentworth's Machinery Yard. By the second day the snow had stopped but already the earth was covered and Darrell could not tell what machinery Malcolm Pitt had selected from the yard.

78

That afternoon Malcolm went into a dozen stores, buying for Miriam and for Leta Pitt and for Roger. Finally he said, "Now, son, we're going to fix ourselves up." He bought an overcoat for himself, a strong rich camel's hair brown, and almost before Darrell knew what had happened Malcolm was holding his shoulders and telling the clerk, "Now I want something fine for my boy. The best knickerbockers and the finest jersey coat you've got."

He twisted away from Malcolm Pitt's hands to protest, but knew that he could not, not there.

"A Christmas present," Malcolm whispered to Darrell, and to the clerk he said, "You can get it ready for us right away? We're leaving on the boat tonight at seven."

"Sure. Sure," the clerk said. "You going to New Orleans on the *Ringbolt*? Huh?"

"To Vicksburg," Malcolm said.

Darrell could not say anything, even when they were back in their room. He could not even thank Malcolm Pitt. It did not seem right that Malcolm Pitt should give him clothes, almost anything would be all right except clothes.

Malcolm sat in the hotel room, in his stockinged-feet, and went over the list of all the pieces of machinery he had bought. He did not seem to notice Darrell's silence. An hour later the clothes were delivered. Malcolm opened the door and took the boxes and pitched them on the bed beside Darrell. He got into his overcoat and went to the mirror and gazed at himself. Then he pointed to Darrell's suit box and said, "Put it on and let's see again how it looks. We're going to be the best dressed men on that boat tonight."

Darrell did not move his hands. He looked up at Malcolm. "I can't take it."

It was not a frown that came to Malcolm's face; it was no

79

movement at all, but only the slow fading away of the light in his eyes. "Now come here. You can't do that. You want to be my boy don't you?"

"Yessir. I want to. But I'm not your son."

"It's only a Christmas present. Just a little old Christmas present. And you saw all the things I got for Miriam and Roger." He went to Darrell and tilted his face upward with one hand and with the other he pushed back the soft blond hair. "Are you going to be that way with me? I thought you loved me a little."

Darrell could smell the new heavy coat.

"Don't you?" Malcolm said.

"Yessir."

"Then everything is all right?"

"Yessir."

"All right now." Malcolm opened the box and held out the suit to Darrell and he took it.

They ate supper before they went aboard the *Ringbolt* and by seven o'clock they were aboard and had everything stowed in their stateroom. They came out and stood on the narrow deck and watched the snow-covered bluffs of Memphis move away from them. The deck in places was iced over and the wind was heavy and damp. The other passengers, all men, were somewhere inside. Above them, on the top deck, the pilot and the helmsman seemed to cower against the cold breath of the river. There was only the sound of churning water.

"I thought you'd rather go back this way than by train," Malcolm said. "Just for once, to see what it's like."

"I had."

"If you're too cold we'll go inside."

"I'm not too cold."

"Good. Not much use riding a boat if you're not going to look at the water."

The whistle sounded two short toots and the boat swerved

80

slowly in the water. "We're passing somebody," Malcolm explained. They turned a little to see the hulk of something to the right of them and one green light showing above the water. Higher up, three lights seemed to hang vertically to nothing in the darkness: two green and one red.

"Finally we've got our gin," Malcolm said. He leaned against the rail and took a plug of tobacco and a small knife from his pocket and sliced a corner from the plug. It was the first time Darrell had ever seen Malcolm Pitt chew tobacco and it made him feel the same way as when Malcolm had put Aaron Gammel's whiskey bottle to his lips. He gripped the icy handrail and watched Malcolm's face: it was very solid and strong when he spat over the side. Darrell could feel his own face tighten, for the tobacco had stained a little the lips he watched. Malcolm looked down at him while his face was still tight and he said, "You don't want me to do this?"

"I don't know," Darrell said.

In a few minutes Malcolm said, "I'll throw it away." He spat the tobacco out and took his handkerchief from his coat and rubbed his lips briskly. "It's not clean, is it?"

"Nossir."

Malcolm put his hand on Darrell's head and tilted his face a little. "You look like a million dollars. Did you know that?"

When they could no longer see the lights of Memphis, another of the passengers came on deck and stood for a minute against the rail. He had a very broad hat and his ascot tie seemed to cover the front of his shirt. "Would you like to join us at cards, sir? You and the young fellow?"

"Well," Malcolm said. "Yes. I'm freezing out here."

There was a table in the center of the room, between the two stateroom beds. Two men rose beside the table. They were handsome enough, a little like Malcolm Pitt, Darrell thought, though not as tall; and they also wore broad ascot ties. Darrell liked both of them. One of the men pushed a bottle and a glass across the table toward Malcolm, making a path through the scattered cards. "This will warm you a little. To begin with."

Malcolm sat down at the table and looked at the bottle and smiled. "Gentlemen, I'll drink with you, or I'll gamble. But not both. It would be a bad example for my boy here."

The man who had pushed the bottle across the table said, "Cards then. That's a fine-looking boy. Are you going to join us, sonny?" He laughed and winked at Darrell.

"No," Malcolm said. "He's my good influence. Keeps me from anything rash."

"I'll go to our room," Darrell said.

"Do you want to?" Malcolm said. "You don't have to."

He wanted to stay, but he was afraid that Malcolm Pitt had meant that he should go. "I'll go."

"All right," Malcolm said. "I won't be long."

Darrell lay in the three-quarter bed under the light covers and was cold and could not sleep, for the wind seeped through the port and down upon him. Once he went to sleep for a few minutes and when he woke he looked quickly toward the other bed to see if Malcolm Pitt had come. The bed was empty and he began to dislike the men who were keeping Malcolm. He thought that perhaps he ought to dress and go make certain that everything was all right, for many things could have happened while he slept.

He was almost asleep again when he heard the door open. He moved under the covers and sneezed and Malcolm said, "Hey! You awake?"

"Yessir."

"Have you been asleep?"

"Yessir. Did they . . . did you win?"

"You can bet your bottom dollar I did. Not much. But a little."

82

"Did they try to make you drunk?"

"No. They were all right."

He watched Malcolm undress and get into bed. But still he did not sleep. He could hear the water outside and the wind faintly through the port, and could feel the sway of the boat. He sneezed twice, quickly.

Malcolm moved in his bed. "What's the matter?"

"Nothing."

"Are you cold?"

"Yessir."

"Come over here and sleep with me."

He sat up in bed but did not move any farther until Malcolm Pitt lifted his covers and said, "Come on." He crossed the room and climbed into bed beside Malcolm and the warmth seemed to swallow him. He turned once and his face was against Malcolm's shoulder and Malcolm pulled him close so that Darrell could feel the great maleness of him, soft and warm and weighty. He shivered a little.

"Are you still cold?" Malcolm said.

"Nossir."

"You can sleep all right?"

"Yessir."

But he knew that he was not going to sleep. He lay very still for a long time, feeling the movement of the boat and listening to the barely audible seeping of the wind and lashing of the water. His heart began to pain him with its wild beating, for now he touched the great clean strength of Malcolm Pitt. The strength grew, and the beat of his heart sounded in his throat and ears and he knew that Malcolm Pitt could hear. Their hands touched for a long time, as if it were part of some old ritual binding them together. Darrell could feel himself shivering, knowing that he had put a certain past behind him, that in the enormous silence the time was like all the early mornings he had ever awakened and looked out upon the frozen earth and suddenly felt—as if it were a new thing—the great and beautiful warmth about him. He could feel Malcolm's lips against his cheek, partly touching his ear, saying, "You go to sleep . . . honey-boy." But Darrell knew, still, it would be a long time before he slept: through all the past corridors of darkness something had reached out to protect him, to shield him. Their hands rested lightly together. Then, as if to complete the ritual, Malcolm put his arm around Darrell. Darrell did not move. He knew that, somehow, there was nothing fleeting about the moment, that he was bound forever to the great strength against him. And he thought he would never be afraid again, not of Roger nor of anyone.

four

On Christmas Eve morning Darrell and Malcolm and Yancey went to the Biggs place and cut a tall lamp-globed cedar for Christmas. That afternoon they set it up in the hall and Miriam and Leta Pitt brought out the bells and the silver stars and the webs of crepe paper. When they had finished, Darrell did not go with Malcolm to the depot to meet Roger but instead he went home to dress for the party that night. He put on his new suit which Malcolm had given him in Memphis and half-expected that his grandmother would fuss again when he left, though she too had been invited not only to the party but to supper that night, and would not go. She did not say anything when he left.

He went into the big house without knocking, because he never knocked, and while he was looking at the tree Miriam came skipping into the hall trilling "Christmas comes but once a year . . ." She stopped very suddenly, as if Darrell had been a stranger, and just as suddenly marched on to him, then turned

her back to him and said, "Tie my sash. I was going to get Roger
to do it but he's not even got his underwear on yet and Father's
shaving and won't let me come into where he is and Mother's
got Louella making . . ." She faced Darrell. "You know what?"

"No."

"Eggnog." She turned her back to him again. "Now tie it."

"Like a shoestring?"

"No, silly. You and Roger can't do anything. You're all
thumbs." She pulled away from him and ran down the hall saying, "I'll get Father to do it."

He watched her to the end of the hall and saw her open the
door and heard Malcolm yell, "Get out of here! I'm going to
blister me a pair of bloomers." Then quickly a figure was running down the hall toward him again, very small and pretty
and agile.

She came up to him again and turned and said, "Here. I'll
let you do it."

He said, "Go away from me, little girl."

She pouted and tilted her head over her shoulder to him.
"Are you going to be mean to me?"

"Yes."

"Tie them."

"No."

"Please."

"No."

She ran into the living room. Darrell followed her to the
fireplace. She said, "You're mean to me because Roger is here."
Then she ran into the dining room calling quickly, "I hate you!
I hate you! Mother. Mother. Mother. I hate Darrell and Roger
and Darrell and Roger . . ."

Leta Pitt called, "Miriam! What's the matter with you?"

"I want you to tie my sash," she said.

"Come in here."

85

Darrell went to the desk in the big living room and stood studying the pattern of the china lamp, running his fingers across its smooth base. He raised his head slowly when he heard steps in the room and knew before he looked that it was Roger.

Roger, half in the lamplight and half in the flickering shadow of the hickory wood, stopped at the edge of the room. He was in knickerbockers and his shirt was open about his neck so that the collar lay smoothly over the rich brown coat. Darrell had not seen him since summer; there was no trace now of the sun he had got during his camping trip in the mountains, but his face seemed to pulse with a certain lean strength. Roger began to smile. Then Darrell began to smile too, though not at first, for the old feeling was not entirely there: last Christmas was such a long time away. But the moment was more than he had expected and he was suddenly very much ashamed that he had not written many letters to Roger, and was a little afraid there was a quietness about Roger that he liked more than ever.

"Hello," Roger said.

"Hello."

They walked toward the center of the room but they did not touch hands. They stood on either side of a big chair, smiling at each other. And Darrell's eyes searched Roger again, from head to foot. He knew that Roger was trying to bridge some gap which lay between them, and he read in the flash of Roger's dark eyes a peculiar condescending, about which he understood only enough to be a little ashamed and a little hurt that Roger should look on him with anything but pride, even if the pride had to do only with heavier muscles and a face filled with the afterglow of the autumn's sun and wind. He wanted to tell Roger how many books he had taken home, from that white house, and read because Malcolm Pitt had given them to him; how, almost every Sunday afternoon, he had sat in that room reading some book

86

while Malcolm Pitt thumbed to and fro in the Vicksburg paper —until it was time for them to walk together in the fields. But he only looked at Roger, thinking that his own eyes were a fraction higher than the ones he looked into, and that his own were not as kind. Then he turned quickly and sat in another chair, halfway across the room, and would not look directly at Roger.

Roger did not move. He said, "You didn't write much. You're not mad with me?"

"No. I don't guess I'll ever be mad with you." He looked into the fire when he spoke. Behind him he heard steps tripping along in the dining room and he knew it must be Miriam. He got up.

Miriam said, "Roger, Mother wants you."

Roger left the room. He walked like his father, only his step was quicker.

Miriam studied Darrell. "Well, are you going to say hello to me?"

"I said hello once."

"O you didn't. You just said did I want it tied like a shoe-string and called me a little girl and told me to go away. You treat me like I wasn't twelve but I am—nearly. You could say hello."

"Hello."

She curtsied. "Do you know who all is coming after supper?"

"No."

"Nolie and Teeny and Richard and . . . you don't care if they come or not. Do you?"

"No."

"Let me whisper something to you?"

"In my ear?"

"Yes. Bend down."

He bent over a little. Her lips touched his ear and he moved quickly.

"Bend down again. You're so touchy."

He bent down.

"You want to sit by me or by Roger at the table?"

Darrell stood straight again. "Why? Because if I sit by Roger I can look at you?"

"Meanness."

"It doesn't make any difference," he said.

The pigtails dangled around Miriam's neck. "All right. I'll put you at the end of the table beside Mother, in a high chair. Baby." She skipped out of the room.

Darrell sat beside Roger at the table. Across from him Miriam waited for her father to serve, heaping style, each plate. At the top of the very long waistline of Miriam's yellow dress, near her throat, the green bow spread like a cluster of pine cones so that Darrell thought Miriam's delicate baby-like skin would be scratched when her chin brushed against the bow. He half winked at her and she frowned. Silently she formed with her lips, "I hate you." Aloud, Darrell said, "What did you say?"

Miriam frowned again. "I said that plate's for you."

"No, it's not." Darrell passed the plate on to Roger who passed it on to his mother.

At the end of the long table Leta Pitt reached to receive the plate, then with a little wave of her hand, said, "No, keep that, Roger. That's too much for me." To Darrell she said, "You'd think your grandmother would be afraid at home, after a night like this."

"I don't think she's ever afraid," Darrell said.

"Mother says that because she'd be afraid," Miriam said.

Leta Pitt fingered the small service bell and finally found

the precise spot to place it. "Now you eat, Roger. Sometimes I think you don't get enough at school."

"You want him to be big as Father," Miriam said. "He wouldn't be that big if he ate a bushel a day."

"You're the sweetest little sister I've got."

"And you're the sweetest little brother. You won't ever write me."

"I can't write. There's a bone in my hand."

"You write Darrell."

Darrell's hand slipped suddenly from his glass.

"How do you know?" Roger said.

"I know."

"Is there anything wrong with it?"

"I hate boys."

Malcolm suddenly stilled the carving knife. "Miriam! Do you want me to make you get up and hug Roger's neck here before company?"

Miriam did not answer. Malcolm, his face turned down toward the carving once again, said, "Have you learned a whole hell of a lot, Roger? In your books, I mean."

"I can factor."

The carving knife stopped momentarily. "That must be fine. White, or dark, or both, Darrell?"

"Both, please."

Leta Pitt rang the little bell quickly. "Coffee for us, Louella; milk for the children." Then she added, "With so many darkies drinking here at Christmas time I don't know whether I'd be afraid or not, if I were your grandmother."

Malcolm said to Miriam, "All white, honey?"

"Yessir."

"Christmas is one time I want some men folks around the house, and after night . . ."

"By God, Leta, will you hush talking to this boy about his

89

grandmother being afraid. If you're concerned, send Louella over there. He's come here for a party."

To Darrell, when he thought back about it, the party was more like the thin smoke of a candle than the bright flame. It was as if all the rooms had been too dim and the figures had walked in shadows. The Ropers had come and the Potters, all except Brother Potter, who, Nolie said, had stayed home working on his Christmas sermon. Aaron Gammel was there, and Richard Gammel, not as tall as Roger but a little older. They had all come almost at the moment when the last dish was cleared from the table and the rich foaming bowl of eggnog was placed between the candelabras.

Always there was Malcolm Pitt's loud, warm voice laughing, Leta Pitt keeping the glasses herded back to the table, Roger talking when they called to him. In the kitchen once with Nolie and Miriam and Teeny Roper, Darrell could hear the voice in the living room, "Tell Aaron about Alec, Roger. Alec and Stella clean up the dormitory where Roger lives."

Then Roger's voice was like his father's, only quieter: *Alec and Stella were both about seventy but their mama was still living. Three weeks ago Alec died. About a week later when Stella came back to the dormitory she was talking to Walter, that's my roommate. Walter said: How did your mama take it? And Stella said: We ain't told her yet. We jist afraid of the shock. But one uh dese days we gonna break hit gently. First day she feels like it we gonna take her fer a walk. We go by the cemetery. Den we go in. We take her all around it, headstone to headstone. Finely we come to the new dirt and she'll say: who dat? We'll say gently: Dat's Alec.*

Darrell listened to the laughter of Aaron Gammel and Malcolm Pitt and the high chuckle of Elazer Biggs. Then he turned away from the laughter, because he did not belong, and without intending to be anywhere was on the back porch with Nolie. They stood beside the screen, she fingering her glass. Her face, even in winter, was a bright vinegar brown and it was smooth almost to a glossiness. She was thin and dark and the near frailness of her body always made him think that she was waiting for something, impatiently. Her eyes flashed up at him while she nibbled the foam with her flushed lips.

"I love this stuff, don't you?" she said.

"I guess so, but it's awfully rich."

She held her glass up to his lips and he turned away.

"No, you don't love it. You don't love anything. But you're always looking at Miriam."

"Aw, Nolie."

"Well, you don't ever look at me. It might as well be Miriam all the time. She tells me lots of things at school."

"Like what?"

"Like . . . well, that she's going to Vicksburg next year to school. And she's going to study singing."

"I know it. That's no secret."

"I hope she goes and I hope you get as lonesome as a scarecrow after all the watermelons are gone. There!" She threw part of the eggnog from her glass onto his cheek, then quickly reached out and wiped the spot away. He stood looking at her and did not say anything. She said, "Kiss me."

"No."

"Why?"

"You guess why."

She threw eggnog onto his cheek again. He slapped her lightly, and caught her hands and held them.

"Turn me loose you little devil! Everybody knows you're so good-looking. You think it too. Turn me loose."

"You don't want me to."

"I do. I'm going to scream."

91

"Go ahead."

"I can."

"Go ahead."

From the kitchen Teeny Roper called to Nolie, "We're ready to go home, Nolie. Where are you? We're ready to go."

"Blah! Teeny! I don't want to go home." She whispered to Darrell, "Kiss me."

He began to laugh and they followed Teeny, who ran tittering into the living room.

Then everybody was gone and Malcolm Pitt was saying to Darrell, "Where the devil you been? You're not going yet. You and me and Roger have got things to talk over. Come back here with me."

He took Roger and Darrell to the kitchen where he refilled his glass, and with his unsteady arm he reached out and gave each boy one sip of bourbon. His warm voice was thick. "That's absolutely enough. Now don't get near your mother."

Back in the living room Malcolm leaned against the mantel. His voice was stumbling. "Roger, you ought to see our plantation now. It's really beautiful. It's not green, being December, you see, but it's beautiful. You're going to be a doctor, but me and Darrell—Darrell and I—know how to make things grow. We work alike. Two and two." He held up two fingers.

Leta Pitt said, "You've had enough to drink. You better come to bed."

Malcolm placed his glass on the mantel. He walked with awkward certainty across the room and kissed her on the cheek. "Women," he said. "I don't know what gets into 'em." Slowly he wiped his hand across his lips. "Or maybe it's what doesn't." He turned and began to feel Roger's arms. "No," he said. "Too soft. I'll show you a strong pair of arms, Roger. Come here, Darrell."

Darrell did not move.

92

"Dammit, don't you like me any more? I'll come to you."

"You've had enough," Leta Pitt said. "Too much to drink."

Malcolm looked at her and then crossed the room to Darrell and put his arm around Darrell's neck. "This is my real son. We're just farmers and we can't factor, but we by God can raise the best cotton in the county. Roger is a schoolboy, soft; well let him be a doctor." He pulled Darrell close. "We're going to build a gin—half and half. You couldn't work like we do, Roger —us men. You're pale—like winter butter. But look at Darrell . . ." He began to feel Darrell's arms.

Roger's lips clenched and his throat grew red. Leta Pitt, with preciseness, took hold of Malcolm. To Miriam she said, "Fix your father's bed."

Miriam left the room. Malcolm bent and kissed Leta, and again he wiped his hand across his lips. They followed Miriam.

Roger watched them, then slowly turned to Darrell. His eyes were no longer free and bright, and his mouth was caught as if no smile had ever crossed his face. "I guess that's why you quit liking me. You think I'm soft, too. We'll go out in the yard and see."

"You're acting foolish, Roger."

"In the yard or here one."

"You ought to know he didn't mean it . . ." But before Darrell finished speaking, Roger, face trembling as Darrell had never seen before, swung desperately toward the harder muscles. Darrell caught him, struggled to hold Roger close to his own body so that the fists had no power. His fingers could feel the flesh of Roger, softer than his own, could feel the muscles weaker than the rows of cords that ran down his own arms to the wrists. He could feel this, and knew also that the flesh beneath Roger's clothes was whiter than his own—then brown from the wind and the leftover glow of the fall sun. He drew Roger tighter and tighter, his breath opened and locked in gaps, almost smiling at his own power against the body in his arms, until Roger with one final plunge lifted his knee into Darrell's groin, hard, quick and accurately. A dark wave of weakness ran down the whole of Darrell's back and a rope of pain crossed his stomach; then the rope, in a half-mist sickening to any taste or smell, seemed to close around his throat. Quickly he released Roger, stepped back, and his fist shot solidly beneath Roger's jaw, against his throat. He watched Roger sprawl unmoving upon the rug.

He saw the sudden sweat on Roger's forehead. In that fleeting moment he wanted to take his handkerchief and touch Roger's brow. Breathless, he stooped, lifted the body into his arms, and started toward Roger's room.

When Roger's head touched his pillow he opened his eyes, looked up, and grasped Darrell's arm as if to keep him from leaving. "I didn't mean to. I didn't mean to kick you, Darrell . . . not there . . ."

"Why did you do that?" Darrell whispered.

"I don't know. I didn't mean to. Will you forgive me?"

"Yes."

"All the way?"

"Yes."

"Bend over." Darrell leaned over close and his hand, half on the pillow, touched Roger's hair. Roger touched his other hand.

Then Darrell kissed Roger's lips. They were soft and warm and the very touch seemed to pain him with tenderness. Darrell stood up. Roger let his hand go.

"We won't ever fuss again, ever."

"No," Darrell said.

"And when I go back to school will you remember me more —write me?"

"Yes."

94

"And when I go to New Orleans to school you won't ever forget me?"

The face before him was the finest image that Darrell could imagine. He kissed Roger again and said, "I won't ever forget you."

Then quickly he went out of the room and in the cold light of that December night he walked a lonely way home; everything he knew was as far away as the mind could reach and had less warmth than any star. There was no understanding of the night or the people who lived in that night, for his mind was numb and awkward and his body ached, which had never ached before. He walked along the path ashamed that he had ever thought of Malcolm Pitt being to him as a father; ashamed that he had loved the times Malcolm Pitt had talked to him not as a boy but as a man; ashamed now and hurt and afraid too because only in a little while Roger would go away again, though Malcolm Pitt might be with him forever.

He began to run along the path, clenching and unclenching his fists. At the creek bank he sat down and, crossing one hand over the other, gripped the calves of his legs, his thighs, and finally the biceps of his arms. His muscles seemed softer and smaller than they had ever been. Then he got up and hurried because his body was chilled and he thought that in any other place he would be warmer. There was no light in the house when he reached home, so that he climbed the front steps noiselessly, thinking that his grandmother would be asleep. He turned the doorknob to her room and slowly pushed back the door, as if he must see her and know that she was there. The fire in the room had died, leaving only the heap of gray ashes against the andirons. He stood in the doorway and let his eyes adjust to the faint moonlight that shone through the windows. His gaze moved a little and he saw that his grandmother's bed was empty. Then he saw his grandmother in the rocker beside the machine, her head tucked against one shoulder, a book closed on her thumb. He called to her and she stirred quickly.

"There's no light," he said.

She sat up and one thin hand massaged her face. "I was tired of the light. I wanted to sit in the darkness and wait for you."

"It's awfully cold in here."

"Maybe it was warmer where you've been."

"It was warm."

"Come a little nearer to me."

He walked around the foot of her bed and stood near her.

"I've been alone. Did you think of that, over there? Where it's so warm?"

"I thought of you."

"Well. Did you?"

"Yes ma'am. Do you want me to build a fire?"

"I want you to listen." She pulled the shawl about her shoulders. "Light the lamp so I can see your face better."

He went to the machine and lifted the globe of the coal-oil lamp. From the machine drawer he took a match, but for a moment he did not light the lamp. He stood looking into the tall oval-shaped mirror that hung above the machine. He could see the dark faint image of himself. Then he lit the lamp, backed away from the machine, and stood looking into the mirror where his image was now brighter. Slowly the heat from the lamp clouded the mirror until he could not see himself, and it seemed that he no longer existed.

"Look at me!" The voice of his grandmother was like a spark from a hickory fire. "You don't love me. Do you?"

"I do." He faced her. His throat was cold.

"It's not me you love. It's the Pitts. I should have got you away from here long ago. Malcolm Pitt. Roger. Miriam. They all mean more to you than I do." She stood and took the shawl

96

from her shoulders. Then she walked to him and bent forward. He thought of Roger lying on his bed, his body curled against the cold. He wanted to go back to him. "Kiss my cheek and go to your room."

Darrell moved to kiss her. His lips had hardly parted when a sound, like the fierce and sudden ripping of strong cloth, jarred the room. He jerked away from his grandmother. His stare fell on the mirror and the long dark crack that ran from top to bottom of the glass.

"The mirror," he whispered. He heard his grandmother gasp heavily.

"It may be a sign to warn you," she said. "You're getting beyond me. I'm just an old woman sitting in the cold waiting—while you found the light and the warmth. So you've been one of them. Well you're going to be fooled. You're going to be lost where nobody can find you. It's like a serpent, isn't it?"

"What is?" His tongue was heavy.

"The crack. It's like a slender black serpent."

He stood staring and she came close to him and took his chin into her hand. "I smell your breath. I knew it would be, had to be. The smell of whiskey coming between those beautiful lips. The Pitts will destroy you. Mark my words . . ."

He wanted to turn his face from the mirror, from her, as though the mere wheeling around would draw a curtain for him across the future and he could go back to something: to a warm still night beside the pond; or to a time on a certain red knoll when he stood at Otho watching the curling smoke, having never heard the name of *Pitt;* or even farther back to something less than night and less than smoke, which he could not name.

part

· THREE

one

On the morning of Roger's graduation from boarding school Darrell went with the Pitts to Jackson. As they rode together on the train Darrell thought that Leta Pitt was kinder to him than she had been for a long time. A year ago he and his grandmother had moved to the Biggs place because Malcolm had arranged the deed and Darrell would pay for the land with the money he would make at the gin. That summer he and Roger had re-painted the Biggs house and built a new fence with arrow-head palings and put a new roof on the tenant house for Yancey who had moved with Darrell to work the Biggs land. While they were painting the house Roger had said, "I believe Mother thinks you're getting ahead of me—now that you own land and a house."

Darrell had said, "What do you think?"

And Roger had said, "I don't give a damn if you own all of Leighton."

It had pleased Darrell, not only the words, but because Roger had said them as Malcolm Pitt would.

So, as they rode on the train that graduation day, Darrell

98

thought that Leta Pitt was unusually kind to him because her son was now, and forever, well on the road beyond anything that Darrell might ever reach. He smiled and at once both Malcolm and Miriam asked him what he was thinking. But he said, "Nothing."

When they came to the school the people were crowding the walks and seemed to be milling about with the color and carelessness of October leaves on the wind. Malcolm led the way into the lobby of the boys' dormitory and then he said, "Darrell, you know where Roger's room is. Go up and tell him we're here."

"I want to go too," Miriam said.

Malcolm said: "Honey, this hall belongs to breeches. Skirts are not allowed."

Darrell climbed the steps to Roger's room almost with the same eagerness that he had climbed them once before and pushed the door open quickly. Roger was standing beside his bed, his black graduating robe about him, and his cap in hand. The cap fell onto the bed and the tassel lay curled like a hook.

"They're waiting for you," Darrell said. He closed the door behind him.

Roger did not move. "I'm almost ready. We had to go over and practice walking across the stage this morning and I just got back."

Darrell looked around the room. One bed was stripped and one bed-table was bare. He knew that Roger's roommate was gone. "Why haven't you packed?" he said.

"I'm not going home." Roger lifted his cap off the bed and fingered the tassel.

"Where are you going?"

"The superintendent told me yesterday that he wanted me to go to camp as a group leader. And I said I might go."

Darrell sat on the bed and lay back with his hands locked

99

beneath his head. After a while he said, "Are you really going, Roger?"

"I think so."

"Why?"

"You already know."

Darrell sat up quickly. "I don't know either."

"I'm going because of you, Darrell. I always seem to be following after you. Sometimes I think it would be better if I didn't see you at all. I don't want to live different from you, but I guess we have to."

"What does that mean?"

"I don't know what it means—any more than you do. I just think I ought to go away this summer. Don't you?"

"I don't know. You'll have to go away soon enough. To the University this fall."

"What do you think I should do—about summer?"

"I know what I want you to do."

"What?"

"Go home with us."

Roger sat on the bed and looked at Darrell for a long time. Finally he got up and said very quietly, "All right. I'll go home with you." Slowly he reached out and took a small box from his bed-table and handed it to Darrell. "I wanted you to be the first to touch it."

"What is it?"

"The Silver Triangle: for scholarship, declamation, and athletics."

"Is it the highest honor?"

"Yes."

"I figured you would get it."

"Did you really think that?"

"Yes."

Darrell opened the small box and put his finger on the

100

medal. After a while he held out the box and said, "I'm as proud as I can be, Roger."

Roger did not take the box. He said: "We've got to hurry. I have to be in the auditorium in twenty minutes."

Once again Darrell held out the box, but Roger said, "You hold it. You had more to do with my getting it than you think."

"What did I do?"

"It's not what you did. It's what you are. When you stayed at home and I went away to school, I knew then I would get it . . . I knew I would. It's more for you than for me."

Their hands were on the foot of the bed and suddenly their fingers touched and even more suddenly drew apart. They looked at each other for a minute and then they went out of the room as if too much of something lay ahead of them.

They were sixteen that summer, almost, and they worked with the men at building the gin. All the timbers and the machinery were ready and slowly the gin rose through the heat and slowly Roger and Darrell bronzed so thoroughly that they did not wear shirts even in the still-of-noon heat. Six days a week they worked and on Saturday afternoons Malcolm always sent them home early and they would go usually to Vicksburg, sometimes for no more reason than to ride horseback, and sometimes they went to the Yellow House to bring something for Malcolm Pitt.

They read Shakespeare that summer, every Sunday afternoon and some weekday nights, under a big oak in front of the church. When it was dark Roger lay with his head against Darrell's thigh and quoted long speeches very quietly, sometimes improvising. If Darrell did not detect the error, Roger scored one point; if he did detect the misquote Darrell scored two. They never remembered from Sunday to Sunday how the record stood, so that each week they started the score anew.

101

Only one thought bothered Darrell: he had always walked in the fields on Sunday afternoons with Malcolm Pitt. Now Malcolm walked alone, and Darrell felt that he himself had betrayed some secret understanding between them. He did not have to think about Miriam, for she had gone to Natchez to spend the summer with her Aunt Susan, because Roger would not go with her to a camp in North Carolina—and she was not allowed to go alone. But he had to think of the end of summer, and it came like a shadow moving across the field in the brightness of noon. The gin was almost finished; Miriam returned from Natchez; and Roger packed his trunk to go away to the University in New Orleans.

The day before Roger was to leave, he and Darrell took Miriam to the Garden City School for Girls in Vicksburg, where she had gone the year before, and they stayed late that afternoon to hear Miriam sing in the opening chapel exercises. She was in the center of the white-robed all-girl choir and when she stepped forward, very much alone on the front of the stage, Darrell thought she was completely certain of herself. If she had been less certain he would have been sorry for her. He watched the lemon-gold of her throat move above the fluffed white collar and, for a moment, he believed that she was more beautiful than any other Pitt; he wished she had not gone away for the summer and he was glad that she would be no farther away than Vicksburg that winter—when Roger went away. But then he forgot again after they had eaten supper at the Waterview and he and Roger rode home alone.

Darrell was going to spend the night with Roger, and when they got home they turned the mares into the lot and went to the church, as they had done so many times that summer, and sat under the oak. But Roger did not quote anything that night, nor did Darrell. Roger's head lay against Darrell and they did not say anything. They could see the gin with its tall silver suction pipes rising in the moonlit darkness and the smokestack towering higher than anything else in Leighton. A quarter mile away was Roger's house, and after a while they saw the light go out in the house. They seemed to see it at once, and to sense in it some signal, for without speaking they got up and walked along the road toward Leighton, not toward the house. They passed Gammel's store and the little post office beside it and crossed the railroad tracks as if each knew where both of them were going. They stood beside the new gray depot under the sign labeled Leighton and looked down the tracks for a long time. They had not spoken a word until Roger said, "I'm always going away."

Darrell said, "I won't come to the train with you tomorrow. Do you understand?"

"Yes," Roger said.

Then they began walking down the track toward the gin and the millpond. Roger said, "To see the store and the depot and the gin and everything makes some other things seem like a long time ago."

"Yes," Darrell said.

"I wish it wouldn't ever change. I wish it was like it was when you first came here. But things will keep on." He pointed to a block of land and said, "Already G. Roper wants to build another store there. He wants Father to sell him that acre."

"Is he going to?"

"No. They had a fuss about it last night."

"Why won't he sell it?"

"I guess he thinks Mr. Gammel might not want another store put up. I don't know. Maybe Father doesn't want things to grow up either."

They turned off the railroad track and before they reached the pond they took off their coats, which they had worn only because of the trip to Vicksburg, and carried them over their arms. At the pond they hung their clothes in a willow tree and sat on the bank without saying anything, like two old men busy at their work. There was no movement of the water and the night was very warm. Then they shoved each other into the pond and played in the water with each other but not one word passed between them until they had dressed and started for the house.

It was midnight when they went to bed in Roger's bed, and still the night was warm and the room was hot. Once or twice they talked quietly to each other as if to wake no one, and then they were silent. But each knew that the other did not sleep. The night bore heavily, like a warm blanket, upon Darrell. His fingertips were damp against the sheet and he could not understand how Roger, stretched unclothed beside him, could look so cool.

Early in the morning Roger sat up in bed and said: "We better put on some underwear. You know Father will be in here pulling at us before good daylight."

Darrell laughed quietly. "I thought you were not afraid of him."

"I'm not," Roger said. After a while he put his arm across Darrell and said, "I think I'll tell you goodbye now."

Darrell said, "Let me ask you one thing, and I want you to promise to tell as near the truth as you can."

"All right. What?"

"If you could have just one wish given to you now, what would it be?"

The night seemed to move on and away from them and finally Roger said, "I would wish that you were my brother, so we wouldn't always have to be leaving each other."

two

Roger had been gone a week when the whistle sounded
for the first time at the gin. Darrell stood away from the boiler,
beyond the gin-well, so that he might see better the first beautiful mushroom of steam from the whistle. The men were crowded
about Malcolm Pitt waiting for his arm to yank the cord. Elazer
Biggs and Eastland Street and G. Roper stood closest and back
of them another group gathered beside Aaron Gammel whose
cotton, the next day, would be the first bale to go through the
gin. Finally Malcolm's hand lifted and pulled the cord and the
sound of the whistle covered them; then slowly his hand turned
the big brass valve and the wheels moved quicker and quicker
until the earth itself seemed to quake beneath Darrell's feet.
Malcolm waved his arm to Darrell and his lips moved but Darrell did not hear. At times the men's faces were covered with
laughter and other times they listened as intently as if the sound
had been no more than the ticking of a watch. After a while
Malcolm closed the big brass valve and the sound and the quak-
ing seemed to go on long after all movement had died away.

Malcolm un-boxed a half dozen bottles that he had brought
from the Yellow House in Vicksburg and the men began to
drink. Darrell left them and went around the gin to the weighing platform and climbed the ladder. He sat for a while on the
ginner's stool and played with the copper weights scattered
along the scale-desk. Then he went through the gin touching
the belts and the ginheads and looking at the glass windows of
the bins until he came to the compress, where he leaned out the
window and watched the men drinking. For a little while he
wondered why he was not down beside the boiler and among

105

the men, but to keep from thinking of that he moved away from the window and wished he had something to do. He returned to the weighing platform and looked at the scales and decided he had not polished them well enough the day before. From the seed bin he brought out the woolen rag and the half-gallon of ashes he had been using. He drew the suction pipe up with the rope provided and fastened the end securely and threw the trip-rope over the scales down to the ginner's stool.

Then he took off his shirt, as if Roger were there, and climbed onto the suction pipe as he had done before, and using the ashes began to polish again. Sometimes he let the sweat from his face drip onto the rag so that the ashes would adhere to the cloth and polish better. Sometimes he made believe that Roger was standing down on the platform and watching the scale-numerals shine in the afternoon sunlight. Now and then he heard the men on the other side of the gin, calling and laughing and swearing, but he did not listen to them.

He had worked out to the highest angle of the pipe and had almost finished the polishing when he heard steps on the platform ladder. He expected the man to be Malcolm Pitt but when he looked up it was G. Roper. Darrell kept polishing, as if he had not seen, until Roper had climbed all the way to the platform and said, "Hey, boy. This a fine gin you got."

Darrell looked down at him, fifteen feet away, and nodded. He could not think of anything to say.

Roper gazed up toward the pipe and his lips stuck when he talked. "Don't you think it's fine?"

"Yessir."

"I think it's fine too. Make a man rich. Did you know I almost built it myself?"

"Nossir."

Roper leaned against the wall. "They's two ways to make money around here. A gin or a sawmill. When you got a gin you got both." He scratched his head, and Darrell wondered what he had done with his hat, for without it he did not look tall. "That ain't hard to figure out how you got both. A good-looking youngun like you ought to figure it. You no good in mental arithmetic?"

"Not very good."

"You reckon a man could run a sawmill without a boiler, huh? If you already got a boiler? Well. You a little slow . . ." Roper began to laugh. "Don't let me get your goat, kid. I was joking you." He crossed the platform, coming closer to the scales and seeming to stumble over the rope. "Who told you to polish them?"

"Nobody."

When Roper looked up, Darrell could see that his eyes were red and watery.

"You don't take orders from Malcolm Pitt no more?"

"He didn't tell me to do this."

Roper began to laugh again. "You a card, kid. The way you handle that old man. I got it all figured out. I got it figured he's going to put up a store for you, right acrost the road from Gammel's. Maybe put Gammel out of business."

"I don't know what you're talking about."

"You a card, kid. You heard me say that." He pushed the trip-rope off the ginner's stool and sat down. "You gonna be the ginner?"

"Yes."

"What you think about Malcolm Pitt anyways?"

"I think he's all right."

"He likes you a lot, huh?"

"I don't know."

"Maybe he don't like you as much as you think; he didn't send you to school, with that fine boy of his. Did he?"

"I wouldn't have gone anyway."

Roper laughed again. "I got it figured. If you went away to school you might meet some little thing that was prettier than Miriam. You know you good-looking, don't you?"

Darrell moved down the pipe closer to the gin-wall. Roper stood up and Darrell stopped.

"You afraid of me?"

"No," Darrell said.

"What if you was to fall off there? What you reckon Malcolm Pitt would bury you in? Let me tell you something—I meant to build this gin. Didn't you know that?"

"No."

"He'll beat me to the sawmill too, then the store. He's going to build the store for you, ain't he? That's the reason he won't sell me that acre. Ain't it?"

"No. He's not going to build anything for me." Darrell moved closer toward the gin-wall and Roper reached down and grabbed the trip-rope. "You pretty little liar. Don't you move. He's doing it for you. I'll pull this thing if you move another inch." His laugh came again, quiet and ugly. "You think he's giving you everything for nothing. He'll get it back some day when you marry Miriam. Keep it in the family, see? You think he's giving you half-interest in the gin for nothing?"

Darrell tried to grip the bucket of ashes tight enough and cock his arm enough to throw, but he could do neither. "The gin's not half mine. I get half what we clear, that's all. I work for it."

"They record things like that in the Chancery Clerk's office. Anybody can see." He held the trip-rope tighter. "Don't move. You going to tell him you don't want that store. You hear . . ."

"Roper!" Malcolm Pitt was climbing the stairs. "You goddamned drunken fool. Put that line down."

108

The bucket of ashes fell away from Darrell. Roper turned, half-facing Malcolm, and the line tightened. "Don't you crowd me . . ."

Malcolm moved slowly, as if gripping something, his eyes set and his face very white. His voice was faint, "I'll break your neck—with my hands."

The line fell away from Roper and he stepped on it and began to laugh. "I was joking the kid."

At the top of the platform Malcolm hesitated, then reached out and caught the bib of Roper's shirt and pulled him forward as if to lift him up. His face seemed as tight as his hand and he said quietly, "I ought to throw you off this platform."

Roper had stopped laughing and the wrinkles had deepened upon his face. "Go ahead. Throw me off. Break my neck and go to jail—go to Parchman. No. They wouldn't put you in the pen. They never would put you in the pen . . ."

"Shut up."

"Go ahead. Throw me off. Give him half the gin, build him a store, then you can marry him to your daughter . . ."

Malcolm struck with the back of his hand, only once. Roper fell across the coil of line and a little trickle of blood came from the corner of his mouth. Then Malcolm reached down and pulled him up by the shoulder and pushed him toward the ladder. "Get away from me G. Just get away from me."

Roper went down the ladder. Malcolm turned and climbed onto the scale-desk and reached up to help Darrell.

"I'm all right. I can get down," Darrell said. But he kept trembling even when his feet touched the platform.

Malcolm said, "Two sensible grown men fighting. Is there anything more sickening? Is there?"

"I don't know," Darrell said.

"I never hit a drunk man before in my life. Certainly not

109

somebody who drank my own whiskey." He took out his handkerchief and wiped his hands and looked in the direction that G. Roper had gone.

"It's not the truth, is it? About half the gin."

Malcolm moved his face slowly around to Darrell. "Yes. It's the truth."

"I don't want it."

For a full minute they looked at each other and Malcolm seemed to grow old as he stood there. "I didn't mean to tell you, Darrell. But you listen to me. Half is yours and half is Roger's. I did it because I wanted to and you better not let G. Roper spoil this for us. I'm not going to make you work down here day and night and dole you out a salary. I want you to be proud of this gin. The worst thing in the world for a man is to work at something he's not proud of. You're going to run it and pay for your half. Don't you understand that?"

"Nossir. I don't know why you'd do it."

"Dammit to hell. Do you have to know?"

"Yessir. I want to know."

"Because I like you. And if anybody asks you about it, you tell them to kiss your behind. It's a matter between you and me—only."

"But I don't know whether it's right or not."

"Have I ever been wrong with you?"

"I don't think you have."

"Then you ought to trust me."

"I do trust you."

Malcolm ran his hand over Darrell's shoulders. "Put your shirt on and let's go."

The next day Malcolm Pitt went to Vicksburg and deeded one acre of land to G. Roper.

110

three

The time went swiftly for Darrell, but only because of the gin and Malcolm Pitt. He could not be lonely when he was with Malcolm nor would he let himself, at those times, think of Roger. Miriam came home every weekend and usually he went to church with her, but on Sunday afternoons he walked in the fields or the woods with Malcolm Pitt—except the Sunday during Christmas when Roger was home.

Sometimes on Sunday night, after that Christmas, he would drive Miriam back to school and hold her hand and think that summer was not very far away. But he had never kissed her then. The first time he kissed her was in the gin early that spring. He had been measuring seed from the gin's seed bin all that day, getting ready for the spring planting, and it was already sundown when he finished. But he did not go home immediately. He stretched out on the tons of seed in the bin and did not want to leave. There was something about the gin at times that was like an animal; and in the spring the animal was very quiet and gentle. He was tired and the strength seemed to flow back into his muscles as he lay stretched on his back. He heard steps on the ladder and knew someone was coming but he did not see Miriam until she stood in the toll bin doorway. His only movement was to reach out his hand for his shirt, which lay beside him, but he only touched the shirt and let his hand fall still. He was a little thrilled to have her look on his naked arms and shoulders and chest. She took off her poke bonnet, and still without saying anything, remained standing in the doorway. Her hair fell long about her shoulders and he found him-

111

self imagining the shape of her beneath the pleated bodice of her dress.

"Darrell?" She called as if she did not see him.

His fingers moved across his shirt again and he thought it was the darkness that made him want to cover himself. Then everything was suddenly very funny to him and he thought of the Bible and Isaiah and the Sunday School lesson. "Here I am. Send me."

"Are you ready to leave? To go home?"

"No, my child. I am weary."

"What's the matter with you Darrell?"

"I am weary of well doing. Knave! Show the woman out of here. She disturbs my rest, my peace, my heart's core." He lifted his arm. "Nay. Stop, rogue! Unhand her. She must not go. Now, fair one. Speak. Why steal you so quietly upon me?"

"You act worse than Roger."

"Yes, fair one. Worse . . . worse . . . worse . . ."

"Father wants to see you."

"Ah! Let the good king wait. Come sit beside me."

"You are silly."

"No doubt. But I have something to ask you."

"Well?"

"If a hen and a half could lay an egg and a half in a day and a half, how long would it take a rooster to sit on a doorknob and hatch a keyhole?"

She threw her poke bonnet at him, and without moving she said, "Give that back to me."

"Come after it."

"I'll go tell Father you've taken my bonnet."

"And he'll take my word for a thousand pounds. I'll say, 'My good lord, I did it not.'"

"He'll believe me."

"You are much mistaken. He will believe me."

112

"I'll show you."

"I wouldn't, if I were you."

"You are the most conceited, unmannerly little nothing I've ever seen. Give me my bonnet."

He sat up and threw the bonnet at her. "Take it! And go home. That's all you think I am. Somebody to work and get grease on my hands, so your father and Roger won't have to do it."

She picked up the bonnet and kept standing, looking at him. "Go on home. I don't want to look at you."

She came over and sat down beside him and put her hand on his stomach and did not say anything. He kissed her on the very edge of her lips and held her close because she did not try to explain anything to him.

"Don't you like me a little?" she said.

"Yes. A little."

"I like you more than you like me. Sometimes you're not good to me."

"I'll be good to you from now on," he said.

"To when?"

"Till doomsday. Maybe."

She moved her hand along his stomach and they kissed again, quickly, like two frightened wings touching.

"You better go, Miriam. You better go now."

"Go with me." She moved away from him and waited.

"I can't."

"But Father wants you."

"I can't go now." He reached out for his shirt and pulled it across his thighs.

Half the distance to the doorway Miriam stopped. "What shall I tell Father?"

"That I'll be there in a minute." She started on. "What does he want with me?"

"To go with him to New Orleans to buy gin supplies. And to see Roger too, I guess. He's playing in a tennis tournament tomorrow afternoon." She ran down the ladder, and he thought the sound was like the running of one who had escaped a terrible thing.

four

While they were on their way to New Orleans Malcolm turned from the train window often and nudged Darrell to share the view with him. Once the tracks curved very near the river and at a distance on the water, where river and sky seemed to meet, was the faint speck of a steamboat. Malcolm said, "Maybe we should have caught the *Ringbolt* in Vicksburg and gone down on it." He laughed.

But Darrell did not understand the laugh, for even the name of the *Ringbolt* made a deep color come to his face. He did not answer, and after a while the tracks left the river and Darrell slept.

When they came into the station in New Orleans, where the smell of crowds and fog was like metal under rust, Malcolm said, "We'll go to the hotel first."

"We don't have much time, do we?" Darrell said.

"We've got time," Malcolm said. "We don't want to see Roger before the match. If he knew we were in the stands watching him he might get over-anxious."

They did not take a hack to the hotel but walked along the narrow impersonal streets, with Malcolm carrying the overnight bag which they had packed together. With the first thrill of the city still about him, Darrell kept his step lengthened so that his stride would equal the stride of Malcolm Pitt, who, he

114

thought, understood all the mystery lurking in the gray shapes of houses and buildings and shops that they passed. Halfway to the hotel Malcolm put his hand on Darrell's shoulder. "They'll have the match on the tennis courts behind the stadium. And Roger won't know we're there until it's all over. He's a little more excitable than we are, Darrell."

The late afternoon was still full of sunlight. The stands seemed far away, like great hillsides in October covered with sumac and hickory and tupelo gum. In the north end-stands a few hundred freshmen sat with their red skullcaps and yelled. Darrell and Malcolm had found early seats along the net-line near the top of the stands. Beside them was a lean wiry student with hornrimmed glasses. He looked at Malcolm and then at Darrell and said, "You a soph?"

"I'm not a student," Darrell said.

The student fumbled with his shirt and pointed to the block of freshmen. "They don't know how to act at a tennis match. I'm a freshman but I wouldn't sit over there—the way they act. Like it was a football game." He took his skullcap from the bosom of his shirt briefly and then deposited it again. "A freshman never has won the intramural championship before, but we're going to win this time. Perch is a junior and on the tennis team but Roger has defeated him several times before—at least twice. Roger Pitt is a freshman. He'll be on the varsity next year."

"Is that right?" Malcolm said.

"That's right, sir. He's our man."

Suddenly the block of freshmen leaped like a wave and Darrell saw the two white-clad players coming onto the courts together.

"That's Roger Pitt on the left," the student whispered.

"On my left?" Malcolm said.

115

"That's right, sir. To our left and walking on the right of Perch."

Darrell felt Malcolm's elbow slightly against him. But the sight of Roger, his gait and his easiness and his bright blue-stringed racket, seemed to press against him more heavily than the arm. He leaned forward a little and put his arm on Malcolm's knee so that his body would not move. He was thinking of the race in Vicksburg and the first time he had ever seen Roger, and he wondered what would have happened if Roger had run that day. In that moment he was certain that he never would have defeated Roger in that race. Then, as if he must bring himself to the present, he whispered to Malcolm, "Have you ever seen him play tennis before?"

"No," Malcolm said.

Darrell took his arm from Malcolm's knee and let the little chills run along his body as they would. He did not remember the games. He remembered the time and the faces and the easy movements of Roger. He remembered the slow sound of the ball like some echo from a deep well and the red-capped block of freshmen yelling wildly when Roger won the first set; he remembered the scorer, perched in his seat at the west end of the net, his face moving like an old woman's fan; and then he remembered the utter quietness and the stark knowledge that Perch had won the last two sets, that Roger had lost the match. Beside him the lean wiry freshman had taken off his glasses and was crying.

They met Roger at the end of the net and the three of them seemed to touch at once and nobody said anything for what seemed like a long time until Roger said, "Dean Longstreet, this is my father, and this is my friend, Darrell Barclay."

Darrell could hear Roger calling other names while the little drops of sweat seemed to leak from his face. Roger handed his racket to Darrell and he took it with a great carefulness.

116

Then the Dean caught Malcolm's arm. The wrinkles in his face were like small rolls of muscle and his gray hair, very long down his neck, was curled at the end. "We're mighty proud of your boy. He's making a wonderful record."

Roger touched his father's shoulder. "I'm going to dress. I'll only be a minute."

Malcolm nodded and listened to the Dean again. Roger said, "Come on, Darrell."

They went toward the gymnasium and once inside the dressing room Roger sat on a bench and without a word slowly removed his jersey. Darrell could only stand and watch him, holding tight to the warm damp racket in his hands. There was some overwhelming need in him to watch Roger's face, to see the tiny waves of tenderness about him now that the moment of triumph was gone. He took Roger's jersey and held it. Roger dropped his face into his hands and Darrell said, "Roger . . . don't be that way."

Finally Roger raised his head. "I wouldn't care so much if you hadn't been here to see me lose."

"What happened to you?" Darrell said.

Roger tried to smile but something deep inside him seemed to hold his face still. "I feel so foolish. I saw you and Father and I didn't know you would be here . . . and I thought maybe I didn't really see you . . . that maybe I just wanted you to be there that much . . ." Roger suddenly stretched out on the bench and turned his face into his arms. "Go tell Father I'll be out in a few minutes . . ."

Darrell went out and behind him he could hear the quiet crying. And for him, Roger was like some king brought suddenly to his knees.

They ate that night at the Galleo and by that time the old easiness flowed in Roger's face again, as if he had put away

117

from him any thought of the afternoon and now looked only toward the day when he would conquer bigger things for his father and for Darrell. Later they went to the Bluegrave where Malcolm drank and talked to the men and watched the floorshow and played two games of cards. Twice he offered Roger and Darrell drinks from his glass of whiskey. After one striptease he took them back to the hotel. While he was getting the room key and buying cigars, Roger whispered to Darrell, "Father thinks I have to be back at school tonight, but I don't. Now you listen. He's ready to go to bed. You can see it in his face. Soon as he gets to sleep you take the key and slip out. I'll be waiting for you down here. We'll do some streets that Father's never seen." Roger winked.

Darrell shook his head. "No. He's liable to wake up and that'd fix you and me both, good."

"No, he won't."

"He will, too. We got a double bed. You know he'll hear me if I get up."

"He'll never know you've moved. He'll be dreaming about the woman at the Bluegrave."

"And when I come in . . ."

"Aw, Darrell, you got to take some kind of chance in everything."

Then Malcolm had come over to them. He said to Roger, "Are you going up with us, or have you got to go back to the dormitory?"

"I reckon I won't go up," Roger said.

"You'll be down early tomorrow?"

"Yessir."

Malcolm turned to go to his room. Roger pointed to a chair in the corner of the lobby. He whispered to Darrell, "Be there. In one hour."

Then Darrell turned too and went with Malcolm Pitt.

118

Later, Darrell lay in bed on his stomach. The room was not completely dark because he had left a shade half drawn. He had placed his coat carefully in the closet, to one side, and left the closet door open. His pants and shirt and tie lay across a chair. He was thinking that Malcolm Pitt would not talk, would soon be asleep, and thinking of how heavy he seemed in bed because the mattress sloped toward him.

The covers seemed tight about Darrell's feet. He had to move a little. Malcolm was breathing steadily, but suddenly in the stillness he said, "That hoochy-koochy woman in the Blue-grave beat anything we've seen in Vicksburg. She was worse than a tadpole in the palm of your hand. Wasn't she?"

"Yessir . . ."

Malcolm was laughing quietly. His laugh changed into long breathing, and finally he was snoring. Darrell waited. He tried to judge the time. With his right hand he cautiously found his left wrist and began counting pulse beats. He counted to sixty-nine times. Still he waited. He began counting pulse beats again. The snoring seemed longer and deeper. Then almost breathlessly he slipped out of bed, pulled on his clothes and went out. He had the key, but he did not lock the door. Once outside the door he waited to hear some sound inside the room and when he could not even hear the breathing he went down the hotel hall.

Roger was standing beside the chair in the corner of the lobby. "I thought you got locked in."

"No," Darrell said. "We talked a little while."

Roger led the way out of the hotel, along the unpeopled streets, through alleys that smelled like damp cold cornbread with a touch of sage.

"I'm glad you got out. It'd be a rollicking shame for you to miss seeing Nanette down at the Criscross."

"Is that where we're going?"

119

"Yes. I thought you might like to see some pretty little girls come down a winding stairs without any clothes on."

"Who's Nanette?"

"She's usually the first one down the stairs."

"A friend?"

"Acquaintance."

The Criscross was halfway down another unlit alley. The entrance was through a split in a tremendous rock. The door itself was nothing more than two thin curtains. They pushed the curtains aside, Roger going first, and entered the room dimly lighted with three chandeliers that hung from the high ceiling. In one corner of the room the winding stairs dropped like a huge augur. The tables, which were not crowded at all then, faced the stairs. They sat down near the center of the room. Roger leaned toward Darrell and whispered, "There are rooms upstairs. You want one?"

"I don't know," Darrell said.

Suddenly Darrell thought he did not know Roger at all. He wanted to touch the arm or wrist stretched along the table before him to make sure it was the same body which he had slept warmly against in another and younger day, the body that had whispered to him beside a creek bank in the nights of another and younger time, and whose voice was always clean like the sound of bright polished silver. For a moment he wished they had not come. His elbows were heavy on the table to steady himself against that something which raced inside him.

"Roger," he said. He whispered.

Roger leaned toward him again. The part through his black hair was perfectly straight. His teeth suddenly shone hard and smooth and white, like Malcolm Pitt's. His face was flushed a little from laughter, and seemed thin, and his dark eyes brighter than the light from the chandeliers. "Have you ever seen one, Darrell?"

120

"What?"

"A naked woman."

Darrell blushed. He did not answer, could not, for his throat was choked with a liquid-pounding.

"I thought you hadn't," Roger said. He seized Darrell's arm. "They're coming down."

A pair of bright green slippers showed on the stairs.

"How many are they?"

"Usually three."

"What do they do?"

"Talk to us."

The feet were moving down the stairs and suddenly Roger slumped a little upon the table. "Aw, kiss my foot! They've got things on tonight."

Darrell breathed deeply. Roger got up. "I'm going to talk to Nanette, before anyone else does."

The three women reached the bottom of the stairs and stood for a moment in a little circle facing each other. Darrell could see only that they had on rich-colored robes, and that all of them were very dark haired. In less than a minute Roger was talking to the one with the green robe and Darrell was sure she must be Nanette. An anger arose in him and he looked away from the women and Roger toward the other side of the room. When he looked toward the stairs again, Roger was coming toward him and Nanette was leaving the room through a side door. He was both angry and thrilled with Roger's daring.

Roger leaned over the table. "You want to go up and talk to Nanette?"

"Talk to her?"

"Well . . . anything you want to do. Come on."

He followed Roger through the side door and to a room upstairs. Roger knocked, then opened the door before Darrell heard any answer. Nanette was standing at the foot of a tall

121

canopied bed, fingering either an earring or a strand of her heavy black hair.

"Come in, little one."

"Nanette, this is Darrell."

"Well, so this is your friend."

"Yes."

"You come in too."

Darrell entered and closed the door. He felt that all the heat of his body was in his face. "Thank you," he said. He kept looking at Nanette and he thought she might be beautiful, except for her eyes: they were too old and too large.

Nanette went to the head of the bed and sat down and leaned back against a pillow. "Sit down, little one." Darrell's eyes moved to the chair nearest him. "Not you," she said. "You stand. I want to look at you. You are very beautiful. The little one has told me. You have excellent hands, good strong wrists. Yes. Come a little closer."

Roger leaned against the foot of the bed and laughed. Nanette turned her eyes quickly to him. "You are a wicked little garçon. But I love you. M'ami, you have a *rich* soul. I hope you are good for your friend. Darrell, you have a beautiful body and you have a beautiful soul. I can see one. I can feel the other. But your name—no. You should be Roger and he should be Darrell. You are the good one."

"I am the good one," Roger said. "Darr is neither good nor bad."

"Darr?"

"Yes. That's my special name for him."

"He does not need a special name. That is for those who have nothing else to offer . . . But, if it is what you want . . . Ah, you do not know what you want. You do not know what you think. Why did you come here?"

"To see you."

"Do you want me to sing?"

"No. I have a sister who sings. We came to love you. Both of us."

"Go home and love your friend. When ten years have gone, you can come to me. I am not for you, now. Some day you come back to me, and one shall be on one side and one on the other. I will love both of you."

"Love both of us now."

"Go away. Your friend is angry with you. You are yet a wicked little garçon." She reached over and patted his cheeks.

When they had reached the door she called to Darrell, "You are the good one. You will be a fine lover some day, beautiful and strong."

They said goodbye and she said, "Goodbye, my little ones."

Down the long dark stairway Darrell kept hoping that when they came to the street and the fresh air, their voices would seem clean again and they might reach each other with words.

In the street Roger said, "Let's take a hack."

"I want to walk," Darrell said.

They turned to go through an alley and Roger said, "I think you're mad at me."

"I'm not."

"I wouldn't blame you if you were. I always go spoiling things for us, showing off when I don't mean to. Maybe I wanted to make you believe I know a lot that I don't know. Maybe I did all this tonight because I didn't want you to think about this afternoon."

"I'd rather think about this afternoon," Darrell said. "I don't care if you lost. Then you were clean and good . . ."

Roger suddenly caught Darrell's hand and they stopped in the shadows of the alley. "I only came down here once with Perch and two others—that's all. I wouldn't do something up there for anything."

123

"Have you ever . . . anywhere?" Darrell said.

"No. Have you?"

"No."

Then they started to walk again, close together, along the quiet, deserted streets with no thought of direction until they came to the very edge of the river, and turning they came along the streets again through the smell of age and dampness. They did not talk and their silence was like the sheet lightning that played about the edge of the city—something strong and sound-less, almost the conqueror of time and space.

At the hotel Roger whispered, "I'll see you early tomorrow. And don't wake the governor. We might incur his displeasure."

But the sudden and aloof pleasantness of Roger's voice did not hide anything from Darrell. They looked at each other for more than a minute, and then Roger went away slowly and at the corner he turned to lift his hand to Darrell who was still waiting outside the hotel.

Darrell entered the hotel room almost noiselessly and listened for Malcolm Pitt's breathing. The room was darker than when he left and he did not try to put his coat in the closet. He slipped under the covers and lay on his back staring up into the darkness which seemed heavier toward the ceiling and thinking, It will not be long until Roger will come home for the summer. He could count his pulse beats then without touching his wrist. Time seemed like rain dripping from a roof. Malcolm Pitt turned on the mattress. His arm touched Darrell's shoulder and in the dark stillness he said, "Where did you two go?"

Darrell's tongue seemed to pull the words from his throat: "A place on Basin."

"What was there?"

"Girls. And a stairway."

"The Criscross?"

"Yessir . . ."

124

Darrell knew then that Malcolm Pitt had been whispering and now the whispering was low and fierce, "Dammit to hell!"

Malcolm got out of bed and lit a cigar and sat in a chair and blew the smoke into the window. When he came back to bed he put his arm around Darrell and held his hand against his side. "Did you do anything?"

"No sir . . ." He was cold and he was afraid he was going to tremble.

"Tell me the truth."

The arm was heavy about him, holding him. "It's the truth. We started to but we didn't . . ."

There was no movement about the room, as if everything in time was too swift to be heard. Darrell kept staring into darkness. He could feel the pulse of Malcolm's heart, for the arm did not move. It lay heavy against him and his body began to grow warm.

five

On the first Saturday night that Roger was home that summer he and Darrell had saddled two horses to ride to Waycrest, for no more reason than to ride, when Leta Pitt refused to let them go. She said, "Malcolm's gone to Vicksburg for Miriam and all the Negroes gone to Waycrest. I'm not going to stay here alone tonight. You two come to my room. I want to talk to you."

They were slow to unsaddle the horses and when they went into the house Roger sat down at the piano and played a vulgar tune. Then he played the tune again and sang certain phrases with proper omissions:

". . . rode so fast he skint . . .
and tore them off behind him . . ."

Darrell said, "Your mama is going to skin something if you don't stop that."

Roger began the tune again and then stopped and leaped to his feet and lifted his arms and cried, "Stand and sing you dear sweet good people of Leighton. One and all. Blend your voices to the glory road."

"Roger!"

"Yes, my dear mother. I will come to you by and by."

"I want to speak to you two."

Roger caught Darrell's arm. "Now could I drink hot blood . . ."

"My good liege, does a little matter of missing a trip to the humble village of Waycrest disturb you so?"

"No. No. No. You will see. She is concerned about our souls. We are five years beyond the age of accountability. She has worn my armor thin. Lend me your arm and let us go forth."

In her room Leta Pitt leaned back in a chair beside the window, and across her ankles, where her skirt did not cover her, she placed a big square doily. She motioned with her fan and Roger and Darrell sat on the bed near her.

"You are a big baby," Roger said. "You are a big overgrown baby and all you need is for Father to spank you where you sit down. You're not afraid to stay here by yourself. Darrell's grandmother stays by herself." Roger lay back on the bed and Leta Pitt's face changed, as if the words she had meant to say had flown completely from her lips.

"Man was born in a state of sin," she said.

Roger sat up. "So you want me to lock my hands behind my neck and crack my elbows together?"

126

"If you show me no respect, Roger, I dare say you show none to anyone."

"I'm sorry, Mother." He lay back on the bed.

She put her fan on the window sill. "Any one of you could be killed any minute. Did you think of that? A horse could fall. Lightning could strike. Or your heart could just quit. Snap. That's the end. They do that sometime for no good reason. It is the truth, isn't it, Darrell?"

"Yes, ma'am."

"You know how quick your father went. He certainly didn't have any month to repent. Did he?"

"No, ma'am."

"They swooped without warning when they took him. And it might happen to you, Roger. Then it's too late to think about the soul. I don't know much of what your father was like, Darrell, but I think he might give a lot right now to trade places with one of you—to have the chance you've got. You're nearly seventeen. Both of you. It hurts my heart, Roger, to think about you in New Orleans and not on the church rolls."

"Father's not on the church roll, talk to him."

"I gave up hope on him before you stood alone, at least before you were talking."

"I wish you would give up on me. Father pays Brother Potter, and he goes to church sometimes, and I think he's going to Heaven. I'll settle for wherever he goes. He's not worried about our souls."

"I'm your mother. It's my business to worry about it. I'm not going to let this summer go by and you go back to New Orleans until you've made your peace."

"You think Darrell will be safe in Leighton?"

"No. I want him saved too. I'm certain you won't join until he does."

127

Roger got up. "May we go now? We need time and meditation."

"Yes. And I'll be praying for these little seeds to fall into your heart and spring like the mustard plant."

Roger went to her and kissed her lips. "I guess you're right about all this, Mother. I'm such a wayward son. I ought to be good like Miriam."

She hugged him and the tears rolled down her cheeks and with her throat tight she said, "You two go on to Waycrest. Go on if you want to. I'm not afraid . . ."

Roger turned from her and winked at Darrell.

That night, after they had gone to Waycrest, they lay in bed in Roger's room and Darrell said, "You know you almost made a promise tonight."

"About joining the church?" Roger said.

"Yes."

"I guess it doesn't matter. I'm going to have to join sooner or later anyway."

"I'm not going to join, not now."

"Why?"

"Because I don't believe all they say."

"You don't have to."

"You have to say you do. I don't want to say I do if I don't."

"You're not fair with me. Haven't we always stood together? I've nearly got to join. Mother will make me. But I'm not going to if you don't. You hold two destinies in your hand, lad. Not one but two. If you want to tamper with my soul, go ahead."

"I don't want to be a hypocrite."

"You wouldn't be. Please do this for me."

"If I do I won't ever spend the night at your house and you won't stay at mine. How about that?"

128

Roger smiled and Darrell knew that Roger did not believe him.

"You promise to join then?"

"Yes," Darrell said.

They joined the church that summer and were baptised and Leta Pitt cried in the church and hugged Roger and whispered to him, "He heard my prayers and He brought you here and I knew He would . . ."

Darrell did not stay overnight at the big house again that summer nor did Roger stay with him. When summer was gone and Roger went away to school, Darrell believed for a little while that something had ended forever.

six

The next summer Roger did not come home at all. He went with two of his classmates to Mexico, and once when Leta Pitt asked Darrell to mail a letter to Roger for her, she said, "It's such a blessing that Roger joined the church last summer. I couldn't bear to think of him going way off down there—and him not a Christian. I think I just wouldn't have let him go. And anyway, I don't know why he suddenly didn't want to come home this summer."

Darrell knew that he was the cause of Roger's not coming home. While he was in the fields or working beside Malcolm Pitt, his separation from Roger seemed right to him. But alone in his room at night he always wondered. Sometimes, after he had eaten supper quietly with his grandmother, he would lie in bed and compose letters to Roger: *I do miss you but I know that it is better for things to be as they are . . . You belong to*

129

one thing and I belong to another . . . I know that some day you can be a great doctor . . . but everybody who is great must be defeated somewhere (He liked that line, though he was never sure what he meant by defeated) *. . . Last week I was getting some books from your house. One was* A TALE OF TWO CITIES, *that I guess you probably read before you ever saw me . . . It makes a difference when I think that I am reading something that you have already read . . .*

But he always fell asleep thinking of what he would write, and no sentence of it ever reached the page.

Late in the spring of the following year, just before school was out, Roger wrote Darrell a letter which read: *Dear D: Do you want me to come home this summer? Faithfully yours, R.*

That night Darrell composed a long letter in his mind which said neither Yes nor No. The next morning when he sat down to write he replied: *Dear R: Yes. Faithfully yours, D.*

Roger had a suntan when he came home that June and he seemed stronger than Darrell ever remembered: something about him was like Malcolm Pitt when he stood beside the hard machinery of the gin with the sweat breaking through his shirt and across his wide shoulders, or when Malcolm stood on some knoll, lifted his hands steadily, fired, and the cock-bird skimming across briars and sumac tumbled. Darrell saw it all the moment he saw Roger's face and he was glad. For a while they talked and then they planned to meet at the millpond that night and fish.

It was hardly dark when Darrell came to the gin that night and because he thought he might be early, he stopped for a moment and looked at the gin that loomed in the dusk like the steep cliffs at Vicksburg rising above the river. The huge dark form made his heart leap, for he remembered the touch of each

130

shingle and wheel and belt, and the hours he had worked there beside Malcolm Pitt.

He set the bucketful of minnows, which he and Roger would use for bait that night, on the ground and it covered a small patch of dwarfed cotton that had sprouted from last fall's cotton seed. While he watched he thought of how he had grown with the gin, his arms and shoulders swelling with each lifting of heavy beams and with the expert grooving and tapping of heavy wheels. Then he picked up the bucket and walked on in the dusk toward the pond, thinking of Roger's hands and face, the new-tanned muscles, and of the tennis matches he had talked about. He turned into the heavy growth of willows and suddenly he stopped. He knew that Roger was not alone. Faintly through the twilight and early moonlight he could see Roger standing on the pond bank stuffing his shirt-tail into his pants without unbuckling his belt. A few feet away from Roger, Nolie stood. She said, "What you doing?"

"Putting my shirt-tail in."

"What you been doing?"

"Patching my boat."

"When did you come from school?"

"Today."

"You get it finished? The boat."

"No. What are you doing?"

"Nothing."

"I don't reckon you ought to be here," Roger said.

Nolie stood fingering and smoothing the long strands of sandy hair that fell over her eyes. "Where's Darrell?"

"I don't know."

"Thought you were going fishing."

"We are. After while."

She began a low trickling laugh. Darrell was watching not so much her face now as the slender figure in the dusk.

"Where've you started?" Roger said.

"Nowhere," she said. "I've been to the church though. The ridge of white candles . . ." She took her hand from her hair and waved it in a small housetop motion.

Roger went nearer to her. "To church? What for?"

She laughed again. "To see the candles, the ridge of white . . ." Then she sat down. From where Darrell was standing, her sitting was like the slow soundless falling of a leaf. Her left hand fingered her hair again and she looked up to Roger. "You think I'm pretty?"

"I think you're a little doxy."

"What's that?"

"You wouldn't know."

"Does Darrell think I'm pretty?"

"I don't know what Darrell thinks."

"You like him better than you do me. You want him for your sister, don't you? Well, she won't ever get him."

"You're talking silly, Nolie."

"Sit down," she said.

Roger sat down by her and she lay back, her elbows pressing into the soft turf.

"You're a lot like Darrell," she said. "Yes, you're a lot like him, except . . ."

"Except what?"

"Except when you're not like him."

"That's crazy."

She raised a little on her elbows; her neck and back made a slight curve. "You don't like me."

"I like you all right." Roger's voice was almost a whisper. Darrell could hardly hear him.

Nolie dropped her head back. Darrell could hear her saying faintly, "No you don't. Just because I'm the preacher's daughter you don't want to touch me."

132

Suddenly Roger moved against Nolie and caught her into his arms. A quivering surged throughout Darrell's body so that he turned quickly, and quietly, back into the clump of willows, telling himself that he had not looked upon Roger at all, that it was only a wild and fleeting image. And when he heard again the fierce whispering and the caught breath he clutched at his thighs to stop his body's trembling. Slowly he sank down to the ground and would not listen. He thought he would never look on Roger's face again. The Roger he had known was lost forever in another world. But finally the whispering became words again.

"Nolie . . ."

"I'm going to hell," she said. "I know I'm going and nobody can . . ."

"Don't talk that way."

She said, "I hope you're satisfied." Then louder she said it again.

"You're acting drunk."

"I am. I am drunk," she cried. "Behind the candles I found it and I took it. The whole bottle, all the wine they had left from Sunday. He'll find it gone and I know what he's going to say. He'll tell me what he's always told me. Lost in the shadow of the devil. Thy nakedness shall be uncovered, thy shame shall be seen . . ."

"Who are you talking about?"

"Father," Nolie said. "Father knows I'm going to hell. He told me and told me . . ."

Slowly Darrell turned, and stood, and watched them again. Roger was sitting beside Nolie. They were not touching each other.

"You don't have to feel like this," Roger said.

"It's not this," she said. "I've done worse things than this. I've . . ."

"Don't be a little fool."

Nolie jumped up and stood looking down at Roger, and even in the darkness Darrell thought he could see a wildness sweep across her face. "Now go tell Darrell! Go tell him what you've done. Tell him tonight when you're fishing. He won't ever speak to me again. He won't ever look at me."

Roger reached up and caught her hand and said, "Why would I tell anybody?"

Nolie jerked away from him and ran, crying, her long sandy hair streaming in the quiet dark.

For a while Darrell did not move. He thought he would go home, that he did not want to see Roger at all. But he stood looking toward the pond bank. Roger turned and lay on his stomach. Finally Darrell started walking toward the pond, as if something was drawing him. Roger turned over quickly when he heard the footsteps. His face was sharp in the darkness. When he looked up at Darrell the incisive line of his lips quivered into a laugh.

"You're early."

Darrell looked away from Roger. "Yes."

"Where are the minnows?"

Darrell could feel his shoulders cool, his face flood. He had left the bucket of minnows in the willow bushes. "I didn't bring any."

"None at all?"

"I didn't have time. I had to help Louella cook supper. Grandmother's gone."

"South Carolina? I never thought she'd go."

Darrell talked quickly. He wanted to forget the minnows. It was not really a lie he had told; it was something, he thought, to save Roger. "I didn't either, but Uncle Turner is her only brother living now and she hasn't seen him since the War. She's gone for a month."

134

They were both suddenly quiet. Then Roger began to laugh. "What are you scared of?"

"Scared?"

"You're shaking." Roger's laugh quieted. "Well, if you don't want to tell me, I'm no mind reader. Some folks strain their guts out trying to factor $a^2 + b^2$."

"You don't have to be smart, Roger."

"What's the matter with you?"

"Nothing's the matter with me. Why did you do it?"

"Do what?" Roger began to laugh.

"You know what." Darrell started down the pond bank.

"Where you going?"

"Home!"

"Darrell . . . ?" Roger's voice carried a long way.

But Darrell was already walking away from the pond and away from the slow, almost soundless, movement of water against the bank. Roger belonged to another time, to another world. And they were lost to each other forever. He thought, Roger does not need me now for anything; he is beyond me. Darrell heard his name called again. He quickened his steps, carrying with him the fierce whispering he had heard only a few minutes before, the echo of Roger's calling, and the purling night-sounds that came out of the hedge, the grass, the trees and dashed in waves against his ears.

All of this (what he had seen) might have started when Roger went to New Orleans, to the University; or it might have always been. He wished he could say it was not Roger at all, it was someone else. If it had been Malcolm Pitt, Darrell could have looked on what he had seen with no more than a certain envy moving within himself. But with Roger he was ashamed, and hurt, and betrayed. It was here and there a man left a little of himself. A share for the pond, for the gin. A share for the trip to Vicksburg, for the mule auction. A share at the barn

135

when Malcolm Pitt's voice shot out in whole-framed laughter. It was here and there; even remembering would not bring it back. He was going to an empty house. There would be no laughter, no footstep, only his own quiet breathing, or the sound of his own turning in bed. But it did not matter. He would be alone anyway. He would always be alone.

The moon was high and strong enough to cast his shadow along the damp inch-a-night grass. He looked once toward the gin, saw the moonlight carom on the silver suction pipes. But he did not go home that way. He went instead along the damp narrow path of sedge, through the patch of small willows. He crossed the road without seeing anyone and passed the small Presbyterian churchhouse which seemed to huddle under the acornless limbs of the tall oak where he and Roger had read to each other. Ahead of him, in the cemetery, the tombstones probed the night like stubby fingers.

He had neared the clay bank and was ready to step down into the road when he heard his name whispered among the bushy hedge. The sound was separate and distinct, as a live peppering of fire, "Darrell."

His stomach jerked in breath to run, but he stopped quickly, half-turning.

"Darrell," she said. Even before his eyes found her leaning against the small trunk of a tupelo gum, he knew it was Nolie. "I thought you would come this way."

"Nolie."

Her hands moved from the trunk behind her, and small pieces of bark fell into the old leaves. Her mouth moved toward a laugh but he did not hear anything. He only felt that a certain fey beauty was shadowed in her face.

"Come here," she said.

He moved toward her. "What's the matter with you? What are you doing here?"

136

"I went in there again," she said.

"Where?"

"There. In the church." She pointed.

"You *are* drunk."

"I'm not, Darrell. I'm not. I didn't mean to do it. I know now you don't love me. You won't kiss me."

"Nolie."

"You kissed me once. You already forgot. You did. But you won't ever any more because he told you what I did."

His hand had closed lightly about her shoulder. He shook her. "Nolie, what're you talking about?"

"You won't ever look at me again. You won't ever touch me because he told you." Both her hands closed about his arm.

"Roger didn't tell me anything."

"He did."

"He didn't."

Then both her hands went around his body. He caught her wrists and pushed her away.

"Touch me. Touch me with your face."

"You want me to walk home with you, Nolie?"

"No. I want you to touch me."

He backed away from her. "Let me take you home."

"No. I want you to touch me with your face."

She crouched down beside the tree, and he watched her bright hair fall over hands and wrists. If she cried he did not hear her. Then he went down the bank into the road.

He had left her with certainty, huddled there in the hedge, but in his mind he had carried her with him all along the road and into his empty house. He did not light the coal-oil lamp on his dressing table. He raised the window which opened on to the front porch, then stepped back out of the square of moonlight. He seemed to pull open, more than to unbutton, his cover-

137

alls, then sat on the edge of the bed to remove his shoes. His broadcloth underwear seemed tight about his body and he wanted to rip it off too; but instead, he threw himself diagonally onto the thin feather mattress which his grandmother had made for summer sleeping. He did not cover his body at all with the unironed sheet, but lay heavy on his stomach, his face turned toward the window, and his mind saying, Why didn't I? She is a little like Miriam. I could have. But I didn't even touch her, only her shoulder. And maybe it was because of Miriam, maybe that was it. But if I had it to do over again . . . And I didn't touch her, only her shoulder.

He turned in the bed with a sudden fierceness and pulled the sheet over him, though he was not cool, as if to intervolve the sheet with the surging that stretched itself throughout his taut body. It was the same pounding as when Malcolm Pitt had come out of the Yellow House in Vicksburg with the wine bottles caught beneath his arm, to say, "Did you see that little stripling? Little witchy eyes? Lead you right out of the Garden. Hell. If I was eighteen . . ." Malcolm Pitt could never have said that to Roger.

The bed was damp to his back, and Darrell was angry that he could not quiet his charging mind as he could close his eyes or press his lips tight together. So a thing lived in him which would not lie down, but in his anger there was no fear, because Malcolm Pitt, with the cigar tight within his fierce smooth lips, had really meant: Reach out, for a man is made for the pounding to rise and die and rise again. Malcolm Pitt, with his firm lips shaped, would laugh at being afraid.

For a moment his body had eased, and he curled a little in bed. His mind had lifted from the certain plunges to a drifting without thought. He was not dreaming, nor was he asleep, but the imaged incidents of the day moved before him, slow and defined, though soft enough that he thought any second he might

138

be asleep. When the shadow passed through his window he told himself that, too, was another image. He did not even open his eyes at the faint sound of steps.

He could hear, suddenly, other steps like the ticking of a watch, and he felt the foot of his bed give to the slightest pressure. His body hinged upright in bed, tense and pounding again, and his eyes dashed wide.

She stood at the foot of his bed, her face almost beautiful in the moonlight that spilled from her and from the bright blade of the lifted knife.

"In God's name, Nolie!"

He thought she laughed. He lifted his hand as if to shield himself. "That knife!"

"I have it," she said.

He moved in the bed away from her while her empty hand clutched the foot-rail.

"Give it to me."

"No."

"Put it down. Put it in the window."

"No. I got it from the church, too. They cut bread with it."

"Nolie . . ."

"You come touch me." She moved around the foot of the bed.

"You put it down."

"Not now."

She was coming slowly, almost gliding, toward him in the shadows with the knife pointed more than drawn.

"Nolie . . ."

"Are you going to touch me?"

"Yes."

"With your face?"

"Yes."

She stopped. He reached out to grasp her wrist. She drew away, turning a little, and the knife slid along the floor behind her.

"I wouldn't have hurt you," she said. "I got it out of the church to open the wine."

"The wine?"

"But I'm not drunk, now. I'm not. There wasn't any more. I didn't want to do that down at the pond. Because of you. But I did and Roger told you."

"I'll go home with you, Nolie. I'll take you home." Again his hand had reached out and touched her shoulder.

"You promised me."

He was closer. His arm had circled down to her back and he was breathing deep and quick against her, remembering the Yellow House in Vicksburg and Malcolm Pitt saying: *Hell. If I was eighteen* . . .

"What did Roger do?" he said.

"You know." Her arms went around him and he did not pull back.

"Tell me . . ."

"I didn't want him to," she whispered.

The surging plunged in him until his arms quivered tight about her. Her lips had caught his and she was falling beneath him like a slow feather to the thin mattress. He wanted to laugh then, with depth and certainty: if Malcolm Pitt knew this his firm flushed lips would break to a full-throated chortle, man to man. His own lips slipped away from Nolie for a moment; and he smiled, believing, having to believe—for he was eighteen— that now he would walk with a certain honesty toward himself and toward Malcolm Pitt, and that his flesh would stand the sunshine, would tan as any man's.

Nolie went away from him quietly, without a word, and he was alone again and afraid. Deep into the night he lay awake and finally he got out of bed and knelt so that his face touched the sheet. He wanted to pray but he could not, because he was unclean. Then in the darkness he washed himself and knelt again beside the bed. After a long time he prayed: *God, let me forget Roger, his hands and his eyes and all his face. Let me forget that he ever was. I am not sorry for what I have done tonight. But let me think about Miriam. I know it is right for me to think about her* . . . For a moment he could see God in a big leather jacket looking down upon him.

part

· FOUR

one

On his twentieth birthday Darrell sat alone in the gin's office looking out into the damp grayness of November and thinking that twenty was such a long, long time away from eighteen. He was watching the bright pea-sized raindrops stick underneath the guy-wires that angled up toward the tall smokestack. There was no rain, only the dampness of November and the low-flying smoke from the boiler.

He had sent Yancey for the mail and when he heard steps on the ladder he turned and waited. But it was Malcolm Pitt who came through the doorway with his face beaming with color, and he was wearing his work clothes—a big leather jacket, a gray tie, brown shirt and brown pants. His soft high-topped shoes were polished as always. Darrell got up and moved to the desk and leaned against it.

"Have you had a good day?" Malcolm said.

"Very busy till an hour ago."

Malcolm put his hand out and gripped the back of the chair. "I should have been here to help you. But I had to go to Vicksburg this morning. Miriam wanted to come home early.

Nolie rode over and back with me. To see her old painting teacher, I think."

They looked at each other, as two people look when they seem to know what each is thinking. The year before, Nolie had gone to the Garden City School. Malcolm had paid the tuition, though Nolie did not know it then. At first, nobody knew it except Malcolm and Darrell and Brother Potter. But Nolie found out—from her father, Malcolm said—and the next year she would not go back. Sometimes, when they talked about Nolie, Malcolm would stand with his face motionless, as if the thought that held him was very painful; and he seemed to say, "I couldn't send you off to school. I couldn't get along without you." Malcolm stood that way now. Darrell kept looking at him and then he said suddenly, "We made it all right. Stafford was sweating over the compress—a little. But we made it all right."

Malcolm turned slightly and looked away, as if Darrell had done a very kind thing for him. "Yancey have any trouble keeping up steam?"

"Nossir. But those cords of pine burn awfully quick. We need more oak."

"Yes. When we get our sawmill we'll have plenty of oak slabs. That'll do away with our wood problem. Pine is quicker than a rabbit." Malcolm went to the window of the office and looked out. "We ought to be bird hunting now, but I guess it's too late to go today. And I've got to go to the store a minute anyway." He put his hands on the window sill. "Don't you think it's time we took another trip to Memphis—just a little spree?"

"I don't know."

"Don't you want to go?"

"Yessir."

"Well, hell. We're grown. We'll just go." His back was still to Darrell and he reached into his pocket and brought out

143

something hidden within his cupped palms. He turned and held out his hand and with a half-laugh let his tongue play across his lips. For a minute both of them were like two children playing a game with pecans. "Hull gull?" Malcolm said.

"Hand full."

"How many?"

"One," Darrell said.

"Right. One what?"

"Does it move?"

"More or less."

"A craw-dad."

"No."

"You're sure it moves?"

"Well, it wouldn't walk off by itself."

"Mousetrap."

Then Malcolm began to laugh and uncupped his palms and opened a small square box. He held out a golden pocket watch to Darrell and the golden chain swung to and fro between them. Darrell did not move. He watched the arc of the chain and slowly lifted his eyes to Malcolm's face.

"Isn't this your birthday?" Malcolm said. He pushed the watch into Darrell's hand and wound the chain about his fingers. His eyes winked slightly and the smile gave way to something else in his face. "A jewel in it for every one of your years, boy, and one extra to grow on. It's all for you." He went quickly out of the office and down the steps, and Darrell stood holding the watch and listening to the endlessness of something.

After a while he put the watch into the bib of his coveralls and walked about the gin, trying to feel that the watch had always belonged to him. When he returned to the office Yancey was standing in the doorway with the mail. He took the letter that Yancey held out for him and said, "Thank you, Yancey."

"Mista Darrell, I don't thank we gonna have no more cotton today. You want me to keep the fire up?"

"Better keep a little up."

"Yessuh." Yancey left.

Darrell sat down at the desk and looked at the envelope. He saw Roger's name in the corner and the sound of the watch in his pocket seemed louder. Little by little he tore the stamped end while, almost smiling, he thought, Roger's got something good planned for Thanksgiving or Christmas.

He unfolded the sheet. The words in the letter seemed to move quickly on the page as the words always moved quickly, yet vividly, from Roger's lips. *Dear Darrell, This letter may put you back a little seeing as how you never heard anything about Anne. We have set the date and you must of course be here to hold the ring and to add strength in that hour. You will be surprised at this suddenness but things go that way. At least it has gone that way with us. It will be here on the campus the 25th in the famous little Chapel that used to be called the Hitching Post and might well be called that now. Anne not so incidentally is the daughter of Dean Longstreet. There is nothing like love brother and when you see her you will know. Do not mix Anne in your mind with any of the other little ones that I have told you of . . .*

He was sweating. Though no one was looking, he knew that his face was rigid, controlled, and he stared out of the window again. He felt cheated, felt that his days and the days of every man he knew were out-of-rein. He could hear the thin spew of steam from the boiler, which never before had sounded like a grating file. He did not know how long he stared, but finally, with a decisive calmness, he got up and walked about the gin. As he walked by the gin-heads he reached out and let his finger slide across the glass. The trace of his finger was left in the thin moted

145

dust. Roger getting married, he thought. He could hear the words, and they seemed to fall like acorns into a dusty and graveled street.

He went back to the gin's office. After a while he leaned forward in the desk chair and took one sheet of the gin's stationery which bore in the upper left-hand corner his own name below the name of Malcolm Pitt. He wrote: *I was not much surprised. Please do believe that I wish you all the happiness in the world. But I cannot be best man. We are still ginning and there are other things. You must understand . . .*

He slipped into his heavy coat, took the two letters, and went down to the boiler where Yancey was raking among the live coals with a short hickory pole. He watched Yancey pull a sweet potato from the hot ashes, feel it, then put it back into the ashes again.

"If a bale comes on the yard do you think you and Stafford can take care of it?"

"Yessuh," Yancey said.

"If I'm not back by five, you can lock the toll bin and leave."

The letter *from* Roger was in his right coat pocket and his fingers were about it. The letter *to* Roger was in his left pocket; his fingers were about it, and he told himself: "If I leave it here it won't go off today. I'll drive to Waycrest to mail it. I'll ask Nolie to go with me."

That was one reason to leave the gin, and he wanted to leave it now. He went past Nolie's house, and then past the church and the cemetery because the Negro woman washing in Nolie's backyard had said, "She's paintin', way beyond the church."

He found her on the knoll, and when she saw him coming she stood and waited for him. Her sleeves were pushed high on her wrists and the opened edges of her thin sweater moved like sedge tops.

146

"You're going to freeze, Nolie."

She laughed, a frail laugh, like her body, and he wanted to wrap the frailness inside his heavy coat. She was smaller than Miriam; not much, but a little.

"Are you going to let me paint you?"

"I didn't come for that."

"You never come for that. But I'd like to paint you in the wind. That would make your cheeks sharper. The wind would dull your eyes a little and you wouldn't stare."

"You can paint the churchhouse."

"I want you standing with the wind across your face. The cleft in your chin would be only the tiniest shadow. And your lips parted only enough for the wind to touch the whiteness of your teeth."

"Or the gin," he said. "You can paint the gin."

"The veins in your hand would break a little through the smoothness, shadow against gold. But in the summer, I'd like to paint you dripping wet."

"In swimming, maybe?"

"Yes."

"Without clothes?"

"Yes. Without clothes. The blend of buff and white would be perfect for you all over, except . . ."

"You better paint the gin."

"No. When can I paint you?"

"Never." He laughed as if the strained laughter would quell the need for warmth which simmered then in him. "You want to go with me to Waycrest?"

"What for?"

"To mail a letter."

"Some letter."

"You want to go?"

"When can I paint you?"

147

"Never. You want to go?"

"You want me to go?"

"Yes." Again he wanted to touch her, to pull her inside his coat. She pushed the hair back from her cheek and held it between her fingers against the wind.

She laughed. "Don't trifle with my affections. You're never afraid around me, are you?"

"Are you going to act foolish?"

"But you are afraid around Miriam. You're afraid to look at her because of her father. Why don't you grow a mustache?"

"The devil, Nolie. Are you going with me?"

"No. In about three or four months when you start to Waycrest to the Pilgrimage Ball, reckon you'll come ask me to go?"

"Aw, Nolie."

"You want to be nice to both of us—you want to take me now and take Miriam then . . ."

"Miriam may be at Vicksburg then—at school."

"School . . . it'll be spring and she'll be home, and you'll be love sick. No . . . it'll be just like November, for you, because you don't love anybody. Go get Miriam. She's home this weekend."

Nolie was not moving. It was all within him, the throbbing and the dashing of simmering waves. He thought that with one touch she would go, but he would not reach out to her now.

"All right," he said. "I might do that."

She laughed again, but the laugh was not so frail as before though her body was still thin and small in the damp wind. He could hear the laugh, or thought he could, even when he had passed the cemetery and the church.

He had already turned into the door of Gammel's store before he saw Malcolm Pitt leaning against the counter, his big leather jacket swinging open, his solid teeth showing whiter because his face was red from the wind.

148

"You going home now?" Malcolm said.

"Nossir."

"Where you going?"

Malcolm Pitt's face could make a thing seem small, like saying: *What in the hell you want with Nolie this time of day?*

"To mail a letter. Then I'm going back to the gin. I may clean the gin-heads."

Malcolm's seasoned hands began fastening his big jacket. "Wait a minute. I'll go with you."

After Darrell had mailed the letter they walked together toward the gin, he a half-step behind Malcolm. He watched the shoulder muscles wrinkle the leather jacket while the two moved in step, and he felt that his own muscles had no strength beside such power. His hand, in his right pocket, closed about the letter *from* Roger, and his damp fingers crumpled the envelope into a tight ball. He wanted something now that seemed forever gone from him, as a child after night has come, wishes he had gone out to play. He was saying to himself that he knew a gin and the color of good earth, that he knew nothing of a University, nothing of Roger's world of $a^2 + b^2$. At the gin he climbed the ladder quickly ahead of Malcolm Pitt, and almost with a fierceness he began tearing into the gin-heads which he had not meant to clean at all that day.

Once in the quietness Darrell said, "I don't know what to say about the watch . . . I'm awfully proud of it."

"I don't want you to say anything." Malcolm did not look up.

Again they worked without speaking until accidentally Malcolm turned a revolving spool too soon so that it scratched Darrell's finger. Almost before the spike caught his finger, he yelled: "Goddammit, Roger, let me get my hand out!" Then quickly he looked up, ashamed and afraid, his scratched hand shaking. "I don't know what I was thinking about. It didn't

149

hurt. It's nothing. I was thinking about Roger." He put his finger to his tongue for a second.

Malcolm took Darrell's hand and looked at the little streak of blood. "You better put some coal oil on it." He squeezed the finger gently and made the blood rush out. "Did that hurt? It ought to bleed a little." He turned quickly and went past the gin-heads to the office and returned with a bottle of coal oil. He turned up the bottle and let the oil drip through the pine-needle stopper onto Darrell's finger.

"It's only a scratch," Darrell said.

"I know," Malcolm said. He put the bottle against the wall and they bent to their work again. After a while Darrell said, "Did you know Roger was getting married . . . at Thanksgiving?"

Malcolm raised up and held the file with both hands and his eyes seemed at first not to believe. "Well, I'll swear. I knew my little boy would grow up." Then he shook his head slowly. "It's awfully quick, Darrell. I hope it lasts."

"Why wouldn't it last?"

"Why? I don't know why. Except there's more fire in Roger than's in me and you. Maybe not any more but a little different from ours."

"Is mine like yours?"

Malcolm began to laugh quietly. "I think it is."

Darrell could feel the watch ticking heavily near his heart.

two

On the night of the Pilgrimage Ball, in the spring, Darrell ate in the kitchen, standing, because he was in a hurry. He stood at the end of the cook-table and fashioned his boiled ham

150

sandwich with salt-rising bread while his grandmother moved about, now and then brushing her finger-tips against her apron. Busy-walking, he thought.

"You look more journey-proud than I do," he said.

"You ought to have coffee tonight, before a party," she said.

"Yancey said Louella would come stay with you while I'm gone tonight, if you want her to."

She pursed her lips. "Why, I don't need Louella." She took a gold-rimmed Haviland china cup, went to the stove, and poured out the coffee for him. He took the cup carefully, hot against his forefinger.

"Thank you."

She watched him drink. "We used to have nine of these cups. By the time the War came there were five left. But bury these? No sir. I filled each one with leaf-mould and set out a flower. They stayed right there in the front window of the old place and the Yankees didn't touch a one." She turned back to the stove, and he thought: I've heard that over and over; it's almost as if she thinks I cannot leave while she talks. "That's something you didn't know about the Yankees: they didn't bother flowers much—woman-like. But moving and such have broken them all down to one now . . ."

He went to the kitchen window and looked out through the dusk toward the henhouse and garden. It was April and each row of the garden was defined with stalk and leaf. He said, "Grandmother, inch-a-night grass is getting the best of the beets."

"What time are you calling for Miriam?" she said.

"At seven." He had not really meant to say any more, but suddenly he was saying, "I'm going to get married soon. I'm going to marry Miriam . . ."

His grandmother lifted her small chin only a little, but very

151

quickly, as if the high stiff collar of her black rep dress were choking. She pulled the shawl tighter about her shoulders, her incisive eyes shone through the dim coal-oil light of the kitchen; and she spoke in the same way he had seen her speak of church or the certainty of the devil's flesh, "Listen to me, Darrell. You've no right to marry anybody till you own a piece of land for yourself. No member of this family has ever married when he couldn't show his wife a clear deed to a few acres . . ."

"I've got a deed," he said.

"Not a clear deed. Married! You listen to me. You've seen nothing of life, and it takes money. Let me tell you a family takes money."

He laughed. "Why, when Roger got married last fall he said he didn't have . . ."

"Roger Pitt! Must you follow every track and turn of the path as Roger Pitt?" She snapped her fingers. "Just like that the Pitts could take all we've got."

Then almost without his knowing, the nearly empty cup crashed between his feet, and the handle, like a perfect washer, rolled along the kitchen floor. He said, never once looking down at the shattered pieces, "It's my business, this is my business, and you can't help me."

"You're such a child at times," she said.

Without speaking he went out the kitchen door, around the house, and climbed into the surrey which Yancey had waiting for him. He did not speak to Yancey. He took the heavy check-lines in his left hand and the fine-plaited whip in his right. Quickly he lashed out twice; the bay mares leaped and he reeled back into the seat. He turned into the road in a long gallop, the narrow wheels sliding on the sand. Again he lashed out, still speechless, and again, until his left hand shook with the gripping of the lines. When he crossed Winter Creek he dropped the whip at his feet and pulled the reins heavily until the surrey stopped. He jumped out on the sand and went in front of the mares. He watched the specks of white foam drip from the bits. He put a hand to each bay nose and felt the hot breath go up his sleeves, then turned and looked back toward the house, remembered the countless pieces of thin china scattered on the kitchen floor.

"That was a sorry trick," he said. "All of it was a sorry trick, but . . ."

He stood in the surrey again, took the fine-plaited whip, folded it in his hands, scanned the flimsy tapering end of the leather, and finally, his arm swinging with a quick twist, he threw it into the shallow water of the creek. Then he drove on slowly.

While he and Miriam rode in the front seat of the surrey toward Waycrest, he thought that he might tell her what had happened back home, and that once he had told her he could forget it had happened. But each time he brought himself to the beginning of the words he stopped, and tried to think that he stopped only because Miriam's mother was in the back seat. Once Miriam said, "I don't think you feel good." He did not answer her with words. He only leaned his face against her hair, thinking, I'll do this no matter what your mother says.

At the Edgeworth House they danced in the long room with the high Dutch-carved ceiling and chandeliers of finger-like pieces of overlaid glass. There in the candlelight he gazed down at the strange likeness of Roger and Miriam. It seemed to him suddenly that she and Roger had drawn every incisive turn of their cheeks and lips from Malcolm Pitt. But while he held her and looked at her, small in the yellow dress, she seemed as far away from him as Roger, who was still in New Orleans.

"You never seem close to me," he whispered.

153

"I don't understand."

"I mean, sometimes I want to tell you things, and, well, I don't tell you."

"Why?"

"I don't know."

"Maybe we're just older," she said. Her hazel eyes seemed warm and deep as topaz.

"You know the first time I ever saw you, you told on me and Roger and got us both in trouble."

"But I didn't know you then."

"Reckon you know me now?"

"I don't know. I ought to. I used to be jealous of you and Roger. Every time you rode off together on a horse, or went somewhere with Father, I wanted to be a boy and go too. I thought boys had a better time than girls." She turned her face away from him toward the end of the room where the Negro orchestra was playing the *Emperor Waltz*. "Do you know the name of the orchestra?"

"No," he said.

"It's from Natchez. When they play for balls like this they call themselves The Royal Dance Orchestra." Then she whispered as if the sudden drop of her voice would separate the two of them from every other couple. "Their real name is Blue Jesus and His Twelve Disciples from Natchez Under the Hill."

"How do you know that?"

"Roger told me. Last summer when we spent a week with Aunt Susan, he slipped out one night and went to The Black Biscuit down in Natchez Under the Hill. He told me all about it and said it was really something to hear them play down there. He never told you about it?"

"No. Let's go out on the porch," he said.

They went out of the room to the back veranda and stood by the cement cistern under the low ceiling light of three candles.

154

"You know what Roger said? The fountain overflows, but the cistern contains."

"He didn't think that up," she said.

"I guess not."

"Help me up on the well-box."

"You might fall in," he said.

"Don't be silly," she said. "That's the last thing I'd ever do."

His hands closed about her waist, but he did not lift her then. He pulled her quickly to him and his lips were heavy against her, then light, then heavy again. Only after it was over did she push him away.

"Right here? Mother's in the hall."

"She's not watching us."

"Are you going to help me up on the well-box?"

"I guess I am." He lifted her.

"You lift me like Father does."

"Do I?"

"Yes."

She looked down at him, her hand no more than a foot away from the candlelight.

"You danced with Vera," she said.

"Yes."

"And you danced with Phyllis . . ."

"Yes. And with Karin and . . ."

"But you danced mostly with me, mostly."

He looked up toward the light, and then his eyes came down again to the brown hair (golden in the candlelight) and then to the parted lips that lit his flesh from having touched them or knowing that he would. He said to himself, "She is thinking: You belong to me, all of you. Your lips have never really touched anybody but . . ."

She said, "Did you know they started to cut this house half in two one time?"

155

"No."

"Well, they did. Old man Edgeworth left it for his two old maid daughters, and they couldn't get along so they decided to divide it. But then they couldn't decide which one would get the East side and which one the West side. Don't you want to know how it ended?"

"Yes. What happened?"

"Nothing. They died."

He moved away from her and stood with his hands behind him, against the wall of the house.

"This light is too much," he said.

"I like it," she said. "I want to watch . . ." If she finished he did not hear her. She leaped lightly from the well-box and laughed as if saying, "I was afraid to let you lift me down, the way you stand looking at me. I'm eighteen. And you're not Father . . ."

He put one arm around her and they walked off the veranda into the garden. The small new leaves from the shrubs brushed against his thighs and there was a different quickness, heavy and firm, in him then. He picked a thumb-sized rose (that was something to do when you couldn't say anything), which Miriam took from his hand and touched against her mouth.

They stopped under the low thick limbs of a walnut tree. The night was too dark for shadows. He stood behind her with his arms around her waist and his cheek against her ear. He could not whisper anything to her until he curbed the quick staccato beating of his heart, but he could still hear the sudden milder purling within his ear when he said, "I want to talk about us." She did not answer and he said, "We're going to get married."

He waited in the darkness under the low limbs, the gray moss near enough to touch. He felt first the slight shaking of her

156

body in his arms and then he heard her laugh, beginning softly and then full and loud as if she was calling to someone across the garden. "I thought of the silliest thing," she said.

He took her arm quickly and wheeled her so that she faced him and looked up, her lips breaking apart slowly and her hazel eyes so still that she did not note the fall of the rose from her hand.

"You didn't hear me," he said. "You didn't hear."

"No, what?"

He did not answer her then, for he remembered her face under the candlelight only a moment ago and the certainty he had seen there was gone.

"Don't stand so close to me."

"Miriam . . ."

"Don't, Darrell. I can feel you."

"I want you to. You love me. Do you?"

"You know."

"Tell me."

"Sometimes I don't love you, sometimes I don't even want to like you because I know what Father thinks. I know what he feels and sometimes I've cried because he loves you more than he loves me or Roger even. Father can't help it and you can't, he just does . . ."

"You know he loves you more than anybody in the world."

"He doesn't. I know he doesn't. I wish he did. I've heard him talking about you to Mother, not to me, but to Mother. And he loves you because . . ."

"Miriam . . ." He made her stop, covering her mouth with his hand. "I like to feel your lips. Did you know that? With my fingers. It's . . . touch mine."

"I can't."

"Yes, you can."

"I can't."

He tried to keep his thoughts on anything but the curious shaking in his mind of, *You're such a child at times* . . .

He pulled her closer and still closer, feeling her whole body against him tightly. "You listen to me," he said. "I don't care what *she* says. *She* doesn't know anything about me; *she* doesn't know what it's like to want somebody and to . . ." He stopped; chilled and mute he pressed his cheek against her cheek, then lips against lips, and her warm body gave to the closing circle of his arms.

Beyond the walnut tree, beyond the edge of the garden and the hedges he whispered to her fiercely, trembling, until almost like a child, daring and unsure, she answered, "I'm afraid, Darrell. I'm afraid. What would Father . . ." He was lost, like a child's breath lost in the fierce upward arc of a pushed swing that rises, rises, stands momently transfixed while fingers seek to hold the height, seek and close on empty air; and the swing plummets earthward again.

He could not even whisper to her as they drove home. *I've sinned. I've sinned. My fingers damp in the bruised grass and she saying to me, whispering: Get my cloak, get my cloak, what if Mother saw? I'll wait by the well. And my face dropped into the bruised grass and my wrist in the bruised grass and one on the hem of her yellow dress. Get my cloak. Darrell, did you ever? I said: No, never anywhere, not this. I can't leave, I can't leave you now. And she said: Get my cloak, get my cloak. I said: Don't cry, I don't want you ever to cry.* And home seemed a long way off; the surrey crawled, on the clay and the sand, it crawled. He kept thinking: *Her mother is looking at our backs, but I found her cloak and I brought it to her standing beside the well-box.*

He could see himself standing before Malcolm Pitt: *I've sinned against you and her, beyond name, and now you can put*

158

*your hands on my throat, curse me, say anything, do anything,
but don't call me son, not now, ever* . . .

Nolie was different. It was not the same at all when she
came into the room that night, came through the square of moonlight and he saw her there with the hand lifted and the bright
blade. Malcolm Pitt could laugh about that. *Hell. If I was eighteen* . . . Nolie was different, because he didn't love Nolie; he
had to do that to walk with a certain honesty toward himself
and toward Malcolm Pitt. Now he felt there was no honesty left
in him.

"Darrell . . . Darrell," she whispered.

He put his arm around her.

When they reached home he and Miriam stood inside the
big gate and watched her mother go up the steps into the house.
She went slowly. They saw the dim light come on in the hall.

"Mother's not feeling well," Miriam said.

Darrell did not answer. Still in his mind was the scrouging
sense that he had sinned against Miriam and Malcolm, and his
grandmother, and God. He was looking down at Miriam.

She tried to smile, her mouth quivering as Roger's had
quivered often toward laughter; but her lips were stalled where
Roger's lips were always free.

"Miriam."

Then her lips broke the soft, painful quietness. "I don't
know what you think of me, or what I think of myself."

He tried to tilt her face to his, but she turned away from
his lips. His arms slid down about her waist, and it seemed that
her whole body was in his hands.

"Say you'll marry me."

"I don't know. I don't know how I feel."

"You do know. You know about both of us. I don't know
why you're afraid."

"We didn't even talk, Darrell. We didn't even talk at all. You just touched me, and . . ."

His lips then were against her face and he whispered, "You don't want to cry, not now."

"But all you did, all you did was . . ."

"Just promise me," he said. "You don't have to tell me when. Promise me we'll get married."

"What would Father say?"

"About us?"

"No. About tonight."

"You talk like everybody knew about it, Miriam."

She cried again, so easily that he was sorry for her, and he kissed her lips.

"I've got to go in, Darrell. I think Mother's sick."

"You'll tell me *yes* tomorrow."

"I have to go in now . . ."

He kissed her. Her lips did not give to his, but she did not pull away. At the door he kissed her again, and again he felt no warmth of her body. But when she turned away from him she was crying. He stood there after the heavy door was closed, and waited until he could no longer hear her footsteps down the hall.

He climbed into the surrey and drove toward the low full moon. He was proud. He was ashamed. For every pleasant beat of his heart there was also the sharp pain and the thought of sin.

But he kept saying to himself that the day would come now when Malcolm Pitt would stand in the church beside the altar flowers, stand tall and wide in the blackness of his suit, and Roger would stand with the ring, never afraid: *Who gives this sister girl daughter away?* He could not know what Brother Potter would say because he had never been to a wedding.

He stood in the surrey and cracked the check-lines against

160

the mares. He was going to get married. She would say *yes* to-morrow, and tomorrow she would not cry.

The mares galloped through the open gate into the lot. Darrell stood rigid in the surrey, leaned his body backward and jerked against the reins. He had not meant to hurry, even though it was after midnight; he had wanted only the wind to cool whatever it was that burned in him like a fever. But nothing had cooled. He was glad it was after midnight, because Yancey would not be there in the lot to unhitch the mares. He did not want to see anybody. Yancey would be sleeping beside Louella in the house across the field.

But his grandmother would be waiting. He dropped the lines and turned to look past the big oaks toward the house. The light was there, motionless in the window. She had always waited. And when he went into her room tonight it would be as though she held out her arms to him while her eyes said, *You are such a child at times.*

Then the asking would start. Her searching eyes would shine through the lamplight and would speak in one compelling tone, asking, always asking.

It might have started years ago when Malcolm Pitt had said, "You ought to buy that land, Darrell. The timber alone is worth it, and it's got a good house." Or the asking might have started when his father died, or farther back to a time he could not remember.

But she was there watching for him when he came home at night from running the gin, or when he came home late from the fields or from Vicksburg with Malcolm Pitt. Always she would be waiting.

He leaped out upon the ground and though the mares did not start they seemed to quiver forward into the collars. His hands gripped singletree and chain to unhook the tight traces.

He strained, then he jerked the heavy check-lines again. "How in the hell can I undo the traces with no slack?" He had not said the words to anybody, but he thought, She couldn't have heard me, up there in the lamplight, but if she had she would say, "There you go talking like Malcolm Pitt again."

Well, he was twenty now, twenty and one-half.

He would not answer anything she asked tonight, not anything about Miriam, even to say yes or no. What had happened belonged to him. When he went up the front steps he ought to turn right in the hall, go into his own room without speaking, for it might be that the wind had sharpened his face, had worn away a cover, and she could look upon the scars. He did not want to see her now, not until the night had brought back his cover for the heart which she might probe.

He turned the mares loose in the lot and while he walked from the barn toward the house he watched the light spilling through the window onto the porch and running like a painted stream across the new spring grass.

At the gate he stopped, outside the path of light, and watched his grandmother moving about in her room. She went to the mantel. She took the key, hanging there, and opened the face of the clock. He knew she was not winding it, but her finger had moved the hands ahead one hour, perhaps two, as if he did not have in his pocket the watch which Malcolm Pitt had given him. He wanted to laugh. I guess it's about one o'clock, he thought, and she'll tell me it's two or three. It was like the way she had always said, *Your father lost the use of his limb in the battle of Vicksburg.* But he could not go inside and say that he had watched her move the clock ahead any more than he could go inside and say, "You don't know half the things I've done. You don't know about tonight and about the time Nolie came here when you were gone to South Carolina. I guess maybe

162

Malcolm Pitt would have laughed about Nolie. Maybe Roger would have, too. But they wouldn't laugh about tonight."

He tried to climb the front steps quietly. He stopped in the hall and waited, as if a great thing must be decided underbreath. One answer led to his grandmother's door, one to his own room. He heard the scrape of page against page; she was reading. He stepped quickly toward his own room, his hand caught the cold knob. A chair moved in her room. His throat was locked against breathing.

"Darrell?"

"Yes."

"Is that you?"

"Yes, ma'am."

"What are you doing?"

His hand still held the knob, unturned.

You are such a child at times. Lying in the bed and looking up toward the ceiling with the cover heavy over the stomach. A part of you but not your stomach, a part of you belonging to somebody else and you touching what does not belong to you. Then turning on your side because the cover is heavy, and being a child. It was strange being a child because you could never really know other people. Lying alone in the bed and looking out the window, and the shade was not drawn because the shade did not go up and down as the shade in Roger's house. But in the dark it did not matter whether the shade was up or down, for only the window mattered. It must be up or down; it must be down. Lying there alone neither in darkness or light and the window down and the covers heavy over the pounding within the body and she comes through the door. You close your eyes and think, It will be all right, it will be all right, if she thinks you are asleep. You were such a child, once . . .

"Darrell?"

He turned and opened the door to her room. The high starched collar of her black rep dress looked as though she had sat stiffly there in her chair all night without moving and waited for him. He leaned back against the closed door. She tugged at the shawl about her shoulders.

"What are you reading?"

"It's late," she said. "Very late."

"The Ball is always like this."

"The hour. Do you know the hour?"

"It wasn't really over when we left."

"You might glance at the clock." He did not look at it. "Sometimes, you are stubborn, boy. I forgive you for being late tonight. I say, I forgive you."

"Thank you."

"But you are stubborn. You begin a little here, and a little there—you begin to fail me. Or maybe you think I'm an old woman who couldn't instruct a fine young man."

"No. I don't think that."

"There's good blood in you. But there are spots that quiver. You have to find an anchor, so that the wind of God will not sweep you away as a frostbitten leaf."

While he looked at his grandmother, suddenly quiet, he thought of Miriam, for her faint perfume was about him, on his cheek, or his hands; and maybe it was strong enough to reach across the room to his grandmother.

"I'm not an old woman afraid of a spider's shadow. Not fear I'm talking about, but respect. Was it becoming to leave me until this hour, alone?"

"I offered to get Louella to stay with you."

"Was it becoming?"

"I don't know."

She looked up at the clock. "The hour is three. Ten minutes past. I hope you had a good time."

164

"I did."

"The preacher's daughter. Was she there?"

"Yes. Nolie was there."

"The way she flaunts her ankles, even in church. And worse, wearing that harem skirt, split up the front. Vanity always leaves its mark. Miriam had a good time?"

"I suppose so."

"Leta Pitt went with you two?"

"Yes."

"You in evening clothes. I've seen you quiver, Darrell. Against little things. One by one. Even strong men have spots they must guard against . . ."

"I don't know what you're talking about."

"About the Pitts. They're slowly buying you. The gin, the land, because you are fine and good and—handsome."

His head jerked back against the door. "How could you sit here in this house and be that cruel? Maybe I have worked hard for Malcolm Pitt. But I never deserved half what he's done for us. You wanted to say it. You meant to say it. But I despise to hear . . ."

She was coming toward him and with her was the dry smell of rose geraniums.

"You're upset because it's late. You'll be ashamed for this tomorrow. Tomorrow you'll go with me to church and you'll pray forgiveness."

She was closer to him. His hand clutched the doorknob behind him. "I wouldn't go with you tomorrow to your goddamned church if I never saw another one." He was crying when the door jolted closed behind him and when his own door opened.

He lay across his bed and when he finally went to sleep he was still dressed, giving no thought to the new full dress suit cut in Vicksburg by Malcolm Pitt's own tailor.

He remembered the light now and then coming through the undrawn curtains, and he remembered the sound of the surrey at the front door which meant that Yancey had come to take his grandmother to church that morning. Once he went to the kitchen, and while he drank milk quickly, he listened as if any step would catch him like a thief. He lay in the bed again and pulled the sheet over his face as though to cover his mind, too, so that it could not remember anything outside four walls. He heard the steps in the hall when his grandmother returned from church.

It was almost dark when he poured out a basin of water from the pitcher on his dresser and began to shave with his father's razor which he had taken three years ago from the oval-topped trunk in the hall. He did not really want to shave. He finished only because he had started.

When he had dressed, it was dark; but he did not light the lamp in his room. He turned around to the knocking on his door. Yancey stood in the doorway.

"Mista Darrell?"

"Yes."

"You sick?"

"No."

"You been sleeping all day."

"What time is it?"

"I'm gettin' ready to take your grandmama to church. Yo' face is red. I think you sick."

"I slept on my arm."

"You don't want nothing?"

"No. Thank you, Yancey."

Yancey moved back into the hall. He walked past the grandmother standing before the hall-mirror, angling her soft black beaver hat over one eye. She turned her back to the mirror. With one gloved hand she brushed a fleck of lint from the black

166

grosgrain ribbon that trimmed the buttoned front of her gray suit.

"Come in," Darrell said.

She stopped in the doorway. "You feel better?"

"Yes."

"I prayed for you today in church. I knew nothing else to do. I'll pray for you again tonight."

"Thank you."

"I don't know what God has done, but I've forgiven you. I hope it makes you feel better."

"It does."

"Where are you going now?"

"Walking."

"If you're going to the Pitts, you might as well ride with us."

"I said I wanted to walk."

"I won't insist then."

"Thank you."

"You are much too thankful, Darrell."

"No. People usually are not quite thankful enough."

She pulled at her gloves. "Are you ready, Yancey?"

"Yes, ma'am."

Then she was gone down the hall.

Darrel left no light burning in the house. He walked among the tall pines and along the honeysuckle hedge; and in the muscadine grove he could hear the small marble-like fruit falling like a finger thumped into dead leaves. There was a nearer way to Miriam Pitt, but he did not take that path.

The Spanish moss was silver, hanging beneath the heavy green of the oaks. The house was still. He had never seen it so still and quiet. But early dark on Sunday evening was always quiet. He wished that Malcolm Pitt would not be in the house. He wished, too, that his own muscles were not full, that he was not tall, that Malcolm Pitt might take his brown whetting thong and erase any sense of guilt with the flat cracking strokes. A whipping always cleansed. But he was old now, much older than he was last night. No blood stirred in quick veins; there was only the sense of having reached out beyond the mark of forgiveness. The gate was half open. He closed it behind him.

He knocked on the door and then he called. There was no moving within the rooms, but he heard the voice, "Come in!"

Malcolm Pitt was stretched out in his chair. The Vicksburg paper was spread about his stomach, one section covering his stockinged-feet that pointed up from the ottoman. He lifted his arms above his head and stretched.

"Come in, Darrell. I've got a little surprise for you. You'll have to talk to me tonight. Miriam and her mother have gone to Littleford Springs."

"When?"

Malcolm's face seemed not to change. "I'm worried about Leta. She thought the water would help. They left on the train this afternoon."

"For how long?"

"Month maybe. Leta thinks it will help."

"But she didn't say a word. She might have told me last night."

"Miriam?"

"Yessir."

"She didn't know. It was all her mother. Women, Darrell, the cross of man. They don't know what they want."

"I better go." Then he looked at Malcolm Pitt's face and saw the bright brown tobacco streak across the flush of his lips. Within him was a quick division, so that blood seemed both to rise toward his face and fall below his stomach. It was as if he came suddenly upon Malcolm Pitt standing naked. He remembered the river and the snow-covered bluffs of Memphis and the boat swerving in the water and the cold stateroom. And he knew that Malcolm remembered too, for his face was suddenly red.

Malcolm leaned over and put the tobacco from his mouth into the cedar tray of ashes on the hearth beside him. "Is that better?" he said. He took a handkerchief from his pocket and rubbed his mouth vigorously. "You're such a clean person, you make me ashamed."

Darrell watched the face and the lips, and he thought, How can I stand here and talk to him and can not tell the truth to him—after last night? The tears came into his eyes and he knew that no shame would hold them back.

Malcolm came over to him and took his arm and said, "What's the matter with you, son?"

"Because you're so good to me, I guess. And because I love you."

three

Darrell came out of his room and put his bag in the hall and looked at the watch which Malcolm Pitt had given him. Then he went through the dining room into the kitchen where his grandmother stood with a cup of black coffee. She placed the cup down carefully on the table when he came into the room and stood holding him with her eyes. He drew his arm across his waist and bowed deeply. "Madam, I humbly beg leave of you." He smiled and adjusted the handkerchief in his coat pocket. "I beg your blessings for this journey. I must to Little-ford Springs."

"Well, you're going even if you haven't heard from her in a month?"

169

"Yes. I must go. The spirit moves me. Here." He touched his heart.

"It's painful to see a fine young man swept completely away." She brushed a crumb from the tablecloth with a flick of her wrist. "But all the good strong men are gone, like the fine old apple trees we used to have, big as an oak. Now they're puny bushes." She braced her hand on the back of the chair. "Why are you going to Littleford Springs?"

"To drink the water. I am lily-livered."

"You are lily-brained. So now you've come to the end of your rope. You think you love her?"

"Yes . . ."

"She's playing with you, Darrell."

"She's not playing with me."

"Well, then. It's her mother. Now you listen to me. I know more about Leta Pitt than you'll ever know. She may be nice and good to you but she never for one minute thinks of you except as a sharecropper's son. You can mark my words: she'll never let Miriam marry you. Leta Pitt knows what it is to have forty acres of land instead of a plantation—and she knows it well enough that she'll never forget it."

He was afraid to listen, and because he was afraid he talked back quickly. "I didn't expect you to understand my going, but you will understand this: I intend to marry Miriam and every time you say anything about it, I'm just that much more certain."

"You may not listen to anything I say, Darrell. There are things about life that you don't know, things that you learn only by living. Water tastes different when you drink it from a china cup instead of a glass. I don't know why. But it's true."

"I'm trying to understand you."

"Life is always the same. It's how you taste life, how you drink life."

170

He looked at her hands and the little knots on her wrists and the small blue ridges that ran along her arms. If he looked at her hands while she talked to him, whatever she said seemed to clothe itself with more truth. He said quietly, "Are you telling me not to go?"

"Yes."

"Why?"

"I suppose Malcolm Pitt is sending you."

"He doesn't even know I'm going. One minute what you have to say is clear, the next minute nothing has any meaning. I believe you think there's something dishonest about everybody who has more than we have. Why do you dislike him? All the Pitts? Because they've helped us?"

"You're quite wrong. I like the Pitts."

"I wish I could believe it."

"You are stubborn."

"I'm ready to go. Is that all you have to say?"

"No, it isn't all. There's another thing to tell you. They have you now. They have you because you're determined to marry Miriam Pitt or anybody. You don't really know what you want. You are merely determined. It was in your grandfather. It's in you. Good blood, but it boils and boils, and I never know what's to come of it."

"Is that all?"

"Yes."

"Yancey is taking me to the train. I'll get my bag." While he turned he could see her hand tighten and seem to shrivel.

"Darrell?"

"Yes, ma'am."

She walked toward him. "I've forgiven you for everything. I want a pleasant parting, no matter how brief your trip is to be. So many things could happen. And you're all I've got. I say I've forgiven you. Kiss my cheek."

171

He kissed her cheek. His lips were dry against her face, dry when he sat in the surrey beside Yancey, and dry while he looked through the train window (where the rails curved) and saw the engine and the low smoke ahead, like some part of himself which he had never seen before. Then the tracks were straight again and that part of himself was gone. He thought of the train engine as plunging into softness and warmth.

It carried him away from something and it carried him toward something. That was easy: you could never go away from anything without going toward something else, whether you wanted to or not. Yet, he might be doing both. Maybe that was what he would say if he stood out in the field and watched himself pass. It sounded like nothing, like Roger's $a^2 + b^2$: mystic because of its nothingness.

He thrust his arm through the window again and let his wrist give to the wateriness of air.

Even before the train came to a complete stop in Jackson, Darrell could hear the cry along the rails, "Fried chicken!" He had heard the same cry along the rails the day he came with the Pitts to Roger's graduation from boarding school; and he had seen the same Negro woman with her clean starched clothes and a brown stocking stretched over her head. Malcolm Pitt had said to him, as if telling a secret, "See that Negro woman, Aunt Docie Castle. Made a fortune selling fried chicken. It's good too. She had a daughter, Connie, almost white. They sent her up to some northern school. During one summer vacation her roommate at school was going to New Orleans and on the way down she stopped off uninvited to see Connie. She was a federal judge's daughter. When she asked in the station how to get to Connie Castle's the station keeper just pointed toward the tracks and said, 'Go out there and ask that lady selling chicken. That's her mother.'"

The train seemed not only to stop but to jerk itself back-

172

ward in a squatting motion. The Negro woman moved along the cinders, handing out the small brown bags of chicken, taking the quarters. Darrell held his arm out, dropped the quarter into the basket. He was not hungry. He was never hungry when he rode on a train. But he had reached out for the small bag because it was something Malcolm Pitt would have done if he had been along.

The train jerked again, the station seemed to slide away, and behind him Darrell could hear the cry again, "Fried chicken!" It was deep and clear and sharp, without tone, without fear, and without ending. It made him want to be back home. He threw the small paper bag out the window.

The train seemed to slow with the coming of dusk. The fresh brown of new turned earth was dark with shadows. Back home, his own land was dark. Yancey and Stafford and Mark and Fleet would be coming toward the barn with the mules— either his barn or the big barn of Malcolm Pitt. The mares would be nosing against the lot gate with a puling sound. That was back home.

He wanted to ask the conductor, "How much longer to Littleford Springs?" But the conductor was going forward toward another car. Even if the train was an hour or two hours late, Miriam would be waiting for him. She would have his letter, the one he had written three days ago. That was his third letter to her.

His first letter to Miriam was less than half a page because he could not say to her anything that he really felt. Roger could have. He could put the meaning into short vivid words and even on the white linen paper it would be clear and defined as the warm feel of a pulse-beat.

But Darrell had said little more than, *Why did you really go away?*

And in the second letter, *Why have you not written to me?*

173

Three days ago he had written, *I do not understand you. Today I saw the letter to your father. He showed it to me. No matter what has happened, you might have written once to me during this month. Friday I shall see you. I wish it was the day before or even the day after. You know your father never likes to start anything on Friday. I think he misses you almost as much as I do. Last week we had fifty acres ready for early planting, but he would not let us start on Friday. Why do I tell you all this? I will see you in three days . . .*

The conductor, with his alpaca coat bulging around the pockets, was coming through the coach door. The man in the seat ahead of Darrell said, "Watch him thread the aisle like a Saturday night Baptist in the south end of town."

"Littleford Springs," the conductor said.

Darrell reached for his bag. There was a hack beside the station, and the tall Negro in the forward spring seat was calling, "Two mile to Littleford Spring, folks . . ."

Darrell dropped his suitcase in the wagon bed and climbed up over the front wheel. "I think I'll sit in front with you," he said.

"Yessuh," the driver said. "You gonna be all?"

"I don't know. Looks like it."

"I usually has a load at night."

"You do?"

"Yessuh. Most generally and usually."

"You're out of luck tonight."

"Nossuh. It don't make no difference. Mista Littleford don't pays me fer the people. He pays me fer coming and going."

"That's the best way."

"Yessuh."

The horses moved quickly to the rip of air sucked between the Negro's lips.

"Is this water any good here?"

174

"Yessuh. They says it is."

"You ever drink any?"

"Nossuh, I don't like its elements. You ain't sick, is you?"

"No."

"I was gonna say you don't look sick. Course a lot of folks heah don't *look* sick."

"No. I'm not."

"Where you comes from?"

"Leighton. You ever heard of it?"

"Nossuh."

"It's the other side of Jackson, close to Vicksburg."

"Yessuh. You gonna drank the water?"

"No. I came to see somebody . . ."

The hack stopped at the big stone gate. On the slope of the hill, lights came from four buildings. The Negro driver pointed. "Doctor Littleford lives to the right. It's the awfice."

"Thank you," Darrell said. He reached up for his bag which the driver was holding for him, and between his fingers he held out a dollar bill. The driver's teeth shone in the darkness.

He walked over the old pine needles, matted into new green moss, toward the small building. He waited a minute on the porch before putting his bag down. To the left was the office. He could see through the open door the nurse, or at least the white-uniformed woman sitting at the desk. He walked to the doorway.

"Come in," the woman said.

"Thank you. I'm looking for someone here. Miss Pitt. She's expecting me."

"Miss Pitt?"

"Yes."

The nurse watched his face, and he thought she was going to say, "Are you ill?" When she did not speak, he said, "I'm Darrell Barclay. And Miss Pitt is . . ."

"Miss Pitt?" she said.

"Yes."

"Oh, Miriam . . ."

"Yes."

"There's a note for you."

"A note?"

"I think so." She handed him an envelope from the desk.

"I don't understand." He had not opened the envelope.

The nurse said, "It's just a note saying they left for New Orleans this morning."

"Left here?"

"This morning. Did you come for the water?"

"Why did they leave? She knew I was coming."

"The note . . ."

"Oh," he said. He took the small sheet from the unsealed envelope. . . . *because Mother had to leave for the clinic today or thought she did . . . but I didn't know until this morning . . .*

"Have you come for the waters, Mr. Pitt?"

He did not lift his eyes from the small sheet.

"Mr. Pitt, I say, have you come for the waters?"

"No . . . And my name is Darrell Barclay."

"I'm sorry, Mr. Barclay."

He folded the sheet with the original creases fitting and put it back into the envelope. "I'm sorry too."

"You will want a room here for tonight?"

"Yes, thank you."

"Dinner is still being served in the dining hall. If you go now." She pointed to the long building. "There."

He did not see where the key came from. She held it out to him.

"Rooms are above the dining hall. Number twenty-one. I'm sorry there's no boy here after six in the evening."

"That's all right."

176

"How long do you plan . . . ?"

"Tomorrow. I'll leave on the morning train." He backed away toward his bag.

He stood before the dressing mirror in room twenty-one and looked at his cheeks, unflushed and smooth. Then he turned and looked down at the note in his hand. "I don't understand her," he said. "I don't understand anybody, not even myself." Something seemed to fret inside him and say, "She's gone, heedless, like a child, and for all your three letters and a trip you have only a note." He did not tear the paper, but instead, he crumpled it into a small hard ball and laid it on the dresser. Strangely, he could remember Roger saying, "Women get over love quicker than men." He could not remember when or where Roger had said it.

But he did not want to believe anything now. He fretted, too, because nothing welled up within him and nothing welled in his eyes. It was like looking down a long dry row, and smelling the dry dust in the wind.

He leaned against the window and looked down on a moss-covered shed. Six people with cups in hand stood beside the stream of water that gushed up through gray rock. He watched them.

"Hold your nose, honey."

"Got it with both hands."

"Ruin a good supper."

"Unhnnn . . ."

"Like axle-grease. You ever taste any?"

"Fool."

"It's my liver."

"Liver? Set it afire with Tennessee Dew, quench the fire at Littleford Springs."

"You got it."

"Hold your cup, honey."

177

Darrell pulled the window down, but he could still hear the voices outside, and the hum of voices in the dining room below. He did not want to eat. But he wanted to leave the room and the note crumpled upon the dresser. He unfolded the note and read the ending again, *I don't know why you didn't get my letters. I wrote twice.*

It was easy to understand. His grandmother had taken them. Slowly he tore the note into small pieces. He was angry with everyone he knew. He was angry with his grandmother for taking the letters. He was angry with Miriam because she had gone. She might have said more in her note, he thought; she might have said, *I'm sorry* or *wait* or *something*. He was angry with Leta Pitt because she had taken Miriam away; with Nolie because she would laugh at this; with Roger because he was married, and his wife was beautiful, and he was happy—perhaps. Least of all he was angry with Malcolm Pitt; but he was angry with him, too, because he could not be like him. He could neither laugh nor walk nor whisper as Malcolm Pitt. He could not hold anyone as Malcolm Pitt. He was angry because of a perfection which was not within him, but was only something he could look upon.

He jerked off his shirt and flung it against the wall. His stare followed the shirt and his words were quick and bitter, unnatural to his tongue, "Goddammit, I don't care. Goddammit!" He sat down on the bed and dropped his face into his hands. Then he cried. He did not know exactly why, though he whispered, "Nothing really belongs to me. Nothing is really mine. They have *given* me everything."

After a while he got up and looked into the mirror. He swore that he would never cry again, and while he swore he thought of what Malcolm Pitt would think of him then.

He poured water from the pitcher on the washstand into

178

the large china basin. The water, splashed against his face, smelled like heated iron. He kept his lips tight.

When he had changed into a clean shirt he went out of the room, locked the door carefully, and started down the long hall toward the stairs. The figure, though slender, that moved toward him from the other end of the hall seemed at first more woman than girl. But he had not then seen the deep V of the neck, the wide, sharply pointed bretelles, like detached wings of white lace, on each shoulder, and on each bretelle a knot of gold ribbon.

They met at the stairhead. He watched her mouth almost open into a smile or into words. But they did not speak. He stepped aside so that she might go down the stairs with her hand touching and skipping along the polished hardwood rail. She nodded to him.

They went down the steps side by side. Her gold watch on the small bright chain about her neck was swinging light against her green dress. He wanted to touch the watch. He wanted to touch her too, maybe because she was beautiful, maybe because he thought she had never heard the name *Pitt*.

With each step of the stair it seemed that his whole body was capering in a circus swing. He was breaking from a shell, becoming something all his own. And while he was afraid to break away from Leighton, afraid that it was wrong, he knew that he must. This was only the beginning of a game. Whatever she said or felt or thought, after tomorrow he would never see her again. Suddenly his hand had caught her arm and his fingers could feel the cold bracelets about her wrist.

"I'm sorry. I thought you stumbled." He was playing the part. He was playing it as well as Roger, almost as well as Malcolm Pitt; and after tomorrow she would not remember his face and he would not remember hers. "Or maybe I wanted you to, so I could catch you."

179

She waited a step below him and looked up. She was small, almost like a child, below him. Then she laughed, the flush from her lips moving up toward her eyes. He dropped her arm as if all the reaching out had been a foolish thing.

"You might have asked my name," she said.

"Well," he said. "What is it?"

"Emily Townsend."

"Do you want to hear mine?"

"Yes."

"Darrell Barclay. Farmer, gin operator, or maybe just hired hand. I don't know." He watched her eyes grow darker. He knew that she did not understand at all, but he did not care. He felt that he had, at least for the moment, unbound himself.

She talked quickly. "I'm already late for dinner. We only got here today and Father had to go back to town. I was waiting for him."

"Does it matter, if we're late?"

"I guess not."

"You've been here before?"

"Yes."

"Well, I haven't. You can show me the dining room."

They started down the stairs. He was a little sick inside. It was such a game. And maybe he did not really want to be unbound. Somewhere, sometime, over the noise of the gin or the man-laughter beside the barn he might tell Malcolm Pitt about this.

They had come to the door of the dining hall. A Negro in a starched white jacket and dark pants handed each a menu, handwritten in old English style.

"Miss Townsend." The Negro bowed.

"Thank you, Bolivar."

"Is it all right beside the window?"

180

"Yes." Then she turned to Darrell. He nodded. Bolivar drew the chair for her. Hardly a dozen people remained in the room. At the end of the dining hall a baldheaded man with a long beard smoked alone.

"Who is he?" Darrell said.

"That's the doctor. If there's anything wrong with you he'll patch it up."

Darrell closed the menu over his thumb. "He couldn't fix what's wrong with me. It couldn't be patched."

"What's wrong with you?"

"I need a new heart."

"That's a big order."

"Too big for the average country doctor." He opened the menu, but he was still looking at Emily.

"There are only two choices," she said. "The second one is much better."

"That's nice to have only two choices. But it would be perfect if there were no choice. Nobody would have to worry. Like predestination, what is to be will be—even if it never happens." He looked up at Bolivar. "We'll have the second one."

Bolivar nodded and took the menus away.

"Are you here for the water?" Emily said.

"No. Are you?"

"No. I came with Father. Daughter's duty."

"Are you the only one?"

"Daughter? Yes. But I have twin brothers. They're in Canada for six months. There until Christmas."

"What for?"

"Oh, they just went with my uncle. He's a mining engineer. They work for him."

"That's where you should have gone—to Canada." He did not mean anything.

181

"If I'd been a boy I would have."

"Oh . . ." He nodded toward the door where Bolivar stood. "I see they know you here."

"I come here every summer with Father. He always stays here from the last of May until the middle of June. It strengthens his voice for protracted meetings."

"A minister?"

"Presbyterian."

"That makes you have to be good?"

"I don't know. Haven't you ever heard that preachers' children were always the meanest in the community?"

"I guess I have at that. But it's not always true, is it?"

"No. Not always."

He toyed with his silver. "Where is your father's church?"

"Jackson."

"Jackson? You already see I know about predestination. But I might come to hear a sermon sometime. What's he like?"

"Father?"

Darrell nodded.

"He's nice."

"That's good."

"He's not like a preacher."

"That's good too."

"He doesn't have a double chin but he's almost fat. I guess he is fat but I don't think about it that way. If you love anybody you see them the way you want to see them."

"Yes. That's right."

"He parts his hair in the middle and he has a mustache— just a thin, little one."

"No beard?"

"No. No beard."

"I know a preacher who has a beard and he's very strict with his daughter."

182

"Father's not strict. It's Mother that's strict. She's small, almost smaller than I, and you know small people are sometimes very strict."

"How about your brothers?"

"They're just brothers. One is blond and one is brunette—even if they are twins—and Roland outweighs Leland almost twenty pounds."

"Let me guess which one is blond."

"All right."

"Roland . . ."

"Why?"

"Am I right?"

"Yes. But how did you know?"

"That's my deepest secret."

She laughed, and he thought he might touch her hand. But he did not touch her because Bolivar was bringing the food.

They ate slowly, cautiously, as if someone, older and wiser than they, stood watching them; as if both knew that they were playing little tricks which were against the rules.

Darrell was not angry any more, for he was certain now that he had broken some shell. He could choose paths he had never chosen before; he could walk with no looking back. He kept thinking, After tomorrow, if I remember her face it will be only to recall the role I played with the ease of Malcolm Pitt. He wondered what Emily would think if she knew that only a few minutes ago he had said, *Goddammit, I don't care. Goddammit!* He wondered what color would come to her face, what light would break from her eyes. She could not know that she had carried him across some rugged surface, safe to the other side. And he did not need to look back.

He would stand now beside Malcolm Pitt, not as a son, but as a man. He would stand tall at the gin in the midst of hard man-talk and man-laughter, because he was beginning to

183

understand the secret, concerning love and night and pleasure, which men always have with men. He would stand tall in the forest of long leaf yellow pine and smell the fresh whiffs of resin from new cut logs while Malcolm Pitt would say, "There's more than a baby fortune in this—with our own sawmill, Darrell." But most of all, the day would never come when Malcolm Pitt might need to say, "I've helped you all I could, son, and now you want my daughter."

He would find another way. It was something that could not be given to him, not by Malcolm Pitt or anyone. It was something he must find for himself.

He knew suddenly that Emily was standing. Her body was slender and beautiful. She was smiling. Quickly he stood too.

"I have to go now," she said.

"Don't go . . ."

"But Father may have come. Will you be here long?"

"Until tomorrow."

"Good night," she said.

"Good night."

He watched her until she had left the room. He was thinking, After tomorrow she will not remember my face nor will I remember hers.

four

Darrell remembered well the face which he had thought to forget, so that once or twice each week through the long summer he stood at the depot waiting to catch the train to Jackson. Each time he had seen Emily, and after her father had announced the bedtime (always at ten o'clock), he would go to the Lenmore Hotel, spend the night, and return to Leighton on the early morning train. His grandmother did not listen to what he said of Emily. Only Malcolm Pitt listened, while they worked, or while they loitered about the barn; and Darrell knew that he understood, for in his eyes was that secret between men. The image of Malcolm did not change.

Darrell waited at the depot, one August afternoon, sometimes looking down the tracks for the train, sometimes kicking into the cinders. He was not impatient with waiting. He was impatient with himself, for he believed that he had made a decision which would anger his grandmother, and would, no matter the understanding, hurt Malcolm Pitt. But he had started on a path, and he could not turn back.

After an hour of waiting he left the depot and went toward the gin and the millpond because he knew that Nolie would be on the pond bank with brush in hand. He could see her from a long way off, bending toward the canvas like a steeple on edge, and from a long way off he called to her as if it would not be safe to come suddenly upon her. Her head and bosom lifted slowly until her back was erect.

"Come here, Darrell, and sit beside me and I'll show you what I've got new."

He went on toward her, across the damp inch-a-night grass of August.

"What have you got new?"

"I want to paint it at dusk, the gin, but there's never enough light on the pipes. Sit here beside me."

"And stain these pants?"

"What're you doing with Sunday clothes on, anyway?"

"I've started to Jackson."

"To see Em-i-lee again? That's her name, isn't it?"

"Yes."

"Did you ever know a train whistle was tall?"

"Hell, Nolie."

"Well, if you ever thought about it that way you wouldn't admit it. Can she paint?"

"No."

"She's a preacher's daughter, isn't she?"

"Every preacher's daughter can't paint."

"How true. And see how special that makes me. I wish you'd strip off naked and jump in the pond. I want to paint you floating with your face up."

"If I strip off, it won't be to jump in the pond."

She laughed and stood up, her charcoal pieces dropping into the grass. "Dripping wet, hair and all, and water-beads rolling down your stomach. You've got little hips. Did you know that?"

"You're just a pretty little stripling, Nolie."

"They match your face because they're narrow, and they're tight. When can I paint you?"

"You're talking like the tall train whistle now." He jerked at his coat in mock motion. "Right now. Naked as that gin pipe, in daylight, too."

She was laughing quickly, watching him reach for her. With one arm he snatched her tight against his side, and his nose brushed into her hair.

"Put your coat on, Darrell." She pushed him away.

"You keep talking . . ."

"Put your coat on."

He stood searching her with his gaze, straightening his coat. She sat down with all her easiness, like a leaf settling into grass.

"I thought you were going to Jackson."

"I am going. The train's late."

"And you're glad. What will little Em-i-lee say? And what will Miriam say when she hears about all this?"

"What do you think?"

186

"You're a fool. You ought to be going down to New Orleans to see Miriam."

"Is that right?"

"She loves you."

"Miriam doesn't love anybody. She has everything she wants. More than I can give her."

"That's it. You won't love anybody until you can give them more than they can give you. I guess that's why little Em-i-lee has got you. I'd like to see her."

"You probably will."

"Oh, so you think she's going to marry you?"

"More or less."

"There you go again. Thinking everybody will love you. I guess you think I'd marry you, if you asked me? No . . . don't answer. We'll skip that." She put her hand to her face, brushed back her hair as if she meant to erase something. She was suddenly quiet.

Darrell looked away from her, like someone looking into another time and changing with his mind what he could not change with his hands. "I wish I hadn't been brought up so close to Miriam. She's like my sister sometimes." Quickly he turned back to Nolie. "I don't know what it is. But I want to do something all by myself, without any help. I don't want to be given everything."

"You're not angry with the Pitts?"

"Angry? How could I be? They've done everything in the world for me. But I have to keep some pride, Nolie. I know it's all mixed up, but you can understand."

"Sit down beside me," Nolie said. He sat down, watching her face change as if she had let go a mask. Her hand rested lightly upon his knee. "I understood before you told me. I don't blame you. I think Malcolm Pitt would rather you would marry Miriam than anyone. But her mother doesn't want you to. She may be sick, but part of it is to keep Miriam away from here."

"I don't know, Nolie. I just don't know."

"You do know. You just don't want to admit it."

"It's not something I'm proud of."

Her fingers stroked his knee while no other part of her hand moved. "Do you really love Miriam?"

"I don't know any more."

"How about Emily? You love her now?"

"Yes!"

"Don't talk so loud. Just whisper. I love for you to whisper."

"All right." He smiled, meaning that his quietness was such a little thing for her to ask of him.

"I hope you marry Emily. And when you get old and ugly and Emily doesn't love you, and Miriam doesn't love you, then I'll love you. We can sit before the fire and gossip."

"I'll think about that."

"But then, I reckon you won't ever get ugly. Likely as not you'll stay handsome all your life. And always have somebody to love you, besides me."

He touched her hand, then covered it with his palm. "You're funny, Nolie, but sometimes I like you an awful lot." He took her hand into his. It was warm and soft. He held it against his thigh and then their hands, still locked together, dropped to the earth. Their fingers pressed into the grass, and finally, without any sense of breaking apart, their fingers no longer touched. Darrell stood up. "I better go back to the depot."

"I never thought you'd go to Jackson tonight, not with Roger home."

"Roger?" He knelt suddenly beside Nolie. He wondered whether her eyes were really laughing at him, whether she was looking into his heart which had quickened to the name he

188

spoke. "He's not here . . ." As he spoke he stood up again, his look fastened against Nolie, trying to tell her she had played a mean joke.

"He is. He came in this afternoon. He was looking for you. Didn't you see him?"

"No." Now he could see the truth in Nolie's eyes, and the faint understanding, as if she knew already what he was going to say. "I'll have to stay and see him."

"And stand little Em-i-lee up?"

"I can call her."

"They've got a telephone?"

"Yes."

Nolie laughed.

"Did Anne come with Roger?"

"I don't know. I don't think she likes Leighton. Do you?"

"Maybe not," he said.

"What do you think of Anne anyway?"

"I've only seen her two or three times. She's all right."

"I guess she is. But when I first saw her I thought: unhnn, just like milk—sweet one day and sour the next, then clabber and sweet again. But she was always sweet around me. Is Emily as pretty as Anne?"

"Yes."

"Well, be sweet to her—whenever you see her."

"I will."

"Tell Roger . . . no, you better not tell him anything. His little wife might be present."

"I could tell him—in private."

"No." She waved him away.

He turned away from her almost reluctantly. Yet, he wanted not only to see Roger immediately but to ask him many things; for Roger, now being married, had suddenly grown old

189

to Darrell, and wise, and full of knowledge that came only from spending nights in the world of husband-wife. He hoped that Anne would not be with Roger.

But it was Anne who met him at the door, and for a moment he thought she was going to kiss him. He did not move to embrace her because he did not think it would be right for him to kiss her, though he wanted to.

"We've been looking for you," she said. They went from the hall into the living room.

"I didn't know you were here."

"We went to your house and you had gone."

"I was going to Jackson."

"I know," she said.

She moved toward the wide windows and touched the curtains for no apparent reason. Darrell was watching her closely, every movement. Her body was small, though not delicate; perhaps a little smaller than Emily's. Her face was a little darker than Emily's, and the very darkness seemed to give a brightness to her. He breathed deeply, watching her. She was beautiful, but she was not more beautiful than Emily.

"What's happened to you and Miriam?" Her eyes lighted, and Darrell was sure that she had taken his side.

"It's hard to say what happened, Anne. I guess it doesn't make sense."

"I hope it works out for both of you."

He wondered then whether she was older than Emily, whether she really understood what had happened. She turned to face him fully. "We might as well sit down. Roger and his father are at the barn. They'll be here in a minute." She took one last look through the window. "This is such a beautiful place. And so much cooler than New Orleans."

"I like it," Darrell said. They sat down. It was almost like the first time he had gone to the manse to see Emily.

190

"Why don't you take off your coat?"

"Yes," he said. "I will." He put his coat across the back of a chair and sat down again.

"I don't know why I'm making all these suggestions," she said. "I guess you're more at home here than I am."

He did not answer. There was a need for silence because he thought she was beginning to understand him.

Suddenly she stood up, her eyes smiling. "I hear them coming. And I promised to have some lemonade ready."

Darrell stood; she left the room quickly, as though the thing which took her away was of great concern. He could hear steps in the hall, and then Roger's voice, "But what a doctor!" Darrell moved a few steps toward the sound.

"As a doctor he's one thing, son. As a man he's another."

"Maybe so . . . ."

Then Malcolm Pitt's voice again, so clear and vivid to Darrell that it seemed to take shape as a face or hand; he held his breath, hearing, "I hate to say I don't trust him. But I swear I don't. He strikes me as the type of man who'd read the Bible while sitting on a privy stool . . . ."

Roger came first through the doorway. He stopped. "Well, where've you been galavanting? I tried to track you down, at the gin, asked Nolie about you, and even rode out to your house."

Behind Roger, Malcolm tilted his head a little and winked. Darrell said, "You just missed me all around."

They shook hands. Then Roger crossed the room, as if he could see Darrell better from that distance. "Where's Anne?"

"In the kitchen."

Darrell, with his face turned to answer Roger, felt Malcolm's hand on his shoulder, then heard him saying, "God, boy, it's hot. Feels like my heart's going to shrivel up like a fried gizzard."

191

Darrell looked up at him and laughed. Then Malcolm said, "I'll go back and help Anne. Maybe I'll find something besides lemonade."

"I'll bet you do," Roger said.

Malcolm went out of the room toward the kitchen. The back of his shirt was spotted where the sweat broke through.

"He could stand more hot weather than I could," Roger said.

"I expect so," Darrell said. "More than either of us. But you've had some sun."

"Tennis," Roger said. He came across the room and stood close to Darrell, his hand light against a chair. "Well, kid, are there any new wrinkles on anybody's horn?"

"I reckon not."

"Nothing new at all?"

"No. How about you?"

"New Orleans? There's always something new there. No. I really haven't done much this summer. I've been working as a student assistant at Starhart Hospital. And getting ready for examinations to medical school in September. With me it's mostly come day, go day, God send Sunday."

"That's a holiday—Sunday?"

"Yes."

They sat down. So many questions came to Darrell's throat that he could, for a time, only look at Roger. Finally he said, "You seem so much older than me . . ."

Roger laughed. "It'll make an old man out of you—marriage will."

"Will it?"

"Maybe it's not quite that bad."

"What's it really like?"

"It's a lot of fun—at times."

"You ever wish you were not—you know?"

192

"Everybody does I guess, at sometime or other."

Like someone caught unaware, Darrell drew back a little in his chair. After a moment he leaned forward. "I like Anne, Roger. I really do."

"Tell me about this new girl of yours."

"Emily? What do you want to know?"

"Is she pretty?"

"Yes."

"And what else?"

"I don't know what else. What else should I be looking for?" Darrell could feel his own face redden as he watched the color come into Roger's face.

"I'll tell you sometime, but not right now. It would take a long time and I wouldn't want an audience." Roger stretched his legs forward, in a way which Malcolm Pitt had always done. "Is Emily really that pretty?"

"Well, I can't prove it."

"And she's a preacher's daughter. I don't know about a preacher's daughter."

Suddenly Darrell stood up. "I don't understand you, Roger. I don't know what you mean."

Roger stood, too. He took Darrell's arm. "I didn't mean anything, Darrell. I wasn't even thinking about Miriam. Whoever you marry I hope it's right for you . . ."

They stood in silence. Darrell thought he was about to talk to Roger as he wanted to. Yet there was something standing in the way. He could not go on.

Roger's hand dropped from his arm. Malcolm came into the room.

Darrell realized for the first time that Roger's and Malcolm's sleeves were rolled up in identical small folds. Malcolm held a glass of scuppernong wine in his hand. Cautiously he took one sip, frowning a little. "This is reserved for age," he said. Then he said to Roger, "Your wife wants you a minute."

Roger and Malcolm were looking at each other, studying. Darrell watched both of them: their tan faces, their muscled arms, their knowledged bodies. They were men with wives, he thought. A wall was between him and these two men. He could not talk to them now.

But soon, very soon, he would be married to Emily; and the wall would be torn away.

five

On that September morning of his wedding day, Darrell rose early and walked from the Lenmore Hotel to Emily's house. He knew that he should not go that early to the manse, that he should not go at all before eleven o'clock. But he went, as if he must break the rule, and stood on the brick steps of the manse and twisted the doorbell in quarter turns.

Emily opened the door, and her black eyes gathered him for a moment as if she had never seen him before. She did not speak, only her lips seemed to break a little like a child blowing bubbles. They did not say anything to each other for a minute. When he was inside she closed the door and looked up to him with what he thought was a little awe and a little anger. "You shouldn't be here. What if Father had come to the door?"

"Nothing. I didn't come to see him." He studied the morning whiteness of her face as if he might find some new curve or shape; and he thought, I know more about you than I know about myself, have learned all this in hardly four months, darling. But his thoughts halted with the word *darling* as his speech always seemed awkward with *darling, sweetheart,*

194

honey. It was easier to say *Emily.* Then suddenly her face changed to a deep color. The room was quiet, like a moment in church when the sacrament is passed and the wine is spilled.

"You shouldn't be here. You know better. Why did you do it?"

"Because I stayed up in that hotel room and listened to nothing as long as I could . . ."

"You want everything to go wrong?"

"Nothing is going wrong." He put his arm around her and she turned away from him.

"It is. It is already." She became very still and looked up at him. "I don't want to go to Memphis."

"What do you mean? Why, Memphis was your idea. You're the one who chose it."

"It was what Mother chose." She came to him and caught his arm. "I want to go to New Orleans. I want to see something new. Please. Everything will be all right if you'll take me there."

He let his hands drop. "We can't change now. Where would we stay?"

"Uncle Vaughan can take care of that. I told him that I wanted to go and he said he could wire the St. Charles. He knows somebody there. He . . . you're mad. You're angry with me."

"I'm not angry, but it's the strangest thing I ever heard of."

"It's no stranger than your being here right now. What's so strange about it?"

"Why didn't you say something before?"

"Because of Mother. I told you it was Mother. She thinks New Orleans is awful. She thinks brimstone might fall on it any day. She doesn't have to know until we're gone. Uncle Vaughan will take us to the station."

195

He turned to the window and let the back of his hand slide along the curtain. She said: "You're thinking of the Pitts. I know they're there."

"Yes, they're there."

"And that's why you don't want to go."

"I don't know, Emily."

She came and stood behind him and put her arms around his waist. "Please, Darrell. I want to go because they're there, because it's New Orleans. I've always wanted to see it and know what it's like—only for a little while . . ." He tried not to think of her hands touching him; he tried to believe that she had not said anything to him, and that he would go in a few minutes to the train station to meet his grandmother and Malcolm Pitt. And as he stood there looking through the window into the autumn-bright morning, he remembered the snow-covered bluffs of Memphis, the dark water of the river, the boat, the wind across the deck that night. He caught her hands around his waist and held them; he knew then where they would go. Slowly he turned and looked down at her. "We'll go to New Orleans," he said.

She kissed him and then they stood holding hands for a minute. "I'm going to the train now. I have to meet them at nine o'clock."

"Yes," she said.

He turned quickly to the door. He went down the brick steps of the manse and once he looked back to make sure that nothing followed him. He wondered whether he would tell Malcolm Pitt that they were going to New Orleans; and he knew, somehow, that he would not.

He walked down the hill into the sun with the light fluff from the cottonwood trees falling like sparse heavy snowflakes over the brick walk. It was the sun of September that he faced and the fluff of September that fell, and he tried to think of cot-

ton and the gin which would start running in two days. It would
be the first time the gin had ever started without him. Malcolm
Pitt would see to everything until he and Emily returned. *Go
ahead, boy, and forget about the gin. Hell, I can run it a few
days. And if I can't run it we'll let the damn thing sit until you
get back. A man doesn't get married every fall. September is
the right time, too. They don't turn the heat on in Memphis until the first of October.*

Yet, he wanted to deny the swift feeling in him that he
wished this day was over, or wished that it would never be, so
that he might start the gin two days hence with the same busy-
thrill which the wheels always turned to; and so that he might
lean out the upper window of the gin's office and looked down
at Malcolm Pitt's stern and gripping face studying the boiler
gauges through the thin whiffs of steam.

He waited on the cinders beside the small gray station
hearing but not listening to the cry, "Fried chicken!", and the
train's whistle and the train's bell. He had heard the same cry,
the same whistle, and the same bell yesterday; and through the
window of the slowing train he had seen Emily waiting for him
beside her father who stood tapping his cane, his hair well-
parted in the middle and his mustache shining brighter than his
hair in the sunlight.

He had not thought there would be any loneliness crowding inside of him as he sat in the candlelight at the rehearsal
supper in the manse. But it was a time of loneliness and he sat
across from Emily thinking that everything would be all right
if he could touch her hand.

At the end of the table Emily's mother sat like some overgrown and over-polite child, and her little brown eyes seemed
triumphant though not unkind. Her long thin fingers seemed to
control the table and all the people there with much the same
sureness that Malcolm Pitt's hands would control the gin

197

valves. There was a strange, eager pleasantness about her, but there was no smile on her face.

At the head of the table Emily's father sat plump and scarlet-faced and over-attentive, as though everyone was gathered under his wing, and he seemed peculiarly restful, free from worry about any soul in his presence. He talked chiefly to Del, Emily's roommate from Belhaven College, who kept her eyes always on her plate.

There was also Emily's Aunt Laura and Uncle Vaughan who had come from Corinth for the wedding. Her Aunt Laura sold hats at a department store in Corinth and her Uncle Vaughan had been a baseball player, a tall left-handed first baseman, before he began to travel for a machinery company.

Darrell sat like a puppet before all of them. It was a time of sadness, and there was about him the sense of being a child manipulated in a grown-up world. It was the end of something and he was not prepared for it, like summer dying too quickly upon the fields.

When the supper was over and when he started for the hotel, the loneliness was with him again though he would not admit to himself that the dull peculiar sense of being lost in an unpeopled land was a pain he wanted to feel. He walked south outside the city toward the cool September haze which seemed only in that direction. In that direction he knew, too, that Miriam waited or slept in the clinic near her mother; and in that direction Roger sat at some table over some medical book: he was taking entrance examinations, he had written. Yet, Darrell could not help thinking, *I did not go to his wedding, and now he is not coming to mine.*

He pushed these thoughts away and turned back toward the hotel, and toward the aloneness which had crowded his room through the night and through the long morning until he had dressed quickly and gone again to Emily.

198

Now at the station he could not see her or touch her, but there was no feeling of aloneness, for the train was moving in, and soon Malcolm Pitt would walk through the vestibule and come down the train steps with his grandmother. The Negro woman passed him with her basket of fried chicken. He had forgotten her name though he knew that Malcolm Pitt would remember it. Like a horse's hoof sliding along gravel the train stopped.

Malcolm Pitt's foot had touched the cinders before Darrell saw him, alone, with his gloves, his cane, and his small square bag all in one big hand. With the other hand he waved to Darrell who knew suddenly what he should have known before now: his grandmother never had intended to come.

"Boy," Malcolm said, and he fingered the brim of his black derby while his crisp-clear eyes looked down as if he had suddenly decided against something he had meant to say. "Am I late? That train's been scrooping along like an old galled terrapin."

"No, sir. Grandmother didn't . . ."

"She didn't feel like coming, Darrell." He lifted his eyes over the city as he had often lifted them from field to pine hills to look for rain. "We're going to your room where I can wash my neck and put on another shirt?"

"Yessir," Darrell said. "At the Lenmore."

"Let's walk," Malcolm said. "Even scissors rust if they're not divided now and then."

Over a protest and a firm grip, Darrell reached for the small square bag. Finally Malcolm released it and said, "Don't drop it. That might start it to leaking."

"Leaking?"

"Something I brought along for us."

A blue-clad Negro took the small square bag at the entrance of the Lenmore Hotel and led the way to Darrell's third floor room, while Malcolm Pitt with every turn of the stairs asked questions.

"What's your name?"

"Vallard."

"Is this town any good? I just want to know what you think?"

"Yessuh."

"You always lived here?"

"Nossuh. I used to live out on Mista Jim Lyman's place. You know Mista Jim Lyman?"

"No. I'm a Yankee. I don't live around here."

"I don't believe you no Yankee."

"Why?"

"I don't hear you like you is."

Vallard opened the door and stood with his back against the facing. Malcolm Pitt took the bag from him and said, "How about a bucket of ice and two wine glasses? You can bring it right away?"

"Yessuh."

Malcolm closed the door and went to look out the window. He shook his head suddenly like a man shaking rain from his face, and moved back toward the mirror. "I'll swear I never could look down without feeling dizzy, not even from a back-yard swing." He was stripping off his coat and tie and shirt.

Darrell was thinking, I should have known. He could remember his grandmother brittle and unwavering: "Well, you're bound to do it. Just bound to do it. So with what little you've made out of the gin and the land you can be the young squire to Emily. It's something boiling inside you, something you got from your father, not from me. Because you can't stop either. You can't stop whatever it is that's in you. And you think it'll be all over when Emily comes. But drive on, just drive on, you're beyond the reach of my words . . ."

He watched Malcolm Pitt lay his coat and tie and shirt across the bed.

"Is Grandmother all right?"

"Don't worry about her. At her age weddings are not as important as they are to you. Never are to a woman anyway. Not really. They're fussy about clothes and flowers and food. But the real thing means more to a man. You afraid?"

"A little. Not like I thought I'd be."

"You ought to be. I've never yet seen a man go through it without shaking a little, at least coloring. Hell, it's a big test. A man afraid on the battlefield can fight back; today you'll have to stand up and smile. Even if you could laugh it would be easier." He turned back to the mirror again and pushed his palm upward over his face with a whisking sound. "Damned if it don't look like I shaved with the butcher knife this morning."

"You're all right."

"Well, son, I get to kiss her too. Remember that."

"I'll remember it."

"More than once, pretty as she is." Then he laughed the laugh which Darrell had heard often beside gin or barn or in the open field, only it was quieter now. "You can trust me. How much time have we got?"

"Nearly an hour."

Malcolm opened his bag and pulled out a new white shirt. Then he drew out a tall clear bottle and tossed it onto the bed.

"I got it at Vicksburg yesterday, for you and me. That shirt too. With Leta still in New Orleans I figured I'd never find the right kind of shirt, so I bought this one to make sure. A wife's right useful."

"Is she any better?" Darrell said, and before he finished the words he wished he had said nothing. He was afraid that he would have to tell Malcolm Pitt that he was going to New

Orleans; and it seemed important that Malcolm should not know this now.

"I don't know, Darrell." Malcolm fumbled with his shirt. "What they say doesn't hold very long. Miriam wrote yesterday there was some change."

"It seems a long time since May," Darrell said.

"It has been a long time, and I'm not used to being a bachelor. Nolie said tell you to keep your windows closed."

"Windows?" Darrell flushed.

"What does Nolie know about your windows, boy?"

He had waited for Malcolm Pitt to ask this, and now he could not answer. "That's Nolie talking."

Darrell did not hear the door open. The blue-uniformed figure of Vallard was already in the doorway with the bucket of ice and two thin conical glasses.

"Right here," Malcolm said. He picked up the wine bottle and bored it down into the ice. "Good white Rhine wine. You can't get it in Jackson, not like this. You can't get anything here but good bourbon." From his right front pocket he took a ten dollar bill. "Vallard?"

"Yessuh."

"Tell the clerk I want this room for tonight. This young man is checking out. Here. I want the best bottle of bourbon you can find in this town. I won't be here when you get back, but you leave it up here for me."

"Yessuh."

"We're just having one mild glass or two now, but I may get good and damned drunk tonight."

"Is it trouble?" Vallard said.

"No. It's a celebration."

"It a' be here."

Vallard was gone. Malcolm Pitt sat on the edge of the bed and stooped over the ice-bucket, whirling the wine bottle be-

202

tween his hands like a man in the cold warming his palms.

"This is your big day, son, and I want it to go off right. Roger wrote you why he couldn't be here?"

"He said he was taking entrance exams to medical school."

Malcolm nodded. He had filled the glasses and was standing with his back to the mirror holding his glass to his lips. For a long time he did not drink. He let his arm fall quickly. "I guess you think I ought to give you some advice. Well, there's not a goddamned thing I can say to you. You always do everything right anyway."

Darrell held his breath. The glass was again to Malcolm's lips and he drank. Then he set the glass down and put his arm around Darrell.

Darrell's caught breath slowly released. "You think this is right?"

"I'm afraid anything you might do would be all right with me."

"Will you really get drunk tonight?"

"Yes. Dammit."

"Why?"

"For you, maybe." He lifted his glass again. "Give me the ring now."

It was not the wine that made the room swim before Darrell's eyes while he held to Emily's hand, nor was it the wine that pushed the sweet scent (almost a funeral-smell) of flowers about him until his very pulse seemed clotted to inertia. He knew the sweat filmed across the shallow wrinkles of his forehead; and in his armpits it beaded and dropped cold against his sides while he heard, *Dearly beloved, we are assembled here in the presence of God* . . .

Emily's father stood before the mantel with the book in his hand and even while he read, his fingers moved, soft and slow

203

and gentle down the page. His voice coming from a throat ridged with fat was strong in its very quietness, was lost in word reverence to an image, to a *Greater Father;* and he seemed never mindful at all of the white and pink chrysanthemums between which he stood.

As Thou has brought them together by Thy providence, sanctify them by Thy Spirit, giving them a new frame of heart for their new estate . . .

Darrell heard the words, not separately but as one breath of speech after another; and while he watched the ever-flushed face moving in a room of stillness, he could see in the mirror above the mantel the back of the minister's head, and could see how the collar seemed to cord the neck. He could not move his eyes away even while he repeated:

And I do promise and covenant . . .

As long as we both shall live . . .

There was strength in the voice he heard though the strength was not the same either in degree or kind as that of Malcolm Pitt, who stood to Darrell's right, not so much a figure tall and broad as he was someone certain and quick and unchanging. The words and the patterned movements became staccato images: Malcolm Pitt's hand held out the ring; his own hand did not tremble, only his fingers moved as cold baling wire bends.

Whom God hath joined together, let no man put asunder . . . The Lord bless you and keep you: The Lord make his face shine upon you and be gracious unto you: The Lord lift up his countenance upon you and give you peace: Both now and in the life everlasting. Amen.

Then he could no longer see the collar in the mirror, the cord about the neck. His own lips were light against Emily's. For one keen and crisp moment Malcolm Pitt bent slowly forward and covered her lips.

204

Then the room was amorphous again though he could feel hands in his and hands about his shoulders. The punch, the laughter, the cake seemed absorbed in the room, like lightbread saturated and sinking in milk. Now and then he heard distinctly:

"So lovely, my dear, but a pity it was not in the church where the whole congregation could see your daughter."

"Yes, I know. But a wedding ought to be small and held in the sanctity of the home. To have a big wedding is too much like giving in to the flesh."

"Of course. It was best here."

"And so we invited only the elders and their wives."

"Irish lace is so pretty, but I never remembered the seed pearls when you wore it, Aline. You added those for Emily, didn't you?"

"No, Laura. Not a stitch was touched. After all, if there is a wedding dress in the family I believe in handing it down from generation to generation. And unchanged, my dear. Have you seen the wedding gifts? Over here."

"Beautiful silver, Aline. Not too ornate, but not slippery, either."

"From the deaconate. And here. Eleven soup toureens. They got eleven."

"They can break one a year for ten years and still have soup."

"And Elder Duncan, over there talking to Vaughan, sent . . ."

"Darrell. Darrell, dear. Aunt Laura and Uncle Vaughan . . ."

"Del. Del Tubber. I roomed with Del at Belhaven before we moved here from Corinth."

"Oh, yes, I keep forgetting . . ."

The room suddenly took shape again; each substance defined itself in vivid flash: Malcolm Pitt was whispering to him. "I'm going . . . Hell. Make sure you don't up and decide not to come back to Leighton."

Then the lines and the edges and the angles; the color of eyes and the smell of punch; and the weave of word and breath and laughter was undefined again, was undefined until he was on the stairs with Emily, going up to her room, his arm half about her shoulder, half about her waist.

"I never knew what it would be like, Darrell . . ."

The words and laughter and the sound of glass against glass below was finally clear and real to him, like the taste of spring water. In a few minutes he and Emily would be going away.

"I don't even know now," he said.

"But I'm glad we didn't have a church wedding. I like it this way."

"You couldn't have found any pulse in me an hour ago. But it's coming back . . . I think." He stopped on the top stairstep.

"Let me feel it," she said.

"Feel it."

"Darrell. I don't know why I love you. I just know . . ." She caught his hand. "We better hurry. We have to get ready to leave. Uncle Vaughan is waiting."

"Do I carry you through *this* door?"

"No." She went ahead of him, across the room, and fingered the draperies aimlessly. "Come here, to the window. I want to tell you something."

He followed her. "What is it?"

"I hope you love me as much as I love you."

He played with her hands, and then he kissed her. "I'm sorry my grandmother didn't come."

"It doesn't matter, Darrell. To me it doesn't. I told Mother she was ill. Mr. Pitt said she was. I liked him."

206

"I'm glad you did."

"You like him a lot."

"Of course."

"He's like your father, isn't he?"

"I don't know. I don't remember too much about my father. Not too much." He knew he was closing a part of himself away from her, and he could not help it.

"I mean . . . I mean he's like a father—to you."

"He came, and my grandmother didn't. You said we had to hurry."

"Yes. We have to hurry. You're not angry at all because we're not going to Memphis, are you?"

He took her hands and played with them again. Suddenly he could feel the sweat on his forehead, and he could feel the drops on his face like the drippings from a candle. He said, "Honestly, it's all right."

six

Three blocks from the St. Charles Hotel, Darrell and Emily turned into an alley, and halfway up the alley they turned again and entered the crib-like door of The Galleo. The room was a long hall with a sawdust-covered floor that seemed to rise, moving back toward a little stage where a wine-colored woman sang in French.

"Over there in the corner," Emily said. "Let's sit over there."

Darrell nodded. He was glad of the shadows and the dim light, and glad that the endless roar of the train was no longer cracking in his ears. For, all the way from Jackson the sound of

207

the train had seemed to bind him, to tie him motionless within a certain time and space so that he could not escape. Now that the sound had stopped he thought that he might break the bonds, break anything that might try to hold him. They stood beside the table for a moment before he reached for Emily's coat.

"Are you glad we came?" she said.

"What?"

"Glad we came here instead of Memphis?"

He had turned his back to her to place the coat on the hall-tree. "If it's really what you wanted," he said. He did not turn again to her immediately. He was looking down to the sawdust upon the floor, thinking how foolish it was to feel that suddenly in one day, that since this morning when her father read the ceremony, she had come to know far more than he; and that she in a few hours had grown older than he and understood so much that he could not treat her as a child.

"Darrell?"

He turned and watched her, with her hands lifted, pull at the fingers of her white gloves.

"I've got a smudge on my gloves."

"You sound like Grandmother."

"Oh . . ."

Quickly he said, "Nobody will see it in this light, darling." He withdrew the chair for her, then carefully seated himself as if he must act like a child at Sunday dinner with the minister as guest. "Are you tired?"

She shook her head. "I was tired when I got to the hotel, but I'm not now."

"Hungry?"

"Yes."

"We won't even have to order here. They'll bring us whatever they choose."

She leaned over the table to whisper to him, "You know all about it. How many times have you been to New Orleans?"

"I don't know."

"What did you come for?"

"Business."

"You came with Malcolm Pitt?"

"Yes."

"I don't believe it was for business."

"Well, once we came to see Roger when he first entered school here. Once we came to . . . you shouldn't pin me down."

"Did you come here? To this place?"

"Yes."

"Where else did you go?"

"To The Bluegrave."

"Will you take me there? I want to go to every place you went to."

"No."

"Why?"

"It's not a place for a lady."

"What's it like?"

"Like something you've never seen. It has a bar that looks like burial vaults. The bartenders are in undertaker's clothes and when you order something they open the vault and pull out a small silver-handled coffin . . ."

"Is that all?"

"No. It's called a concert-saloon. You wouldn't understand the other parts."

"Where else did Malcolm Pitt take you?"

"Honey, you want to know too much." He took her hand and played with her fingers almost as if he thought it was a thing he should do. He withdrew his hand when the dark wiry waiter brought water to the table. The waiter bowed.

"Apéritif, monsieur?"

"No thank you," Darrell said.

"Non?"

"No."

The waiter turned and his heels left dark square holes in the sawdust along the floor.

"Why didn't you drink something?"

"I didn't want to."

"You drink with Malcolm Pitt."

"But he's . . ." Darrell looked down into his water glass which was cupped within his hands.

"Oh, I didn't care either way," she said. She moved her glass against his. "Did he want you to get married?"

"Who?"

"Malcolm Pitt."

"I don't know. I didn't ask him."

"He didn't. I know he didn't."

"You sound like Nolie."

"Who's Nolie?"

"I've told you about her."

"When?"

"Well, if I haven't told you then you'll get a good surprise. You'll probably like her."

"Do you?"

"Of course. Why not?"

Before she could answer, the waiter brought crayfish bisque, put it down with precision and turned away again without speaking. Darrell watched Emily dip into the soup, watched her lips play with the spoon, and he smiled a little, thinking, Now she is not so grown-up.

"Do you like this?" she said.

"Yes."

"Maybe I could learn to make it."

210

"We wouldn't like it so much at home." He saw the faint beginning of a hurt smile, and put his hand out quickly and covered her wrist. "I didn't mean it that way. It sort of goes with New Orleans or Vicksburg more than with home. I remember the first time I ever had crayfish bisque; it was with Roger and his father in Vicksburg. I guess Roger and I were twelve then."

"Will we see Roger down here?"

He pulled his hand away from her wrist. "I don't know."

"I'd like to see him. And Miriam too."

"We're not visiting. We're on a honeymoon. You'll have plenty of time to see them. It takes eleven minutes to drive in the surrey from our house to Miriam's house, when you hurry."

"You know exactly?"

"Yes. I've driven it enough."

"Oh . . ."

He heard himself saying, almost without meaning, "I'm sorry, darling." He held her hand again, held it as if he must do so no matter what the dark-haired dark-eyed waiter thought when he came silently with the trout amandine that burned the throat with the faint bitterness of peach seed kernel.

And afterwards, while the waiter held the crêpes suzettes in one hand and the match in the other, he smiled for the first time and said, "Honeymoon, monsieur?"

Darrell nodded, and over the blue flame he could see the waiter look down to the tight cluster of small white roses pinned to the left above the vestee of Emily's green dress. When the waiter was gone she said, "He likes my hat. I thought you would notice it, but . . ."

"I've been looking at you, not your hat." He looked then at the silver gray velvet and the feather about the hat, curling down to her hair.

"Aunt Laura smuggled this to me from Corinth. If Mother

211

had seen it I never would have gotten out of the house with it. When we go home, maybe I won't get by your grandmother so easily."

"Maybe not, but don't worry about it now. Are you ready?"

She nodded toward her coat. They walked out into the dark coolness of the street and Emily turned to the right. Quickly Darrell had grabbed her arm. "This way. This is the way," he said.

"I'm always getting lost," she said. "I never have any sense of direction."

"I'll show you. I won't let you get lost." She was close to him, and she was small, and he was strong. He thought that all the constraint and awkwardness he had felt in The Galleo was ended, perhaps ended for always; and now he must reach her with words, must with words pull their minds together until they touched like bodies, with his own mind firm and dominant while hers listened. He was whispering fiercely to her, holding her arm tight while they walked; and his lips were close to her ear. "I know every inch of this street because I've been up and down it a dozen times, late at night and early in the morning. No matter how many people are around you, you can always hear the hard sound of your own feet on the cobblestones. But even in the daytime I never like to walk this street by myself because of the smell—the chicory and the river-damp odor makes you hungry for something you've never had. The last time we were here there were four women at that corner dancing in the street and a Greek fellow was trying to get a cart by with a barrel of molasses. He got mad and jerked one woman's skirt . . ."

"Darrell?"

"What?"

"You're hurting my arm."

"Oh," he said.

212

"Where are we going?"

"To the hotel."

"Now?"

"Yes. We can see New Orleans tomorrow. Or the next day, or the next. We've got five days."

She pulled her arm loose and held to his hand.

"I wouldn't get married any time but in September," he said.

"Why?"

"Because September is the youngest month of the year, whether you know it or not."

"The youngest month . . ." she said.

He thought of Nolie, the tall train whistle.

At the desk in the hotel lobby he took his hand away from hers and leaned slightly against the counter to receive the key to their room. Then he held her hand again, without speaking, until he had closed the door of their room behind him. He locked the door.

"Come here."

When she stood a little way from him he drew her closer and tilted her head, but he did not kiss her.

"Did you like where we ate?" he said.

"Yes."

"You like New Orleans?"

"Yes. Do you?"

"Only for a little while. Sunday I'll want to leave. I'll want to go home. Wait till you get home and you see the hills there now. Wait till you see the hickories above our house in solid gold, and the blackgum trees a dark wine red, and the dogwood turning purple all in the middle of tall pines." He was whispering.

"I'll like it, Darrell . . ."

He kissed her then, pushing against her until she bent away from him and said, "Will you light the gas?"

"No."

"But I need to put up my clothes and . . ."

"You can do that tomorrow. I want the room like this now, and after a while I'll close the curtain where no light will come in at all . . ."

The room, to him, seemed to lock itself from all motion save only the sound of time moving, time moving like the slow burning of a weak gaslight. He broke the spell by walking to the window and looking out over the buildings rising through the mist. He turned and pulled off his coat, then fingered the buttons of his shirt. Emily, without looking at him, unpinned the roses and laid them on the edge of the dresser. He stooped over at the foot of the walnut bed and opened his suitcase.

"Even in the dark I can find my blue pajamas. I hope they match . . ." He stopped because his lips felt heavy.

"Darrell, I . . ."

"I'm not looking."

He went back to the window and pulled the curtains closed. His pajamas slipped out of his hands. He picked them up.

When his knee touched the bed the sheet seemed to break like crisp taffy. The pillowcase against his ear was like dry fodder leaves shattering. Emily was beside him and he felt suddenly that if he spoke to her his head must be lifted above her. He propped his head so that his elbow dug into the pillow beside her and he was looking down to her face. He could tell that she was looking not into his eyes but at his chin or the hollow of his neck. Her finger touched the hollow.

"Did you ever sleep under a feather comfort?" she said.

"No."

"I have. Mother has a . . ."

"Emily . . ."

"I'm . . . a little afraid," she whispered. She let her hand drop from his neck.

214

He leaned down, his arm bending, and his cheek covered her face with slow movements. "Darling . . ."

"Because I never . . ."

"I know it."

"Not with anybody, Darrell. Have you?"

"You shouldn't ask."

"Mother said . . ."

He was touching her face with his lips; his fingers stroked tight against her throat in short feeling movements.

"Precious . . ."

"What if we have a child because . . . of tonight?"

"We're married."

"You won't . . ."

"Don't move."

"Wait . . ."

"No, darling . . ."

He thought that nothing in the room seemed real, had for the moment no shape as the rise and fall of music has no shape. Time seemed to move then like the thin sound of gas which any minute might burst to flame. He was always measuring time and now it was moving by him quickly, like something leaving. In the midst of the naked sound of time a faucet dripped water, staccato steps went down the hall, and the open window shook once with the night's September breeze.

The room was warm. He stood beside the window and opened the curtains a little. The pounding was not gone from his body; the pounding was only half spent. And the blood was like time in his body. Time kept moving inside him because she had not drawn from him the half he could not give alone—the half he could not name; made up of a whisper, a quivered lip, a touch of fingers in the dark; and all of this was something warm, to be seen in the dark, to be heard in silence, to be called with no movement of the tongue. He looked out again through the mist and saw the tall buildings rising.

"Darrell?"

"Yes."

"What are you looking for?"

"Nothing."

He pushed his body against the window sill. He thought, She saw me. His hand went out against the windowpane and his knuckles slipped along the smooth surface. He was thinking that she could not see his mind leap the brown building and fall somewhere on the edge of the mist where the houses became low, where Miriam waited. And even if his body had been quieted to its very marrow in that room, his mind would still have leaped beyond the palm trees and the light posts and the car tracks where Roger leaned over his opened book, his elbow on the desk, his fingers jabbed like a pitchfork in his hair.

"Darrell?"

"Yes."

"Are you glad we came to New Orleans?"

The mist was rising, like a heavy layer of smoke from the gin, and the ground seemed farther away though he could not see it.

"Are you?" he said.

"Yes."

Or it might be that Miriam and Roger were down below, somewhere. It might be that they had walked the streets tonight and somewhere in the shadows below the mist he had passed them without touching.

"Will you bring me a glass of water, please?"

"Yes . . ."

He thought, She is bringing me back to her. He turned away from the window, leaving the curtains undrawn. He found the glass and the pitcher on the marble-top washstand. He lifted

216

both and went back to the light of the window to fill the glass. The sound of the water was like a half-open steam valve at the gin.

"When are we going to see the Pitts?"

Suddenly the glass and the pitcher were no longer in his hands. Broken bits scattered about his ankles and his feet were wet and smarting with tiny stings. "Why must you keep asking me about the Pitts? We're not going to see them!" Then he went to the bed and took her into his arms and held her like a child.

seven

Darrell lifted the razor and looked at it. For a minute the polished concave sides seemed soft and pliable in the morning light. Four mornings he had shaved in the room, and each morning the room had seemed strange and smaller to him. Suddenly he wondered why, when he pulled with a short downward stroke, the razor would not leap into his flesh. The blade touched his temple lightly; he pulled slowly. His hand shook. Behind him he could hear Emily breathing in sleep and each cautious stroke of his razor matched her breathing.

His mind gave shape to the silent times within this room when their bodies spoke in quickened breath. The days seemed quick with breathing. The hours along the gray impersonal streets were again remarked. The raw wine on the wind, the green odor of hemp, the soft and seeping smell of coffee each morning, the heavy fish-fume from the wharf where he and Emily had stood, the sawdust-sprinkled floors in dim lights, all intervolved itself into a sense of taste and smell which became less a city and more the sharp definement of one room

217

where buildings plunged upward through mist or hovered like a shoebox along the narrow streets.

Somewhere in this strange sphere of taste and smell, in one of the rooms of one of the buildings, he had drawn back the curtains of another person's life; and in doing this he had drawn the curtain to part of his own secret self, sensing while the razor scraped a path down his lathered cheek, while his fingers fumbled with the buttons of white broadcloth underwear, while he turned to look at Emily almost diagonal across the bed with her hair dark as bird wings against a bright sky and her lips pressed a little open like a child's because her cheek was flat against her pillow, sensing in all this that man was made so that whatever gave him pleasure would give him pain.

Now for the first time he did not lose the loneliness when he looked at her, or even when he touched her.

He wanted to go home. He was not looking at Emily but he could feel her perfume about him, and it became not her own but the perfume of a city that crowded heavy against him and heavy inside him. Day after day it was stronger and stronger and his whole insides seemed weak under the weight of it, until he wanted to rise in quick violence and smash a windowpane with his bare hand to let fresh air in, knowing even before his fist curled tight that whatever would come through the window would not be the air of home but the heavy rich sultriness of New Orleans. He was glad it was Sunday, and glad that Sunday was the day of leaving, because he believed then that the air of home, that something as simple as the smell of autumn leaves, would heal whatever gall he felt.

He went back to the bed, almost laid his fingers playfully on her throat, thinking how her whole body would curl under the light blanket. But he did not touch her, for it seemed to him that no stroke of hand nor gentleness of voice would atone for having taken from her a full measure and having returned only a part. Then suddenly, as he stood watching the easiness of her sleep, he knew what he must do. It was like reading a puzzle and understanding no part of it until the whole meaning flashed vividly across the mind. He knew exactly where he would go and he would go in secret, and the thought of secrecy was like having a strange new power in his hand. If Emily awakened before he returned then she would think simply that he had gone out to walk along the streets as he had done two other mornings. He finished dressing hurriedly and went to the door and opened it carefully. He stood for a moment holding the door ajar before he turned and went slowly down the hall.

He walked block after block of the quiet streets and the sunshine, though not bright, was warm against his face and hands. There was nothing in the air but dark pigeons and the sound of church bells. He had to think about what Miriam would say, or what he would say to Miriam. Even in the endless daylight along the palm-lined street he could see her face, though in the darkness he always remembered her face as curving to a more precise and accurate shape. When the trolley behind him grew louder than his own footsteps he turned and waited. At the corner he climbed aboard and asked the conductor directions to Brockner's Nursing Home.

He stood in the front of the car, which was empty of passengers except for himself and two Negroes, and wanted to talk to the conductor. It did not matter what was said. Maybe he might say, "Funny thing. This girl I grew up with, childhood sweetheart, out here at the nursing home with her mother. I just got married, that is to somebody else, and I'm going out to see her a minute. Funny thing, at least . . ."

But the thin dark-suited conductor looked straight ahead, swaying a little with the car, and working his lips like a man about to whistle. He did not turn to look at Darrell when he called out, "Brockner's."

Darrell opened the wrought-iron gate at the corner of the street and the weights closed it behind him. The grounds of the Home spread over two blocks and in the center was a three story yellow building with white banisters and four white columns. He did not see anyone on the grounds though somewhere beyond the building someone was whistling. He climbed the steps and without knocking on the tall doors he entered into a large hall. At one desk a nurse stood up when he entered. Halfway across the hall he could see the small brown mole on her chin and her middle-aged face smiled at him.

"Could I see Mrs. Malcolm Pitt or Miss Pitt?"

The nurse took a cedar pencil from her cap and pointed to him as if she must have time to think before any word was uttered. "Your mother is upstairs in her special bath this morning. But Miriam is in her room. Number seven." He opened his mouth twice but he could not interrupt her quick speech. She pointed with her pencil down the hall. "And I know she's waiting for you because just this morning I was talking to Miriam and she said you were coming to take her to church . . ." She stopped suddenly. "You are Roger?"

"No."

"Oh . . ." The nurse smiled and her mouth went into many shapes while she nodded complete understanding. "Sweetheart?" She smiled again.

Darrell repeated, "Number seven?"

"Yes." She nodded her understanding again.

"Thank you."

Even when he had knocked on the door where the card on the facing read Pitt, he wanted to turn away. And better still, he hoped that no one would answer, that Miriam might already be gone to church. He heard her answer and with it was a quickened sweep in him like heavy snow against an ungloved hand. He held the doorknob tight. He heard her call again, "Come in."

220

He pushed the door back slowly and waited, knowing that his lips quivered like a small bird's wing. He saw first her cheeks, and then her nose shrink and swell with breath, pulsating. Her lips and eyes were fixed momently like something stopped in mid-flight.

"Darrell! I thought you were Roger."

"No. It's . . . me . . ."

"What are you doing here? In New Orleans?"

"We came here instead of Memphis. You know all about it, don't you?"

"The wedding. Yes. Father wrote me. And I got your letter."

"I never got any of yours . . ." He tried to smile. "Nothing seemed to work right for us."

"The letters didn't matter, Darrell. It was more than that."

"Yes. It was more . . ." Then his words were quick and blunt, as if they marked the end of something. "I thought it was what you wanted."

"Maybe we didn't know what we wanted, either of us."

"Maybe we didn't, but let's not make it worse by quarreling."

She turned a little from him, not listening, not speaking, her eyes no longer hazel, but a mild gray. His lips could not then shape her name. He watched the profile of her nose, again pulsating, golden in the dim light. It suddenly seemed odd that they were more than children.

The room was not warm but his shoulders and arms stung with heat, as if her very breathing lashed him. "It would be all right, Miriam, everything would be all right if I didn't remember. But I do remember. I always remember, even when I don't want to. I know you're wondering why I did it."

"I won't ask you why. It's not your fault . . ."

He took her arm. "But I want you to know. I want you to

221

listen. I did it because I thought it was right, or because I had to. I love you, Miriam. You know I love you. And you know what I feel for your father and Roger . . ." He stopped and pulled his hands away from her. "I don't know why I did it, but it wasn't to hurt you. It wasn't to hurt anybody. You've got to know that. Believe me."

"I believe you, and I want you to believe me. I hope you're happy. I hope it will be all right."

He waited for her to go on talking, as if speech gave him the right to stay there while silence made his staying there wrong. He thought of Roger. He did not want to see Roger then.

"I have to go, Miriam. Tell your mother . . . tell her I'm sorry I didn't see her. We're going home today. Can I tell your father anything?"

"Father?" Her eyes seemed to light a little, to gather a new strength. "Tell him they think Mother is better and we'll be home before long."

He stood looking at her, waiting. Suddenly he took her wrist. "I had to come by, Miriam. It was all right to come, wasn't it?"

"It was all right," she said.

He went out and when he reached the lobby of the clinic he saw Roger coming through the door. A very small laugh came to both of them. They blushed and then they embraced each other and Roger said, "Well, you've gone and done it. And you look just the same."

"You thought it would change me?"

"No. Nothing will ever change you." Roger moved another step away from Darrell and shook his head as if some great delight had come to him. "You are yet a wicked little garçon. But you're a good one too, a really good one. Where is she?"

"At the hotel."

"I'll bet she's lovely. You never liked anybody that wasn't

222

lovely in one way or another. But I'm irked. You've been here all this time and didn't even once say a word. Why didn't you?"

"I don't know."

"No matter." Roger laughed. "It's a great life if you don't weaken."

"And if you weaken?"

"You won't be by yourself. Have you seen Miriam?"

"Yes."

"The little priss. She ought to have her behind blistered. Nolie never acted half as silly as Miriam has in the last four months. She got just what's coming to her and I'm glad. Let her little heart ache; I hope yours doesn't. I'm glad you showed her —her and Mother too."

"You're not glad."

"No. I'm not glad. She's my sister. But don't think I didn't tell her what I thought. Now she'll have plenty of time to devote to her voice, just plenty of time—she's going to sing at the church this morning. I hope you don't blame yourself for any-thing."

"I'll never blame myself too much."

"I don't know."

For a minute they did not say anything. Then Darrell said, "Is everything all right with you?"

"I'm at least on the edge of happiness."

"And that's all?"

"That's all," Roger said.

"But that's something."

"Yes."

"I have to go now. Emily doesn't know I'm here. Goodbye."

"Goodbye, good one. And be good to her."

"I will."

"I believe you. And I hope she's good to you."

eight

The singsong of the train was ending. Darrell had been quiet, slumped a little in the seat beside Emily and looking beyond her through the train window. He said, "Riding in a train or anything always makes me sleepy."

"Are we nearly there?"

"Yes."

"Will anybody know enough to meet us since we changed our plans and went to New Orleans instead of Memphis?"

"They'll know," Darrell said. "This is the train we'd come in on from either place. Everybody changes in Vicksburg."

The post office and the tall oak beside it came into sight. A surrey was hitched to the oak. The sound of the train whistle seemed much longer than it was, but the sound was like Leighton. It belonged to the time of dusk, and it belonged also to the time of leaving rather than the time of coming home. It made the darkness outside seem cold and unpeopled.

Darrell stood up. Through the train window he saw Malcolm Pitt standing alone beside the tall oak watching the cars choke to a stop, and his face was at once like something familiar and something bright with newness. Darrell smiled because Malcolm Pitt looked strong and unyielding standing alone in the dusk; the figure was the strength and the warmth of a land he had come home to. He smiled again. Then suddenly he was searching the cinder-sprinkled area around Malcolm Pitt, but he did not see his grandmother. The train was abruptly still. He was holding Emily's coat.

"I see Mr. Pitt," she said.

"Yes."

224

"Is he meeting us?"

"I guess so. Grandmother is probably busy making a feather bed for us. You see, September is the time to pick geese."

"Don't try to be clever, Darrell. This is Sunday."

"I forgot. It is Sunday. Maybe she's at church."

"She may not be feeling well."

Darrell turned to a porter and pointed out three bags. He held out a bill and the porter nodded, then bowed. Emily followed Darrell down the aisle, holding his hand.

"You're not only clever today, but you're generous."

Darrell thought, Maybe I gave him a dollar because that is what Malcolm Pitt would have done.

At the end of the coach he let Emily pass on to the vestibule ahead of him. A dozen feet from the train steps Malcolm waited, his face set to laughter and his shining white teeth playing a little over the flush of his lower lip. He did not offer his hand, but instead, he put one arm around Emily's waist and the other about Darrell's shoulders. "You two don't look like you've been traveling. Where are your bags?"

"The porter is bringing them," Darrell said. He could feel the big hand in his side, the fingers close in his ribs as if the sudden pressure of the touch was sign that some deep secret lay between the two, some particular man-knowledge that Emily would not understand, like: *Hell. If I was eighteen* . . . He looked up into the seasoned and knowledged face and thought that the eye teetered slightly, and in the brief movement the message was: *You're on the right road, son, but tell me, how was it?*

Malcolm started toward the bags which the porter had placed side by side on the cinders. "Your grandmother had to go to Vicksburg for something or other today. Yancey and Louella drove her. They'll probably be late getting back. I want you two to come by the house for a little while." He picked up one of the suitcases and nodded toward the surrey. Darrell had already

225

gathered up the other two bags. Malcolm walked close beside Emily. "Maybe you wonder where the rest of Leighton is?"

"No," she said. "Darrell told me it was smaller than Jackson—a little bit."

"I know you two are anxious to get home, but I went to Vicksburg yesterday for the sole purpose of a little champagne, just for this. From the Yellow House, Darrell. I promise I'll have Stafford drive you home early."

"Oh, we're not tired," Emily said.

"Maybe you're like me," Malcolm said. "Love to ride a train."

At the surrey Malcolm put the bag down and his hands circled Emily's waist. She tried to shy gracefully away from him, but he laughed and lifted her into the spring seat. "Always make a man lift you into the seat. They'll appreciate you more."

While the three rode together with Emily sitting a little forward in the middle of the seat, Darrell wished that nobody would have to speak. For that moment New Orleans was behind him, and the smell of Leighton was clean and swelling with freshness, was Leighton's own, as the sudden autumn smell of crayon dust and wrapped lunches belonged only to a schoolroom. And then he wished that Malcolm Pitt would speak and he might answer: *Yes, Father. No, Father.* But the time for that, if the time had ever been, was gone too, like the crayon dust.

The narrow surrey wheels knifed into the loose dry gravel beside the front gate of the big house. Malcolm jerked the lines with a short flick of his arm and climbed out over the wheel. He lifted Emily to the ground. Darrell sat for a moment before he suddenly leaped out. He had forgotten the smell of Leighton, and in his mind was the one thought: She knew we were coming home today and she went to Vicksburg. Malcolm Pitt had to meet us and if he hadn't . . .

226

Stafford, tall and brown, had opened the gate and was standing to one side smiling so that his teeth were a streak of whiteness in the dusk. Malcolm Pitt waited for Darrell and Emily to enter.

Darrell said, "Stafford, this is my wife."

"Yes, ma'am." Stafford bowed.

"Just leave the bags in the surrey, Stafford. I want you to drive Darrell home after while."

"Yessuh," Stafford said.

"Hitch the mares and come on back to the kitchen."

"Yessuh."

Once in the hall Malcolm walked to the middle bedroom and opened the door. He motioned to Emily. "Put your coat in here. You may want to refresh yourself for a minute."

"Thank you," she said.

"We'll be in the living room here," he said.

Darrell followed him into the big room, and the two stood on the hearth, both leaning slightly against the mantel. Darrell was looking down though he was not searching for anything with his eyes. He was trying to find some word to say to Malcolm Pitt who stood, Darrell thought, now ready to hear whatever he felt. But the words would not come because the feeling would not shape to any words he knew or had ever heard. If he was a child (as he had been once in this room) he might say: *Father, lean over and let me touch the color in your face,* and if he was a child he might think: *Tomorrow I will smell the crayon dust in the schoolroom.*

He was remembering two things: the way Malcolm Pitt looked at Emily, which made Darrell proud; and remembering what Malcolm Pitt had said a long time ago, "Hell, son, when a man gets married he wants the mattress to slope toward him."

He knew that Malcolm Pitt was looking at him. He heard,

227

"I'm glad you're back. I had a time keeping everything in line around here, not being used to it by myself."

So now he stood alone in a room with a man who was like his father, and not his father, and the words would not link themselves into anything that should be heard. How could anybody ever hope to say anything without meaning too much or too little? Perhaps meaning nothing.

"I'm glad you met us," Darrell said. "It was bad enough for Grandmother not to be there. I don't know what Emily would have thought if nobody had come. I'm grateful because you . . ."

"You know you mean enough to me not to have to be grateful for that." Malcolm turned his back. He had spoken with no effort, suddenly. "Let me see if Stafford's in the kitchen." His broad shoulders seemed to halt in the dining room doorway, as if he might look back.

Then he was gone and Darrell was thinking it had all been too quick, this being a man and standing taller than the mantel. It had come all too suddenly, like blackberry winter.

"Darrell . . ."

Emily stood in the hall doorway. Like the half circle of a falling leaf her eyes swept from the dark green damask curtains across the Rosewood sofa and chairs to the mantel and above the mantel to the painting of Malcolm Pitt's grandfather. Darrell thought he knew every line and shade of the painting without looking again. Then she walked over to the bookcase and picked up the small framed picture of two boys on a spotted pony, the dark-haired one in front, the light-haired one behind. Darrell had not seen it there until then. He knew instantly it was out of place. It belonged in Roger's room.

"Who is this?" she said.

"Roger and I."

He walked over and stood beside her, and touched the

228

frame too, a grooved frame carved from the heart of long-leaf yellow pine. "How old were you two? In this picture?"

"Eleven or twelve."

"I'll bet you two were mean."

"Naturally."

"And fought everybody. Even each other."

"Sometimes."

"He's good looking. Some pair."

Malcolm came into the room. "How about it, Darrell? Can Emily have some champagne?"

"You want some?" he said to her.

She shook her head. "No, thank you."

Malcolm said, "Then some really good scuppernong wine?"

"Just milk," she said. She looked hurt, as if Darrell had turned against her. "You know Darrell didn't drink anything stronger than coffee on our honeymoon."

"He didn't want to miss anything," Malcolm said. He went back into the kitchen.

"Take the wine if you want it," Darrell said. "I won't tell your father."

"Father thinks you don't drink anything."

"If Father wants to know what I do Father ought to ask me."

"I didn't mean that."

He took her hand. "This is one place I do whatever I want to do." They looked at each other and he knew that she did not understand what he meant.

Then Malcolm came into the room and behind him was Stafford with a tray. For a while they drank and talked and Darrell was thinking of hands that seemed to pull at him and he wanted to touch all of them; an open palm, empty, was a very lonely thing.

"Is it that strong?" Malcolm said.

"No," Darrell said.

Stafford came again with a tray and after a while Darrell said, "I think we had better go."

"Not now. You haven't told me about Memphis."

"We didn't go to Memphis. We went to New Orleans."

"New Orleans? Did you see any of my folks?" Then his face was flushed, swiftly, deeply, and the sudden damp film across his forehead was like a breath against a cold windowpane. Darrell had never seen his face so fixed and molded.

"I saw Roger, and Miriam, for a few minutes . . ."

Slowly Malcolm nodded and Darrell knew that he could have told nothing but the truth in that house. He watched Malcolm's fingers turning the champagne glass, leaving heavy grooved fingerprints. He saw Emily's face suddenly check itself and smile, as if she had known all about it. And all their breaths seemed like three winds meeting, going away, and meeting again, until Malcolm, turning to Emily, put words upon his breathing.

His words came out like sudden green buds through a mist of gray Spanish moss. "And what did you think of New Orleans?"

"Oh, I wanted to go there. Darrell didn't."

"He doesn't like the city. He's like me—wants the smell of the country."

"I guess you are a lot alike," Emily said.

Darrell got up. "We really should go."

"Let me get Stafford for you," Malcolm said. "He'll drive you."

As they rode home Darrell watched the shadow of the mares skimming the gravel and bending across clay ridges beside the road. He pulled his watch out of his pocket. The moon was

230

light enough for him to read the watch-face but his mind did not record the time, for he was wondering what he would say if Emily asked, Who gave you that? He put the watch into his pocket again, as if to hide it.

"You're glad we stopped by, aren't you?"

"Yes," she said.

"The ladies here will give you a shower before long. I don't know where. Maybe at Brother Potter's or Aaron Gammel's. I don't know."

"And you'll be at the gin?"

"Gin or somewhere else. You never heard of a husband going to a shower, did you?"

"No," she said. "If it's at the Potter's, I'll see Nolie."

"Don't worry. You'll see Nolie."

"You're awful sure of Nolie."

"Aw, darling, don't get disturbed." He knew she was deliberately not mentioning Miriam's name. He smiled to himself, not knowing why, except that he was thinking it was like saving pennies until you could buy a big piece of candy.

"I guess you know that's the first time you've called me *darling* since we left New Orleans."

"It makes a difference—being in the country. We're not very affectionate. After a while I might start in calling you *woman*."

"I wouldn't listen."

"You'd have to."

"I'd leave."

"No, you wouldn't."

"Yes I would." She touched his chin.

He kissed her.

"What will you do tomorrow?" she said.

"Tomorrow? I don't know. We'll gin a little cotton and then I think we're going to look at some timber."

231

"Big business men. I never know what to say around you two. Looks like Mr. Pitt would be lost if he didn't have you."

"You reckon?"

"Yes."

"Well, I'll think it over. You come by my office tomorrow and I'll let you know."

"You're so clever at times."

"So you found that out too."

"Yes, and right clever of me to find it."

"Maybe."

Stafford turned off the road into the drive and Emily was suddenly sitting straight and rigid beside Darrell.

"We're here . . ." she said.

"Yes. This is home . . ."

Stafford stopped near the gate. Darrell held Emily's arm, kept her sitting beside him. Though there were no tall white columns, the house loomed white before them. On either side of the gate Cape jasmine bloomed. The windows of the house were dark.

Stafford was already on the ground and taking out the bags when Darrell released her arm. He got out of the surrey and lifted Emily down.

Stafford said, "On the porch, Mista Darrell?"

"Fine," Darrell said.

Stafford took all three bags at once. Darrell leaned over the gate and broke the tallest jasmine bloom. "This is very special. My grandmother brought this cutting back from South Carolina three years ago. It always blooms very late."

"Maybe she won't like our taking her blooms."

"She's not here."

"How do you know? She may be back by now."

"The surrey shed is empty. Very simple."

"You're clever again."

"I can't help it. It's just in me. People can't help what's inside of them."

"Not as long as they keep it inside."

Stafford came back through the gate, his body straight almost to awkwardness, his long arms and full-set wrists swishing against his clothes.

"Thank you for bringing us home, Stafford. If I don't get to the gin until noon-time tomorrow, you take care of everything for me."

Stafford smiled. "Yessuh." He seemed to spring into the surrey and drive away.

"You want another one?" Darrell said.

She held the small bloom against her lips. "No. One is enough."

They went up the bricklaid walk, slowly, but not touching each other. At the front steps he put his arm around her, and his arm was still around her when the other hand reached out to open the hall door. The knob turned. He pushed. His arm fell away from Emily. "It's locked."

"Locked?"

"Yes. She might at least leave the door open."

"She had to lock it, Darrell."

"People around here are not that bad to steal. We hardly ever lock it."

Emily began to laugh. Darrell took his hand away from the knob.

"I'm glad it strikes you funny."

"It does. I guess we can sit on the steps and wait."

"No. We can go through the window. I'll bet a Yankee-dime it's not latched." He went to the window. The sash lifted easily. "You see. It takes a little forethought." He crawled into his own room, holding the window up with one hand. He fitted the latch into the notch so that the window would remain up.

233

"Well, I can't very gracefully lift you over the threshold but come on in."

The square of moonlight was suddenly there, the figure in the window, the arm lifted, only there was no glimmer of moonlight from bright steel. He wanted to back away from her then as he had backed away from Nolie once, but he stood rigid, staring into her face.

"What's the matter?"

He tried to laugh. "Everything but the bright blade," he said, suddenly, not meaning to.

"What is it?"

"Nothing. I was thinking about something that happened a long time ago."

"Tell me," she said.

"Nothing. Something about the window."

"Why don't you tell me?"

"All right," he said, as if something was being drawn from him. "It was nothing but Roger coming through the window one night with a knife opened trying to scare me. It was a long time ago. We were little."

"I thought you didn't live here when you were little."

"Did I say it was here?"

"No."

"Well."

"I didn't mean anything."

"I know you didn't."

"But sometimes you are strange to me," she said. "Like all of a sudden tonight you tell Mr. Pitt you saw Miriam in New Orleans, and I felt right foolish, because I didn't know when or where or how or anything."

"Do you want me to tell you what happened?"

"Would it be the truth?"

"I don't know whether it would be or not. He asked me a

234

question tonight and I told him. I never have, and I never intend to lie to Malcolm Pitt."

"What about me?"

"What do you want to know? Just now you kept asking about that window. Something foolish. Something that would never mean anything to you either way. But I had to tell you something, because you couldn't take No."

"Yes," she said. "Something . . . anything . . ."

He was breathing long and hard and labored, and with each breath his heart was thudding. He seemed lost in the moon-lit shadow of her figure, smothered beneath a dark woman-shadow which his hands could not push away.

"You don't think I love you," she said. "Do you want me to go home? Do you want to take me back?"

"Do you want me to?"

She was suddenly against his body, her face under his chin, crying so that he could barely hear her whisper, "I love you so much, Darrell . . ."

"I know you do, darling. It was all my fault, and everything was wrong here . . . hush crying . . ." He was taking her coat off and then his fingers fumbled with the cone-like buttons of her blouse. She was close against him.

In the darkness he turned the covers back, and then he could feel at once the sudden chill of the fresh, unironed sheets and her body quivering a little against him. "Are you cold?"

"I'm not cold, but . . ." Her voice seemed to choke. She was close against him again.

"We'll be warm in a minute."

"I'm not cold, but . . ." She stopped again, still trembling a little.

She seemed to grow still in his arms, to feel the warmth between them. He was gentle with her, more gentle than he had ever been. His moistened lips whispered in her face, his whole

235

body waited. Her fingers sought him slowly. He followed her touch, waiting, whispering, following again. She pushed him. He moved away. He thought she was going to cry, but she only called his name in smooth whispered syllables that seemed to hang on the dampness about her lips.

Her fingers pulled him and again he gave to her touch, breath-drawn, slow, stalling, though he wanted then to be fierce and sudden. But in the very stalling was a new tenderness for him. Again he waited, as if she could belong completely to him for a space so brief that it could be measured only by heart-beats in his ear. He held to that time which was slipping swiftly away from his gripping, searching muscles; and in the center of this, faint and sharp, he heard the surrey stop at the gate, heard his grandmother's voice darting in the moonlight and darkness, "Just leave the surrey at the barn, Yancey. And remember to come early. You wake him, Louella . . ."

He held his quick breath, raised his lips slowly from her face; his fingers could feel the heart-beats in her throat. Against his cheek her lips whispered, but he did not hear her. He heard only the steps along the porch, the snap of handbag, the twitch of keys, and the easy flick of the lock.

"It's Grandmother," he said. He tried to move away from her, but her fingers were tight in his back.

"Don't. You can't now . . . don't . . . she'll think we're asleep."

"With our bags still on the porch? She'll come in here."

"Darrell?"

"What . . ."

"Please don't."

"She'll come in here I tell you."

"Are you afraid of her?"

"Dammit . . ." He moved away from Emily. "I'll have to dress."

236

"Your robe's in the suitcase."

"I've got another one in the closet." He lifted the covers a little, waiting, listening. The footsteps were in the hall.

"Hurry, Darrell . . ."

"Wait till I see if she goes to her room first. I'm not burdened with clothes."

He heard the door to the living room open and close. He pushed the covers away from him. "I reckon the Lord did give folks darkness so they wouldn't go crazy, and I'm included."

"What are you talking about . . . ?"

Without answering he took his underwear from the chair, then went barefooted toward the closet and found his robe, and a pair of house shoes. At the washstand he poured out a basin of water and fumbled in the darkness for soap.

"Do you want a glass of water?"

"Please."

He took the water back to the bed, but before he gave it to her he leaned over and touched her face with his cheek though he did not kiss her. She took the glass and drank. He put it back on the washstand.

"I'll go in for a minute. I'll tell her that you are already in bed."

Emily did not answer, but she touched his hand as if to keep him there though she knew he must go.

He opened the living room door only wide enough to slip through it, and closed it cautiously behind him. His grandmother stood as if she was waiting for him, as if she knew that he would come at that very moment. On the dresser beside her the lamp burned steadily. He thought she stood straighter, more unbending, than he had ever seen; he thought, too, that she looked much older than that time when he had last thought to mark her age.

"Well," she said. "You've come home."

"There was nowhere else to go," he said.

Her chin snapped quickly in a movement which he could not tell the direction of, but he knew it snapped. She seemed not to expect what he had said; nor to know whether she had won the first brief skirmish. He walked nearer to her, toward the hearth, with the rope-belt of his robe threading his fingers and circling his wrist.

She came closer to him and stood on the hearth. "That perfume about you is much too strong."

"There's no perfume on me."

"Well, maybe it's from her, or from Memphis."

"We didn't go to Memphis. We went to New Orleans."

"New Orleans. So you stepped into the quickest quicksand you could find. I wish you could know how much it hurts me to see you shaken away from everything you ought to hold on to. What does Malcolm Pitt think of you now?"

"I guess he thinks whatever he always thought."

"Look at me when you answer. You don't want to talk about it because you're ashamed. We all are."

"Well, he met us at the train. That's something."

"He forgives too easily. You'll pay when the time comes. And now that you have a wife I suppose you feel like censuring me."

"No."

"Let me tell you that what I have done is for your good. It was to remind you . . ."

"I want to forget it. You've kept my letters. You didn't come to my wedding, you didn't meet the train, and you locked the door knowing we were coming home. I don't want to talk about any of it any more. It's over and done with."

She turned her face and all the rest of her body was perfectly still. She whispered, as someone trying not to cry. "I don't know what's come over you. It seems no time ago that you were

238

sweet and kind and good, and now you don't act like my child at all. You trample . . . trample . . ."

He took her arm. "Grandmother . . ."

"Where is she?" she said, turning close to him.

"She's already in bed." His hand dropped from her arm. About her was the scrouging smell of rose geraniums, the dead petal-smell like stifling dust.

She straightened the shawl about her shoulders. Her eyes seemed focused on his mouth. "I tried to save you. But I started fifty years too late. I can see the paths a long way back, paths you can never look back on. It was a blessing your grandfather died at Vicksburg. You think I wept for him. I never did. He was weak. We didn't lose our land because of the War. It was dribbling away from us before Vicksburg fell. And your own father came to nothing, because he was afraid, because the blood was weak in him too. I didn't weep because a strong man died. I wept for him because he was my son."

"Grandmother . . ."

"But I couldn't falter, because of you. Your face promised everything to me. Such beauty in you and such strength and I hoped for so much. Even from the time I washed you in a dishpan I could feel the strength in you. I couldn't even begrudge the land we had lost because I thought the hard days we had come on, the shoes you needed and didn't have, would test your mettle. I lived through a time when men fell because of luxury and vanity."

"Malcolm Pitt doesn't think my grandfather failed."

"Because Malcolm Pitt came back. He was stronger than the rest."

"He'd never say that. He remembers as well as you and he never forgot what my grandfather did."

She gripped the lapel of his robe then, not for need of

strength, but as if her arm would be the bridge over which even her thoughts might travel with a new force that he could not shy from.

She said, "Your face hurts me. Favored at once with something strong as hickory and soft as damp roses. If you were so determined I wish it had been Miriam. It would have been better. I don't know what you're searching for. You know so little of what life can do. You don't know how God can try you, try you until you cry out at midnight, until you come to an end like the others before you, without love. Your grandfather never loved me, your father never loved your mother. I can't bear to watch this again—in your face . . ." She touched his cheek. He did not move at all.

She turned quickly to the clock on the mantel and, opening the glass face, moved the hands back one hour. "I know what time it is . . . and I know now how many years of my life have come to nothing. Tomorrow, before you get up, I'll be on the train for Charleston. I'm going to my brother's. This is my last goodbye." She was crying, so easily that it was almost beautiful to him. She kissed him, partly touching his lips, and again he did not move at all.

He said, "Grandmother, you're upset over nothing. You'll feel better in the morning. Good night." Then he walked out of the room, and after he had stood on the porch for a while he took the three suitcases at once and went into his room.

Beside him, under the covers, Emily was warm and soft; but he turned away from her though he reached behind him and pulled her arm around his body.

She whispered, "What's the matter?"

He only held her hand tightly and with his arm pressed her arm against his body. He was ashamed that he did not want to turn to her, that he should lie with his face toward the window listening to breath and to time outside four walls. He did

240

not believe that his grandmother was going away, but he could hear her words now even with more clearness than when he stood, robe-clad, upon the hearth. And something was twisted, coiled as easily as he had coiled the robe's belt around his wrist. Perhaps it was in him, maybe not new at all but reaching a long way back, hidden from eyes, lost from touch, and intervolved in breath and thought and pulse beats. *Until you come to an end like the others before you, without love.*

He lay now beside warmth, smelling the perfume on clean tender flesh; and the perfume was at once stronger and more pressing than the scent of rose-geraniums had ever been. He drew his knees up a little and tucked his head down as when he, being a child with Roger, had often placed himself, head between knees, in a barrel and rolled down some grassy slope. Now in his half-sleep and half-dreams he seemed to be rolling slowly into a warm damp nothingness, scentless and safe. Finally he slept.

Before full light came, he heard steps in the hall, heard the surrey once again at the gate. He shoved the covers away from him and ran barefooted to the window. He saw Yancey helping his grandmother into the surrey. Against the frosty half-light of morning he saw her ride away, straight, slender, unbending, not once looking back.

Behind him Emily was calling, "What is it, Darrell? What is it?"

But he did not answer her.

· FIVE

one

In the months that followed, Darrell sometimes remembered the straight, unbending figure as clearly as he had seen it ride away in that frosty half-light of morning. Sometimes he thought fleetingly that he was compelled to a strange path which his grandmother had certainly foreseen. But always he was able to deny it, though he could not always shut her face from his mind's eye, could not always erase: *You don't know how God can try you, try you until you cry at midnight, until you come to an end like the others before you, without love.*

He did not try to tell Emily why his grandmother had gone because he knew only a part of the answer. Twice he tried to tell Malcolm Pitt, who listened with his eyes unmoving though fingering his chin so that even his well-shaven beard scraped against the touch; and each time Darrell knew that words tricked him. He stopped, speechless; and Malcolm had said, with the hearty crinkles about his eyes, "Well, boy, she's not as young as we are. Maybe it's better . . ."

He did not know, until his grandmother was gone, how her words and even the silence in her face had sometimes held him,

242

how often she had pointed to something so that he did not have to decide for himself. It was suddenly, like a bird-flock swooping at dusk, that everything lay in his hands, the little answers, the little plans. For this, too, he missed her. But with this change before him he thought to become more a part of that realm of vigorous, hard-tanned men about the gin, the store, the barn, who had come to accept their days with a vigorous peacefulness, who seemed to need no more than what they had, either in light or darkness, and whose desires, unlike his own, seemed never to change.

He walked there among them, his arms strong, his face lean and tanned; and it was he who turned the brass valve so that the gin belts moved into that steady drone. But somewhere in him where the gin's drone did not fathom, where the sun's rays did not touch, there seemed a need for something more, and the need was compressed and bound, harder than any cotton.

On the day before Thanksgiving, almost three months after his grandmother had gone away, Darrell had his first real quarrel with Emily. It was very brief but it seemed to tear something within him beyond mending. That morning he had started to the gin and Emily said, "I want to go to Mother's tomorrow for Thanksgiving and I want you to take me."

"But I can't take you," he said. "A lot of cotton is coming in. We've got to work tomorrow."

"On Thanksgiving day?"

"Yes."

"That's almost a sin. You might as well work on Sunday. Nobody works on Thanksgiving."

"We do—if there's work to be done."

"You and the Pitts."

"Yes, me and the Pitts."

"It couldn't be that you don't want to take me because Miriam is back. She came home yesterday."

"I told you I had to work."

"Have you seen her yet?"

"No."

"And you won't take me."

"Emily . . ." His face trembled a little in anger. "We've got seventeen bales of cotton coming in tomorrow."

"I don't care. I don't ask much of you. I'll go without you. I'll go by myself and stay until I get ready to come back."

"Go ahead! And don't ever come back if you don't want to." He went out of the house quickly and when he reached the gate Emily was calling after him.

He went back to the porch and kissed her and she stopped crying and said, "I'm sorry . . . I'm sorry, darling. Tell me you didn't mean what you said."

All that day at the gin he was quiet, even while he worked with Malcolm Pitt. Early in the afternoon Malcolm left and Darrell, as if he were twelve, felt lost in a world of man-talk and man-laughter. He thought he might never belong to the men in overalls who squatted in a circle about the boiler, now and then spitting brown juice, and whose hands were hard and clumsy though their eyes burned with a kindness that seemed sometimes to say, "There is only one religion: to visit the sick and care for the poor." They laughed, and he was among them, touching them, brushing against clothes far more faded than his own; and the desire to be more than among them, to be one, mounted in him slowly like the whetted appetite of a child mounts who stands beneath the tree and gazes up toward a mellow September pear hanging far beyond his reach.

He was glad that day when they were gone and the gin was quiet. At dusk he stood alone looking out the office window of the gin. The air was warm, too warm for November, so that he had his coverall sleeves rolled above his elbows in small neat folds, and had the office window open. He was watching Nolie sitting straight and slender on the millpond bank; only one arm seemed to move. He thought that he might call out to her, not that he had formed any words to say, but he wanted to call, to be daring. But before he said anything he saw Malcolm Pitt in the gin-yard below him, getting out of his surrey and coming toward the gin-ladder. The sight of Malcolm Pitt made his whole body ease. He turned to face the doorway and to listen to the steps on the ladder. Malcolm came through the door, husky and grinning, and even in the dusk Darrell thought he could see every crinkle about his eyes.

"What you doing here this late? Your wife will think you fell in the gin-well."

"How did you know I was here?"

"I saw your surrey. I thought something might be wrong."

"Nothing's wrong. Not with the gin anyway."

"With what then?"

"Nothing. I was joking."

"I'm going to Waycrest for a little while. Betran Wilcox is meeting a few over there to talk politics. They're picking somebody to run for the legislature. He asked me about you. Said he could put you in just like putting a teat in a calf's mouth."

"What did you tell him?"

"I told him to go to hell." Malcolm moved to the desk and sat on the edge of it. "I wish you were ready and could drive over there with me. I hate to go by myself."

Malcolm reached into his pocket and took out a small bright bladed knife and a plug of brown tobacco. He cut off one corner of the plug and said, "Here. Have a chew with me. You're a married man now." He held out the tobacco and Darrell took it. Then Malcolm began to laugh and took the tobacco from Darrell's hand. "You're too clean for this, and politics."

When Malcolm put the small brown square between his

bright teeth Darrell could feel his own body flush all over. They waited in the dusk not saying anything to each other. Then Malcolm got off the desk and spat out the window and said, "I've got to go." Darrell watched him go down the ladder and listened until he could no longer hear the surrey in the darkness.

He went out to the weighing platform, leaving his leather jacket in the office, and watched Nolie on the pond bank. There on the platform he could see the light from Malcolm Pitt's house. After a while he ran down the ladder and when he was halfway to the house he began to walk. At the front gate he waited. He did not want his face to be damp when he went up the front steps. He pulled the gate ajar and leaned upon it. He could hear the piano.

He entered the hall without knocking and stopped and waited in the living room doorway. He was directly behind Miriam and she was the distance of the room away from him. For a minute he thought, This is not really Miriam or else I am not really here; we can not both be here together. He could not call the name of what she played, but he knew it because he had felt it before in some other age too far away to remember. It did not matter—not knowing the name—because it needed no name anyway.

He waited, like standing at a window with nose and forehead against cold glass, not seeing the glass, only feeling it, and watching the snowbirds come closer and closer to the window sill outside, knowing the fingers could not touch even one quivering feather.

He believed that he did not call her name. But her hands dropped on the keys. She turned. Then she stood up. "What are you doing here?"

"To tell you what a little priss you are."

"You knew Father was not here."

His laugh mocked her. "Your conceit makes me laugh. If

246

you think my heart has skipped any beats over you—you might as well know it hasn't."

"Neither has mine. Why did you come?"

"To laugh at you."

"You make me tired."

"You've made me tired for a long time."

"You can go home. With those greasy coveralls you look worse than Stafford."

"I'll go when I get ready. This place belongs to your father."

"Why he likes you, I don't know."

"I'll tell you why. He's got more goodness in his little finger than you've got all over you."

She came a step toward him and he watched her hands, the slender fingers buff in the lamplight, as if his eyes could not move upward. Her fingers curled. "I despise you," she said.

"Do you think I love you? I don't. I never have. You're a conceited little nothing. I don't see how you could have come from Malcolm Pitt. You're not Roger's sister. You're a little . . ." The tears came into his eyes and onto his cheeks and he could hardly see her. She was coming toward him and suddenly she stopped and something seemed to stop within him too. Her face trembled and she was crying very hard.

"Please go, Darrell . . . Please . . ."

"Don't make me go."

"You know you must . . ."

"Miriam . . . what are we going to do?"

"Leave . . . I'm going to Europe after Christmas . . . with Aunt Susan . . ."

"You can't."

"Please don't make it any harder . . . I hate myself . . . Please . . ."

He went away from her quickly, remembering that her hand

was lifted as if to hold him. He did not remember exactly, for he had turned so that he could not see her at all. By the time his mind was clear again he was already outside and closing the gate.

He did not go directly to the gin. He went toward the lot gate and the pasture. All the Negroes were gone from the lot and he walked in the alley of the barn alone, slowly, smelling strong stallion scent and the rich odor of clover seed packed in the hayloft. He crossed through the lot fence and went toward the railroad tracks. He walked on the crossties toward the millpond, long step, short step, smelling the creosote and the dew-damp steel. When the pond was adjacent to him he made the right angle like a well-trained soldier and went toward the gin. He wanted to find Nolie and he found her.

She was standing up as though to take one more last look at the gin before leaving. When he climbed up the pond bank she turned to face him, her eyes bright in the dusk. She shook her head, a smile weaving across her face.

"There's a cricket in the thicket. You've been trifling with her affections."

"Whose?"

"People don't always come back the same way they went. What did Miriam tell you?"

"Nothing. I didn't ask her anything."

"Why didn't you? Mr. Pitt is in Waycrest."

"Is he?"

"Yes."

"You ought to be a spy, Nolie. You'd be good at it."

"I'd like that. Let's you and me join up and be spies."

"I'm ready."

"Is Emily jealous yet?"

"Of you?"

"No. Miriam."

248

"She may be."

"She will be."

"You've got it all sketched out. Do you know the colors in it and what the end will be?"

"You mean this sketch here?"

"Hell, no."

"Oh. You mean your own private circlings. No. I don't know the end."

"It wouldn't surprise me if you did. You're a little devil." He took her quickly and kissed her.

"Turn me loose before I charcoal a picture on your cheek."

"You want me to drive you home?"

"No. What would folks think of a married man taking me home?"

"A lot less than staying out here. You want me to?"

"I guess so if it'll give you any pleasure. You are sweet sometimes. I don't know why."

They started toward the surrey. He took the canvas for her. She walked a little ahead of him. He began to feel cold. He thought to roll down his sleeves but he did not. He watched her hair, long and soft-looking, bounce over her ear and touch her cheek. She pushed it back. At the surrey he gave her the canvas. She put it in the front seat.

"I've got to go up and get my jacket and lock the office."

"Don't forget your hat," she said.

"Go with me."

"You don't need me."

"Well, I could get along without you, but it'd be better with you." He pulled at her arm.

After a moment she followed his pull. On the ladder she said, "I wonder when I'm going to start hating you."

He did not answer her. On the weighing platform he turned her hand loose, still without speaking, and went into the office.

He jerked the window down, took his jacket and put it on without rolling his sleeves down. Then he locked the office door.

"What's the matter?" she said.

"Nothing. We're going home."

"Darrell . . . I didn't mean . . ."

"Nothing is the matter. Except that I sometimes act like a goddam fool, hurting people one after another without any sense about what I've done until it's too late. I'm ashamed of myself. I don't know what's the matter with me."

"Come on," she said. She took his arm and they went down the ladder to the surrey. He thought, I guess I didn't want to partly because she said yes so easily.

They drove to her house without speaking though twice he touched her hand lightly, warmly. When she stepped out of the surrey at her gate, he thought she understood something about him which nobody else knew, perhaps even himself.

Half the distance home he kept his eyes closed, not for tiredness, but to shut out things around him which he did not want to see nor to touch nor to remember. His hands were aimless on the lines; he knew the mares would trot toward home. He did not put the surrey in its shed. He left it in the lot and stabled the mares, leaving the stable doors open so the mares could water at the pond during the night. He walked to the house slowly, telling himself there was nothing to be afraid of now, that he knew the path which he must walk, that he would walk it with the same space between his chin and chest as Malcolm Pitt.

His step was slow and mechanical, as if every maneuver which he would make had been planned in detail. It was a little like a man might walk in a time of death, not as one might go crying, but too proud and too strong to give way that much to flesh. He believed, or seemed to believe, that he knew what he was seeking, and he would go straight to it, forgetting all the devious ways.

It was then, at the gate, that he began to remember Emily's face, her body, the shape of wrist, the shape of breast, that he had touched and thrilled to in another time which seemed far back though it was no more than two weeks ago. He thought he had suddenly become old. He did not have much time to find what he was looking for. He saw her through the window, in the lamplight.

Emily met him in the hall. She was trim and neat, smelling of lavender soap so that in her presence he suddenly knew the gin-odor-man-smell was about him, perhaps in the same way it was sometimes about Malcolm Pitt. Her apron strings circled her waist tightly twice, and the bow, double knot style, was tied in front.

"I thought something had happened, Darrell."

"Nothing. I should have been here before now." He pulled his jacket off. She took it.

"Your water is ready."

"Thank you." He started to turn from her, then he stopped. He took the apron bow and unloosed it. Then he went on to his bath, remembering her smile, glad that he had unloosed the bow, glad that he had her smile to remember.

He was slow bathing, looking at his body for a long time, now and then flexing his leg so that his thigh-muscles and calf-muscles bulged and shone in the lamplight that fell on his over-soaped skin. When he had bathed he went about the house in his robe seeming to do nothing but breathe quietly. He drank two glasses of milk. He did not eat at all. He told Emily that he was not hungry, which was the truth, but was a thing she did not understand until he had kissed her. Then she seemed to understand.

251

His voice was harsh only once that night. He was already lying in bed and Emily was moving about in the room. He did not know what she was doing because his eyes were closed, to shut out something. At first he called to her quietly, gently, as a man who is thinking about something other than his speech. The light remained on. He put his arm across his eyes and heard her moving in the room again. He thought a long time had passed while he waited for her. It was then that his voice leaped too harshly, "Come on to bed . . ."

He felt the light go, the darkness come. He turned on his side and held the covers up for her. When the covers were settled again he began to take off his underwear which he had put on only a few minutes before. He thought she might say again that he ought to wear pajamas. But she did not say anything.

He touched her and pulled her to him, feeling her smooth silken gown against his unclothed body. It was neither warm nor cold, but it seemed almost like sensitive flesh. He put his lips against her ear. "Do you know what tonight is going to be?"

"No."

"The night of our first son . . ."

After a long time of stillness she said, faintly, "It may not be a son . . ."

"It will be," he said. He was touching the gown. "Take it off." He thought she was crying so he touched her lips with his fingers. He whispered, "Are you crying, darling?"

She said, "No . . ."

"Don't," he said. "We've both learned enough by now to want him born at least from gentleness."

252

two

There were two sons instead of one, and almost the first thing that Darrell thought when they were born was that neither of them could be named Malcolm. Emily's mother was there—moving about with her bird-like precision—and she insisted that the naming must be done by Darrell, for the twins *were* boys. She also insisted that her grandsons would have Emily's eyes, their grandfather Townsend's hands, and (being male) Darrell's body. And one day while she stood beside Malcolm Pitt and watched the twins she said, "I hope they have my nose. People have always told me that I have a good nose."

"Yes, ma'am, you have," Malcolm said, as if he was much younger than she.

After that she led him to the porch and talked to him for hours. When he left she came into Emily's room as if her little body moved with a new energy and said, "Now, daughter, that's a gentleman from head to foot. I wish you could name both your sons after him."

At the end of her week's visit she stayed an extra day so that she might see Malcolm Pitt when he came to the house again.

When the twins were two weeks old Darrell lay on the bed beside Emily one night and watched Louella diaper his sons. He watched their pink bodies which seemed all hands and feet and a shock of pleasure seemed suddenly to come upon him as if he had only then realized that they were sons, the very heart of strength.

When Louella left the cribs and went out of the room Darrell sat up in bed and looked at Emily propped against her pillows reading. A completeness had come over him and he imagined that he was feeling now what Malcolm Pitt had felt when Roger was born. But with his pleasure was a sadness, a feeling that he had taken everything from Emily now to make himself complete. She held a hand to her cheek as she read and he could see the dark orbs of her eyes moving across the page in little gaps. Her face was clear now, not flushed, and her body looked young again. That was something he had not taken away. He took the book from her hand pulled her face to his gently and kissed her. "I want to talk," he said. He pointed to the cribs. "We're going to have good sons—they've got their nights and days straight."

Her hand was in his and both their hands lay across the open book.

"I'll have Louella stay here all the time and help you. You'll need her, with two boys to see after."

"I'm glad they were boys," she said. "I'm glad for you." After a while she said: "But you can't name either one of them Malcolm now, can you?"

"No," he said. "I can't name them Malcolm, or Malcolm and Roger either, now they're twins."

"Let me name them."

"All right." He leaned over and kissed her. "You name them."

"I want to call them Leland and Roland, after my brothers. Is that good?"

It did not seem right to him, for in his mind he still saw names of others who were closer to him. But he whispered, "That's good." He looked at the cribs again. "They won't remember a thing that's happening to them now."

"What is the first thing you remember?" she said.

"The first thing? Standing on a hill holding a rim in my hand."

254

"And the second thing?" They were whispering now.

"I think it was putting my finger in hot cornbread. It was on a green plate. What about you?"

"The first thing was about Father. I think it was touching his teeth and feeling him bite down on my fingers."

Darrell held her hand to his lips playfully and pressed his teeth against her fingers. Then he got up and put out the light and came back to bed and held her hand tightly. He would have given her anything that night.

By the time the twins were two years old Malcolm took them in the surrey with him, usually on Sunday afternoons, and drove across the fields, though he never took them away from the house unless Darrell, not Emily, gave permission. By the time Leland and Roland were three, Malcolm no longer asked permission, for they were always dressed and waiting for their trip and when the surrey arrived they ran to the gate and waited for Malcolm Pitt to lift them. Sometimes Darrell stood on the porch and watched his sons leave with Malcolm, and though he was proud he was also hurt when he saw the light on their faces as they rode away; but he was hurt only because he was not going along.

Malcolm taught them to call him by his first name and Emily quarreled with Darrell that he should allow such a thing to happen to his sons. Darrell said, "I wouldn't feel right to change a teaching of Malcolm Pitt. If it must be undone, you'll have to undo it."

"Whose sons are they?" Emily said. But she either did not try to change that one particular of their manners or else did not succeed.

At the gin Aaron Gammel had said, "Your family is growing faster than Leighton, Darrell. Two at a time." And it was

Eldon Roper who had said, "He's just gettin' while the gettin's good."

When Malcolm Pitt held the twins he sometimes said, "We better go ahead and buy another sawmill, Darrell, so you'll have something for these boys to do in a few years. I reckon if I'd had twin boys I'd 'a' made me a fortune in cotton or lumber or something." Then he would put them down and say, "Hell, more than likely I'd 'a' ruined them."

Darrell wrote to his grandmother about the twins. Almost at regular intervals each month afterwards she wrote a letter, always addressed to Masters Leland and Roland Barclay, that she was well and that Uncle Turner was well, and that they wanted to see the twins.

Once, while Darrell and Malcolm were filing the ginsaws, and when there was reason to speak of nothing but the work before them, Malcolm suddenly said above the scrape of his file, "Dammit, Darrell, looks like you're gonna have to give Roger one of your boys if I'm ever to have a grandson."

Darrell had laughed, because it was during those days that he felt he had conquered some turbulent will inside himself, though perhaps he felt, too, that he had conquered it only for a space of time. Yet he must have felt, also, that time and chance and circumstance had helped to defeat whatever part of himself that he was fighting against. After that night when he saw Miriam at the piano, when he had said everything that he did not mean, he did not see her alone, for soon after Christmas of that year she sailed to Europe with her Aunt Susan.

There were cards from Miriam, always addressed to Mr. and Mrs. Darrell Barclay. Perhaps it was a year later that the first letter came. It was from Italy, postmarked Napoli; and in the letter, Darrell thought, was nothing more than what a sister might have written: "We live on the very edge of the bay here, on a tall cliff, so that the waves seem almost to lash beneath us.

It makes Aunt Susan's head swim even to look out our window. I know that with a little practice I could land a coin in the salt water below. To our right is the Isle of Capri, and looking directly out of our window we can see the smoke curling above Vesuvius in the daytime and at night we can see the flame, a little like a globeless lamp in distant darkness. Yesterday, when we came back from the San Carlo opera house (which Aunt Susan is determined to go to at least three times a week even if it means seeing a repeat performance) our mail had caught up with us. Along with letters from Mother, from Roger and Anne, there was even a letter from Father. Father's letter is a triumph because Roger accuses Father of never having written him but two letters during all his time away at school. Half of Father's letter was about your twin boys . . ." And when he could find nothing in the letter that belonged only to him, he tried to imagine the letter's being only for Emily.

That was the first letter. There were others which came to the gin because Yancey brought all the mail there. Each time that Darrell looked at the blue envelope which was at once foreign and familiar, seeing no more than the postmark Napoli, and before he even took the letter from Yancey's dark hand, his certainty, his grip, his sure control which he believed he now possessed, would suddenly give way. It was after he had read the letter and when he would begin to fold it back into its envelope that his stomach seemed smothered in water. He would go down to the boiler, talk to Yancey and Stafford, trying to tell himself with talk to them that this feeling was only for a moment. He would stand with his face a little feverish, his stomach flushed like a medicined laborer, until finally, ashamed, he would go to the gin's out-house.

By evening, when he rode home from the gin with his hand about the letter in his coat pocket, he would try to decide whether he was glad or whether he wanted to crush the letter

257

in his pocket, fling it toward the clay road-ditch, and curse the crumpled ball in mid-flight. But he always took the letter home and gave it to Emily to read. Each time he thought of Malcolm Pitt saying, "When a man tells the exact truth or acts completely honest folks are apt not to believe him—they're so unused to it." Emily, when she had read the letters, never said anything more than, "Well, she seems to have everything she wants. I wish I could travel like that sometime. But I guess a woman with two babies wasn't meant to get very far from home."

Darrell had written to Miriam twice in the three years since she had gone. Perhaps when he sat down in the gin's office that morning to write his third letter to her he meant to write impersonally of that which would concern anyone who had been from home three years. But when he had written half a page, in his neat though uncompressed style, he stopped. He knew there was something in Miriam's recent letter about which he wanted to write. He closed his eyes and tried to reproduce the last page which she had written. He could remember distinctly two sentences that came at the top of the page, could remember every peculiarity of her spare and unadorned handwriting, even to the heavy crossed t's and the initial vowels always disjoined: *Along with my singing I am learning to paint. Aunt Susan who always was good at painting flowers on glass thinks I have talent. You and Emily* . . . Then he could not remember any more, and though his forgetting might have been a trivial thing he sat fretting at the desk.

Perhaps he did not really want to recall whatever it was that had escaped him, or perhaps some deeper thing, some knowledge too old and too elusive to remark, had made him feel even before he sat down at the desk that he would never finish the letter. He sat tense, staring through the window into the morning light of that November day which no darkness and no time was ever to wipe from his memory.

He took his pen again, ready to write, thinking, I will remember later whatever it is. It was then that Malcolm Pitt stood in the doorway of the office without Darrell ever having heard the sound of one foot.

"Have you seen Roger?"

Darrell turned in his chair while he was still hearing the words. Malcolm Pitt, not leaning, but erect with one hand against the jamb, seemed to fill the doorway. His face was morning-red from the clean shave. The fingers of his free hand played across his chin and cheek. Darrell had understood each word, and knew that he had, yet he heard himself saying, "Sir?", as if to make Malcolm Pitt's lips keep on moving.

"Has Roger been down here this morning?"

"No, sir."

"I thought he might be here. He came home last night for Thanksgiving."

"I didn't know he was coming until today," Darrell said. "Is Anne with him?"

"No. Such a short time off for Thanksgiving that she stayed with her folks." He let his hand fall away from the jamb. He stooped a little to scratch his knee and then he straightened again. "Damn, I don't know where he went to. Just like Roger to mosey off somewhere when he's needed. His mother wanted him to ride out to Cless Bynum's and get the turkey for tomorrow."

"A white one?"

Malcolm's eyes were bright. "Yes. That white flock he's got looks like a young snow storm on foot. They're beauties. The finest I've ever seen. It makes me hungry to watch 'em walk around in the yard. I had him put a couple up and feed them corn-mash in milk."

"Sounds tender enough."

"They will be. And with good dressing." He winked suddenly as Roger might have done. "You can't beat it. But good dressing depends on the right amount of sage." He stopped and touched the brightness of his cheeks again slowly. "Leta said for me to make sure that you and Emily came to eat with us tomorrow."

"Well, I don't know. Emily thinks the boys are so much trouble to move around . . ."

"Hell. Louella can do that. She loves to have her hands full with them. Good for them too."

Malcolm started across the room. Darrell let his arm fall across the few lines of the letter which he had written.

"Is Stafford busy?" Malcolm said.

"He's piddling around the boiler."

Malcolm went behind the desk to the window which was already open, and leaned out. "Hey, down there?"

Darrell could see neither Yancey nor Stafford but in the sudden stillness he heard above the slow sound of steam, "I druther be called a beggar twelve times ovah than a rogue once. But I stood with my lips touchin'. I knowed what might happen. Then they'd be some slow drivin', sad music, dirt throwin', and no dodgin'. And no tellin' who it'd be . . ."

Malcolm called down toward the boiler room, "Stafford?"

"Yessuh."

"What are you doing?"

"Hepping Yancey with the gauge down here. It's not doing right."

"You know where Roger went?"

"He's up town gettin' a haircut."

"Well, I want you to ride out to the Bynum place and get the Thanksgiving turkey. Better be back before noon if you want any turkey tomorrow."

"Yessuh."

260

Malcolm turned to Darrell. "Do we need Stafford down here any more today?"

Darrell shook his head. "No, sir, I don't reckon so."

"Stafford. When you get back, stay up there and help at the house. Just get one now. I've got another one out there, but it's for Christmas."

"One. Yessuh."

"What's the matter with that gauge?"

"I don't know suh. It jist ain't acting right."

"Well, hurry up with the turkey."

"Yessuh."

Malcolm moved back from the window and half-leaned against the desk where Darrell still sat. "You reckon we'll have any cotton this afternoon?"

"I doubt it."

"What you say we clean the gin-heads, splice that main belt again, oil everything, and close up till Monday?"

"Be fine."

"And I reckon right in the middle of it some damned shirttail full of cotton will drive up."

"Likely."

Then Malcolm sat on the edge of the long oaken desk and his stout fingers kept rubbing across his knee. He pulled up his pants-leg and pecked at his knee with one finger. "You see that red spot?"

Darrell nodded, watching the heavy calf-muscle flex.

"If it was a little warmer I'd swear I had a tick right in the center of my kneecap. It couldn't be a chigger so I don't know what the hell it is." He pushed the pants-leg down. "Who you writing to?"

Darrell knew he was going to ask it, knew even before the pants-leg slid downward. What he did not know was how he

261

might answer, or even if he might try to laugh and not answer it at all. He gathered the sheet up, could feel it crumpling in his palms, for he was not looking at the sheet but looking up to Malcolm Pitt's face. He thought he might say, "To my grandmother." He even adjusted tongue and lips to say it. But his heart seemed suddenly to unspin like the tight-wound spring of a toy. He shaped his lips again to say, "To my grandmother." But again his heart was unspinning while he watched some infinitesimal shadow of all-knowledge and all-understanding crawl slowly across the face waiting to hear him. He knew the sudden sweat stood on his forehead because he had almost lied to Malcolm Pitt, who knew the answer already. It was like looking over a cliff, then moving quickly backward for fear the guard-rail or even the earth itself might give way and leave the body in mid-air plunging downward, forever damned.

"To Miriam," he said. It was no more than a whisper. He stood up. His eyes left Malcolm for a moment.

Malcolm Pitt did not move off the desk. His hand moved up and down his thigh slowly. His cheeks caved neither to smile nor laugh, but the color around his eyes seemed to wrinkle and the small muscles about his temples moved outward. "Do you love her?"

"I don't know."

Only then did Malcolm Pitt let his eyes fall away from Darrell's face. He looked down. He was opening and closing the hand not on his thigh, dragging his fingers across the smooth surface of the oaken desk. "I reckon I didn't have to ask you that, Darrell. I just didn't want either one of you to be hurt, any more—any more than you could help." Then he stood up quickly, his big hand clamped upon Darrell's shoulder. "Come on, boy, and let's get this thing cleaned up. When we start smelling sage in dressing tomorrow we won't feel like working any."

262

All day long they worked side by side. By then, by that year, they had filed enough saws and spliced enough belts so that they did not need to speak to each other. A nod, half a sentence, a brief glance were directions enough for each to the other. There, beside Malcolm, a calmness was about Darrell. It seemed always there in those times because it was a moment of completion for him, his body and mind at once joined to the world of quiet action—an action of which he knew as much as Malcolm Pitt. It was the only sphere of complete calmness he had ever known, a sphere set up by half-sentences which seemed always understood even before they were shaped by his or Malcolm's lips:

"Just a fraction . . ." The voice was halfway between whisper and casualness.

"Yessir . . ." The saws turned.

"A hair more . . ." The saws moved again.

"On the button . . ." The hand reached over. "File."

"Long?"

"Long."

"More?"

"Split the hair . . ."

"Right?"

"Just a wink more . . ."

"Yessir."

The cryptic half-sentences went on so that it seemed to Darrell some urgent communication was passing between them. It was as if they were no longer talking about machinery at all but were speaking about themselves with such natural calmness that sometime, someday, he would be able to tell the shape of his own life to Malcolm Pitt, tell it to him without looking up to him in a voice somewhere between whisper and casualness.

Then he heard a sudden long breath, felt the body beside

him straighten and mold itself tall and strong again. The saws were filed. Together they looked at the bright sharpness and the pale steel-dust they had filed away.

"We put the raw edge on that baby."

"Yessir," Darrell said. He saw the shirtsleeve across the wide brow, and the brief glance from Malcolm meaning: warm, too warm, for Thanksgiving. The tiny creeks of sweat were on their faces.

Then the machinery was oiled; again no directing, only the half-sentence, the nod, the brief glance.

It was three o'clock when they began to splice the belt. Malcolm was saying, "After Christmas we'll go to Memphis and buy another good sawmill from Wentworth. He's got some cracker-jacks . . ." He stopped because Yancey had called to him. Malcolm turned. "What you want, Yancey?"

"These gauges still doing wrong."

"All right. Get up some more steam and we'll be out there after while."

"Yessuh." Yancey went back toward the boiler, talking to himself: "Awright, git to bending, boy, the big man want some steam. Sho. Sho."

The leather splicer cut into the palms of Malcolm's hands again. He looked up at Darrell. "Have those gauges gone bad before?"

"Last week we had a little trouble, but they got all right."

"It may be those damned geese in the millpond have stopped up the tubing. It'll cause the water to foam when the pond's low."

Darrell nodded. They bent to splicing again. Each time that Malcolm jerked the splicer tight Darrell, who was holding the belt in place, thought he could almost hear the wrist muscles leap. The sweat rolled off the back of Malcolm's hands.

"You want me to splice some?" Darrell said.

264

"I'll get it. Not much left."

It was still warm but the sun was almost down when they finished the splicing and stood in the thin misty steam beside the boiler, studying the gauges. Malcolm tested one valve, then another.

"What do you think it is?" Darrell said.

"The damned geese."

"We let it cool off and drain last week," Darrell said. "That might be better."

"I don't know, Darrell." Malcolm opened the drain-valve for a second. He looked back at the gauges. "Hell, I can't tell whether we've got ten pounds of steam or two hundred. What do you think you've got, Yancey?"

"I don't know, suh. I had some steam up all day."

"I reckon you'd better turn the water on," Malcolm said. He moved back from the gauges as if to stand clear of the steam that drifted by his face.

Darrell went to the gin-well, thirty feet away, watched Yancey climb over the boxing, lean down. He watched the hand turn the brass valve. It was then that Malcolm Pitt yelled through the thin steam, the first time Darrell had ever thought that any fear could come into his words. The cry shot through the pale, cheerless light of November, high, too high, for Malcolm's voice, "Wait! The damned thing may be dry!"

Yancey raised up from the valve, slow, unthinking, not hearing. "Suh?"

Darrell shoved at Yancey's shoulders, pushing him back down toward the valve. "Cut it off, dammit, cut it off!" Then Darrell leaped into the gin-well beside Yancey. His hand found the damp brass. He had turned once when the lightning blast of steam sounded above them. The well itself shook. Yancey was hanging madly to his arm. Darrell jerked his arm free. He leaped over the well-boxing, wildly, into the rain of steam and ashes

265

and bark, which was not hot by then but only warm against his skin.

For a moment he did not see anything except the jagged end of the blown-out boiler. Then he saw Malcolm Pitt dimly through the steam and ashes, not tall but slumped, his right arm straining across his chest. Darrell could not move. He only stood, knowing while his body was locked inert that his thoughts were foolish and irrational: *What if I had lied to him this morning? I almost did* . . . Twenty feet away, with face clenched, Malcolm Pitt stooped a little and pulled the piece of copper tubing from his chest. When the piece dropped at his feet, with a sudden release of caught breath he said, "Good God . . ."

He did not fall. Darrell was suddenly beside him, lifted him, held all his weight as if he had been no heavier than a child. The caught breath released again quickly. "Let me down, Darrell . . ."

Still holding Malcolm, Darrell yelled, "Yancey! Get somebody. Get Roger! Roger . . ." Then slowly he put Malcolm down. He did not see Yancey leave. He heard him running.

"I pulled it out," Malcolm said. "It went here." He touched near his heart. His fingers closed and his hand fell away.

Darrell was holding Malcolm's head in the cradle of his arm. He did not speak; his mind was quivering more than his lips. *Roger will know what to do. What if I had lied to him this morning? I almost did. Roger will know . . . .*

Malcolm said, "The damned geese messed up those gauges."

"Roger will be here in a second. Roger will know what to do."

"I can't move my hand . . . son. It feels like . . . cotton."

Darrell touched Malcolm's hand, rubbing it.

266

Twice Malcolm tried to speak. His mouth made a quiet dry sound. Then he said, a little more than a whisper, "I'm glad you're here . . ."

A fleck of blood had settled on Malcolm's lips. Darrell did not know where it had come from, but it was there, shining, bright red on the suddenly pale lips. He took his finger and wiped it away.

"It's better this way," Malcolm whispered. "Here . . . at our . . ." He stopped and breathed easily for a moment. "You never saw me sick in bed . . . ?"

"No . . ." Darrell whispered.

Malcolm turned his face a little toward the gin though his eyes hardly moved. "It's yours and Roger's now . . . every time you're here . . . remember . . . we built it together . . . I rather you'd be here now . . . than anybody . . ."

Darrell could not then see Malcolm's face. He did not even see when Malcolm closed his eyes, but he felt it. He was crying when the men came. He knew each of them, yet their names did not cross his mind, nor did he speak when they took Malcolm Pitt from his arms.

It may be that he did not sit a full minute alone on the cinders and ashes before the boiler. His mind did not record any sense of time at all. He sat there in the suddenly bleak light, trembling. It was more than his flesh quivering. His very bones shook. He heard the sound of Roger's steps a long way off. Still quivering he stood up. He met Roger at the gin-well.

"Where is Father?" Roger's face was thin but it was not pale.

"That goddamned boiler, Roger. It went in here. In his heart. The gauge-stem."

Some of the trembling seemed to leave Darrell's body and move directly to Roger's lips. "Dead?"

267

"In his heart. Here."

Roger's eyes were dry, staring. There was a pulsing along his throat but his face was suddenly still. His mouth opened slowly, as if to curse; but no sound came, not even of breath. His fingers tightened.

Darrell said quickly, "I know I'm responsible for the gin. Maybe you think I could have helped it. Maybe you think I left something undone that caused it. It was the geese I tell you. But go ahead and strike me, face, anywhere, I wouldn't lift a finger."

"I know you're stronger than I am."

The pulsing raced along Roger's throat again. His body was not moving at all.

Darrell said, "You think he meant nothing to me?"

The pulse beats leaped in Roger's face then. "I guess I know. He built this gin with you. You've been with him to Memphis, New Orleans, ate with him, slept with him, been with him twice the times I ever have. I wasn't his son. You were. How do you expect me to feel?"

"I don't know . . ." Then Darrell put his hand on Roger's shoulder. "Nobody could help it, Roger."

"Take your hand off me."

His hand fell away. They stood facing each other, both breathing quickly. Darrell heard only their breathing and the drip of water from the valve in the gin-well. He turned his back to Roger and walked away. He was walking beside the cordwood with no knowledge of distance or direction, not seeing anything nor hearing the bark snap beneath his feet. But he had not gone thirty steps when Roger called.

"Darrell . . ."

He stopped and turned. Roger was still standing beside the gin-well. His face was lifted but he was crying then, his long breaths quivering in and out slowly.

268

"Darrell . . . Don't leave me. Walk with me to the house."

He waited for Roger. Together they walked in the bleak dusk of November.

three

Rain against a window had always moved Darrell, and he stood that night, like a child, with his fingers touching the cold pane. He thought of the week-old grave of Malcolm Pitt and the heavy rain eating into the soft earth and seeping downward. He whispered to himself: *I will build a canopy myself. Roger will let me.*

In another part of the house, in the living room, Leland and Roland were calling, "Pop us some snowflakes. Pop us some snowflakes," and Emily was saying, "I'm going to put you two to bed if you keep on. I can't fool with popcorn tonight. I'm busy with this sweater. Don't you want a sweater?"

"No, sir."

"Ma'am . . ."

"No, ma'am."

"Mother . . . mother . . ."

"Yes."

"Leland always says *no sir* to you. Doesn't he?"

Darrell pushed the window down tighter, though the rain was not leaking through, and held his hands tight along the sill. The thought of the water seeping through the grave-mound which was not yet the color of the earth about it made his body tremble, and his eyes began to fill. He might have kept from crying if he had known that Emily was coming into his room. But she was suddenly there and holding his shoulder and he was staring into the window.

269

"I can't see a minute's peace, Darrell. They want you to pop them some corn. Come on."

"Not now."

She pulled at his arm, turning him. "Come on. Before they start crying . . ." Suddenly she saw his face and let go of his arm. "Now it's you. Oh, I know you're worse than they are."

"Leave me alone, can't you? Just for a little while."

She touched his arm again. "Darling, I know you miss him and you're hurt, but you ought not to cry. What would people think if they knew? You're a grown man."

He only looked at her and she moved away from him and went back to the living room to Leland and Roland. After a while he got his coat and went out into the rain. A few hundred yards from his house he stopped on a knoll where the earth was soft, and he said to himself: *I will build a house like his, here. I will go to Vicksburg tomorrow and have it planned. I will build the house and I will build a canopy over his grave.* The thought of it seemed to make him a part of some indomitable force; he would build something which could not be destroyed and which would not let his name lie idle on the tongues of those who came after him. Then he left the knoll and walked slowly along the road toward Leighton and the Pitt house.

When he reached the house he stood in the shaft of light that came through the window and cleaned his shoes carefully. The front door opened quickly when he stepped upon the porch and Anne stood in the doorway, each side of her face seeming to smile alternately, as if she was a sister he had not seen for years.

"Aren't you drenched?" she said.

"No." He took off his coat and hat and put them in the porch swing. He followed Anne into the living room.

Roger was standing before the fire in shirtsleeves with

his collar opened wide. The firelight played on his throat and the hollow of his neck. "Hello."

"Hello, Roger."

"Come dry your feet." Darrell went across the room to the hearth. "Is there anything the matter?" Roger said.

He caught Roger's eyes quickly. "No. Why?"

"Nothing. It's not a fit night out—for man."

Anne came and stood beside Roger. "Your mother has been wanting to see Darrell."

"Where is she?" Darrell said.

"Upstairs," Anne said. "I guess she was feeling worse today."

"I'll go see her," Darrell said.

"Warm your feet first," Roger said. "Your feet are wet." He pulled up a chair for Darrell.

"I promised to read something to her," Anne said. "But I'll wait until Etta leaves."

In a few minutes Etta came down the stairs wearing on her head a silk stocking, rolled almost its full length, and covering her hair like a tam. She was Stafford's wife and a very large Negro woman. In the doorway she stopped. "I'm gone on home now, Mista Roger."

"Have you got a coat?" Roger said. "It's pouring out there."

"Nossuh. I didn't bring none this mawning."

"Anne, get one of my old slickers for her. There's one in my room."

"I bring it back in the mawning." She turned toward the hall. "How you, Mista Darrell?"

"All right, Etta. You all right?"

"Yessuh. The Lawd doing all right by me." She went into the hall and Anne followed her.

"What does your mother want with me?" Darrell said.

"I don't know."

"Is she sick?"

"No. No more than usual."

Darrell got up. "I'll go talk to her." He went up the stairs and when he entered the room he could hear the quiet sound of the piano below, but he did not know what Roger was playing.

Leta Pitt was propped up in her bed, very near the outer side, as if she might slide onto the rug at any moment. Her face did not seem much older to him than when he had first seen it, but her hands were old and webbed with veins and her knuckles shone like little marbles.

"Darrell! Did they send after you or did you just come?"

"I just came."

"In all this rain and lightning." She held out her hand and caught his and the tears began to roll upon her cheeks. After a while she motioned for him to draw the ottoman nearer her bedside and sit down. Then she took a fresh linen handkerchief from the box beside her and commenced to dry her face. "It's so terrible, Darrell. I wonder if God is just. Do you think He is? Sometimes I think He isn't, but I know it's because we can't see how things are going to be. Now tell me. Tell me what were the last words he said."

"I don't remember them."

"How could you forget? I can't believe you've forgotten. You do remember. Did he ask for me?"

"No."

"What did he say? His very last words."

"I don't remember."

"Oh, Darrell . . ." She began to cry again and she took another fresh handkerchief and stopped the tears before they touched her cheeks. When her eyes were dry again she said, "Do you think God sent it on me for a punishment?"

"No. I think it's just something we don't understand."

"He wasn't saved. You know that. And it was all so sudden he didn't have a chance." The tears almost began again, but she stopped them. "What will God do with him? He can't send him you-know-where. Do you believe he's there?"

"He's in heaven, wherever that is."

"I'm glad you said that, Darrell. You don't know how much I loved him. You've never lost anybody that meant as much to you as he meant to me. I slept in the bed with him for forty-two years. Sometimes he was you-know-how in the day-time but he never scolded me once after dark. Never. But I've thought all day I wished we were Catholics. Then we could pray him out. We could make sure. But you don't believe he's there."

"He's in heaven."

"Darrell, you're so sweet and good. You're still a beautiful child. You are my boy."

He touched her hand and got up. "I'd better go and let you rest."

She held to his hand. "You can't go. I haven't told you yet. Do you really think it could be a punishment sent against me? Would God do that to me?"

"No."

"But I've wept over it. Miriam away over there, and couldn't be here even for her own father. I've got to tell you. And you've got to forgive me. I've had enough sent on me to bear. You will forgive me?"

"Yes. For what?"

"You and Miriam. I've always loved you. But I didn't want it to happen between you and Miriam. It was my fault. I took her away from you. The Lord might take me at any time, we never can tell, but I want you to know and to forgive."

"It's all right."

"You're so good, and you're so much like my own. I knew

273

you would forgive me and now the Lord can't send anything else against me . . ."

"It's all right," he said again and stood up. "I'd better go and you'd better rest." Slowly she began to cry and she was crying quicker and louder when he went out the door.

At the foot of the stairs he met Anne. She carried a book in her hand and she said, "I'll go up and read her something. She likes for me to read to her."

Darrell did not say anything. He nodded and went on toward the living room and the sound of the piano. He stood near the hearth for a while and watched Roger's hands. Then he picked up the medical journal beside him and thumbed its pages until he saw the page he was looking for. It read:

THE LAST OF MIDWIFERY
by
Roger Pitt, Obstetrician
Starhart Hospital

He had already read the article and now he counted the pages. There were seven. Suddenly, without turning from the piano, Roger said, "She's certainly in a mood, isn't she?"

"Yes," Darrell said. He put the journal down and went across the room and stood beside the piano.

"What did she want to tell you, anything?"

"No."

"Do you like this piece?"

"It's very sad."

"Yes. It's heavy on the heart. Shall I change?"

"No."

"We like to punish ourselves, don't we? We get that from Mother."

"I don't know."

274

"Tonight is the first time I've played. It lets something out through your fingers, instead of other ways. Moping maybe. Do you understand?"

"Yes."

"Why did you come tonight?"

"Because I had to. Do *you* understand?"

"I always have, haven't I?"

"I think so."

"I'm glad you came. I have something to tell you before I leave tomorrow."

"Are you leaving tomorrow?"

"I have to go back. Anne will stay another week, but I have to go."

"Without her? New Orleans is bad for you without her."

"Are you thinking of Nanette?"

"No."

Roger stopped playing and sat quietly for a moment. "That was a long time ago. But I always think of it as the end of something."

"What is it you're going to tell me?" Darrell said.

Roger got up and went to the hearth. "My internship ends the first of the year. I'm coming back to Leighton."

"Leighton! Why?"

Roger laughed. "Maybe because I like you." Then his face clouded. "A man doesn't forget where he's born. I'll build me a hospital here someday that a lot of people will be proud of."

"Out of what? There isn't enough practice here and at Waycrest to keep Dr. Edgeworth busy."

"He's getting old. And maybe he's busier than you think."

"I think you're making a mistake. I'll take care of the gin for you. I'll do whatever you want done on the place. Anything. But you're making a big mistake to come back."

"How do you know?"

"I know because I feel it's wrong."

"Don't you want me to come back to Leighton? Tell me the truth. Do you?"

Darrell's eyes did not move from Roger. Finally he said, "No . . ."

"You're not telling the truth, not all of it."

"How could I tell you everything?" Darrell came to the hearth and stood at the other end of the mantel from Roger. "I've always wished our families could grow up together, that our kids could play together . . ."

"You remember that I haven't got any sons, like you."

"I remember."

"You want to be like Father in Leighton."

"Yes. Here or anywhere. Why not?"

"I won't keep you from it."

"It wouldn't be like brothers, Roger. You may think it would, but it wouldn't. Maybe we'd envy each other, I don't know."

"Envy. Well, how do you think I've always felt about the way Father treated you?"

"I don't know."

"I've been jealous just as far in me as jealousy would go. And envy too."

Darrell's hand clutched the mantel, and his knuckles showed white. "If he ever gave me anything that you want back, you can have it. Anything. The whole gin . . ."

"Don't be a damned fool! You know perfectly well I'm not talking about anything that Father gave you. You worked for it. I'm talking about the way he felt about you and the way you felt toward him. That's something you don't buy and sell. And you don't give it away either. I know how much he loved you, even if you don't."

"What do you want, Roger?"

"To come back to Leighton."

"Why should you ask me? It was your home before it was mine."

"If you are going to be angry with me, I won't come back."

"I've never been angry with you. It would be hard for that to happen." Darrell looked down upon the floor like a man who stands beside a trading barn and gazes upon the ground, afraid that he may purchase something unsound at an undue price. He did not want Roger to see this fear. "There's Anne to think about. You know she doesn't like Leighton."

"That's her choice. Not mine."

"Would you really come without her?"

"Yes. But she'll come."

"To a post office and a few stores. You're a doctor, Roger. You can be something in the world. What's here for you?"

"Everything. Isn't that enough?"

"Yes. I guess that's enough." He watched Roger's shoulders, held square and straight so that little valleys ran along his shirt and he thought that Roger would never belong to any world of time. "I've got to go," he said. He went into the hall and Roger followed him. "I'm sorry I talked the way I did about your coming back."

"Maybe there was nothing else to say."

"Maybe there wasn't." Their hands touched briefly and it was awkward for them.

"You can do this for me, Darrell. Anne has to leave in another week. I hope you won't mind coming to see Mother and letting us hear if she needs us. Miriam will be here right after Christmas. We got a cable this morning. You'll do that, won't you?"

"Certainly."

They suddenly laughed quietly with each other.

four

A few days after Christmas Darrell came home from the gin and the sawmills and instead of going to the lot he stopped the surrey at the front gate. He had been to Vicksburg that day. When he opened the gate Leland and Roland came running, breathless, toward him, their four-year-old faces so much alike, as the dusk seemed to open before them, that he could hardly tell them apart. Leland was yelling, "Papa! Papa! Roland tried to catch my calf and he ran it through the fence and cut its teat." Then Roland, catching Darrell's hand and pulling hard, cried, "Down in the crib a big ole rat stuck his tail through a crack and Yancey twisted it off, clean off. He killed it . . ."

Darrell caught them, lifted one into each arm, and walked on toward the house. In the hall Louella took them, and Darrell went into his and Emily's room, where Emily was standing in a chair taking the holly from the window.

"I want to show you something," he said.

She stepped down from the chair and came across the room to him. "What?"

"Something across the road."

They went out into the yard and crossed the road and stood on a knoll among a group of big oak trees.

"Today I saw the architect," he said. "We'll put it here. It should go here, shouldn't it?"

"Yes," she said.

"It'll be like Malcolm Pitt's house. Don't you think he would be proud of it? Just like his."

"Exactly like his?"

278

"Yes. Unless you want something changed on the inside."
He put his arm around her. "You can have all the closets you
want. You can talk to the architect. He'll be here tomorrow.
Aren't you happy about it?"

"You know I am."

"It doesn't show enough in your eyes."

"How much will it cost?" she said.

"How much? What does it matter? Every tree in sight belongs to me. I could build two houses. Three. I'll use my own
lumber . . ."

"You're getting too proud."

"You're getting cold." He took off his leather jacket and
put it around her shoulders. "Here."

"Sometimes you're very good to me," she said.

"Sometimes."

They walked back toward the house and when they reached
the gate Emily stopped and looked at the mares still hitched to
the surrey. "You had better put the surrey up," she said.

"I'm going to use it after while."

"For what?"

"I think you and I should meet Miriam. She's coming on
the train tonight."

"I know it." Emily walked on toward the front steps.

At the porch Darrell caught her arm and his jacket slipped
away from her shoulders. He put the jacket around her again.
"I told her mother we'd meet Miriam tonight."

"Why?"

"Somebody should."

"It's not my place to meet her."

"Her mother's not well . . ."

"I'm not well either."

"All right. You ate too much for Christmas." He patted
her waist.

She pushed his hand away from her. "You needn't laugh at my figure. We're going to have a child."

"A baby? How do you know?"

"How? I've been knowing for a month."

"But you didn't say anything. You didn't tell the truth . . ."

"I don't want it."

"That's a pretty thing to say."

"I don't care whether it's pretty or not."

"Emily . . ." He put his arm around her and the jacket fell from her shoulders again and lay on the porch. He stooped and picked up the jacket and held it across his arm. "You don't mean that. What are you angry about?"

"Nothing."

"You're glad about the baby. We'll hurry the house and move in. He'll be born in the new house. You want him born in the new house, don't you?"

"What does it matter where anybody is born? You weren't born in a house like the Pitts."

"How do you know? You never asked me where I was born."

"You can tell me some other time."

"You won't go tonight?"

"No."

"Do you want me to go by myself?"

"You wouldn't be fool enough to do that."

He took her hand and his thumb moved up and down her wrist. "You don't have to act like this. Sometimes I think you don't want anybody to be kind to you: daylight, bed, anywhere."

"You never hurt me in bed."

His fingers sank into the softness of her arm and he shook her, and his own body shook in anger. In that quick moment he

280

wished that he had never been gentle with her. He turned away from her, his whole being outraged with his own tenderness.

"Were you being kind so I would go with you tonight?" she said.

"You can go or stay," he said quietly. "I don't give a damn. Do whatever you like."

"I owe her nothing. None of the Pitts."

"All right. Be certain you pay out no more than you owe."

"You and the Pitts. Always you and the Pitts."

"Yes. Me and the Pitts."

She started into the house. He reached out and touched her arm. "The baby, Emily. I'd better take you to Dr. Edgeworth's tomorrow."

"That's better," she said. "I thought you were going to recommend Roger. I hear he's coming back too."

He went to the depot alone that night and while he waited for the train he thought that his heart might quicken when the train came in sight. But nothing seemed to change, even when he saw Miriam through the coal-specked window. She was standing in the aisle of the car and for a moment he could see only her hand. He wondered if her fingers would feel the same in his hand as they had in that other time.

The porter came ahead of her with three bags. Then Miriam stood on the ground holding a small round box. Her light yellow coat closed well and tight about her waist, and her shoulders were tipped with fur. Her eyes had grown darker since he had last seen her. She looked at him, smiling, as if measuring him against a former time, and neither of them moved.

"Hello," he said.

"Hello."

He wondered why it was not there, the old feeling, and he thought it might have died with Malcolm Pitt. She came to him and took his hand for only a moment. A few yards away from them the conductor lifted his hand and waved toward the engine and the train crawled away.

"I wondered how it would be to see Leighton again," she said. She looked past him to the post office and then to the stores.

"How does it feel?"

"I don't know yet."

"You've been gone a long time."

"In a way it doesn't seem so long. You don't look any different."

"None at all?"

"Yes. A little. When I first saw you I thought of Father."

Slowly he looked away from her. Then he went to her bags and gathered all three of them into his arms. She followed him and then turned and walked beside him toward the surrey as if her nearness would take some of the weight from his arms. "There's everything in there," she said. "You can't imagine all the things I've collected and two trunks are on their way. I thought they might get here ahead of me. I stopped off a night with Roger."

Something moved within him then, like the old feeling in that other time.

"How is Mother?"

"She didn't feel like meeting you. I told her that Emily and I would come. But Emily is sick."

"Serious?"

"No. Nothing much." He placed the bags into the surrey and then helped her into the spring seat. He did not feel anything. It was like helping Emily.

They started along the graveled street, riding in silence, and he was sorry that nothing moved within him. He wished he could have felt some little kind of pain when he looked at her.

"I want to see Father's grave," she said.

"Now?"

"Yes. Before I go home. It will only take a minute."

He stopped the surrey under the big oak by the church and they walked together into the cemetery, not touching each other at all. Twice his hand drew across the brighter stones that shone in the moonlight. They came to the newest grave and stood. For a while they did not say anything; then she talked quietly, almost whispering, and her face was clear and dry.

"Did you make the canopy?"

"Yes."

"I'm glad," she said. She did not seem at all near to crying.

They stood for another few minutes and then she turned and walked ahead of him to the surrey. When they were halfway home she said, "You know Roger is coming back?"

"Yes."

"Last night he talked about coming home. I felt sorry for him. He seems lost in New Orleans. He is such a kind person. I felt very strange last night. We talked for only a little while, but I seemed all of a sudden to understand him for the first time in my life. Has he changed that much?"

"Maybe it's you. Maybe you've changed."

"I might have. Yes," she said.

At the front gate he helped her out of the surrey and took the bags to the porch. For a moment they stood on the steps and looked at each other. Her eyes seemed to move away from his face to his hair. "This is the hardest part," she whispered. "To go in that door and know he won't be there . . . ever."

He caught her hand and held it tight for only an instant, as if to stop what surged within him. Then he left her quickly, because he could not bring himself to watch her face.

All the way home he stood up in the surrey, driving slowly, as if the mares pulled a heavily loaded log wagon. Emily was

283

standing beside the window when he entered their bedroom. Without speaking he walked to the crib and looked down at Leland. He knew that in the soft light from the lowered wick of the aladdin lamp her eyes followed him. Quietly he turned to Roland's crib. The blanket seemed too near Roland's chin. He pulled it back half an inch and watched the small fingers above the blanket open and close. Then he stood on the hearth and removed his coat.

Beside the window Emily turned a little and said, "I want a separate bedroom, Darrell."

His eyes moved quickly up and down the nightgown that fell about her loosely, except for the tight gathering around her waist. He did not answer her then. He went to the closet, took off his vest, and put coat and vest on a hanger. He went to the foot of the bed and stood as if Emily had said nothing. She was only a few feet away from him. When he raised his head and looked at her it was as if a hand had jerked his chin upward. Her hair fell well brushed about her shoulders. He did not know why such outrage simmered within him. "Emily, if I have hurt you, I never meant to. Try to understand at least that much of me."

"Do you want to wake the babies?"

"I don't care."

"That's it. I'm the one who has to worry with a baby. All a child means to you is a moment of pleasure."

She waited for him to answer. Finally he went to her and pulled her body against his gently. "It doesn't have to be this way. Why can't we understand each other? Sometimes it seems as if we don't even try."

Her hands caught his arms. She whispered, "Let me go to bed, Darrell."

He moved away from her and stood between the two cribs. He was not looking at anything, because his eyes were closed;

284

but he was remembering his grandmother, straight and unbending, riding away in the frosty half-light of morning, remembering the words she had left: *Until you come to an end like the others before you, without love.* The words he remembered seemed now to fall upon him with actual sound, each like a green locust-bitten plum falling too early upon the earth.

The day Roger came back to Leighton the foundation was already laid for Darrell's house. Late in the afternoon of that day Darrell was standing near the base of the chimney when he saw Roger's buggy coming up the new-cut driveway. Roger was standing as he drove and from a hundred yards away he lifted his hand and waved to Darrell. When he came within a few yards of the house's foundation he stopped the buggy and jumped out like an excited child. He came toward Darrell, his face bright as a clean lantern in early dusk. He said, "Hello, you old horse's butt."

Darrell pitched the trowel he held onto a pile of lumber. "Listen at that, you second-rate midwife."

"Second-rate? Brother, I brought nineteen babies into the world last week. Perfect deliveries. Not the slightest hitch." They stood a few feet from each other.

"Too bad it wasn't a score."

"No. Nineteen was enough. Too many people always want one more of something."

"We're going to have one more. Emily is . . ."

"Is that right?"

"Yes."

"How soon?"

"Summer."

"You old rascal."

"Aren't you proud of me?"

"I reckon so."

"Sit down."

"Will you tell me how you did it?" Roger laughed. Then he said, "I can't stay, really. I've got a dozen things to do."

"When did you come in?"

"This morning. I want some good lumber from you—to build me an office beside Gammel's store. Aaron's going to do it for me and I need some good lumber."

"The gin-yard is half-covered with yellow pine. Take all you want. There's tongue-and-grooved ceiling in the seed shed. More than you'll need."

"That's white of you, kid."

"Forget it. I've got something for you. From the gin. We always settled the books right after New Year's. The cotton's in the warehouse at Vicksburg."

"Are you going to sell yours?" Roger said.

"Yes. Right away."

"I think I'll hold mine and play with the market a little. It's going up. If I can hit it just right, I'll build a hospital here that'll make a lot of folks look twice."

"I wouldn't play with cotton now."

"That's all I've got to play with."

"Well, it's your cotton."

Roger stood upon a concrete pillar for half a minute as if to test it. "What's your big hurry with this house?"

"You really want to know?"

"Yes."

"I want my next child born in this house. Does that sound strange?"

"No. Nothing wrong with that." Roger started toward his buggy. "I've really got to go. Thanks for the lumber. I might deliver your next child free."

Darrell moved a few steps toward the buggy. "Roger?"

"Yes."

286

"Dr. Edgeworth is handling Emily's case. She wanted him. After all, he did bring the twins. You understand how she might feel . . ."

Roger laughed. "Of course. I was only joking. I'll have plenty to do around here. More than I want."

Darrell caught his arm then; their hands touched in a playful, almost childish way, and the everlasting magic coursed along Darrell's arm and colored his face and stilled his lips.

"What is it?" Roger said.

"Nothing."

Roger smiled and his face was warm. "Tell me the truth, lad. Are you glad I'm back?"

"Yes," Darrell said.

five

"Where is he?" Darrell said.

Yancey took his hat off and came onto the wide front porch of the new house. Sweat curled around his eyes. "Miz Edgeworth said the doctor wouldn't be back fer a hour or two or more. She'd send him soon as he come back."

"Look," Darrell said. "You'd better go after Roger . . . Dr. Pitt. Tell him Dr. Edgeworth is late."

"Yessuh," Yancey said. He turned away quickly and went toward the buggy at the gate, the unbuttoned sides of his overalls flapping in the afternoon shimmer of heat.

"Yancey! Come back by Mr. Gammel's and get Miss Paralee."

Darrell turned into the house, passed Louella in the hall, and went on toward the kitchen. From the new pantry he took a bottle of wine that sat among the jars of fruit. It was a special bottle. A week ago he had gone to Vicksburg for it and for Emily's present, which had not yet been unwrapped. When it was all over he and Roger would sit in the kitchen as he and Malcolm Pitt had done when the twins were born. He put the bottle on the table and went out of the kitchen toward Emily's room. He stood in the doorway a full minute looking at Emily before he went into the room, which seemed too dark for three o'clock in the afternoon. "Don't you want the shades up for a while?" he said. "It would be cooler." There was a slight damp film above her lips.

"All right," she said.

He raised the shades and pulled a chair near the bed. He sat down and put one hand over her fingers that lay upon the sheet like thin white cotton-locks. "Are they any quicker?" he said.

"I don't think so. I don't know."

"Dr. Edgeworth is on another call. He'll be here before long. I sent after Roger, and Miss Paralee."

"We still have to depend on them. Even in a time like this."

"On who?"

"The Pitts."

He got up and walked away from the bed and stood at the window fumbling with the shade again.

"Have you ever belonged to anybody but the Pitts?"

Slowly he faced her, and as his lips parted he saw Leland and Roland standing in the doorway. Their hair lay in golden heaps; their faces were streaked with dust. "I thought you two were with Mark. Go into the yard. Your mother is sick. Don't make any racket." They went back into the hall and his eyes moved again to Emily.

"I didn't mean to be that way," she said. "But it makes you so sick. You have no idea." She closed her eyes for a little while.

His own forehead became damp from watching her face. Suddenly he remembered the present for her. He went to the dresser and brought out the small package. Back at the bed he said, "I've got something for you."

She opened her eyes.

"A present. You want me to open it for you?"

"Yes. Please."

His fingers tore nervously at the wrapping. In the palm of his hand he held out a gold locket-watch to her. She caught her breath as if the pain had come again. "Oh, it looks so expensive . . ."

"It's Swiss," he said.

"Put it around my neck."

He bent over her, fumbling to fasten the small snap. "There," he said. He kissed her and her fingers stroked his arm. He sat down beside the bed again.

"You are good to me," she said. "I'm sorry for what I said. I want you all for myself. Sometimes I can't help the way I am about you. Women love you, because you never love them —completely."

He leaned over and touched her forehead with his lips. "It will be a boy, don't you think?"

"Yes," she whispered. "I think it will be a boy."

"And you're glad we're in the new house?"

"Yes."

"Try to rest now." He got up and went to the window and searched the road for Roger, or Yancey and Miss Paralee. He thought of the tall slender figure of Miss Paralee at the crest of some clay hill, moving to or from a sick bed in the twilight or dusk, her face seeming never to turn aside. He thought of her small black umbrella that she always carried with her. She did not seem like Aaron Gammel's sister.

"Darrell?"

"Yes."

"Do you see anybody?"

"No."

"I thought I heard something."

"They'll be here soon. Are they quicker now?"

"I think so."

He went to the bed and said, "Can I do anything?"

"No. You go out and take care of the boys. Send Louella in here. She knows what to do."

He called Louella and then he went into the yard and picked up both Leland and Roland. He took them to an oak near the end of the porch and put them down again. "I'm going to let the old chiggers get you." He took a pallet quilt from the end of the porch and spread it out for them. In the stillness he heard the sound of a buggy. Miss Paralee and Yancey came in sight. He met them at the gate and took Miss Paralee's umbrella and helped her out of the buggy.

"The doctor's not here yet?" she said.

"Not yet."

"Emily's not the kind to have trouble, anyway." She took off her wide sunbonnet and gloves and went ahead of Darrell to the house.

When Darrell turned back to the twins he saw Roger's buggy suddenly in the driveway. Roger got out quickly and left his mare to Yancey. He came up the walk with his coat across one arm and his bag in the other hand. His eyes winked in the sunlight and he smiled. Darrell was thrilled at the thought of Roger's arriving so quickly. He watched the boyish face come up the walk. Sometimes it was very hard for him to think of Roger's being a doctor.

Roger said, "Well, Papa, I'm here."

"You made a very quick trip," Darrell said.

290

"'Twas nothing, kid. How is she? Have you timed the pains?"

"Yes. About every twenty minutes."

"Oh, we've got a long while to wait."

"Miss Paralee is here."

"Good," Roger said. He looked at the twins, and puckered his face at them, and then went on into the house.

Darrell went to the end of the porch, near the pallet quilt and sat in the dark egg-shaped shade of the oak. After a while Roger came out of the house with his shirt collar unbuttoned and his sleeves neatly rolled halfway to his elbows. He sat on the pallet quilt between Leland and Roland and pulled both of them across his stomach. Without looking at Darrell he said, "She's all right. Nothing to do now but wait."

"Dr. Edgeworth was on another call," Darrell said.

"He's got his hands full," Roger said. He held Leland up and let him walk along his stomach. Then he held Roland in the same way.

"I've got a horse," Roland said.

"You'll have more than that after while."

"Look how dirty they're getting you," Darrell said.

Roger stood Roland beside him on the pallet. "Tell your old papa to leave us alone. Tell him not to jug with us." Roger sat up and looked at the twins and took out his handkerchief and cleaned Leland's face.

Yancey came around the corner of the house and stopped at the end of the porch. "Is they anything else you want me to do?"

"Yes," Darrell said. "Take care of Leland and Roland. Take them down to the barn or the creek or somewhere."

"Yessuh. Come on," he said.

They ran after him and then ahead of him toward the barn.

291

"What a pair," Roger said. "Why couldn't I have a pair like that?"

"It takes a man, lad. A real man."

"With something special no doubt?"

"Yes."

"Aw, go to hell."

"Listen. I brought us a bottle of wine from Vicksburg."

"From the Yellow House?"

"Yes. From the Yellow House. I think this one is going to be a boy too. We'll celebrate."

"Another son?"

"Yes?"

"Now don't latch on to any holier-than-thou attitudes. You could be the papa of a baby girl."

"It'll be a boy."

"Dammit. You're the worst spoiled . . ."

"Dr. Pitt," Miss Paralee called from the hallway.

Roger got up quickly, though not as quickly as Darrell. He went past Darrell and patted his shoulder. "Don't get your bowels in an uproar, Papa. Just rest in the shade."

It was not quite dark, but already Louella had lighted the lamps in the house when Dr. Edgeworth came. In the dusk he looked taller than Darrell ever remembered him. He threw his tobacco away and wiped his lips and came up the walk slowly with his worn house-top satchel. His hair was very white under the edge of his hat and his face was lean and old and tired. Now that Malcolm Pitt was gone, he was the only man Darrell knew who seemed to live in a world beyond the slightest evil. He stopped at the front steps and put his hand on Darrell's shoulder. "I had another labor case. Metlocks."

"Roger is here," Darrell said. "We didn't know when you could come."

292

"Good boy."

Darrell took him into the house and stood for a while in the doorway of Emily's room and watched Roger in his white tunic, and then watched Roger and Dr. Edgeworth talk quietly. He went out of the house and walked in the yard for a while and finally went to the gate and leaned his arm and head over against the cedar post and waited. After a while he heard steps along the walk behind him, and he turned. Roger was coming toward him, his coat and his satchel in hand. He thought Roger was trying to smile and could not.

"You can't leave now," Darrell said.

"Why?"

"You've got to stay. The wine and all . . ."

"It might be a daughter." Roger laughed.

"What's the matter with you?"

"Nothing."

"You can't go now."

"There's a doctor here. A rather good doctor. And the one your wife wants."

"I'd feel better if you stayed."

"I don't frankly care how you feel."

"Dammit. Go ahead."

"I am. You've got everything you need. House, land, mills, sons. You don't need me. Why shouldn't I go?" His lips remained parted and shaped, as if his spoken words had been only a faint beginning of some uneasiness piled within him. He moved slowly away from the gate, got into his buggy, and drove into the darkness.

Darrell stood and watched until he could no longer hear the sound of wheel or hoof. Then he went along the walk slowly toward the house. At the front steps he stopped and went around the house into the kitchen, took the bottle of wine from the table and held it tight in his hand. He returned to the front gate the way he had come, and then went past the gate into the road.

Halfway to Winter Creek bridge he angled off the road and crossed the ditch. In the hedgerow he found a rock half-buried in the earth. Slowly he pounded the bottle against the rock. The bottom fell away, and the smell of wine was sharp against his face. With each stroke the glass scattered on twigs and leaves, the jagged edge of glass nearing the neck in his hand. When only the neck remained he pressed the splintered end into the earth and turned toward the house. The lights through the windows seemed brighter from the distance and he could see clearly the image of Roger's face—the way it had been at the gate only a few minutes before. "Why?" he said. "Why?"

He went into the living room and turned the aladdin lamp very low and waited. He did not eat any of the supper which Louella prepared for him. "Have you put the boys to bed?" he said.

"Yessuh. In the far room." She whispered and the quietness of her words startled him.

"Is anything going wrong?" he said.

"It's not come yet." Again she whispered and then she went out of the room.

He waited, sometimes standing, sometimes stretched on the sofa with his hands locked at the back of his neck. Twice he went out of the house and walked to the barn and back. He was standing with his arm against the mantel when the doctor came into the room. The sound of the door jarred him. "Something *has* gone wrong," he said quickly.

"There is some trouble," the doctor said slowly. "If you want to send after Dr. Pitt . . . it wouldn't hurt anything."

Darrell looked at him for almost a minute. "I don't want to send after him, unless you think I should."

"He's a fine doctor . . . and it's his specialty."

"Is something bad wrong?"

294

"I want you to know the truth—yes."

"What . . ." He started toward the doctor and then he stopped suddenly. "I'll go after him." He went quickly into the kitchen where Yancey sat beside the cook table. He said very calmly, "Saddle me a horse, Yancey. It'll be quicker than the surrey. Bring him to the gate."

Yancey got up. "Law, I done turned 'em in the pasture. I drive 'em up quick as I can."

"All right. Hurry."

He went into the hall and passed Miss Paralee. She did not seem to notice him at all. He went to Emily's room. The door was closed. His hand touched the knob, and quickly he turned away toward the porch. He rushed down the walk and stood waiting at the gate for Yancey. He could hear the sound of running hoofs in the pasture. "Why did he have to turn them out?" he said. He opened the gate and his hand held onto a paling. "Damn him," he said. "Damn Roger . . ." Every beat of his heart was like a minute of time. He walked a few steps toward the barn and then came back to the gate, for the sound of running hoofs had died away. In a few minutes he heard the chain on the lot gate and knew that Yancey was coming. Then a hand touched his shoulder. He wheeled, shivering against the touch, and looked into the long lean face. The doctor's hand fell slowly; his thick white hair was ghost-like against the night. "Son?"

"Yessir."

"For the second time in forty-one years . . . I've lost a mother . . . and a child . . ."

Darrell only strained to see the doctor's lips in the darkness. He could feel a throbbing in his throat. The doctor took his arm. "I did everything that could be done. The child was stillborn . . . a daughter . . ."

The sound of the horse nearing the gate pounded in Darrell's head. He turned. "Yancey?"

"Yessuh."

"Put him back . . . no. Hitch him there for a while." He put his hand to his face. The doctor gripped his arm tighter. "I'm all right," he said.

He went into the house but he could not then go into the stillness of Emily's room. He went instead to the room where Leland and Roland were sleeping. For a long time he stood and looked down at them. Then he went into the living room and sat down at his desk and leaned his head over against his arms.

A little while after midnight Miss Paralee came into the room where Darrell sat alone in a chair. "Are you asleep?" she said.

"No."

"Doctor Pitt is out here."

He faced her quickly. "Where?"

"In the hall. He wants to see you."

"I don't want to see anybody."

She moved back toward the door. "Can I get you anything?"

"No, Miss Paralee. Thank you."

"Don't you want to lie down?"

"Not right now."

She went out. The door closed, then opened again. "Darrell?"

"Yes, Roger . . ." He got up and faced the door.

Roger himself seemed small in the dim light but the lamp cast a huge shadow of him against the door. He held to the doorknob a long time. Finally he turned it loose and moved another step forward. "I've done a thing I'd give anything to undo."

Darrell saw the shadow on the door instead of Roger, and his lips quivered a little. "I'm angry at you, Roger. For the first

296

time in my life I'm angry at you. I don't want to look at you. I asked you to stay."

"I know you did. I was terribly wrong, but I had a reason for leaving. It wasn't a petty thing, Darrell. Someday you'll understand why I left. You'll know why. I'd give anything in the world if I hadn't gone. It never crossed my mind that anything would happen. There was no way to know . . . I've talked to Dr. Edgeworth . . . nothing else could have been done . . ."

"I wish you wouldn't explain to me . . . if you don't feel any guilt—I'm glad."

"You know I feel guilty. How would you expect me to feel?"

"That's your concern now."

"Darrell. I ask you to forgive me. If I was wrong let God be angry with me—but don't you be." The tears he held back finally rolled onto his cheeks.

"I just want you to leave, Roger. That's all I want."

Roger moved around slowly and went out the door and his huge shadow seemed not to follow him.

six

For a month he did not talk to Roger. He went to Leighton as seldom as possible, and only when he had to did he talk to anyone. Twice he took the twins to Jackson to Emily's parents but he never stayed more than one night. The Townsends were like strangers to him and he could not believe they were the grandparents of his sons. At night, long after Leland and Roland were asleep, he sometimes walked the slopes and hills about Leighton, or his pasture, as if he must forever flee from some shadow.

More than once he thought he would go to Roger and say it had all been for nothing—this anger in him. But when he was no more than a few minutes walk from the house he would begin to think of Leland and Roland, alone, and would return. One night he asked Louella to stay with the twins, and that night he walked all the way into Leighton and stood on the pond bank and watched the light from the Pitt house. It was the end of August and the night was heavy with sultriness. The clouds were thick and dark beneath the lightning in the west, and beyond the darkness, toward Vicksburg, a low roaring hovered over the railroad tracks. Rain came and he stood on the pond bank until his clothes were soaked and all the roaring had passed. Somewhere, he thought, beyond my reach lies what I am looking for; perhaps it lies in the smell of fresh plowed earth, of cool spring water, of early frost, of good clean strength, and with no more form than the shape of darkness, so that my fingers close always on emptiness.

On the way home that night he went into the cemetery and touched the headstone of Malcolm Pitt's grave—the canopy had kept the mound dry. He touched no other markers.

Sometimes he thought that if he could have talked to Roger for half an hour as they had once talked in that old, old time of their childhood, whatever pain he felt would move away. But he did not go to Roger. He thought some sense of duty would not let him go.

Once he saw Nolie for no more than a minute at the post office window and in that brief time her face seemed to draw from him a part of what he needed to say. But when he met her again on the graveled street of Leighton, her face no longer drew him. Twice he saw Miriam and he was sorry for her, because it seemed all at once that any word which might pass between them would be useless.

Slowly that duty, which demanded his anger against Roger,

298

became more vague and he wished that Roger would come to him again. Perhaps he believed that Roger would come, and he waited. But it was Miriam who came instead.

Through the living room window he saw her there at his gate one afternoon and beside the surrey was Stafford, holding her hand as she stepped down. Leland and Roland, who were playing in the yard, met her at the gate and Roland caught her hand and said, "Leland put a chigger in my neighbor."

"Nabel," Leland said. "And it wasn't a chigger. It was just a ant."

She stooped over and pulled up his shirt and looked at his stomach and said, "I'll bet it's gone now."

Darrell turned from the window and went to the front porch to meet her, wishing with each step that it had been Roger instead of her. When she came into the living room she did not sit down. "I've only got a minute," she said. "I don't want Roger to know I've been here."

"Is he your guardian these days?"

Her eyes narrowed against him and became darker. He knew she was angry with him and he was a little pleased. "I didn't come here to quarrel with you, Darrell."

"No. Of course not."

"And I might as well tell you that I didn't come here to make you feel any better. I came because of Roger."

"What about your little brother?"

"I think you've treated him the way I wouldn't treat a . . . dumb something."

"You do?"

"Yes. I do. What you've been through with is no excuse. You're little. That's what's the matter with you. Just little . . ."

"You didn't come to quarrel?"

"Well, you could stop acting like somebody in grammar school."

"How has your brother acted? I asked him to come here, and I asked him to stay. But he walks out like walking away from an elevator—and my wife dies. He can go to hell. He means nothing to me."

"You don't know what's happening to him."

"I don't care what happens to him. He never once asked me to do anything for him but that I did it. Never. Then when I needed him, he left. Can you answer that?"

"Yes."

"Then answer it."

She moved to a chair, as if she must have something between them. "All right. I'll tell you. Roger hasn't got the heart to tell you. He thinks it would hurt you. He left because Emily told him to leave. Ask Dr. Edgeworth. He heard it. Yes. Because she didn't tell Roger to leave before another doctor came . . ."

His eyes moved slowly down her body to the floor and his fingers closed into his palms. She held to the back of the chair.

"I don't care what you think of me for telling you. I don't. But you've got nothing against Roger . . . I don't care now what you think." She moved toward the door.

He crossed the room and held her arm lightly. "Don't you? Don't you care at all?"

"Yes. I'm sorry. If I was half as kind as Roger I wouldn't have told you. Maybe I wanted to hurt you . . . maybe I thought that if Roger lost you, we would all lose you. . . . You know I care how you feel." She pulled her arm easily and slowly from his hand. "Will you come talk to Roger?"

"Of course I'll come."

"He's all mixed up, Darrell. Anne has gone to New Orleans . . ."

"Not for good?"

"I hope not. But they quarreled, and maybe Anne's right.

300

They want him to come back to Starhart and he doesn't want to go. Everything has gone wrong. He lost money on the cotton market . . ."

"How much?"

"I don't know. He's in Vicksburg now. Roger is not like you, Darrell. He's not as strong as you. If you could have seen the way he's been when you wouldn't speak to him . . ."

"I should have known, Miriam. But I didn't. I never have meant to mistreat anybody. You or Roger or anybody . . . you believe that, don't you?"

"Yes, I believe you."

"Why does it happen? Is it something in me?"

"Maybe it's something in all of us."

The next morning he went to see Roger. He had thought the men would be gathered about Gammel's store, for a rain had fallen during the night and the cotton was too damp to be picked. But the men were not yet there when he reached Leighton. He stopped his surrey beside the store and talked for a minute with Aaron Gammel.

"Heard Roger had bad luck with the market," Aaron said. His face was red and sun golden in the early September light. Across the bib of his overalls the leather watch band drooped.

"Yes," Darrell said. "You know how much it was?"

"No. Good bit I gathered."

Darrell walked on toward Roger's office, as if he was glad this had happened to Roger so that he could now hold Roger as he himself had once been held by Malcolm Pitt.

He opened the door without knocking and went into the office. Roger stood beside his desk; his face was clean-shaven, his suit well-pressed. Faintly a smile spread on his face. He was like a little boy, Darrell thought.

"Hello," Roger said.

"Hello." Darrell moved nearer to the desk and put his hand onto a chair. "How much was it?"

Roger laughed. "Did you come to bail me out?"

"No. I just came."

"Why?"

"Because I'm sorry for the way I've treated you. Miriam told me some things. I'm sorry about all this. It's your turn to forgive me. Maybe you'll be bigger than I was . . ."

"Listen, it's all right."

"Completely all right?"

"Yes."

"Then tell me how much you've lost."

"About eight thousand."

"That much? You haven't got that much."

"No."

"What did you do?"

"Bertran Wilcox paid it for me. Personal loan . . ."

"For how long?"

"Until I get it."

"How will you get it?"

"I've got lots of land. I could sell you my half-interest in the gin."

"Don't joke."

"They want me back at Starhart. I could go back there at a nice commission. It wouldn't take too long to save . . ."

"You hadn't thought of me?"

"I had. Yes."

"Are you going to let me do it?"

"No."

"I want you to let me."

"I'm sorry that I can't."

"You haven't forgiven me."

"I have."

302

"Then I don't understand. You and your family have given me in one way or another everything I've got. Now you won't let me do this for you . . ."

"I never have given you anything."

"Let me do it for your father then. What would he think if I didn't? What would he think if you didn't let me? It means a lot to me. You have no right to refuse."

"How would I pay you? Go back to Starhart?"

"You can owe me. Just owe me. I might like for you to always owe me something . . ." He stopped. He knew now that Roger needed him and he did not want the need in Roger's eyes to end. It was like that moment when the log-wagon boomers are fastened against the chains and the lever comes down slowly, moving even the heavy logs closer to each other. "Is it settled?"

"I guess so," Roger said. "I told Bertran Wilcox I'd probably pay him today. He has my note."

"Then let's go today."

"I can't go till late afternoon. And I'll need to stay overnight to get some supplies that are coming in early in the morning."

"I can stay too," Darrell said. "Louella will be with the boys."

"All right. We'll stay and go to the Showboat. And celebrate our being friends again."

"Again? I think we always were."

"Perhaps," Roger said. "You're a good garçon."

Darrell turned quickly then and went out of the office. He saw half a dozen men gathered about Gammel's store. When he came to them Duard Street said, "How much did he lose?"

"He didn't say exactly."

"You mean you don't want to say?"

"If you want to know, ask him."

"Hell," Duard said. "I don't want to know. I think it was

303

a damned nitty trick for a grown man to pull. Any son-of-a-bitch that'd gamble that way ought to lose."

Darrell moved a step and his left hand caught the bosom of Duard's shirt. His right hand landed hard and quick against the jaw before him. Duard staggered back and stumbled to his knees on the sand. Not a man moved or spoke. Duard got up and stood staring at Darrell; his right hand clenched and unclenched. Then Darrell walked toward his surrey. Behind him he heard Aaron Gammel's voice, "I guess you'll learn sometime. They're practically brothers."

seven

It was already dark when they topped the crest of Mission Hill and Vicksburg lurked below them. The sound of whistles was chill on the river, and the water lay dark before them like a stroke from Nolie's brush. A pounding commenced in Darrell. It was like entering Vicksburg for the first time, when he was filled with the childish fear of touching a thing that should not be touched or of looking upon a thing which should not be seen. He thought, I am the master of such fear now. But within him the pounding went on.

When they stopped in front of Bertran Wilcox's house Darrell said, "I could give you the check, Roger. I don't have to go in."

"Come on. You know I want you along."

Bertran Wilcox was in his library when they went in, Roger ahead of Darrell. He raised up straight in his chair to shake hands with them and then he leaned back again. "Don't mind my not getting up. I'm just not as young as you boys. Sit down." They sat in the cushioned armchairs in front of his desk.

304

"I'm sorry about the luck you had, Roger. But it's not too bad. I see you've brought your big brother along to help you out."

Roger's lips stalled. Then he said, "This is Darrell Barclay. I thought you two knew each other."

Bertran laughed. "We do. I'm coming out one day to see that new house of his." Bertran turned a little in his swivel chair to face Darrell. "Malcolm Pitt did raise you, didn't he?"

Sudden coldness moved along Darrell's spine. He said, "More or less."

Bertran shook his head. "I saw him nearly every week for forty years. You know, my finger's not in things much at the bank any more. But every now and then I sit there doing nothing and I get to thinking that old Malcolm's going to walk right through the door—so much so that I wouldn't bat an eye if he did." He turned away from them and looked out the window. "What's on your mind?"

"My big brother is going to redeem me," Roger said.

Bertran faced them again, the fingertips of one hand pushing against the fingertips of the other hand. "You know I wouldn't crowd you."

"I know that."

Darrell put out his arm and let it lie along the dark surface of the desk. His wrist seemed to pound with the quick beating of his heart, and his body seemed to grow stronger with each beat. Bertran placed a draft before Darrell for eight thousand and two hundred dollars. Darrell's fingers dampened the paper so that the ends of the check curled. He took the pen-staff from the desk and when he pressed the point against the paper a dark blot flooded out. He jerked the pen-staff away, as if the dark blot was caused by blood from his trembling fingers.

"A blotter," Bertran whispered.

Darrell took the blotter and dried the ink. Then he wrote his name, cautiously, like one imitating a copy book. He looked up at Roger, with his fingers still pressed over the edges of the check. He lifted the check into Roger's hand so that Roger must touch it.

"It's not mine," Roger said.

"It's yours until you endorse it." Darrell looked away, for he felt that Roger would hate him should they face each other in that moment. And he was filled with an upsurge of tenderness for Roger who until now, he thought, had never needed him. Swiftly, the moment passed and he was walking out of the house with Roger into a night that would shield them. His heart was lifted up and a coolness was upon him, though sweat dripped from his forehead.

"Free again," Roger said.

Darrell laughed and he knew that his laugh was like Malcolm Pitt's. It would be this way forever. He had won. And he wanted to keep nothing inside of him. He wanted to fling out everything that he had ever stored within himself. It was as if his voice might break forth with steel-strong words like the voice of Malcolm: *Goddammit I did it because I could and because I wanted to and because I like you* . . .

They left the surrey at the Yellow House, registered for a room, and took the key with them and went to eat at the Waterview. The time seemed to bristle with something tremendous just in the offing, and Darrell was tense with waiting. *At any moment now* . . .

They finished eating as if they must hurry, must leave and search elsewhere for what they could not find there. It was dark when they crossed Washington Street and went down the steep brick-paved slope toward the canal and the Showboat. Darrell thought that Roger was following him now as he, himself, had once followed Malcolm Pitt. On the Showboat they went first into the gambling room, filled with smoke and walking-canes

306

and tall hats. At the bar they drank bourbon and for a while watched the floor show. A heaviness seemed to settle on Darrell, he felt choked. He leaned against Roger and whispered, "We won't find it here."

"What?" Roger said.

"Whatever we're looking for."

They drank again and the voice of the black-faced comedian was hazy and distant to Darrell. Again he seemed waiting for something to unfold, for some actual sound, or certain clash. Once he put out his hand and touched Roger to make sure that he was not alone. In the midst of sudden laughter in the saloon, Roger caught Darrell's arm. "You're more than right," he said unevenly. "Let's get out of here."

They walked slowly up the brick-paved slope, their arms across each other's shoulders. A thin fog was lifting above the river. The sound of whistles rose and lay upon the air.

"Are you drunk?" Darrell said.

"No. I am not."

"Have never been?"

"Have never been."

"Are you my brother?"

"Yes. I am."

"Have always been?"

"Have always been."

"You'll remember this?"

"I'll remember."

Then their arms freed each other. They turned and walked toward the edge of the river. The fog was still rising over the dark smooth water, and they stood watching.

"You remember this place?" Darrell said.

"Certainly. It's where our father swam the river." Roger put his hand on Darrell's shoulder.

307

"Yes. Our father." Darrell looked at Roger. "I think I'll go swim it."

"Why?"

"To prove what a man I am."

"You're all right."

"How do you know?"

"I know." Roger's hand fell away from Darrell. "Let's sit down."

They sat on a driftwood crosstie, bleached from the summer sun. To Darrell the river seemed so narrow before him that Malcolm Pitt might have crossed it in a dozen long breast strokes. The fog was almost gone, and the dizziness cleared in Darrell's head. He wondered what it would be like to be really drunk. He got up. "Are you ready to go?"

"Yes," Roger said.

They walked in silence to the Yellow House, as if they had been boys for a time and now they were men again.

Once they were in the room, Roger went to the head of the walnut bed and switched on a small floor lamp. Darrell sat down in a chair and dropped his face into his hands. He wanted to go on talking to Roger, as they had talked on the brick-slope, but now he was afraid. He wished that he had drunk more. Without speaking Roger took off his clothes and put them on a hanger in the wide closet. He looked back at Darrell. "What's the matter with you?"

"Nothing."

"You're not sick?"

"No."

"You drank more tonight than I've ever seen you drink. You drank like Father."

"I'm all right now," Darrell said. He got up and took off his clothes and hung them in the closet. He knew that something was slipping away from him, maybe Roger or the image of Mal-

308

colm Pitt. The pounding in him was growing heavier. He stood in the closet and gripped the hanger until the hook bent within his palm. Then he came out of the closet and stood against an armchair.

Roger went around the foot of the bed and raised the window shade. He sat on the bed and leaned over with his elbows along the window sill. Darrell stood and watched him.

"Turn the light off so I can see the river," Roger said. "And come here."

Darrell turned off the light and crawled across the bed and sat beside Roger. They leaned into the window. Below them the wide dark river curved. The black joints of barges and boats lay along the water's edge.

"It makes you feel funny," Roger said. "A river always does. Like one main artery through the body. Do you wish you could paint?"

"Like Nolie? I don't know."

"I wish I could."

"Maybe you could," Darrell said.

"I couldn't."

"How do you know?"

"I know. It's not in me."

"You know what's in you? I don't know what's in me."

"How much money did it leave you?" Roger said.

"Money?"

"Yes. After that check."

"I don't know. Why?"

"I wanted to know."

"It doesn't matter."

"All right. But it does." Roger leaned farther into the window. "You remember the first time you ever saw it?"

"The river? Sure." Darrell got up and went around the foot of the bed. He pulled back the light covers and lay down.

309

"Does it seem like a long time to you?" Roger lowered the shade, but he still sat with his elbows on the window sill. "Does it?"

"I don't know."

Roger turned then and got into bed beside Darrell. For a minute he did not say anything. He breathed deeply. "It does to me. Sometimes it seems that everything that happened to me then was just a dream."

"Would you want to live it over again?"

"Yes," Roger said.

"What would you change?"

"I'd love Father more."

"What else?"

"I don't know what else."

Darrell wanted to put his arm around Roger then. But he would not. "It shouldn't be that way," he said.

"What?" Roger said.

"Nothing."

"Did you love Father? I mean *really* love him?"

Darrell touched Roger's shoulder, as if his hands might speak, for his lips had failed him for a space of time. "Would you make something ugly out of that, Roger?"

"No. I think I'd be the last person in the world to do that."

"Then what do you mean?"

"I think you know."

"Do you want me to tell you, Roger? Do you think I should tell you?"

"If you feel like it."

"Yes. I never saw him in my life but that something moved inside of me. I would have done anything for him. Anything. I wish I'd been killed instead of him . . ." Suddenly he put his arm around Roger, and he said, "I love you, Roger. I always have. But not that much. Sometimes I wish I did. Sometimes

310

I wish with all my heart I did . . ." His fingers moved along Roger's face and he knew that Roger was crying. He leaned over as he had done in that lost and younger time and touched Roger's face with his lips. "You mean more to me now than anybody. I wouldn't hurt you for anything. But what I've said is the truth . . ."

"I should never have come back," Roger said. "But I wanted to be close to you. I wanted to be like you. Any day, any minute, I would trade with you . . . everything you are, I'd like to be. I've always loved you that much . . ."

Darrell's arm was tight about Roger and his fingers kept touching him in a gentle movement. "Do you know any answer?"

"No . . ." Then Roger put his arm around Darrell and they were very still. Somewhere along the waterfront a bell rang sharply, like the clamor of new-sharpened shovel plows dropped suddenly to earth. A coldness came to Darrell and crept along his skin like blackberry winter. He ached with the longing that Roger would speak and hold back the coldness, even for an instant. For a full minute Roger neither moved nor spoke and his arm lay like years across Darrell's body. Suddenly Roger whispered, "Do you think it's right?"

"I don't know . . . we're grown now . . ."

"What did Father ever say?"

"Nothing . . . he never said anything . . ." Darrell held his breath, for they seemed to be on the river: the room swerved and he listened to the barely audible seeping of the wind outside and the lashing of water; he saw Malcolm's white handkerchief rubbing his lips briskly, and he remembered that he had never seen the slightest stain on Roger's lips. It is only a dream, he thought; but he knew the wild tenderness was now upon them.

eight

In the bright light of day their eyes burned with a tenderness against each other, as if to say: now it is done; we have reached the just-beyond; there is no going back to something less; there is no ending. But they knew the time had been too much, that all the time to come would be too much, not for themselves, but for others—for the living and the dead.

They did not see each other for a week. Darrell knew that Roger was going away; his office was closed and boxes were shipped from the depot. He wondered whether Roger would leave without telling him goodbye and the very thought of it crept through his nerves like ether. Every day he moved with an outward hurry, almost a fury, but within him something waited for Roger to come to him. Then one evening at first dark Stafford brought a note to Darrell, which read: *Dear Darr:— I am leaving on the train tonight. Will you meet me at the church?*

He dressed himself quickly, but he walked into Leighton. When the church loomed faintly before him in the darkness, his heart began to pound and he made himself walk more slowly. Under the oak tree he waited, but Roger had not come. He could see the light from the Pitt house and he thought, he is saying goodbye now to Miriam and to his mother; he will be here any minute. He walked about the tree and then he thought of going toward the light and Roger's house—but he might miss Roger in the darkness. He waited, and beneath his arms he could feel the dampness coming through his shirt and even his coat. "Roger?" he said, as if Roger was hiding somewhere near him in the darkness.

312

He took out the watch which Malcolm Pitt had given to him. In a quarter-hour the train would come. Roger would not play any joke on him—not now. Suddenly he turned and ran into the church. "Roger?" he said. His voice echoed in the darkness. He stood straight, his eyes searching. Behind the pulpit, on the stained glass window, slightly illumined, was the figure of Jesus. "Roger?" he said again. He turned and went out into the night. Suddenly his lips parted in a smile and he said, "I know what it is. He's not going away." The thought of it shook him like cold starlight.

He took out his watch again and gripped it within his palm and would not look at its face.

Then Roger's face broke the darkness; he was only a few feet away and the night's stillness seemed gathered in his body. He stood as if holding a breath, his shoulders square and straight. The sculptured lines of his face were flawless, filled with repose like an answer. They moved toward each other. The very tips of their fingers touched; their hands closed together. Then they embraced each other but they did not speak.

The whistle sounded, shattering the night into pieces no larger than tupelo leaves. Roger turned toward the sound and his footsteps measured the darkness and all of time beyond. For a few steps Darrell followed him and then, like a child, he slowly sat down on the autumn grass and dropped his head to his knees as if he would sleep.

When he arose he could see the light from the Pitt house. He turned quickly, putting the light to his back, and walked down to the depot and looked at its emptiness.

Then he went home, and all the way to his gate he kept looking around as though someone followed him.

He went into his room and for a long time stood gazing upon Leland and Roland asleep. He thought he saw upon their faces some vague enduring strength of Malcolm Pitt. They were

313

his sons, and a part of him, and he whispered, "Some day I will have another son."

He went to the window, and he imagined that Roger's face was on the edge of night outside. Strangely, he wanted to laugh. His mind was crowded with their being twelve or twenty and the wild plum smell along the pond bank and the willow fuzz about the gin. He was picturing Nolie's hair streaming in the wind, and seeing the dark red hair of a small Irish setter lifeless from the stroke of an ax. He was hearing the curious sounds of first dark in another day: the crickets in the grassy railroad right-of-way, the bullbats wheeling above his head, the faint sound of a cowbell coming from the hills, and the *belly-deep belly-deep* of the millpond frogs; he could feel the seat of a surrey, a new spring-seat holding him and Roger—and Malcolm Pitt very large between them; and he could feel himself riding northward on a train with Malcolm while the wild geese arrowed southward through December. He leaned farther into the window, his fingers seeming to touch the darkness, and wept.

After a while he lifted his eyes as though once again he might see the light from the Pitt house flowing through the arc of night.